SOFTLY GROW THE POPPIES

In the summer of 1914, Rose Beechworth, mistress of a charming country house left to her by her wealthy father, is not looking for love. But when spoilt heiress Alice Weatherly decides she must kiss Captain Charlie Summers goodbye, she takes Rose along with her to Lime Street station — and straight into the heart of Charlie's brother, Harry. Although they are neighbours, they have never met, for Rose ignores the social round and Harry is immersed in the difficulties of keeping his father's ramshackle estate together. As the war takes its terrible toll and Charlie disappears into the fog of battle, Alice becomes a heroine, while Rose finds herself running two great houses. It seems impossible that any of them will find happiness again . . .

Books by Audrey Howard
Published by The House of Ulverscroft:

THE SKYLARK'S SONG
THE MALLOW YEARS
SHINING THREADS
A DAY WILL COME
ALL THE DEAR FACES
THERE IS NO PARTING
ECHO OF ANOTHER TIME
THE SILENCE OF STRANGERS
A WORLD OF DIFFERENCE
BEYOND THE SHINING WATER
THE WOMAN FROM BROWHEAD
RIVERS OF THE HEART
ANNIE'S GIRL
WHISPERS ON THE WATER
PAINTED HIGHWAY
REFLECTIONS FROM THE PAST

AUDREY HOWARD

SOFTLY GROW THE POPPIES

ML

Complete and Unabridged

CHARNWOOD
Leicester

First published in Great Britain in 2012 by
Hodder & Stoughton

First Charnwood Edition
published 2013
by arrangement with
Hodder & Stoughton
An Hachette UK company
London

The moral right of the author has been asserted

A catalogue record for this book is available
from the British Library.

ISBN 978–1–4448–1660–0

Published by
F. A. Thorpe (Publishing)
Anstey, Leicestershire

Set by Words & Graphics Ltd.
Anstey, Leicestershire
Printed and bound in Great Britain by
T. J. International Ltd., Padstow, Cornwall

This book is printed on acid-free paper

For two special people who have made my life brighter, Gwen and Norman

1

It was warm, so warm that Rose was tempted to remove her gloves. Her hands, despite the fact that the gloves were made of the finest kid, were sticky with perspiration but they held the reins firmly, so she clicked her tongue to Sparky and told him 'Get up there, lad,' which he did for he was fresh so early in the morning.

'I don't know,' Dolly had said, 'why the dickens you have to go to Old Swan at all in this heat. Can't she use plain white to hem that petticoat? Do she have to have that specific shade of cream? After all, no one's going to see it.'

'Dolly,' Rose had said patiently, 'you know how particular the girls are. They wouldn't dream of using the wrong colour, besides which one of them has begged me to buy her some khaki wool so that she can knit socks for the soldiers. She's walking out with the under-gardener and he's bound to enlist like all the young men, so I suppose she's thinking of him; and anyway, I feel like having a ride. I want to find out what's happening. *The Times* is full of war news and yet nobody seems to know exactly what is to happen next.'

'Well, you won't find out in Old Swan, chuck, that's for sure. Why don't you take your book down to the summerhouse and have a read and a rest? This blithering heat's enough to knock the stuffing out of anyone. The gardeners were saying those dahlias need splitting and you know how fussy you are about which plants go where so you could tell him what — '

'Yes, yes, he told me yesterday but I feel I must just get this silk so that they can get on with their sewing. I bet every woman in the country wants to knit something for the troops and khaki wool will be hard to find . . . ' Besides which she was restless, anxious to discover what was going on in the vicinity of Liverpool with regard to the war that had been declared, war with Germany. It seemed Germany had violated a treaty, setting aside the neutrality of Belgium by demanding a passage through the country. Great Britain warned Germany that it should withdraw its troops from Belgium at once and if Germany did not do so by midnight on 4 August a state of war would exist between them. Germany did not do so. The Great War had begun and Rose wished to know how it would affect those who would be involved in it. Not just the men who would be bound to fight but those at home.

There were crowds everywhere, so it was reported, cheering and shouting and singing patriotic songs, especially in London outside the Palace, filled with enthusiasm for this great and glorious war in which they were to fight. Lord Derby was very keen to get a company of local lads to form their own Liverpool regiment and the streets were filled with hundreds of young men eager to be in on it. They were all terrified it would end — it would last a month they had heard — before they got their chance to share in it. War, war, war: the single syllable throbbed through the land and she wanted to get to Old Swan to find out for herself what was happening instead of just reading about it in the newspapers.

She and Dolly were sitting in the enormous kitchen that her grandfather had considered just the right size needed for the life he would lead as a country gentleman, with, of course, the sort of entertaining he meant to do. There were two large tables, solid, scrubbed pine on one of which the kitchen-maid was chopping parsley in readiness for the fish that was to be served at luncheon. A door led off to pantries and sculleries and another was open to reveal the stable yard. A dresser at least twelve feet long stood against one wall, its five shelves lined with pottery utensils of every kind from humble egg cups to large serving platters big enough to carry a roast fore-quarter of lamb, a leg of pork, a sirloin of beef and the game he shot on his own land. The coal-fired stoves, two of them, were the very latest design with a fire between and a hot plate on which, and from which, Cook could produce gargantuan meals. There was a clothes rack that could be hauled up to the ceiling and on which the freshly ironed laundry aired; there were copper pans, terracotta pots, weighing scales, dozens of implements, baskets in which fresh fruit and vegetables from the garden were delivered, and before the fire two rocking-chairs where Dolly Davenport, who was housekeeper and ran the house like clockwork, and Cook rested during their busy days. Nessie, the cook,

3

was married to Tom Gibson who was head gardener at Beechworth House and they had a comfortable cottage on the other side of the kitchen garden, as befitted their station. The rest of the servants lived in, except the laundry-maid who went home to her cottage in Hatton Lane each night: four housemaids and four menservants, grooms and gardeners. The men lived above the stable, the maids shared bedrooms at the top of the house.

It was one of the under-grooms, who hitched Sparky to the gig, holding the reins until Miss Beechworth emerged from the back kitchen. Miss Rose was known for her unconventional attitude towards fashion. Today she wore a full, well-cut, lightweight camel-coloured skirt that reached to mid-calf and was split to her knee, plain white shirt open at the neck, the cuffs turned back almost to the elbow. Her highly polished riding boots were revealed when she swung up into the gig. She wore no hat, the sun picking out copper and golden glints in her short, curly auburn hair. She was an extremely handsome woman of twenty-four years, independent, enormously wealthy and had refused every offer of marriage she had received.

She slapped the reins on Sparky's rump to set him off down the long drive, then she turned out of the wrought-iron gates of Beechworth House and into Hatton Lane. Bertha was in the garden of her cottage hanging out her own family's laundry and Rose waved to her.

'Soon 'ave this lot dry, Miss Rose,' Bertha shouted as the gig passed her.

'You certainly will, Bertha,' Rose shouted back as she picked up speed. The hedgerows flashed past, overgrown with brambles, the fruit almost ready for picking. The fields beyond were busy with men and boys, for, war or no war, the harvesting must go on. Men and boys, most of whom would enlist for their great adventure, were advancing against the golden ranks of wheat in slow rhythm, blades sweeping, flashing in the sunlight. The banks on either side of the lane were covered with toadflax and hawkweed and among the brambles were long streamers of honeysuckle and sweet-scented bedstraw. Some of the fields were golden with ragweed and others bright with a tapestry of scarlet poppies. There was a rowan tree standing sentinel at the corner of the field that was part of Oak Hill Farm and a thrush was gorging on its plentiful berries.

She was just about to turn from Hatton Lane into Dunbabin Road, which led through Wavertree and on to Old Swan, when she caught sight of what appeared to be a child hurrying from the opposite direction. She had time to notice that the child was extremely pretty, finely clad in a white muslin dress with a skirt that reached her ankle bone, a straw hat with a wide brim, its crown covered with pink flowers, and she carried a small pink reticule. She was holding the brim of the hat as she broke into a run, then with a sudden movement she discarded it, throwing it with what sounded like an oath into the hedge. Her hair was revealed, so pale it was almost silver, curls falling softly from

5

the crown of her head to her shoulders. A pink ribbon dangled from one of the curls as though she had rammed the hat on in a hurry. When she saw Rose her face broke into a beaming smile, revealing perfect teeth. Her eyes were clear, surrounded by long silky lashes and such an incredible shade of blue Rose could not help but stare. Not pale blue, not grey, not green, nor the purple of a pansy but a mix of all these shades as the light caught them. She could imagine any man falling into their soft beauty. Her cheeks were flushed a delicate rose pink and Rose could see, now that she had pulled Sparky to a halt, that she was not in fact a child but a young woman, a young woman so slight, so delicate, so dainty her tiny breasts barely lifted the bodice of her fetching dress.

'Oh, thank God,' the young woman began. 'Am I glad to see you. Are you by any chance going into Liverpool? I'm trying desperately to get to the station before the troop train leaves but Papa said I was not to go. He disapproves of Charlie, you see, and it is not a proper place for a lady and he told Matthew he'd lose his job if he took me. I've no money for a cab and when I said I'd take Blossom and ride there — she's my mare — Taylor was threatened with dismissal if he saddled her. Oh, I do beg your pardon. My governess has always said my manners are atrocious and so they are. My name is Alice Weatherly. How do you do.'

By this time she had reached the gig which was headed in the opposite direction from the city and Rose was astonished and speechless, for

6

surely the girl knew that? She was holding out her hand to Rose and Rose took it. It was shaken heartily.

The girl, Alice Weatherly, stood and waited, smiling.

'Well?' she said.

'Well what?'

'Are you going into Liverpool?'

'I had not intended to. I was about to . . . '

The girl's face fell and reluctantly she let go of Rose's hand, which she still held. 'Oh dear, then I'll just have to walk it.' Her face brightened and Rose was quite fascinated by her change of expression. 'Where *are* you going, may I ask? It might take me part of the way.'

'I'm going into Old Swan. My maid needs some thread and the kitchen-maid wants to knit socks for the soldiers so I am going to buy khaki wool and at the same time I thought I might see what was happening now that war has been declared. Anyway, what's so important about the station that you must get there so precipitously?' Rose went on.

The expression on the girl's face turned to one of astonishment. 'It's the troops . . . '

'Troops?'

'The soldiers who are going to fight the Germans. Five infantry divisions and one of cavalry. Charlie Summers is going since he's a cavalry officer, a captain, and he's taking Lady and Duke — '

'May I ask what all this has to do with me, Miss Weatherly?' Rose interrupted.

The upper-class society of Liverpool was

close-knit, the Earl and Countess of Derby being at the very top of the pile and an invitation to Knowsley, the seat of Lord Derby, was much sought after but not by herself. She knew of the Weatherlys of course, for they were a wealthy family living close to Beechworth House.

Arthur Weatherly inherited from his father a thriving business importing and exporting goods to many parts of the world. He was known as somewhat of a bully, keeping his wife, before she died, under his thumb and it was said that he was attempting to do the same with his pretty daughter. A baronet, at least, was what he wanted for her and this Charlie Summers she spoke of and of whom he disapproved came from an old family, land rich but money poor. True, his father was a baronet but since Charlie was the younger son, a soldier and with no hope of succeeding to the title, it was not surprising he frowned on his only child's apparent attachment to him.

'Oh, do please call me Alice.' She smiled her endearing, innocent smile and Rose could not help but smile back.

'Perhaps we could go to Liverpool in your gig, Miss . . . Miss . . . ?'

'Rose Beechworth.'

'Oh, please, Rose,' for it seemed Miss Alice Weatherly scorned the niceties of the day which said that people in their station should use surnames on such a short acquaintance. 'Can we not go into Liverpool for whatever your maids need and while we are there you could drop me off at Lime Street. The train leaves at noon and

Charlie will be so disappointed if I'm not there to see him off. I promised him. Of course he won't be away for long. A little skirmish, he calls it, all over by Christmas.'

Rose sighed, looking about her as though for inspiration. The growing heat of the day and the bright morning sunshine lit the hedges that ran along the field belonging to Lark Hill Dairy with what was called Jack-by-the-Hedge, with white campion, with red campion, with ragged robin and all the lovely summer plants that thrived there. Beyond the hedge the meadow was peaceful, half a dozen cows grazing, the cowman who had just put them out after milking trudging back towards the dairy. A flickering movement caught her eye, which was drawn to a shrew-mouse darting its long flexible nose in search of insects or worms, a pretty, harmless creature that seemed at odds with the violence that threatened to tear apart the calm existence she had known all her life.

Her grandfather had started building the family fortune in the middle of the last century. In 1852 gold had been found in a far-off place on the other side of the world. A foreign place with the foreign name of Yackandandah in Victoria, Australia. Her father had told her that her grandfather William had been one of the first diggers on the scene. He had been a young man with a wanderlust not satisfied with what he had in Liverpool, which was nothing. Yackandandah's nearest town was called Beechworth, and that was enough to convince William Beechworth he should seek his fortune there. He found gold

9

hanging in the roots of shrubs that he pulled up from the creek, which had proved incredibly rich in gold. Grandfather William had returned to England a man of means and from those riches his son, Rose's father, had increased the family fortunes a hundredfold, leaving Rose Beechworth one of the wealthiest heiresses in Lancashire. She had often thought of taking ship to Australia and visiting the area of Yackandandah from which had come her fortune and had vowed that one day she would but life was remarkably pleasant, now that she was totally independent, the owner of shares in a shipping company, the railway, mining in Yorkshire which day by day made her even richer and, more importantly, dependent on no man. She pictured in her mind the beautiful home that her grandfather had bequeathed to his descendants, for despite his low beginnings he had been a man of great taste. The house was set on a slight rise of land, the grounds falling away from it in smooth, well-cared-for lawns, flowerbeds aflame with colour at this time of the year. The beds were surrounded by clipped box hedges, their luscious green setting off the white gleam of garden statues. A covered trellised walk led to a summerhouse set by a small lake, the walk festooned with hanging baskets trailing ferns and pink roses while the lake itself was starred with lilies disturbed only by the smooth glide of the swans drifting effortlessly from bank to bank.

The house was furnished in the fashion of the nineteenth century but with none of the clutter so beloved of the times. The rooms were large and airy which the wives of her father and grandfather Beechworth, women of refinement and taste, had furnished with elegance and flair. A richly carpeted hallway was furnished with a long-case clock that ticked importantly at the foot of the wide staircase, a marble nymph set in a fluted recess, and deep velvet chairs before an enormous fireplace over which hung a gilt-framed mirror. There was a drawing room filled with costly ornaments, a French clock in ormolu and enamel, vases of rococo Sèvres, and ornaments of Coalport and Meissen. Chandeliers created shimmering, dancing light in every room including the dining room, which though high and wide was barely filled by the highly polished oval table and matching velvet chairs, twenty of them. A sideboard ran along one side with niches and shelves to accommodate silver dishes, a crystal lamp and porcelain. Also on the ground floor were a breakfast room, a library, a study and to the side a conservatory, known as a 'winter garden' when it was built. There were a dozen bedrooms, most of them never used, and even the very latest of bathrooms which she herself had designed and had installed.

The house had bay windows to the front and overlooking the gardens at the side and a terrace on which dozens of pots bloomed with geraniums. A vegetable garden, a tennis court, again never used since she had no one to play with, and the whole surrounded by woodland, parkland and at the edge of the property pastures where the horses browsed. She could do exactly what she wanted, go exactly where she

11

pleased and though she was aware that Dolly, who had helped to deliver her into the world twenty-four years ago would fret until she returned home, she was very tempted to take this sweet-faced child into Liverpool.

Alice saw the indecision on Rose's face. 'Please say yes,' Alice begged. 'I'll be no trouble, really. It's miles into town and if I don't get there soon Charlie will have gone.'

'I suppose you . . . well, I suppose you like this Charlie?'

'We love each other.'

Rose smiled and pulled a face. 'Dear God in heaven, little did I know when I set out this morning I'd be . . . ' She was about to say 'playing cupid' but Rose had never been in love so the shining light in Alice Weatherly's face was a mystery to her. Nevertheless it was there, as pure and innocent as that of a child and who was she to scoff at it? The girl's eyes were like sapphires, now so vivid a blue they were startling. Sapphires with a diamond in their depths, or was it a star? Dear God, she was getting all romantic, sentimental, which was not like her.

Alice's voice interrupted her thoughts. 'I'm so sorry. I can see I'm a nuisance. I can probably get a lift somewhere on the route. I've no money for a cab, and I've actually never been out on my own, you see.' She made a face of self-deprecation. 'Isn't that an awful admission at eighteen and in this day and age where young women are doing all sorts of things, college and . . . and then there are the suffragettes and what

12

they are fighting for. I've often thought I would like to be one of them,' she said wistfully, 'but my father is very protective.' She sighed then brightened. 'So if you could tell me in which direction I should go I would be most obliged.'

Rose grinned. 'Oh, for God's sake, hop up. I could do with an adventure myself and there will be lots of things going on in town, especially if your Charlie is there to tell us what's happening and where he's off to.'

Alice's face lit up and her smile threatened to blind Rose. She was utterly amazed by her own behaviour but for some reason this artlessly naïve, childlike young woman who was six years younger than herself appealed to some part of her she did not recognise. She knew herself to be resistant to frivolity, to light-mindedness, to much of the heedless search for *fun* with which girls of her class were imbued, but this child, for she seemed no more than that, intrigued her and she really would like to see the soldiers set off for France. Of course she had read about it in the newspapers but had not really understood why it was happening. It was all a bit confusing and to be honest a lot of fuss about nothing. Who cared whether Russia expanded in the Baltic or the eastern Mediterranean? The British were determined to keep the port of Constantinople from falling into Russian hands. Russia wanted to carve up the Turkish Empire, and the Germans had marched on Belgium at which the British were appalled but she supposed there must be a lot more to it than that. But did the ordinary working man care about it? They had never heard of many of these places and were hardly aware of the bitter conflict that had been going on for a year or more. Now, for some reason, France and Great Britain had declared war on Germany!

And here was this enchanting young woman, alight with love and patriotism, off to Lime Street railway station to see the man she loved take a train for this mad muddle.

Alice scrambled up into the gig, thanking Rose again and again, chattering vivaciously as they moved along country lanes and then the broader thoroughfares of the outskirts of Liverpool, on each side of which were the smart villas of the middle classes. Then they went through the warren of cramped terraced houses on the edge of the city, passing shops, factories, warehouses and the Royal Infirmary, until they reached the top of Brownlow Hill.

And there it all was: the great city of Liverpool and at the bottom of the hill the railway station. The trams seriously offended Sparky who had never in his life been further than a couple of miles from home, driven by Rose along quiet lanes and through country villages. Whenever Rose, with her maid, came into Liverpool on her infrequent visits to her dressmaker or boot-maker, or milliner, they were brought in the carriage driven by Thomas, the coachman. So to Sparky and the woman who held the reins, doing her best to control his panic, this seemed absolute chaos. Not only trams but also horse-drawn vehicles, drays and wagons, men on bicycles impatiently ringing their bells, carriages and, worst of all, the new phenomenon, the motor car.

Alice looked quite relaxed in all the confusion but Rose realised that her little gig with a panic-stricken Sparky beginning to rear and lunge was a danger not only to the vehicles in the road but to the pedestrians who had come to the city to see their boys off. What's more, the khaki-clad soldiers who marched towards Lime Street blocked most of the way. Packing the pavements were huge, cheering crowds, little boys who 'hallooed' and threw their caps in the air, old men with tears in their eyes, perhaps remembering their own enthusiastic youth fighting in the Boer War. Women and girls blew kisses and waved their handkerchiefs and a band played 'It's a Long Way to Tipperary', stirring music to keep the soldiers in step on this great expedition.

Sparky did not care for it at all, causing even more chaos until Rose, handing the reins to Alice who was, fortunately, used to driving a gig about the grounds of Weatherly House, got down and put her arms around his neck in an effort to soothe him.

'We'll have to find somewhere to put him,' Rose shouted above the din to Alice who held on bravely. They were by this time turning into Lime Street and before them was the magnificence of the Adelphi Hotel. A sign pointed to the back of the hotel to stables where guests' horses were cared for. Threading her way through the dangerous crush Rose managed at last to get Sparky and the gig to the stable yard where a groom, delighted to be of service to two such attractive ladies, declared he would keep an eye on the slowly calming pony.

Alice was the daughter, in fact the only child, of Arthur Weatherly, a prominent gentleman in the world of shipping and it was whispered that when the company began in 1709 it had dealt in slaves. The first of the Weatherly Line vessels had sailed from Liverpool to the West Indies and brought back slaves, the trade growing so that by the 1750s over 25,000 had been transported. One street in town where the sale of black men, women and children had been held was even called Negro Street but the lucrative trade came to an end at the beginning of the nineteenth century when Arthur Weatherly's predecessors had turned to other cargoes and the company continued to thrive.

Alice had been gently reared, protected, mixing with families of her own social standing, kept to the schoolroom and accompanied wherever she went at all times by her governess, her mother before she died, or a groom.

The two young women walked close together, aware that they were the object of many inquisitive glances. Alice was dressed in the style worn by all young girls of her class, while Rose prompted utter amazement in her eccentric outfit of short skirt, boots and no hat and this in a day when no decent women ventured outside her home without a hat!

'Hold my arm,' Rose whispered to Alice since she had noticed, even if Alice hadn't, the way the men were eyeing the beautiful girl by her side.

She was unaware that her own handsome looks were, in a different way, as attractive as Alice's. She had a mass of curly Titian hair — she called it ginger! — which was vibrant with copper, a tawny red, streaks of golden brown, quite glorious and quite untameable so she kept it cut short and it rioted over her skull unchecked. As she and Alice struggled through the crowds the curls bounced and fell over her forehead, curly tendrils touching her long brown eyelashes which were tipped with gold. Her eyes were a golden brown, uncompromising, watchful, intelligent, and her mouth was a rich, ripe red with a tiny dimple in one corner which lifted at the side when she smiled. She was as tall as most men, slender but shapely with a fine breast. Her manner at this moment was guarded, protective of the dainty little creature who clung to her arm.

The station forecourt was a heaving mass of men who would be trained to be soldiers and who were all cheerfully being herded on to the waiting train. The Earl of Derby had appealed to the men of Lancashire to volunteer and it must be said they did not need much persuasion. They formed the 19th Battalion, the King's Liverpool Regiment and among them was a cavalry unit in which Charlie Summers was a captain. He and other officers were busy with loading their horses into wagons at the rear of the train, for there would be a great need of horses in the battles to come, or so they believed. Mounted troops would be the main components of offensive warfare. In battle they would carry a sword, a rifle for use when dismounted and a lance. Cavalry units were also equipped with one or two machine guns carried by a team and cart.

At first it was almost impossible to recognise one soldier from another. Most of them were working-class men and the sound of their orders from fierce regimental sergeants thundered over the shrieks of train whistles. Porters shouted, horses whinnied their distress, the men whistled and sang, thrilled by this new adventure they were off to, that of defending their country. The regiments were made up of men who knew each other, who, when they were settled, would be known as the 'Liverpool Pals' and who would in a short time learn to present arms, fight with a bayonet and throw bombs. They did not know in that first month of the war that soldiers were already dying in their thousands.

And in the midst of all this seething mass of apparent turmoil the British Army was doing its best to load all the necessary provisions for battle on several trains that would be off within the hour.

On a narrow ramp that led up into the horse wagons, six sweating soldiers, one of them an officer, were doing their superhuman best to get a grey mare aboard, exercising great patience while the grey's owner stood at her head gently pulling her bridle.

Alice gave an excited squeak. 'It's Charlie, look, Rose, it's Charlie, and that's Lady.'

But Rose was not looking at Charlie, or even Lady, but at the tall aristocratic gentleman who was watching the drama from the platform to the side of the wagon.

2

Harry watched as the young woman approached along the station platform, the most astonishing young woman he had ever seen. She was tall, at least half a foot taller than Alice. Not pretty like Alice who was holding her arm; her face was too strong for that, but with eyes a startling gleaming golden shade, a flawless skin with a hint of honey and hair that was so vivid it seemed to light up the platform. There was a look of humour about her, in the way her full mouth curved upwards at the corners as though she would smile readily. Her figure was fine, graceful with a straight back and high, full breasts but the outfit she had on was highly improper. Or so the women gathered on the platform evidently thought. Nevertheless she was very striking and he could not drag his gaze from her and get back to the job in hand. He had been involved with helping his brother, Charlie, load his mare on to the train, pushing her smooth grey rump with his shoulder in an effort to coax her up the ramp, but at the sound of Alice's excited voice they all stopped and stared, even the troopers, and the grey took the opportunity to back down. Her eyes were rolling, her ears flattened and her big teeth were ready to take a nip out of anybody who put a hand on her, but though Charlie turned towards Alice he kept a firm hold on the reins.

Harry hurriedly smoothed his jacket down and

straightened his tie. Alice was darting through the crowds to get to Charlie and the young woman with her was left standing on the platform, pushed this way and that by the seething mass of people, soldiers and those who had come to see them off, but her eyes were fixed on him as his were on hers. Something was communicated from deep chocolate-brown eyes to those of gold and the chaos about them seemed to recede in the strangeness of that first moment of meeting.

The message conveyed from one to the other had a warmth, a recognition and Rose was conscious of a dizziness — no, not a dizziness, but a feeling of disorientation which surely was not usual in the circumstances. She had got up this morning with nothing on her mind other than a determination to take the gig to Old Swan and here she was in the midst of the confusion and muddle, which she could see all around her, of men off to battle. She could hear Alice's voice chattering her dismay as she helped Charlie — she supposed it was Charlie — quiet the terrified mare — 'Let me hold the reins . . . you take . . . oh dear, what are you to do? She is so frightened . . . what will you do if . . . ' while across the dreadful mix-up Rose Beechworth and Harry Summers looked at one another without a word. Now that he had righted himself after his efforts in helping his brother, he was seen to be immaculately dressed and bore a striking resemblance to Charlie. She had often watched them riding hell for leather across the land at the back of Beechworth House, shouting encouragement as they chased the fox, laughing, young gentlemen at play, but now that they were both concerned about the mare and her refusal to be shepherded aboard the train the likeness between the brothers was even more apparent. They were both tall, with long, loose, powerful limbs but whereas the younger, even now in the midst of this turmoil, seemed to have a merry look about him, the elder had an almost austere beauty that was completely masculine and very striking. There were deep furrows between his eyebrows as though a frown was more his usual expression than a smile. For all that he was not yet thirty it was as though he bore a great weight on his broad shoulders and for some reason it touched Rose.

With a supreme effort he tore his gaze from the fascinating young woman and turned back to his brother. 'It's no good, Charlie. She'll hurt herself. I'll ride like the devil and fetch your horse. You know how she loves her or do you think she'd follow another gig pony?'

'I don't know, Harry. She'll go anywhere with her, you know that, but as for another . . . But you'll have to be quick, old chap. The train is to set off in an hour and if she's not aboard I'll have to leave her. Though how can a cavalry man manage without his horse?'

Charlie had brightened at the sight of Alice, but now he was the picture of dejection. He led the frightened animal into a quiet, or at least less crowded, corner of the station yard while the soldiers who had done their best to get her aboard thankfully left to get on with their duties. Charlie spoke quietly into the grey's swivelling ears and slowly she calmed down.

Charlie Summers was a career soldier and he looked every inch a cavalry man in his well-fitting uniform: a khaki jacket, the buttons on the pockets polished to a golden gleam, beige breeches like those he wore for riding, a leather belt and shoulder strap and a peaked cap with the regiment's badge at the front. His knee-high boots glowed a lustrous chestnut brown with the spit and polish his batman had put into them. He wore his cap at a rakish angle and his dark brown hair curled over his collar. He was twenty-four but looked far younger. He had a ferocious appetite for life and always had, climbing to almost terrifying heights in trees, sliding head first down banisters, leaping fast-running streams. He possessed that indefinable characteristic, a mystical charm that everyone he met, at school, on his father's estate and now in the army responded to. He was popular with his men, displaying a warmth that was irresistible to all those about him, men of his own rank and those he would lead into battle. He was, sadly, not his usual cheerful self now. Alice had spoken to him softly and he touched her cheek then buried his face in her neck to the consternation of those nearby.

'Alice, my love . . . you came.' He lifted his head and took her hand, bringing it to his lips. 'How? I thought your father — '

23

'I escaped, Charlie. I couldn't let you go without — '

'But how did you get here?'

It was as though the two of them were in an enclosed bubble in which no one else existed. They could be seen and heard but neither seemed to be aware of what went on around them. The grey mare stood quietly as though she too were part of this mysterious and unreal moment.

Rose, who was watching them, stepped back. Her heel came down sharply on the foot of Harry Summers's boot and he grunted but nevertheless put out a gallant hand to steady her. For a moment it touched her elbow and she distinctly felt the electricity pass from him to her. Startled, she turned back to him and looked up into his warm brown eyes, gazing into them, mesmerised. They did not smile but were deep in the magic she knew to be important. Fine lines were drawn about his eyes, tracing from the corners. Her heart missed a beat and for an astonishing moment she felt it rise in her throat. His face was strong and his lips were firm but as she watched they lifted into a small smile meant only for her and it told her he was as transfixed as she was.

'I beg your pardon,' she managed to say, 'that was extremely clumsy of me.'

'No harm done,' he answered automatically.

'I was — ' She was about to say something else but he interrupted her.

'Really, please don't concern yourself.'

'The grey . . . ?'

He had recovered his self-control now, and so had she, the astonishing moment over.

'Yes, I'm afraid Charlie — he's my brother by the way — '

'Yes, I know. And you are Harry Summers.'

'And you must be the mysterious Miss Rose Beechworth?'

'Mysterious!'

'Indeed, it is said you refuse all invitations and do not entertain. Mind you' — he grinned boyishly — 'I can't say I blame you. Some of the social gatherings I am forced to attend are a crashing bore.'

'Then why do you go?'

'Surely it is one's duty — ' He was interrupted by Charlie who, leaving Lady in the care of one of his troopers and still with Alice clinging to him, tapped him on the shoulder.

'What am I to do, Harry? Do you think you could fetch Molly in time?'

Rose broke in. 'Alice and I came in my gig. Perhaps Sparky, my gig pony, might . . . perhaps your mare will follow him on to the train.'

Harry looked puzzled for a moment as though being spoken to by a precocious child boasting of a new toy then his face cleared. Understanding, he took her arm.

'Where did you leave him? Close by?'

Charlie, with Alice still almost hanging round his neck, drew closer.

'The stable yard of the Adelphi. I had to leave him there because of the crowds. He was panic-stricken.'

'Come along and show me.' Harry held her

25

arm, pulling her along, forcing his way through the press of excited volunteer soldiers, tearful families come to bid farewell to their departing sweethearts, husbands. There were wagons, horses not yet aboard and even would-be passengers waiting for another train which would leave as soon as the troop train was away.

It was quieter when they reached Lime Street, moving in the direction of the Adelphi Hotel and at last Rose managed to untangle her arm from Harry Summers's strong hand, hurrying along beside him, easily matching her stride to his.

'Are you certain it was the Adelphi?' he barked at her, scarcely turning his head, for he was doing his best to free himself from the state of mind into which this young woman seemed to have thrust him. This was not like him. He had so far in his life evaded the blandishments of many young women and their grasping mamas but this one, despite being almost a neighbour, he had never met. He had heard about her, since her unsociability was well known. There were many young men who would be glad of a wealthy wife but though she was invited to move among her own class she declined all invitations to do so, he had heard. She did not care for parties, it was said, and was that strange being, one who was more at ease with the farmers, cottagers, the working classes and their families in whom she took a great interest.

'Am I likely to mistake it for another?' she snapped back, for like him she could not support the feelings that had invaded her when she came face to face with Harry Summers.

'No, I beg your pardon but — '

'Then allow me to find Sparky and fetch him to your brother. I just hope the mare likes him and that Sparky is willing to lead her on to the train. I myself believe it is cruel to expect an innocent animal to go to war. Men can decide for themselves but horses . . .'

'My brother is in a cavalry unit, Miss Beechworth, and a cavalry officer without a horse is somewhat useless. The British Expeditionary Force are already fighting — and dying — in France. You will not have read about the Battle of Mons in which thousands of our men were mown down and the force was virtually destroyed and so we must rely on a volunteer army. They need infantry *and* cavalry units such as the one my brother serves in and the men you saw at the station will be part of it. But we really do not have time to discuss the question of war at the moment, Miss Beechworth, so perhaps when we have Lady safely aboard you and Alice will take tea with me at the Adelphi where I will do my best — '

'There is no need, Mr Summers. I have read the newspapers and can make up my own mind about such things.' She became quiet then, a thoughtful look on her face. 'Though I must admit I had not heard about the . . . the terrible . . . about Mons.'

'I have a friend in the War Office who keeps me informed, Miss Beechworth,' he replied shortly. 'Now then, let us find your pony and get Charlie and all those young men who are willing to die for their country on their way.'

Not another word was spoken, both recognising the strength of will of the other. As they at last reached the stable yard of the hotel, she realised incredulously that she had been arguing with a complete stranger, a man she had just met and despite what had taken place between them this was baffling in itself. A bizarre episode of what appeared to be mutual recognition had occurred though they had never been in one another's company before. He was a man about whom she knew very little and they had been at loggerheads about something of which she knew even less!

Sparky was still tethered to a ring in the wall, his nose in a bag of oats that the stable lad had generously given him and he did not take kindly to having the nose bag wrenched from him, but, having filled his belly and recognising Rose, he allowed himself to be led along the side entrance of the hotel and into Lime Street. Rose spoke soothingly into his ear since as soon as he was drawn into the bustle of soldiers who were to board the next troop train he began to object, pulling back on his rein.

With an expertise and calm that Harry watched with hidden admiration, Rose settled Sparky in a way that told him she was used to horses and with trust the animal followed her and plodded towards the station platform where the last of the horses were being loaded.

Charlie and Alice were still standing, hands clasped, in the middle of the melée, Lady fidgeting nervously at Charlie's back. They appeared to be oblivious to those around them and Harry tutted with annoyance.

'Dear God in heaven, would you look at the pair of them,' he muttered, then without more ado he took Rose's hand and led her to the corner where Charlie and Alice were marooned, Sparky trailing behind them.

'Charlie.' His brother's voice brought the young officer from his reverent contemplation of the girl he loved. 'What in hell's name do you think you're doing, you young fool?' Harry snapped, 'standing there like some love-sick calf when there is so much to be done. If Jimmy Bentley catches sight of you mooning about you'll be for it.' The name of the major Jimmy Bentley, brought Charlie out of his trance and he straightened up immediately. 'Quickly,' Harry continued, 'get the pony to Lady and let us try to get this animal and you on the bloody train.'

Several ladies in their vicinity were extremely shocked by this language, and from someone they had taken for a gentleman, and looked aghast, not just at his words but at the woman he was with.

His voice softened and he bowed to them apologetically then turned back to the little group and the two animals. 'I'm sorry, Alice, but you must say goodbye. Move over here next to Miss Beechworth. Come along, my dear, Charlie will be all right, won't you, Charlie. Now, Miss Beechworth, will you . . . ' but Rose was already fastening Sparky's bridle to Lady's muzzle strap and with a gentle word and watched by the open-mouthed cavalry men, began to lead the pony up the steep ramp. Despite what he had been through that day Sparky went obediently since he had known and trusted her since his birth, which Rose had witnessed. The mare followed him placidly.

Harry Summers was also open-mouthed with what he was beginning to recognise was more than admiration for an attractive, intelligent and spirited woman. She was, besides these attributes, calm, sensible, practical with none of the airs and graces and the desire for praise that seemed to abound in other young women. She had seen what needed to be done and without any fuss had done it. He wanted to take her hands and say, 'Good work,' and perhaps, 'When can we meet again?' but he damped down his enthusiasm, merely watching as, the problem solved, she led the gig pony back down the ramp and on to the platform. There was a small cheer from the men around her and she acknowledged it with a nod and a smile. God, she was amazing!

Charlie had dragged himself from Alice's clinging arms. He raced up the ramp after Lady who was being lovingly tended by a soldier-groom. She was ready to panic again, he could see, the rowdiness that still could be heard from the platform unsettling her once more even though she was comfortably tethered between two other animals who were quiet. The band played a rousing tune, cries of 'Goodbye' and 'Take care of yourself,' and 'Don't worry, Ma, I'll write soon,' echoed along the platform, the whistles and hooting from other platforms alarming the animals who had been quiet, their distress conveying itself to the highly strung grey and Charlie forgot for a moment the woman who wept for him. If the horses were like this now how would they react to the long swaying drive and clatter to the camp where the men were to receive further training in the art of killing? He could feel the vibration of the wagon and realised they were actually under way, gathering speed. He was off to war and had not said goodbye to his darling Alice.

With a frantic command to Burton, the soldier-groom, he raced along the corridor of the swaying train, shouldering aside the men who still had their heads out of the windows for a last look at a beloved wife or mother, most of whom held their handkerchiefs to their eyes. She was still there, held in the comforting circle of his brother's arm. On her other side was the unknown young woman who had so amazingly helped to get Lady aboard. She was holding Alice's hand. He waved frantically, along with dozens of others, but Alice did not pick him out. He watched as she was led away by Harry and the young woman who was holding the bridle of the gig pony. What a blessing she had been!

He was to revise his opinion in the days to come. In the thick of a battle in which he, like thousands of other young men, had longed to be involved, he was to revise his opinion in the days to come, though it was no fault of Rose's.

Sparky caused a minor disturbance as he, Rose, Alice and Harry fought to get out of the crush in the station. Rose did her best to soothe him and at the same time was aware that Harry

Summers was attempting the same with Alice who was distraught, weeping inconsolably.

'I didn't even kiss him goodbye,' she hiccuped, drooping against Harry's shoulder.

'It couldn't be helped, Alice. He had to get Lady aboard.'

'I know but — '

'Now then, Alice,' Rose interrupted abruptly. 'You saw him off which is what you wanted so dry your tears. Let's get Sparky settled then Mr Summers has offered to take us for tea at the Adelphi. Should you not like that?'

'I wanted to kiss him goodbye.'

Harry and Rose exchanged a look over her head, one in which exasperation and sympathy were mixed. Harry raised his eyebrows, clearly not knowing what to do for the best. He and Charlie had known Alice since she was a small girl and he himself felt about her as he would a sister. But Charlie loved her, not as a sister but as a woman and declared that they were to be married.

The pony was hitched to the wall in the stable yard and the three of them walked down the side passage and round to the front of the hotel, entering the Adelphi through its magnificent arched portico and into the richly appointed entrance hall. The hotel had been a favoured 'stopping place' of the royal family, princes of foreign royalty and there were very few visitors of importance to the country who had not stayed there. Consequently it was a favourite of the elite of Liverpool and as the three of them entered they were watched by astonished porters, open-mouthed receptionists, the under-manager who happened to be on duty and guests who were thunderstruck at the sight of the strange trio. They brought the genteel ladies in the tea room to a complete silence. The well-dressed gentleman was not an unusual sight but with one woman weeping most distressingly on one arm and another garbed in what they could only call a *scandalous* outfit, not at all fit for the tea room — both ladies with neither hat nor gloves — it quite spoiled their afternoon! The woman — they could not call her a lady — with her sleeves rolled up, an open-necked shirt and *riding boots* revealed beneath her *split* skirt would not have been allowed into their own drawing rooms and they did not expect to find such attire in any of the places they visited. And would you look at her hair, for heaven's sake, cut short and in a mass of loose curls around her head!

Harry seated both Alice and Rose, taking no notice of the slack-jawed waiter whose job it was to lead guests to a table of his choosing, then, with that commanding and Rose supposed arrogant manner of his class, gestured to the head waiter who automatically hurried over and took Harry's order for tea and . . . 'Should you like cake, or perhaps . . . ' turning to Rose who shook her head. She held Alice's hand and murmured to her and gradually Alice managed a tearful smile.

'You have both been so kind but my heart feels as though it is breaking. I knew Charlie was to go but I did not imagine it would be so . . . so cruel. Not even a farewell . . . a kiss . . . oh, dear, please don't let me start again,' for she was on the verge of more tears.

'Alice, we were all saddened by the departure of not only Charlie but all the soldiers who are to fight.' Then she remembered what Harry Summers had said to her about the British Expeditionary Force and the men who had died at Mons only a few days ago. 'But we have certainly put the cat among the pigeons here.' She grinned mischievously and Harry fell more under her spell than ever. 'The old dears are having a lovely time wondering what the dickens a woman dressed as I am is doing in their precious tea room. I suppose I look like some wandering gypsy. We have quite made their day so why don't we smile and pretend we are nothing out of the ordinary. Let us think of the day when Charlie comes home with all the other soldiers and you and he can be married. Will you promise that I shall be a bridesmaid? But don't dress me in pink. I look awful in pink.'

Harry watched her as she made Alice smile and even chuckle. He reflected on the distinct probability that this — meaning not only all the soldiers coming home but a wedding between Charlie and Alice — would never happen. Arthur Weatherly, Alice's father, wanted more for his only daughter than the second son of a land-rich, cash-poor, family-proud gentleman, whose father had gambled and wenched away his wealth over the past twenty years. The estate Charlie's father had inherited was falling about his ears and only one son, Harry, was doing his best to keep it all together. Cow sheds needed rebuilding and land draining, not to mention the slow deterioration of the lovely and gracious family home, Summer Place, and there was no money to do it. Arthur Weatherly was not a man to pour money into the hand of the man who had caused such a decline. He would look elsewhere for a suitable husband for his daughter. Harry remembered the struggle he himself had had raising money to buy Charlie a commission, parting reluctantly with some land to do so. They lived on the rents of the tenant farmers with Harry doing his best to manage the estate in his father's place, a thankless task he discovered, and it certainly ruled out any chance of finding himself a woman willing to live on the pittance that came in. One day it would all be his and unless he or Charlie married an heiress, how were they to maintain it?

Alice was sipping her tea, her long, silky hair slipping from the ribbon that did its best to hold it in place. She was dishevelled from Charlie's ardent embrace but she had stopped crying and Harry surreptitiously watched Rose who was totally unaware of the stir they had caused. Typically, she did not care. She drank her tea and discussed with Alice how she was to get back to Weatherly House.

'I can take you in the gig but you must promise to come to Beechworth tomorrow and drink chocolate with me. Dolly makes the best chocolate in the world.'

'Dolly?'

'Yes, she runs my house for me.' She laughed.

35

'You see, I am not at all domesticated and cannot manage without her. I love her as though she were my mother.'

Alice smiled wanly. 'My mama passed away.'

'As did mine.'

'Papa might not let me. He will be furious that I have seen Charlie.'

'Does he not like Charlie then?' looking suddenly at Harry, for surely they should not be discussing his brother with him sitting there quietly drinking tea.

'Don't worry, Miss Beechworth.' Harry smiled broadly. 'I know exactly what Mr Weatherly thinks of my family but it does not concern me unduly. Now, if you are ready, let's go and rescue poor Sparky who has done us all a great service today.'

They were stared at quite openly as they picked their way through the tables towards the wide hallway, for never had such a sight been seen in this exclusive hotel, meaning the tall girl with the cropped hair and what they could only call 'trousers' or so her split skirt seemed to be! The culprit was oblivious to their gaze, Alice was too upset to notice and Harry Summers simply did not care!

3

As Rose steered Sparky and the gig into the stable yard Dolly's voice could be heard from the stable and it was pretty obvious she was giving Fred and Davy what she called the length of her tongue. 'Do I have to light a fire under you, you gormless half-wits, or shall I saddle them horses myself? She's been gone all day and anything could have happened to her on that road to Old Swan. There's hedges on both side where tramps an' such like could hide themselves an' seein' a lovely lass like our Rose could set about her an' ... an' ... so damn well get a move on or you'll feel the back of me hand, Fred Simmons,' despite the fact that Fred was almost as old as Dolly with a grown family of his own. 'I dunno, if you want a job doing properly and quickly you've to do it yourself.'

Rose brought the gig to a stop, smiling at Alice who looked slightly alarmed. By this time the trio in the stable had heard the gig's wheels on the cobbles and the clip of Sparky's hooves. Dolly whirled out into the yard and with hardly a pause for breath vented her anger and worry on to her mistress. 'Where the devil have you been, young lady, I'd like to know, worrying us all to death thinkin' you were dead in a ditch, set upon by thieves and gone all day without a word to anyone. In ter luncheon, you said an' here it is with me gettin' ready ter sort out dinner an' you drive in as bold as you please . . . '

She had begun to eye the pretty young thing who sat besides Rose, her voice tapering off in astonishment. 'And who might this be, if I may be so bold as to ask?' Her young mistress was well known for her quixotic nature and for bringing home waifs and strays to be fed at the kitchen door or given a night's bed in one of the rooms above the stable.

Rose jumped down from the gig, moved round the back of it to Alice who she handed down as if she were royalty. The groom and stable lad were at the door of the stable and their mouths dropped, for this was no waif. Though she might be a bit untidy — no hat nor gloves! — she was certainly a lady and their masculinity observed that she was one of the loveliest females they had ever clapped eyes on. Hardly bigger than a child but with a sweetly curved figure, eyes the colour of a pansy or a bluebell or was it a cornflower with a brilliance in them that was fascinating, silver-gilt hair falling freely down her back and a complexion like a rose.

She smiled at them shyly and they both whipped off their caps and smiled back, which incensed Dolly even though she herself felt quite captivated by the girl.

'Well?' she demanded to know.

'This is Miss Alice Weatherly, Dolly. I met her on the road and decided to go with her to Liverpool where she was eager to see her . . . her fiancé.' She turned to Alice. 'Is that right, Alice? He is your fiancé, is he not?'

'Oh yes. We are to be married as soon as

38

possible,' Alice explained to the dumbstruck trio. 'He is a soldier, you see, a cavalry officer, and was ordered to take his horse to . . . well, even he was not sure where but he is to fight the Germans, but as soon as he has leave we will be married.'

They all melted and began to make moves as though to comfort her. She had been to see her sweetheart off — with Miss Rose's help — to fight in this dreadful war that had come upon them so abruptly, for none of them knew anything about world affairs and often pondered together on why they should be involved. How could they resist her?

'Well, come inside, Miss Weatherly,' Dolly exclaimed. 'Nay, Miss Rose, what on earth were you thinking of, letting us stand about when a cup of tea and perhaps one of Nessie's biscuits — just come out of th'oven — would be very welcome. See, Fred, take the gig and put Sparky to bed. I dunno, poor lass . . . ' Anyone who had a sweetheart going off to fight for his country awoke all Dolly's compassion. You always knew when some emotion was roused in Dolly's breast as she lapsed into her broad Lancashire tongue which had been almost erased since she came to Beechworth House.

Dolly Davenport was just twelve years old when she was plucked out of the Female Orphan Asylum in Myrtle Street by the wife of a wealthy and prominent Liverpool businessman who had his finger in so many pies he employed a secretary to keep his records. She came to Beechworth House as a parlour maid and Jane

Beechworth had been married to William for only six months and he adored her and could refuse her nothing. She was eighteen when he married her and he was twenty-eight and before she died with her son in childbirth she had suffered two miscarriages close together, leaving only one child: Rose Beechworth. Rose took the place in his heart of his beloved wife and though he was — in society's mind — recklessly indulgent of his daughter she remained unspoiled, in fact downright peculiar in their opinion, preferring the company of her father, her servants and those who worked on her estate. Her father had died when she was eighteen, leaving her the owner of the estate and shares in the railway, mines and other profitable businesses.

When her mistress died, Dolly had become head parlour-maid. With her mistress gone and Miss Rose barely ten years old, Dolly had taken over the running of the house. The master had been prostrate with grief and was no use to anyone so it had been up to Dolly to put things to rights. She had done so and for fourteen years had kept order. It was she who had employed a governess for the young Rose, a young woman she herself had thought suitable, and with the master spending much of his time in the city it was not until Rose was eleven that he had noticed her and having done so he found a new outlet for the love he had borne his wife.

Between a loving, indulgent father, a governess who taught her that the only way to learn was by reading, taking her to museums and concerts and any place where learning might be found, Rose was not a conventional product of her era. Her governess, who had unusual ideas about education, was just as lenient as Rose's father and while Dolly loved the child and could deny her nothing she also taught her the difference between right and wrong. Nobody, however, set out to teach her the correct ways of polite society. Her father because he had no time for parties, balls, dinner dances and all the nonsense the upper classes went in for, Dolly and Miss Holdsworth because they knew nothing about them. Even their mistress, the late Mrs Beechworth, who was shy, retiring and content to adore and be adored by her husband and who spent her time on domestic matters, had made no effort to integrate her daughter into society. She had been a compassionate woman who did her best to better the lives of her servants, indoor and out, and local people in the villages about Beechworth House, so was it any wonder that Miss Rose had turned out as she had. *Everybody loved her!*

Now Dolly turned and solicitously took Alice's arm with the intention of leading her towards the kitchen door where a group of women stood smiling. Nessie, the cook, Fanny, Carrie, Polly, kitchen-parlour-and scullery-maid, and even Miss Holdsworth — called by everybody 'Holdy' — waited to welcome this lovely young woman. War fever gripped them all and anyone who was vaguely connected with it was a hero or heroine to them.

Alice looked about her, troubled, it seemed, by

all this attention. 'Oh dear, I'm afraid I must get home. My father . . . he did not want me to go; he will be cross.'

How could anyone be cross with this dainty little thing? their expressions said.

'Don't be silly, Alice,' Rose reproved her. 'You cannot just dash off home without — '

'You don't know Papa, Rose. He forbade me to go and I defied him. I love Charlie so much and I knew it would distress him if I wasn't there to see him off. So I had to choose who I would hurt the most and Charlie is so dear to me . . . But I'm afraid my father . . . '

Tears ran down her face and almost as one those who saw them wanted to take this strict father and wring his bloody neck — or so Davy told Fred later — but Rose put her arm round Alice and over her shoulder told Fred to leave Sparky and the gig and she would drive her home and explain what had happened. She was confident she could make this child's father see that it was not patriotic to send a man to war with no one to give him a loving send-off but even as she led Alice back to the gig Dolly was giving her opinion, which she seldom held back, on the nature of a man who could be so hard-hearted.

'Surely if you were to tell him you were perfectly safe and in good hands with our Miss Rose who everyone hereabouts knows as perfectly respectable he would — '

'No, no, it is kind of you and Rose has been wonderful and Harry Summers is — '

'Harry Summers! What's he gotter do with anythink?'

'He's Charlie's brother and Papa disapproves of the family so you see he must not be mentioned. If Rose were to take me home and just dropped me at the gate then no one can be blamed.'

'Dear God, I never heard anything so callous and I would not dream of dropping you at the gate to face this alone. I will drive you to your front door and speak to your father and tell him . . . '

They were all nodding in agreement since this was the right thing to do and their Miss Rose, who was afraid of nothing, would set this bugger — Davy's words — to rights.

'No, oh no. Please, Rose, do as I ask. If I seem to have gone with . . . with someone who gave me a lift — a casual lift — then I will do my best to convince him. You see, I don't want him to know about you. That way I will probably be able to visit you later; well, when this has all blown over. Please, Rose.' She gripped Rose's arm with frantic fingers but there was nothing Rose liked more than a good fight with someone of whom she disapproved.

She and Alice climbed into the gig helped by many eager hands and with a click of her tongue, turned the reluctant Sparky, who thought he had done enough and had had enough frights for one day, and headed for the gate and the road to Weatherly House. All of them, even the scullery-maid, came to the gate to see them off, begging her to come and visit them as soon as

43

she could. She'd be more than welcome!

She resisted all Alice's pleading to be dropped at the gates and had almost to forcibly restrain her from jumping out while the gig was still moving.

'Really, Alice, your father will be relieved to know that a perfectly respectable person drove you into the city and that you put yourself in no danger with me. I will tell him that I found you on — '

'No, no, Rose, please don't. He never lets me go anywhere unless Miss Price is with me or, if I go riding, one of the grooms. You don't know — '

'Rubbish! I can't imagine — '

'No, of course you can't,' Alice said forcefully. 'You have not met him. As long as I act in what he considers a correct and ladylike manner he is perfectly pleasant but if I cross him he can — '

'Poppycock,' Rose spluttered. She had been surrounded by affection and given perhaps more freedom than most girls of her class and believed that Arthur Weatherly, when he heard the story, would be as her own father had been, prepared to listen to reason.

★   ★   ★

She was wrong. The man who stood glowering on the sweeping steps of Weatherly House was a man who had been disobeyed and at the sight of his livid countenance Alice began to tremble and even to huddle up to Rose as if for protection.

'Good afternoon, Mr Weatherly,' Rose said

pleasantly, thinking to turn his anger away from Alice to herself.

'Never mind that, Miss . . . Miss . . . '

'Beechworth. Rose Beechworth of Beechworth House. I have returned your daughter safe and sound.' Her own voice sounded strained even to her and the man, who was visibly restraining himself from hitting someone, preferably her, she thought, took no notice of her.

'Get in the house, Alice. I will deal with you later. Go straight to your room and wait there for me. And I would be glad if this . . . this person would remove herself and her . . . her *équipage* from my drive.' He made it sound as though Sparky were pulling the local rubbish cart!

'Really, sir, Alice and I have done nothing to deserve your disapproval. She needed a lift and I — '

'I have no interest in this . . . this person, Alice, so if you would climb down and get upstairs I shall — '

'Well, I must say, this is not the way a gentleman treats a lady . . . ' Rose declared, though she started to understand that to tell him that she and Alice had merely been to the station to see the troops away to war would only make matters worse. He was already turning his back on her, following his daughter as she scurried up the steps. He closed the door firmly and Rose sighed, for she realised that Alice had been right and she herself had been wrong. In her arrogance, or perhaps it was really innocence, she had believed she could reason with him and make him see that they had done nothing improper. She remembered, too late, of course, that Alice had told her that her father did not like the Summers family so why in her swollen pride had she not listened to her? Now what had she done? Thrown poor Alice into the centre of her father's anger. What would he do to her? Alice had intimated that he had never hit her but he had looked as though he might do so today.

Slowly she turned Sparky on the smoothly raked drive and headed for the splendid wrought-iron gates half a mile away. She had been glad on her way towards the house that she had persuaded Alice to let her take her to the front door, believing that her father would be pacified by Rose's explanation of their action, but on the return journey, despite the long trudge Alice would have had, she knew now that she had only made things worse. Her own self-confidence had betrayed her. No, not her, but poor Alice.

The grooms both ran out of the stable, smiling, dying to ask her about Miss Alice since they had taken a great fancy to the lovely young girl, but she merely climbed down, shaking her head at them. They had the sense not to say anything but Dolly was a different matter. She was there on the back step, a stout, red-faced woman in a snowy apron, the keys that were in her keeping as housekeeper jingling at her waist. She felt she was entitled to let her feelings be known and to question who she liked about what she considered to be her domain. And guests at Beechworth House were her business and had been since her mistress had died when Rose was only ten years old.

'Well?' she questioned.

'Well what?' Rose answered, too dispirited to give a full account of what had happened.

'Don't you cheek me, young lady. You might be the mistress of this house but you're not too old for a box on the ears. Was everything all right? Did her pa — '

'He's the most awful man I have ever met. Anybody who crosses him had better watch out and what will happen to poor little Alice God only knows. She was brave to defy him and go to see Charlie off but she'll be made to pay for it. Oh, for the love of God, let me get in, Dolly.' And as she spoke she suddenly became aware of a smart trap pulled by a little pony tethered to a ring in the stable wall.

'Who — '

'Nay, what a day this 'as bin. I put him in the drawing room but he didn't want no tea or coffee. I even offered him a glass of your pa's best whisky but he didn't want — '

'Who the devil . . . ?'

'Mr Harry Summers, that's who.'

'Oh, damn and blast . . . '

'That's no way for a lady to talk, Miss Rose, an' your poor mam'd turn in her grave if she — '

But Rose was striding towards the door that led from the kitchen to the wide hallway beyond. As she entered the drawing room he stood up and she was seriously alarmed by something that rose up inside her. What the devil was the matter with her? What was it about this man that he

47

should have this effect on her, she who had held in scorn all the gentlemen who had done their best to ingratiate themselves into her good graces? But her face was impassive and Harry Summers, unknown to her, wondered exactly the same thing. He had brought the trap to take Alice home, or so he told himself, when he had known full well that Rose Beechworth would have already done so. Nevertheless he blundered into what he hoped was a reasonable explanation, stammering slightly. She was having none of it!

'Mr Summers, if you have come to take Alice home, which I believe is your intent, I have already done so. The gig was there so I took her and — '

'Got a mouthful from her father for your trouble.'

Harry Summers, if he was put to the torture, would never admit what prompted him to harness the trap and fetch Alice from Beechworth House. It had nothing to do with Alice, fond as he was of her since Charlie and Alice were madly in love and Charlie was, after all, his brother. But for reasons that vexed him he felt a compulsion to go to *her* house and drive Alice back home. Now, as *she* stood before him he felt the calm wrap round him as he gave in to his feelings and admitted that although it was only this very day that he had met this tall, rather haughty woman who was looking at him with such scorn, she was the only woman for him. He was not to know from her expression that inside she was all aflutter and her heart was beating so

48

rapidly she was afraid he would see it move beneath the fine poplin of her blouse.

'He was not very pleasant,' she admitted, 'and well . . . ' She reached out and absent-mindedly picked up a Dresden figurine, turning it over and over in her sudden distress. 'I was sorry to leave her but there was nothing I could do. He ordered me off his land and shut the door. You don't think he *beats* her, do you? I couldn't bear it if I thought . . . '

'No, oh no, Rose.' He crossed the carpet and took the figurine from her, replacing it on the table, took her hands and looked earnestly into her deeply distressed, golden eyes. 'He's a bully, riding roughshod over everything and everybody who does not do his bidding but he is very proud of her. In his own crooked way he loves her. He is over-protective with her. But not only is she very pretty she will be a wealthy young woman. Many young men have courted her, young as she is, but he sent them all packing. But she fell in love with Charlie and he with her. I believe they met again as adults at a tennis party given by the Fosters . . . d'you know them? . . . no, well, Charlie doesn't give a damn for her money. He wanted a career in the army and has done since he was a little lad. He's longing to see 'action' as all of them are so he and Alice must wait. God knows what the outcome will be.'

Her hands did not pull away from his and she looked into his face which was on a level with hers. He was a tall man but her brow almost touched his lips and for a magical moment he was tempted to kiss it and she held her breath hoping he would but, remembering himself, he took a hasty step back . . . and waited. He didn't know what for and neither did she.

'And what of you, Mr Summers?' she managed to ask breathlessly.

'Me? I am somewhat constrained by the health of my father, Miss Beechworth. You may have heard, for the whole county knows everyone's business. And that is why Arthur Weatherly considers my family to be beyond the pale. He thinks my father a wastrel who committed the cardinal sin of chucking his money down the drain. Gambling, I suppose. A crime in his eyes and he wants our family to have nothing to do with his. That is the gossip, Miss Beechworth.'

She was indignant. 'I do not engage in gossip, Mr Summers.'

'So you have not heard that my father had a stroke?' He smiled ironically.

'Well, yes, but . . . '

'I apologise, I did not mean to infer you were like the rest of them, those who prattle among themselves on how long he will last. They say he deserves it owing to the fast life he led which resulted in him losing everything he had except the house and the land.' His voice was bitter now. 'But he was always a good father to Charlie and myself and I cannot abandon him. I too want to fight in this bloody war — I'm sorry, that is what it will be — but I cannot leave him to die alone. I am doing my best to hold it all together, the farms, the tenants on those farms, the land itself, but when he goes and I go off to fight who will look after it all for me and, of course, for

Charlie? It is his home as well as mine and although I will inherit the title and all that goes with it I have a duty ... Dear God, I'm sorry, I've no right to bore you with my problems.'

'I am not bored, Mr Summers. And if there is anything I can do to help you I hope you will ask. Just ask. I'm not concerned with the meaningless trifles that seem so important to females who exist in what is called 'polite society'. I long to do something *real*. I am becoming increasingly interested in the women's rights movement and have been to one or two of their meetings. But so far I have done nothing and I'm ashamed of myself. Tell me, do you think that it might be — '

'Miss Beechworth, dear Miss Beechworth.' He began to laugh and for a moment she was offended then she joined him. 'Here we are talking of such serious subjects when there are other matters ... '

'What matters, may I ask? Your father is dying, you seem to be telling me, and I suppose you will then be *Sir* Harry Summers and we will all have to curtsey to you but please ... '

'Please what, Miss Beechworth?' he murmured tenderly.

'Can you not call me Rose and may I call you Harry?'

★ ★ ★

She watched as he climbed into the little trap, looking somewhat awkward, since it was a ladies' vehicle and he had trouble fitting his long legs in.

51

He turned at the gate and looked at her, his face quite expressionless but nevertheless she knew that something important to them both had happened this day.

Dolly was behind her, her wise eyes searching her face for an answer to an unasked question.

'Well, what the devil was that all about and don't give me no flannel for I've eyes in me head and brains too.'

'I can't imagine what you're talking about, Dolly Davenport.' Rose tossed her head, her froth of curls flaming round her head like a living flame. There was a deep light in her golden eyes as though a candle had been lit in her head and her cheeks, which were usually a rich creamy colour, had a flush in them.

'Oh yes, you do, my lass. But if you want to keep it to yourself that's up to you. Harry Summers is a fine-looking man and — '

'Oh, go to the devil,' Rose exclaimed and flounced up the stairs, taking refuge in her bedroom. It was simply furnished but every piece of furniture was of the best quality. The colour scheme was mostly white with a touch of apple green and rose pink in the curtains and carpet. The large double bed was covered with a white embroidered quilt, the work of her own mother and very precious to her. The big bowed window had seats round it scattered with cushions, and with the door securely fastened in order to keep Dolly out she sank down on to them, her back against the side of the bay, her feet tucked under her. She looked down the long gravel drive to where Tom, Nessie's husband, was dead-heading the roses in the border. She thought she might pick some later and take them to her mother and father who lay in the same grave in Holy Trinity Churchyard, then, her eyes unfocused, her head on her knees, she wondered how far Harry — she was determined to call him Harry now — had got.

A knock on the door brought her from her reverie.

'What?' she snapped irritably, reluctant to let go of her thoughts.

'Miss Davenport ses dinner's on't table, Miss Rose.'

With a sigh she stood up and moved back into the world she had got up to that morning.

4

Just before Christmas Sir George Summers breathed his last and his elder son, now Sir Harry Summers, though he had been fond of his father, was relieved. He had done his duty but now he was free to join his brother on the battlefields of France. The doctor had gone an hour since and Harry lay back in the deep leather armchair in his study, his long legs stretched out to the fire that blazed in the hearth. There was one thing they had in abundance on the Summer Place estate and that was firewood. A golden retriever in a basket lay beside him suckling two puppies, four having not survived. Of the two, one was a pure gold, the other a mixture of brown, gold and grey and Harry was of the opinion that one of Dan Herbert's collie dogs had climbed the wall when Bess was on heat. Still, they were, as most puppies are, very appealing as they now left their mother and did their best to climb out of the basket. They should by rights be free to roam a little now, for they were seven weeks old but Bess was his dog and fretted if she was not near him so, to the disapproval of Mrs Philips, his cook, and Mary the housemaid, the only servants he had left, he kept her basket beside him.

'Them dogs should be in the stable, Mr Harry,' Mrs Philips had said with a sniff. 'It's not right for them to be in the house. It only makes more work for Mary and I don't care for the smell in here, really I don't. Your mother, God rest her, would not have allowed it, I can tell you.'

'Yes, I believe you have, Mrs Philips, several times, but since Charlie went I have been — '

'Ah, yes, I'm speaking out of turn. You must miss Mr — or should I say Captain Summers and . . . ' Her voice changed instantly to one of sympathy. 'And then with Sir George so poorly . . . '

She had left quietly and the next day, today, in fact, his father had gone.

He did not hear the front doorbell ringing but Bess did, lifting her head to look at him. A discreet knock at the study door brought him from his reverie and Mary appeared, her face still showing signs of recent weeping for, despite his wild ways, Sir George had been liked by all his servants.

'There's a lady to see you, sir. Shall I show her in?'

'Sweet Jesus, can I not get a bit of peace even on the day my father dies? Who the hell is it?'

'Miss Rose Beechworth, sir. Come to pay her respects.' Mary's eyes welled with tears but before he could remove the mask of astonishment from his face there she was, dressed almost as she had been when last he saw her except over her shirt she wore a belted woollen cardigan in a rich mix of emerald and navy with a scarf of the same colours tied about her neck. Her hair stood up around her head, reminding him of a bright, tawny chrysanthemum bloom and her cheeks were flushed to peach since it was a frosty day.

He stood up, alarmed at the way his heart jumped in his chest. 'Thank you, Mary,' he said to the maid who withdrew discreetly.

'Miss Beechworth . . . ' he stammered.

'Rose, please. I thought we had settled that. I came to say how sorry I was to hear about your father.' She walked slowly towards him while the dog growled softly in defence of her puppies, for she did not know this stranger.

'But how did you know? He only died an hour ago.' Their eyes were locked in something that had nothing to do with what they were saying.

'I met the doctor, who is also my doctor, while I was exercising Foxy, and he told me. I presumed you would be alone so I came to . . . to . . . '

Her voice petered out and she simply stood there. The silence thundered on, then was broken by the puppies both yapping at once and another growl from Bess.

'Be quiet, Bess. This lady will not harm you or your offspring.' He put his hand down and clicked his fingers and at once the bitch heaved herself out of her basket and stood up to lick his hand. 'This is *Rose* who is a friend. A good friend,' he added softly.

'I hope you are not . . . that you don't mind . . . I have not seen you since August when your brother . . . and Alice hasn't called. I'm sorry about that. I think she and I might have been friends.'

'She would have been glad of your friendship

but I have heard she is kept close to home since that day.'

'He is a brute.'

'Yes.' He shrugged his shoulders then turned abruptly to ring the bell. 'Here am I, the perfect host who should be offering you some refreshment.'

'You must still be in shock after the death of your father. I know I was when mine died. But the old cliché about time is true, you know.'

His hand stroked the dog's silky head while the pups whimpered for attention, then with a sudden movement Rose moved to kneel at the basket. She picked up the squirming puppies who licked and nipped at every bit of her face and neck they could reach in an enchantment of delight.

'I've never had a dog,' she murmured indistinctly.

'Then have one of these. Have both if you would care to. They are weaned. Mrs Philips and Mary would be your friends for life if you took them away.'

'What about their mother? Will she not fret?'

'Strangely enough dogs lose interest when their pups leave them. They are not like human mothers, you know.'

Rose began to smile and so did he though he had no idea what had amused her. 'Dolly will have a fit.'

'I suppose she would but if you'd rather not . . . '

'Oh no, I would love them. I wonder if Alice would . . . '

His face was a mixture of amusement and dismay. 'You have never met Arthur Weatherly except for . . . No, he would show you the door if you turned up alone, never mind with a puppy for his daughter. I'm sorry, Rose, but the possibility of a friendship between you and Alice is very remote. Now then, will you drink a cup of hot chocolate with me? You can get to know Bess and the puppies. What will you call them?'

'Ginger and Spice.' Her voice was firm.

'But what made you . . . ? Ah, their colouring. Very apt. The multicoloured one is Spice, of course.'

'Of course.'

They sat for an hour while the pups wandered about the room, making little puddles wherever they fancied but Harry did not seem to care. The subject of the progress of the war came up, the war that was already killing thousands of their young men. Already Harry had lost his groom who had joined up and had been overheard doing his best to persuade Enoch who was a hedger and ditcher and at least forty, to come with him to France just as though it were a holiday that Enoch would enjoy. These were country boys and Harry wondered how long they would last in what he called 'the grown-up world' of being a fighting man. Most of them had worked the land since they were thirteen. They had known nothing else so how would they cope in that frightening world across the Channel? He said so to Rose.

'The First Battle of Ypres and at Mons cost us almost the whole of the British Expeditionary

Force and the government is asking for hundreds of thousands of volunteers to replace them. You've seen the posters. The Germans are trying to get to the sea to cut us off but so far, thank God, they have not succeeded. It's quite clear it will not all be over by Christmas, in fact it seems to be stalemate.'

'What does that mean, Harry?' She sat in a chair opposite him, sipping her chocolate, her hands cupped round the mug, one of the puppies determinedly chewing the toe of her boot while the other cried under the table lost in the folds of the cloth and unable to see his mother. Harry casually rescued him then sat down again.

'It means the trench lines dug by our troops and theirs are so heavily defended on both sides they cannot be breached. Miles of barbed wire and machine guns are deployed. Charlie says — '

'You've heard from your brother?'

'Yes, being an officer his letters aren't censored so he can tell me these things. Anyway, I shall find out for myself soon. I shall report . . . '

She scarcely heard the rest of his sentence, for the banging of her heart was in her ears. She could not bear to think of him in danger and her face was white now, the lovely peach tint drained from it.

' . . . so I shall have to get the . . . the funeral over and then . . . I'm hoping Charlie will get compassionate leave. Forty-eight hours perhaps.'

He was filled with consternation when she

stood up abruptly, picked up the puppies and made for the door.

'I must let you get on. I'm sorry to have held you up.'

He stood just as quickly. 'Don't be daft, lass,' smiling as he fell into the tongue of the Lancashire man he was. 'You have been most welcome. And what about the puppies? You can't carry them on a horse. I assume you rode over?'

'I can walk.'

'Let me send them over with Enoch then.'

'I would be glad if your man could bring them. It will give me time to warn Dolly.'

She was terrified he would see the expression on her face which would have told him that she found his going to war was unbearable. At last she understood what Alice had gone through. Stumbling to the front door, not bothering to be *shown out* as was the correct way of doing things in their society, she ran down the steps, mounted her chestnut mare which was almost the same colour as her own hair and galloped off down the neglected drive as if the devil were after her.

When she reached home she dismounted and almost threw the mare's reins at Davy, who scuttled from the stable where he and Fred had been having a crafty smoke, and dashed across the yard to the kitchen door.

'We've got a visitor,' were the first words Dolly spoke, moving to one side as Rose flung open the door, revealing, to Rose's astonishment, the huddled figure of Alice Weatherly. She was slumped at the table doing her best to drink the cup of tea that Dolly had thrust into her shaking hands.

'Alice!' At once Rose could feel the hopelessness that had run through her body when Harry told her he was to go to war begin to drain away from her. Here at last was someone she could talk to, someone who would understand what she herself was feeling, but when Alice stood up, the tea ignored, the change in her was obvious. Dolly was to tell every one of them over and over in the next few days that she had never been so shocked in all her born days. Her lovely bright hair, which had once been so fair and bonny, hung in a lank curtain about her face and down her back. Her eyes were lifeless and her hands wavered like two snowflakes towards Rose as though she might fall. Tom was in the kitchen having a brew and as Alice stood, his newly lit pipe fell from between his teeth and shattered on the stone floor, the noise seeming to bring them all back to life. Dolly took her hand from her face and turned on Carrie and Polly, shooing them into the scullery.

'Why don't tha' come to't fire, my lamb, an' get thi' warm,' Dolly invited and Rose moved at last.

'Come, Alice, you must be frozen. Bring your tea and do as Dolly says.'

Alice did as she was told, moving in a way that told them she was used to being obedient and if they had said, 'Go and peel those potatoes,' she would have done so though she had never peeled a potato in her life. She wore an old shawl that had seen better days and which had probably belonged to one of her father's servants. She could not seem able to stop shivering and when she was seated Rose went to her and knelt at her feet.

'I had nowhere else to go,' Alice said simply, 'but if you are unable to . . . I'll understand.'

'The workhouse, you mean.'

Alice recoiled but Rose put her strong young arms about her and hugged her close. 'You are a daft little thing,' she told her lovingly. 'Dolly and I will take care of you, won't we, Dolly?'

'Course we will, chuck. Now drink your tea and get thi' warm. You've come to the right place, my lamb. Now let's get you settled,' calling to the three maids who were lurking in the doorway to the scullery, not wanting to miss what was happening. 'Carrie, run up to the linen cupboard and bring down some blankets. They're on the top shelf,' as if Carrie, who had been making beds at Beechworth House for years, would not know that. 'Now, Miss Alice, strip off by the fire and let's get you warm. Nay, no one will come in,' she said, as Tom retreated towards the door. 'There's only us women here' she added. 'Nay, my lass, don't cry,' putting a motherly arm about Alice.

Between them they took Alice's garments from her one by one, doing their best not to look at her jutting belly, which in contrast to her thinness seemed all the more swollen. She wore a pretty woollen dress in a soft rose pink which strained over the bulge of her pregnancy, and a corset which, presumably, had hidden her condition until now.

The maids' eyes were wide, not just with dismay, for the worst thing that could happen to a girl was to be with child without a husband, but with pity since Miss Alice was only a child herself. They had seen her now and again going by in her carriage and marvelled at her sweet face. And who on earth could have got her in this condition and then gone off, perhaps to war, and abandoned her? Alice was in such a stunned state she didn't seem to mind her nakedness, forgetting the modesty with which she had been brought up, allowing them to wrap her in the warmed blankets then sitting obediently in the rocking-chair. She stared into the fire while the rest of them tiptoed round her, giving her time to recover a little, when she suddenly began to talk.

'Charlie and I — before he went to France — we loved one another . . . ' She did not know how to word the rapturous lovemaking she and Charlie had shared. 'We were going to be married — run away and be married since my father would not countenance it, then the war came and there was no time. He has written to me, through Harry.'

The maids' faces were a picture! Charlie and Harry! The Summers brothers! And here was poor little Miss Weatherly in the family way!

'My maid wept; she had come into my bedroom unexpectedly and saw me. She screamed in her shock and my father came racing up, and some of the servants . . . I hadn't had time to put my corsets on, you see. He shouted at me, called me names, awful names. My maid — she loves me — tried to stand up to him but he hit her, knocked her down as though it were her fault. He pushed me away when I tried to help her. 'Get dressed,' he said, 'and get out of my house.' Then he swore. I had no coat. He pushed me away again and I almost fell down the stairs — I might have lost the baby, Charlie's child. He followed me, my father . . . The servants were horrified and tried to help me. Dear God, it was like a nightmare . . . my father, he's . . . Gilly — she's my maid — ran after me and put this shawl round me . . . she was crying . . . She'll be dismissed.'

'She can come here, Alice.'

'You are all so kind. I must let Harry know so that he can tell Charlie where I am; just until I can find somewhere . . . '

'Stop it, Alice, stop it, I say. You will stay here with us and have your baby and then we will see what is to be done.'

Rose was aware of the sharp intake of Dolly's breath and the maids, who had been brought up, as decent girls were, to believe that it was a sin to consort with a man to whom one was not married, exchanged glances, for what would their families say if they knew.

'No, oh no, I couldn't. I wouldn't presume . . . my mind was . . . I was in such a state . . . I gave it no thought so I came here. I did try to get out to see you but I was watched, after that day when you and I went to the station. I couldn't even send you a letter. Oh, Rose, please let me

64

rest for an hour then I will see if perhaps Harry . . . '

Her voice was apologetic and she lapsed into silence. They held their breath, waiting to see if she had anything else to say and though they were all shocked to the core like all virtuous women of their time would be, could they be cruel enough to judge the poor little thing? Dolly wondered how many other young women would find themselves in the same condition at a time like this when their sweethearts went off to war and might never come back. Besides, this house was not hers, it belonged to Rose and it was Rose who would make the decisions.

The servants were still standing unmoving, Rose kneeling with her arms about Miss Alice when a commotion at the back door had them all twittering like a flock of starlings. What the devil was happening outside in the yard? A voice could be heard asking for Miss Beechworth and when Fanny opened the door, had they not been in such a trance it might have been amusing. A working man stood there and in his arms were two wriggling puppies. The man looked most put out as though this was not really his job and the quicker it was done the better he would like it.

'Sir Harry sent these little buggers. Rather you than me,' he told the astonished maid, thrusting them into her reluctant arms. She shrieked as though they were live snakes, put them down on the clean floor and stepped back, holding up her skirts. Both of them promptly squatted down and made water.

Alice laughed and as Dolly watched her, she

65

forgave everything and everybody, which included Miss Rose, to hear Miss Alice laugh when moments ago she looked as though she might do herself some harm if left to her own devices.

'Miss Davenport . . . what are we to do?' Fanny stammered, looking as though she were ready to jump on the nearest chair to avoid the excited puppies.

'Nay . . . nay,' Dolly wailed, 'what 'ave thi' done now, Miss Rose? See . . . ' turning to the man on the doorstep. 'Tha'll 'ave ter tekk 'em back.'

The man was truculent. 'Sir Harry — aye, — 'is dad died this day an' it's *Sir Harry* now — ses ter give 'em ter Miss Beechworth, an' that's what I done.' He turned on his heel, climbed into the trap and drove swiftly out of the yard.

Rose got to her feet. 'Lord, I forgot about the puppies with all . . . ' She turned to Alice. 'I thought you might like one, Alice. They're called Ginger and Spice.'

'Never mind what they're called,' Dolly screeched. 'They're not stopping in my kitchen so you can put that in yer pipe an' smoke it. See, will tha' look at that.' It was a sign of her agitation that she was struggling with her words. 'Tell Fred ter tekk 'em to't stable an' — '

'Oh, no, please, Miss Davenport, let me look after them, with Rose, of course. I have always wanted a dog of my own. I'll clean up after them, I promise.' A light had been restored to Alice's eyes, perhaps only momentarily but for the present she was taking an interest in something other than her own terrible dilemma.

For the first time Nessie, the cook, spoke up. Until now she had watched the drama without a word but now she gave her opinion for what it was worth.

'Forget the wee dogs. That lassie needs to get to her bed. Let Fred take the pups to the stable where Fred and Davy and my Tom'll care for 'em. They've got each other so they'll not fret for their mam. There'll be enough goin' on in the next few days to be mitherin' about puppies. Tekk Miss Weatherly to her bed, Miss Rose, get her tucked up an' then later she can have summat to eat. I'll mekk her a tasty dish for she's eatin' fer two now.'

Nessie's sensible suggestion calmed them all down, even Dolly who was not used to being told what to do. She went to the back door shouting for Davy or Fred and told them to take the small animals to the stable and . . . well, do whatever you did with such creatures, wiping her hands of them completely. It was nothing to do with her what Miss Rose did in her own household though she did her best to stop her mistress from acting too hastily over many matters. She was just too good-hearted in Dolly's opinion!

At last peace was restored. A fire was lit in the best spare bedroom, Miss Alice had been bathed by herself and Miss Rose, even to the washing of her hair which looked lovely again, curling softly down her back. She wore a nightdress of Dolly's and was put to bed with a hot-water bottle at her feet and when Rose looked in on her later, replenishing the fire, drawing the curtains in the lovely candle-lit bedroom, Alice was sleeping like a baby, her face flushed, calm, as a well-loved child will sleep.

Rose had sent a message by Davy to Harry saying that if he could come at once she would be grateful. It was to do with Alice and Charlie, she wrote.

He rode in the dark, a lantern fixed to his saddle on a stick bobbing ahead of him and was ringing the bell at Beechworth House within the hour. Fred was summoned to see to his horse. And the question of Charlie and Alice was discussed at length by Harry and Rose. There were so many questions to be answered. Should they call the doctor? How far gone was she? She must naturally stay with Rose, they both agreed about that. Though she was carrying his brother's child it would not be proper for her to live at Summer Place. She must rest and be well fed. Then Harry revealed news that Rose longed to tell Alice.

He nursed the glass of whisky Rose had pressed on him and she sipped her sherry, both aware of the tension in the drawing room and when Dolly was called for, so was she. She had seen the way the two of them avoided looking at one another and her wise old mind put two and two together and came to the right conclusion. So that was the way of it! Her mind rejoiced, because Harry Summers was the man she would have chosen, had she the right, for her Rosebud.

'Well, I think I might have the answer to all

our problems, Rose, and Miss Davenport. I have telephoned a gentleman, a gentleman high in rank at the War Office and he has promised he will take all the necessary steps to get Charlie compassionate leave. For his father's funeral and at the same time, if I apply tomorrow and obtain a special licence, for him and Alice to be married.'

'Oh, Harry, I must go and tell Alice at once. She will be overjoyed.' Rose jumped to her feet and made for the door but Harry stood up and caught her hand, and kept hold of it.

'Let her sleep now, Rose,' and in his eyes were the words, 'dear, dear Rose' which was not missed by Dolly. 'Wait until it is arranged so that she will not be devastated should it not happen.'

Her hand lay in his where it longed to be and if Dolly had not been present they would have exchanged their first kiss.

5

They stood for the second time in two days at the altar of All Hallows Church which was so close to Summer Place it was hardly worth getting out the old carriage to take Sir Harry Summers and his brother Charlie to the lych-gate through which the bride would enter. Still, as Charlie declared, he and his brother, who was to be best man, could hardly walk to his own wedding, could they? The carriage was almost falling to pieces, poor old thing, and it had been kept for sentimental reasons really. Their mother, Lady Summers, had used it for years to take her into Liverpool, driven by the coachman who had long since gone to his maker, but Enoch, roped in for the task, did his best to make it presentable, and with a borrowed horse donated by Dan Herbert, the farmer from Oak Hill, and with Enoch 'done up' in his best suit at the reins, they felt they would not shame Alice. They'd even tied some white satin ribbon to the carriage.

As he waited for his brother in the hallway of Summer Place Harry's mind wandered back to the days since his father had died and Alice had arrived at Beechworth House, pregnant and distraught. He had telephoned his contact at the War Office the moment he heard the news.

'Tom, is that you?' he had asked the moment he was put through to the high-ranking officer with whom he had shared a room at Harrow. 'It's Harry — Sir Harry Summers now, and though I hate to throw my weight about, or rather my title, it certainly helps with difficult folk who are impressed by it. Yes, my father, today . . . Thanks, Tom, that's kind of you. I have a favour to ask and pray that you will be able . . . Yes, yes, that's it exactly. Can you get Charlie a forty-eight hour pass to attend the funeral? I'll be honest with you, Tom. There is also a young woman . . . yes, I know Charlie always was a man for the ladies but this is genuine. They are exceedingly fond of one another, so much so . . . er . . . she is pregnant and has been thrown out by her very respectable family so you can see the difficulties. No, she is not with me but with a very dear friend of mine whom I hope to . . . well, that's another story.'

Tom had pulled many strings and at this time of year with the two armies bogged down in their trenches, German and British facing one another in an absolute stalemate after the Battle of Ypres it was felt that Captain Charlie Summers should be allowed the compassionate leave he so richly deserved. He had been noticed. He had fought like a tiger at Ypres and his command of his men, and the respect they held him in, went a long way to granting him leave. He had arrived home with the mud of the trenches still staining his uniform and though it had only been four months since he had gone to war he was already a changed man. He did his best, teasing Mrs Philips as he had as a boy and cheerful young man but he was not the same. He had seen such horrors, men mutilated, horses with their entrails hanging out as they fought to keep their feet, the death of his own Lady who had been blown to a mist of blood and bone as she was hit by a shell, she and Burton the groom who was fetching her to Charlie.

He had walked silently into Alice's open arms. Harry had offered him his own stallion Corey for the ride to Beechworth, but he had refused as though the killing of Lady was something he would never get over and Harry wondered whether Charlie would ever ride a horse again. Instead they had driven through the winter lanes in the trap. It was a bitterly cold day, sunny with ice thick and sparkling on every hedge and blade of grass, but Charlie had not noticed as though his eyes were so full of other unbearable sights that they had no room for beauty.

He had put his head on Alice's shoulder and stood trembling in her warm embrace and it was not until she reached for his hand and placed it on her swollen belly and he felt the movement of his child that he became himself for a while. He smiled and held her close, kissing her with such tender love those who were in the kitchen felt they were watching something private, something sacred to these two.

Now he was to become her husband and the sight of her coming up the aisle towards him restored him as nothing else could.

As they waited at the altar for the bride to walk towards them Charlie glanced over his shoulder. Present were what Charlie called the same hordes of 'vultures' who had attended his

72

father's interment the day before and to Harry's dismay he had been about to harangue them but he was saved by the arrival at the porch door of the bride.

'Behave, Charlie,' Harry had warned him yesterday, knowing his brother was ready to do battle with anyone or anything that offended him. 'He was their squire after all, and they have come to pay their respects. Not to gawp as you think.'

They were gathered in the church and even among the gravestones to see Sir George laid to rest and now they had come to see Sir George's handsome son marry the Weatherly girl who, it was whispered, was already with child. And herself only a child at eighteen. But then there was a war on and there were hasty weddings taking place up and down the country in these terrible times. Already two young men, sons of farmers and known to them all, had been killed in the trenches. Those hasty marriages were not called 'shotgun weddings' any more, for the soldiers were more than willing to marry their sweethearts before they returned to the trenches. But they were not the proper events that would have meant six months' engagement at least. The birth rate had gone up considerably in the days following the declaration of war! Those of a more charitable nature sympathised as who could blame young men, many of them virgins come straight from school, wanting to know the delights of love before they left for the Western Front. Up and down the country it was beginning to be realised that this war that was supposed to be over by Christmas — which had come and gone — would be a long time in reaching a conclusion as the casualties poured back across the Channel.

As she came down the aisle Alice held the arm of the person who was to give her away and Harry smiled, for who else would have the audacity to take what should have been Alice's father's place but Rose Beechworth! A gasp of consternation rippled round the congregation and the vicar almost dropped his prayer book but there was nothing written that said it was illegal.

They both looked splendid but in different ways. Alice was almost ethereal in her young beauty. She wore the wedding gown that Rose's mother had worn, and let out skilfully. White lace backed with satin with a high neck and long sleeves and between them, she, Rose and Dolly had cleverly draped a length of chiffon across the front of the skirt so that the bump of her child was barely noticeable. Tucked into her silvery hair, which was piled on the top of her head in a froth of curls, was one white rosebud — which still flowered in Tom's greenhouse — and she carried another. In contrast, Rose was dressed in oyster satin and carried a small bouquet of oyster-coloured roses. Her hat was a boater on which Fanny and Carrie from Beechworth had arranged a circlet of apricot-coloured roses around the crown, thrilled to the core to have been given the run of Tom's hothouse. They had even taken the liberty of adorning their own bonnets with pink roses, smiling at their mam as they walked up the aisle behind Miss Beech-worth and Miss Weatherly who would soon be Mrs Summers. Their mams and the rest of their families were as proud of the maids as if one of them were the bride!

Rose was at least six inches taller than Alice but both of them smiled serenely as though there was nothing unusual in one woman giving away another. Most of the women were in tears as the lovely girl became the wife of the brave Captain Charlie Summers who would be going back to the fighting the very next day.

She herself, the bride, had become tearful as she contemplated her wedding day. 'What am I to wear, Rose? I can hardly stand at the altar in the morning gown in which I came to you.'

She looked down at the tailor-made, woollen, button-through frock which, while smart, was not fit attire for a bride who was to marry the man she loved in church. 'Perhaps we could marry in a registry office but . . . ' Although she knew that had she come to the altar in one of Dolly's working frocks with a pinny tied round her waist Charlie would not have cared. But he had stipulated to Harry that he wanted to marry Alice in church for all to see their joy, not hiding away in some neutral office with only strangers about them.

'If we marry in church there must be the calling of the banns. What of them?' Alice had asked but it seemed the new squire had thought of everything in his cool, disciplined mind and had obtained the special licence.

'And who shall give me away, Rose? Do you

think I could walk up the aisle on my own?' looking appalled at the very thought.

'Dear Alice, I know who will give you away. I shall give you away for I feel that you are part of my family now. All of us at Beechworth feel great affection for you and will continue to do so when you become Charlie's wife.'

Rose had begun to love this sweet-natured little creature almost from the moment they had met on the road to Liverpool. They all thought the world of her. Dolly, Nessie the cook and her husband Tom, Esther, Rose's maid, Fanny, Carrie and Polly the kitchen skivvy, plus the men who worked outside who watched over her when she went for a walk about the grounds. Dolly had told her she must not wrap herself in cotton wool just because she was with child. Exercise was what she would need and Tom took it upon himself always to be working where she walked.

They were all to go back to Beechworth House after the wedding ceremony and share the wedding breakfast that Nessie had prepared. With the captain off to France the next day the new Mrs Summers would move to her position as the mistress of Summer Place with Mrs Philips to *look* after her and Rose would visit her every day. They had tried to persuade her to stay at Beechworth House but Alice had felt it was her duty to live in what had been Charlie's home and his child would be born there as generations of Summers had before.

There was champagne to toast the newly married couple and even the outside men and the housemaids were to share in the celebration.

It was noticed that soon after their arrival at Beechworth the bride and groom disappeared to the room that Fanny and Carrie had lovingly prepared for them and they were not seen again until the next morning. And who could blame them, for though the captain had been his old self, making them laugh with tales of the funnier side of life in the trenches — he told them nothing of the other aspects of his soldiering and the men he commanded — and drank champagne and kissed his wife and even Dolly, when he came down the next morning, while he was better than when he had arrived, his face was frozen in that expression every soldier wore when he was about to return to France.

★ ★ ★

So the year progressed and it was February when Harry turned up at the back door of Beechworth House, putting Corey into the hands of a nervous Fred, for Corey was known to be skittish.

'For God's sake, man, be firm with him or he'll lash out at you.'

'That's all very well fer thi', sir, but this un's a bugger, if tha'll pardon me language.'

'Well, do your best. Is your mistress at home?'

'I think so, sir. 'Er Foxy's still in't stable.'

'Right, I'll go in then.'

Dolly was sitting by the fire, a cup of tea in her hand, black, strong, with two teaspoons of sugar, just as she liked it, sipping slowly, a calm look on her face which vanished as Sir Harry strode in.

Nessie was doing something at the stove, stirring a saucepan and Polly was busy in the scullery scrubbing vigorously as Nessie insisted upon.

'Sir, I'm sorry, I didn't know you were expected.' Nessie bobbed a curtsey and Polly would have done the same if she had seen him. She was singing the song popular with the soldiers.

If you were the only girl in the world,
And I was the only . . .

'I beg your pardon, Miss Davenport. I left Corey in the yard so I came in this way. I'm sorry I didn't knock but I just wanted a word with Miss Beechworth. Is she in?'

Miss Beechworth! When last Dolly had been in the company of Rose and Sir Harry it had been *Rose* and *Harry*! Well, who was she to question the new squire? After all he was gentry and she was not and the gentry were known for their peculiar — to the working classes — habits.

'She's in the breakfast room, sir. She was late up and — '

'The breakfast room is where?' His voice was cool.

'I'll show you, sir,' struggling to get up from her comfortable chair.

'No, don't bother.' And without further ado he passed through the swing door that led to the hallway and she heard him looking in one room after another until he apparently found Rose.

'Oh, there you are,' she heard him say, then the door closed and there was silence.

78

Rose was daydreaming by the fire that had been lit in the breakfast room, a cup of coffee on the small table beside her, Ginger dozing on her knee, gazing into the glowing coals. She was dressed in a pair of beige breeches that had been especially made for her and a warm woollen jumper in a soft heather blue. At the neck could be seen a shirt collar, the sort gentlemen wore. Thrown carelessly over a chair was a tweed jacket, again like those young men wore.

She turned, startled by the sudden opening and closing of the door. At once she smiled, for it was of him that she had been dreaming. Then the smile dropped from her face. 'Is it Alice? I was with her only yesterday and she was blooming.'

'Ah, good morning, Miss Beechworth,' he said. 'No, it's not Alice. She is, as you say, blooming and she has settled in nicely. The servants are . . . well . . . it is not Alice but something else entirely. I hoped to catch you before I left since there is much to discuss.'

Her smile showed signs of returning but his tone frightened her and once again it slid slowly from her face and Harry Summers's heart turned over in his breast at what he was doing to her but it must be done. After what had happened to Alice he was not prepared to leave this woman to the same frightening fate. He loved her, that he admitted to himself and he thought she reciprocated the feeling and he knew if he allowed it to bloom even for the short time he was to be at home it might develop into more than . . . than . . . Well, they could not become as

Alice and Charlie; he was probably putting it a bit strongly and anyway he was to be off very soon and the temptation . . . oh, for God's sake, Harry Summers, pull yourself together. You are only imagining that she feels . . . Pull yourself together . . .

'Harry . . . ' she stammered. 'I'm not sure I understand. What has happened to Harry and Rose? I thought we were past all that.' She stood up and her face grew rosy with resentment.

'Please, Miss Beechworth, I know you wanted to do something for the war effort, you said so yourself, so I thought I would ride over and put my proposition to you. You are resourceful, strong and efficient, I believe — '

'What the hell is this all about, Harry Summers? You come bursting into my home and act as though we barely know one another but if that's what you want then I shall do my best from . . . So, *Sir Harry*, what is it that you wish me to be *efficient* about — is that the word?'

'I've not much time to waste, Miss Beechworth, so I'll get right to the point. I have been in touch with the authorities who are in charge of the wounded and they have been to check on Summer Place. They say it's just what they need to become a hospital and it is all now in hand.'

His voice was cool and his face quite rigid in his effort not to let her see his emotion. It was a hard thing to speak to the woman you love as though she were just an acquaintance who was to be asked to help in the war effort. But he must. He wanted to sweep her into his arms and cradle her there. To beg her to wait for him to come home to her but what if he should be killed which, from the figures of the casualties on the other side of the Channel, was more than likely. On the night before Alice and Charlie married Charlie had spoken to him in a voice of despair. He was an officer but he was not one of those who stood behind the trenches and let his men 'go over the top' as it was called. He had gone with them, encouraging them, sharing their danger, seen them mown down by vicious machine-gun fire. He had seen them hanging helplessly on the barbed wire and had even shot one himself to put him out of his misery and terror. Men with horrendous wounds who would die a slow, agonising death. He had recited the horrors of it all in a quiet, monotonous voice, his eyes focused on the sights he had witnessed. And the war was only six months old! How many more months, perhaps years would this go on?

Charlie had predicted years and the longer you were over there the chances of your surviving grew smaller and smaller. He had fought at the Battle of the Aisne, being part of the cavalry charge that had regained a strip of France about fifty miles wide. He had been part of the race to the sea that had ended at Ypres and when the Germans finally gave up, the British were literally on their last gasp. They were reduced by huge casualties, outgunned and outnumbered by more than ten to one but the Germans did not know it and gave up. Ypres was reduced to a pile of rubble but they had held out. Charlie had seen it, suffered it and was no longer the irrepressible boy he once had been.

'I'm going too, old man,' Harry told him. 'I leave as soon as the authorities have set up Summer Place as a hospital. Alice will be given a suite of rooms for her and the baby, or she might prefer to go and stay with Miss Beechworth when the wounded start to . . . '

Charlie had come out of his tranced state, turning to stare at his brother. They were sitting in Harry's study, which was a man's room. A room where a husband might go and sit to smoke his cigar or read *The Times*, leaving the drawing room to the women. It was shabby, as were all the rooms in Summer Place, but the old clock that had been in there for over a century still ticked the minutes away and was the only sound except for the bark of a fox somewhere on the estate. Between them lay Bess, unconcerned that her puppies had gone, dozing with her muzzle on her paws, her eyes darting from one man to the other.

Charlie had sighed. 'I suppose you would be called up anyway,' he said quietly. 'But tell me why is it Miss Beechworth all of a sudden when you have referred to her as Rose in the past? I got the feeling you liked one another. That it was more than friendship.'

'It is, Charlie, but I will not fall into the trap of — ' He stopped abruptly.

'Like I did, you mean? When Alice and I became . . . more than friends we did not know there was to be a war or . . . but I loved her. *HER*. Not just her body. Of course I wanted her as a man wants a special woman but I swear I meant to marry her if only her bloody father had not been so intransigent.'

'I know, old lad. You are an honourable man and I mean to be the same. I will not marry Rose until this damn war is over so I must treat her . . . well, we have been, I think, both of us, more than . . . I know her and she knows me in some way that is nothing to do with the flesh. I will marry her when the war is over but I must allow her the choice of . . . waiting for me or falling for someone else.'

'Oh, Harry,' Charlie said sadly.

And now here he was, hurting her, he knew, by the cold way he spoke and she was bewildered. Nothing had been spoken between them that might be construed as an understanding but their hearts had told them, their very souls had answered and her bewilderment was turning to anger. She would not say so, of course, but her very manner was icing over as she got to her feet. She held Ginger, and Spice had gone with Alice. She bent down and put the puppy on the rug in front of the fire then straightened up and on her face was the exact same expression as was on his.

'Just tell me what I am to do, Sir Harry. I *do* want to help in this war and have been toying with the idea of offering my services as a nurse, or VAD or even to drive an ambulance in France but — '

'Oh no, you must not do that,' he cried before he could stop himself. The thought of this beloved woman being in the same danger as the soldiers, as he himself along with Charlie would be, was unbearable. He did his best to cover up what he had almost revealed. 'You will be needed in the hospital that is being set up very soon at Summer Place. Doctors, nurses, stretcher-bearers: they will all need some sort of supervision and since you live so close by I thought — '

'You thought Miss Beechworth, a spinster with nothing else to do is just right for the job. Well, let me tell you, Sir Harry Summers, I will decide what Miss Beechworth will do to help in this war. I am twenty-four years old, strong, tough and unafraid. I can make decisions and I will soon learn to drive an ambulance since I am a determined woman who likes a challenge and will not be beaten, or ordered about by any man, so set up your hospital and look around you. There are plenty of women, especially if they have a man at the front, to help staff the place. And I think it would be better for Alice to come here. She and the baby don't want to be surrounded by wounded men. It would only remind her of what Charlie is suffering. So, good day to you, Sir Harry.'

She bent again and picked up the pup who immediately started to lick her face in an ecstasy of love. She held it firmly as she brushed past the man she loved and who was off to war with cruel words between them. They both wore fixed expressions, not looking at one another as she opened the door and strode through it. She made for the kitchen where she dropped the pup into Dolly's startled lap.

'I'm going for a ride,' she snapped.

'What about him?' Dolly asked, nodding in the direction from which Rose had just come.

84

'What about him? Sir Harry is quite capable of finding his way out.'

'Now what's happened?' Dolly was exasperated, for she had hoped that these two, who she was certain were just right for one another, might make a match.

'Ask him.'

'Rosie, love, tell me what's up with — '

But Rose had gone, slamming the kitchen door so hard Polly dropped the frying pan she was scrubbing, making such a clatter that Ginger, who had dropped into the sleep that young animals and children can do so easily, woke up and began to bark.

'Oh, for God's sake,' Dolly complained, putting the little creature on the rug where it cowered in fright. The door into the hallway opened abruptly and Sir Harry burst through, striding as wildly as Rose had done moments ago.

'Can't you shut that bloody dog up?' he complained as he made for the back door.

Dolly almost gave him the rounds of the kitchen, she told Nessie later. After all, he was the one who had fetched the damn thing here in the first place. She picked up the puppy and soothed it and, comforted, it fell asleep again.

'I dunno,' she sighed unhappily. 'What a to-do-ment. Men! Why the dickens do they go to war, tell me that? It causes nowt but heartache.'

'Aye, yer right there, Dolly. My Tom'd be off termorrow an' 'im nearly fifty! Silly old bugger!'

6

In the spring of 1915 during the Battle of Neuve Chapelle and the Second Battle of Ypres in April the list of the dead and wounded added up to 180,000, but nevertheless the British Army attacked the Germans with great strength and success. Among those who took part were Captain Charlie Summers and his older brother who was also a captain, Harry Summers. Sir Harry Summers had gone into Liverpool to enlist and because he had spent time in the Officer Training Corps when at school nearly ten years ago it now entitled him automatically to a commission. While in town he had visited his tailor to order his officer's uniform. He looked well in khaki, gleaming riding boots, polished shoulder strap and belt, the leather holster holding a revolver, a peaked cap with the badge of his regiment, the same as Charlie's. All that remained for him to do was get to the 19th Battalion, the King's Liverpool Regiment, which was already fighting on the Western Front.

During the battles it all ended for one of the brothers in the horror of the poison gas the Germans directed at them with malevolent cruelty and a favourable wind. At first it was the French who took the full force. The strange green vapour, which, though the soldiers were not yet aware of it, was called chlorine, was stared at uncomprehendingly by the troops in the fighting. They exchanged anxious glances, wondering what the hell it was. Some quirk of nature perhaps but when the men began to fall, doing their best to breathe, ripping at their own throats because they felt they were drowning, they no longer wondered but fell in screaming agony. Their heads exploded in pain and they were filled with a raging thirst and those who were able reached for their water bottles and began to pour the contents down their throats.

Captain Harry Summers ran along the trenches, seriously risking his own life since he too was breathing in the poison besides being bombarded by the barrage of 'whizz-bangs' that came over the trench. He tried desperately to knock the bottles from his men's hands, shouting as far as he was able, telling them not to drink or they would die, but some did not hear him and some did not care, for the agony of their lungs and throats needed a soothing drink to quench it. Those who drank started to cough and a froth of green liquid erupted from their mouths and most of them fell back and began to die. Shells were bursting around them and their officer kept shouting at them to spit and though he could hardly see with the matter that filled his eyes, he did his best to get the men who were under his command, most of them the 3rd Liverpool Pals, to do as he ordered. All hell had been let loose but he knew it was up to him to make them lie down in the bottom of the trench until the gas drifted off and the effects of it dissipated, if it ever would. The ground quivered and heaved so that the din penetrated the deepest recesses of his brain but he did his best to watch over his men, slithering along in the mud and imploring them not to move. His senses were numbed by shock as were all the men's but they did as they were ordered and it was thanks to him that many of them were saved.

In another part of the trench his brother was facing up to the same horror but there was luckily no gas aimed at them. The thunderous noise made thinking almost impossible and Captain Charlie Summers, through the noise and lack of sleep, made a mistake. What happened came without pain, without even the realisation that he had been hit. He was aware of a soundless explosion like the red-hot wink of distant shellfire. A young soldier in his company, just come from England and whose first action this was, suddenly stood up shouting, 'Mam, Mam, fetch me 'ome, Mam. I don't like it out 'ere.' Charlie rose to his feet and grappled with the boy, doing his best to bring him down but the boy fought with him, tearing at Charlie's chest, dragging at his jacket from which fell his papers. He continued in his maddened terror to tear at Charlie's throat with his slowly whitening fingers, taking with them his officer's identity disc which was quickly buried in the muck of the trench. A shell burst close to them and a splinter of shrapnel tore right through the boy's helmet, taking his brains with it. For some unaccountable reason it ricocheted into Charlie's temple where it lodged. They fell together in what seemed a bizarre embrace and the rest of his men, thinking him dead, stood up and ran away, anywhere, they didn't care as long as they escaped this hell. But they ran the wrong way, chasing one another straight into the machine-gun fire of the enemy and of them all, only Captain Charlie Summers had a flicker of life in him. The trench wall, hastily erected, just as hastily collapsed on to the two muddied soldiers, buried as so many were in the graveyard of France.

★ ★ ★

Alice's son was born on the very day Charlie Summers was pronounced missing, believed killed, and it was Rose who brought her the news. And as if she hadn't enough to deal with, on the same day a telephone call to Summer Place, to where Rose and Dolly had moved, told them that the ambulances were on their way. Dolly was helping with Alice's labour. Rose was there should she be needed and it was a good job she was, for none of the servants would have answered the telephone's shrill ring.

It seemed that the wounded from the battle were pouring back across the Channel and beds were needed at once. All the hospitals in the south were filled to overflowing and though they themselves had nothing but a willingness to open Summer Place to the wounded, as Sir Harry had promised, they could hardly do so without somewhere to lay them. They needed a doctor, she told the disembodied voice on the other end of the line, and nurses for though she and her staff would do all they could they knew nothing about nursing wounded men. They needed beds to fill the rooms that were to be prepared for the soldiers and so many other things because they were not yet set up to care for wounded men. They would do everything that was necessary but . . .

It was all taken care of, the harried voice at the other end of the telephone told her. With the ambulances and the soldiers would come iron cots, mattresses, blankets, bed linen, two doctors, two nurses and three VADs. All they needed was space to put them in and would Mrs Summers please have . . . Rose tried to tell her that she was not Mrs Summers but the voice at the other end of the line was not listening. She was up to her eyes in it, she told Rose, and very grateful and when Dr Roberts arrived would Mrs Summers ask him to ring her. He would know who she was and with that she rang off.

★　★　★

Dolly, who had gently broken the news to Alice about Charlie, had been brought over in the gig by Fred when Mrs Summers started in labour. She was upstairs with Alice, wanting Alice to cry, to cling to her, to show some sign that she had taken in the dreadful news about her husband but she just lay rigidly in her bed, the baby beside her, and stared into God knows what hell the death of her young husband, whose son she had just borne, had flung her. Dolly wanted to comfort her, to hold her in her arms, rock her as one did with the bereaved, but Alice was as stiff

90

as a board and refused to be comforted and Dolly was sadly aware that it was she herself who needed comfort. In giving it to others one helped oneself. Nessie and the three housemaids had made their way to Summer Place so that they would be on hand for the arrival of the wounded. They knew nothing about injuries, they whispered to one another, but any woman would do her utmost to ease the suffering of their brave boys. Both Elsie Smith from Ashtree Farm and Jenny Dunbar from Top Bank had sons 'out there' and dreaded the telegram, those that would be sent to so many homes in the next months.

Dr Smith had gone downstairs to see if he could get hold of his wife on the telephone, for he had been at Summer Place all night and most of the day. He found Miss Beechworth in the hall clutching the telephone in her hand, for the moment her usual resourcefulness seeping away from her like water from a cracked jug.

'They're coming, Doctor,' she managed to say in a quivering voice.

'Who are coming, Miss Beechworth?' His voice was impatient, wondering where the wonderfully efficient young woman who had helped in what had been a difficult delivery had gone to.

'The wounded.' She handed the receiver to him or rather he snatched it from her hand.

'What wounded?'

'They're coming here at this very moment and we're not ready.'

Dr Smith, though he was not young, was

quick to grasp a situation. You had to be in his profession. He had no idea how long it would take the impending arrivals to get here but with the help of Miss Beechworth's stable men and gardeners they must at least clear the rooms that were to be made into wards.

'They'll need to be scrubbed down with carbolic, Miss Beechworth. How many rooms have you available?' forgetting for a moment that Miss Beechworth was not mistress here. The real mistress was lying in a coma-like state unable to help herself, never mind dozens of wounded men.

'I think about twenty bedrooms and then the drawing room and . . . I'm not awfully sure but — '

'Get them all cleared of furniture, Miss Beechworth. An operating theatre will be needed, a sluice, rooms for the nurses, the doctors — '

'An operating theatre?' Rose quavered.

'Come now, Miss Beechworth, pull yourself together. This house has been found suitable and I presume you and Mrs Summers have discussed it?'

'Yes, but it has come so suddenly and this is not *my* house, Doctor. I can't just move furniture . . . and to where? I don't know if — '

'Miss Beechworth, as you know, Mrs Summers is not capable at the moment of making any sort of decision so it is up to you. Good God, woman, these men need your help. Gather all the men and women you can in the area and start right away. I'm sure they will be more than willing to help. These poor wretches will be at the gate any minute. Let us try to be ready.'

Dr Smith was himself exhausted but with Miss Beechworth's men and women hastily summoned from the farms they had all the ground-floor rooms cleared, the furniture stored in attics, in rooms over the stables, in fact any place where there was an empty spot was soon filled. The farmers' wives had rallied round and were on their knees with buckets of water and carbolic soap, vigorously scrubbing the acres of floor, the miles of skirting boards, windows to be leathered, even the two farmer's wives whose sons were over in the mud of France climbing ladders to reach the high walls of the once lovely rooms — breakfast, dining, drawing room — but leaving Harry's study for the doctors as it was. They would need somewhere to write up notes, to give orders and simply to rest when there was a moment from their gargantuan task. The nurses and VADs were allocated temporary bedrooms on the first floor and when at last the convoy drove up the long drive they were more or less ready.

Under the directions of the doctors and nurses, the iron cots were hastily erected, simple beds that were put up in a minute, and the wounded men carefully placed on them. The sounds of the suffering men had most of the women in tears and Polly fled to what had been the butler's pantry which was to be turned into a sluice. Mrs Philips and Nessie were in the kitchen boiling water for the tea women thought was the answer to all life's problems. Polly, crying silently so that her tears fell in her bucket, was scrubbing down for the second time because she could not bear it, she said. Nessie was sorry she had brought her, she kept saying to Mrs Philips, since she was as much good as a chocolate teapot but she was sorry later when she saw the girl doing her best to comfort a man — *man!* He was no more than a lad in long pants — crying for his mother.

They were all non-commissioned men from all walks of life, the wounded officers going elsewhere. Staff Nurse Long had twenty years of nursing behind her, Nurse Heron slightly less, but with fifty wounded men to attend to and the VADs, who had a first aid certificate, they managed admirably. Rose hovered round them, taking orders and performing the most onerous and dirty jobs, for none of the men could get themselves to a toilet, should there have been enough to accommodate them. Dolly stayed with Alice who had not spoken a word since the news about Charlie had been hesitantly given her, taking no notice of the lovely little boy who lay at her side.

'That babby'll die if he's not fed soon,' one of the farm wives told Rose as if they weren't already prepared for it. 'My lass 'as just had one, 'er fourth. She's enough milk for two babbies. Give 'im 'ere an' I'll tekk 'im across,' for his fretful wailing was undermining everyone's strength, everyone except Alice who seemed impervious to anything.

So Charlie's son who had not yet been given a name was taken to Ashtree Farm where Elsie

Jones's daughter-in-law gave him his life back. They decided he might as well stay there instead of 'lugging' him backwards and forward as Dan Herbert's wife said. He slept peacefully by the side of young Jane Jones who shared her mother's breast with him.

Rose found that she had a talent for nursing; well, perhaps not a talent but at least she did not flinch from some of the tasks the nurses were beginning to ask her to take on. She was learning all the time as those first days were got through, standing at the elbow of Staff Nurse Long or Nurse Heron while dressings were changed, injections given and wounds cleaned. One of the men, a sergeant, had a terrible injury to his leg which Dr Roberts had confessed to the other nurses he thought might have to come off because it had turned gangrenous.

'Please, Doc, don't tekk me leg off,' the sergeant begged, and Rose wanted to weep for him, since she knew he was a farm labourer with four children to support and what good was a one-legged farm labourer?

'I'm sorry, old man, but if I don't it will spread and even kill you.'

'I'd rather be dead,' the sergeant said. ''Ow can I work and keep four kids an' a wife?'

'I'll give you work, Sergeant,' Rose told him. 'If you let Dr Roberts amputate you could have a false leg fitted and there will be work for you then.'

''Ow long'll that be, miss?' the sergeant asked hopelessly. And as though he had given up he allowed his leg to be amputated but died on the operating table.

'Can I see you in my office, Miss Beechworth?' Dr Roberts asked her politely, leading the way in to what had been Harry's study. She remembered the night she and Harry had sat there, friends but with something already blossoming between them. They had been discussing the war and he had treated her as though she was an intelligent woman instead of the usual 'you're a woman, dear, and wouldn't understand' which was the attitude so many men took. Where was he now? Dear Harry, where was he now? After seeing some of the terrible injuries the soldiers suffered and hearing their cries of pain, seeing the way they watched as the nurses approached them, starting their work of suction treatment on suppurating wounds, the employment of irrigation with bacterial fluids, making their agony worse, she had this scene in her head of Harry somewhere in a hospital such as this suffering what these men suffered, or, worse still, lying in the muck and muddle from which these soldiers had come.

Some men had stood for days in hastily dug trenches without a chance to remove their boots, ankle deep in tainted water, some of them with gangrenous feet. A soldier who had been wounded would make his way, or be carried to the regimental aid-post in the line. From there, after his wound had been hastily dressed, he would be taken to a field dressing station and with luck then taken by ambulance further back to a casualty clearing station. Then there would be a train journey to a base hospital to be shipped directly home across the Channel. It was an admirable scheme but when a wounded man had been days with the soil and dirt of the battle festering in his wounds his chances of survival became slimmer and slimmer. Even then, if there were no room at the hospitals in the south they were taken to hospitals such as Summer Place, another long and pain-ridden journey.

'Sit down, Miss Beechworth,' the tired doctor told her, which she did.

'I know you mean well, my dear, but you cannot go up and down the wards offering jobs to men with no legs, who are blind or mutilated and it will get worse, Miss Beechworth. Some men, not here at the moment, have such horrific wounds to their faces that their own mothers cannot bear to look at them. You must learn to be dispassionate, detached. I know, I know it is hard but it is something a good nurse learns no matter what is in her heart.'

'Dr Roberts, I cannot — ' she began but he cut her off.

'Then I cannot allow you to help on the wards. You will be kept scrubbing and polishing and working in the sluice. There is always more washing of bed linen than your women can keep up with and . . . well, your friend who has had the baby needs you. She has lost her husband and lies in her bed staring at the ceiling all day. Even her baby has been taken away.'

'She cannot feed him, Doctor,' Rose said passionately. 'Do you want the child to die?'

'There you go again, Miss Beechworth. You

feel things too much and perhaps if more effort had been made to put the child to Mrs Summers's breast she would — '

'Really, Doctor, I find your words very insulting. Mrs Summers is my dearest friend. I would die for her.'

The doctor sighed. 'Then go to her and instead of nursing the men, try to get her up out of that bed and into the spring air. Try to interest her.'

'We do but she is grieving for her lost husband. We are to christen the baby next Sunday and I am trying to get out of her what she is to call him. She has not spoken and unless she does I am left to choose the name for the poor child.' She looked round her desperately as though seeking inspiration.

'You must choose his name then, Miss Beechworth,' Dr Roberts replied.

'How can I possibly?'

'Had you and she not discussed it before . . . before all this?'

'Well, my father and grandfather were both called William and — '

'She liked it?' He looked wearily at her for he had enough problems without what to him seemed a trivial thing, the naming of the child of a missing — perhaps dead — soldier. At this very moment he should have been in his bed while Dr Cartwright took over, since there were thirty wounded soldiers needing attention.

'Yes, she was — '

'Then you must do it because I believe Mrs Summers will not be well enough by Sunday to attend her son's baptism.'

He stood up and passed his hand over his thinning hair. He had been about to retire when this war came upon them and had felt it his duty to continue his doctoring until it was over. The trouble was they had not expected so many wounded or for the war to thunder on as it was doing. The 'lull' or the stalemate was well and truly over and everywhere men like him and women like Miss Beechworth had stood up to the horrendous task set before them. He looked out of the study window and could hardly believe the beauty of the gardens that surrounded the house. It seemed almost obscene when over the Channel it was a charnel house. A mist of bluebells carpeted the woods on the far side of the garden, and a mass of daisies grew round the small lake on which two swans glided side by side, impervious to what the world was up to. In the lawn, which needed mowing, were more daisies and against the wall with the gate to the stables was a great splash of orange, marigolds he thought. At the side of the house a conservatory contained an explosion of colour, trailing ivy and ferns, all very overgrown. White wrought-iron chairs, which his idle mind thought would do nicely for men as they convalesced, were positioned around the lawn, and beyond that the trees were heavy with pink blossom. What a wonderful world this was until men smashed at it with greedy fists.

Then he became aware once more of the young woman behind him who was, after all, doing her best. He turned sharply. This was a pleasant room. A man's room with a big desk, leather-topped with a heavy silver inkstand, deep, comfortable leather chairs, a side table on which Sir Harry Summers would have kept his decanters and glasses and a French window through which came the smell of the country — grass, mayflowers, the smells of spring. And on the walls, pleasing to the eye were old prints of hunting dogs and horses. A typewriter and a telephone sat on the desk, a couple of rugs lay on the oak floor and a clock ticked on the mantelshelf above the fireplace where a cheerful log fire burned.

'Miss Beechworth, you do some good work on the wards and are a great help to the nursing staff but may I ask you to promise you will not give false hopes to the men, those who have lost limbs or their sight. Some of them may recover and be well enough to be sent back to the battlefields so — '

'Good God, Dr Roberts, you mean to return these poor men to that . . . place after what they are suffering, *have* suffered? I cannot believe — '

The doctor sighed again. 'There you go again, Miss Beechworth. I really must beg you to — '

'I will not stay out of the wards, Doctor, and I will not promise that I can stop myself from sympathising with them. They need someone to talk to, to pour out their pain and anguish; so many of them are terrified you will report them fit to return to duties they cannot cope with. This is not my house but while Mrs Summers is incapacitated I am in charge of it and you have no authority over me, nor my women. One of them has already lost a son in the trenches; oh yes, we have had a terrible description of the trenches and two of the women who are helping here know that their sons are still there and what is happening over there. My own . . . I have a person who . . . means a lot to me — ' she gulped and reached for a chair back to steady herself — 'and I can only hope that if he should find himself as some of these men do there will be a woman who will help him, not just physically but emotionally. He is . . . he is very dear to me . . . ' She dashed a hand across her eyes and turned to the door, fumbling with the handle to open it. As she moved into the passage that led from the study into the main hallway, Dolly was stumbling down the stairs, her face like chalk and behind her was Polly who had just taken a tray up with some delicacy to tempt Miss Alice, as most of them still called her, to eat a little something.

She still carried it but her eyes were filled with her easy tears.

'What — God in heaven, what?' Rose stammered, clutching Dolly's arm, for she thought she might fall.

'It's the lass . . . ' Dolly hung on to Rose, showing every one of her sixty-odd years.

'What, Dolly?'

'It's Miss Alice. She's gone.'

7

The man in the bed opened his eyes. His head was swathed in bandages that came down to below his eyebrows and he could barely see. He turned his head, doing his best to get a better view of exactly where he was. There were other beds with men in them all lying very still, and what he supposed were nurses bending over them. Where the hell was he? His brain did not seem to be functioning as it usually did. How had he got here? Why was his head bandaged? It ached abominably and he groaned with the pain of it and as one of the nurses heard him she came across to him from where she had been attending to another man.

She smiled and said something to him but he couldn't understand what she said. His heart missed a beat for he believed he was in hell. He hurt all over, his head the worst, but even worse than that was that he could remember nothing. What had happened to bring him to what looked like a hospital ward and . . . and . . . *who was he? For some frightening reason he couldn't remember his own name!*

The nurse, who was dressed in a snow-white apron and a handkerchief headdress, spoke to him again, laying a comforting hand on his and for a brief moment something she said made sense to him. Just a word or two but it was in . . . in German he thought.

'*Guten tag*,' she said, which he understood. He must have learned the language at school, he supposed, for though he could remember nothing else, he knew he was English. How did he come to be here? he asked himself again. What the devil was he doing in what was obviously a German hospital? his tired brain begged to know but he couldn't recall, try as he might.

She smiled again, a pretty smile that brought dimples to her rosy cheeks and for a flash lasting a mere fraction of a second he caught the end of another smile, just like this one, from other lips, then it was gone and he was really frightened. Had he been in an accident? Was he on holiday when he had had an accident? Oh God! What the bloody hell was the matter with him that he must fight so desperately to understand his situation? It had made his head ache more violently than ever so he closed his eyes hoping that when he woke again it would all become clear to him. That someone would speak to him in his own language, explain how he came to be here with his head in a bandage and the worst bloody headache he had ever had.

When he opened his eyes again the nurse with the pretty smile was talking to a man in a white coat further down the ward. The men in the other beds which were arranged neatly on either side of the ward were very quiet, not moving beneath their tightly made bedclothes. One or two, like him, had bandaged heads and at the far end there was a screen round a bed. Some other poor sod who was so ill no one was to see him, he supposed, though why he should think that he could not imagine. He had never been on a hospital ward before so what had brought him to this one? The bandage on his head must mean it had been hurt in something, an automobile, a . . . a motorcycle, perhaps he had even fallen off his horse; a horse . . . a horse: that had chinked its way into his empty brain — something to do with horses? The man — was he a doctor? and the nurse with the pretty smile were both looking at him and began to walk towards him. The man took his wrist in his hand, glancing at a watch as he did so. He spoke to the nurse and nodded then spoke to him in the same language as the nurse. Again he caught a word or two but not enough to give him a clear understanding of what the doctor was saying.

'*Wie heissen Sie?*'

'I can only speak English,' he told them, wondering how he knew when everything else was a blur.

The doctor looked astonished. 'You are English?' he said, his own speech broken and with an accent.

'Yes.' Was the man a fool? Could he not see by his uniform . . . his uniform? Now why had he thought of that — a uniform? First a horse, then a uniform?

'We were not knowing. We thought you to be from the . . . ' He babbled something to the nurse who shrugged, then answered him in German.

'Ach, now I am seeing. You were picked up by . . . erm . . . stretcher-bearers . . . German. You have no . . . er . . . er papers . . . no . . . ' He made a gesture of circling a ring round his neck. '*Die identifikation* . . . not there and were brought with our own . . . er . . . hurt . . . to this infirmary. I am a' — he tapped his head — 'of the brain. You had no clothes . . . you were . . . ' Here again he made a motion of brushing something from his body. 'Ach . . . mud, much blood and your head . . . splinters . . . shrapnel, so I remove . . . operate on you. Your name is . . . ?'

'I . . . I can't seem to remember.'

'Your rank?' The doctor looked at him sympathetically. 'You remember, hey.'

'Rank? I was a soldier?'

'*Ja*, but of course. You do not recall?'

'*Nein*, nothing.'

The doctor patted his arm. 'It will soon . . . come back . . . yourself you will find.'

'*Bitte*, please, help me,' he gasped as he clutched the doctor's arm. 'I must have relatives who will think me dead.'

'Dead. Oh no, you will not be dead . . . not now.' The doctor loosened the patient's grip, nodded kindly and moved on to another bedridden man.

He reached out an imploring hand to the doctor who turned, sighed, then came back. 'You . . . erm . . . I took some . . . splinters from your head . . . ' He muttered again in German, turning to the nurse who raised her eyebrows. 'I surgeon of the head . . . I did not see you . . . while later . . . they had cleaned you . . . they thought you were about to dead . . . die, but

I . . . ' He waved his slender hands about. 'I . . . '

'Operated,' the man in the bed murmured.

'*Ja*, operate and take out splinters . . . put in small . . . platter . . . no, no . . . plate and here you are . . . ' He waved his hand airily about the room.

'I . . . please, I cannot remember. I must have had papers on me to say who I was?'

The doctor turned to the nurse and said something to her but she shook her head.

'*Die krankenschwester* — nurse — says no papers, so no name.' He shrugged his shoulders. 'This war . . . ' then shook his head sadly as he moved down the ward.

★   ★   ★

'Well, she can't have gone far. She was only alone for a few minutes. Ask the men to search the grounds and . . . and tell one of the men — no, *all* of the men from the farms to search for her.' Rose shook her head and opened the door of the cupboard under the stairs, peering inside as though to find her friend there.

Dolly wrung her hands and tears wobbled in her eyes prepared to stream down her cheeks. She who had been the strong one in the Beechworth family ever since she had come to work for Miss Jane, Rose's mother, when she married William Beechworth, all those years ago. She had been staunch and unruffled through all the family's traumas and joys and had never shed a tear in public though when Miss Jane, Mrs Beechworth died, those she did shed had been in

106

private. She was now old and tired and easily upset. She loved Miss Alice, the girl who had vanished, almost as much as she loved her own daughter, which Miss Rose was although Dolly had not given birth to her. She sniffed and brushed her nose with the back of her hand. 'I only went to the bathroom. I thought I'd give her a bath. In her bed, like. She was weak as a kitten, she ate now't. I filled the basin and got a clean towel an' that. I were goin' in when I saw Polly comin' up wi't tray an' we talked fer a minnit. I were askin' after 't babby. Polly 'ad bin over to Ashtree but when we gorrin' she were gone. Dear sweet Jesus, it were my fault . . . '

Rose put her arms about the elderly woman and hugged her. 'No, Dolly, no, you are not to blame but we shouldn't stand here wasting time; we must set out to find her.' Her face became hopeful. 'Perhaps she's gone to see the baby.'

But Polly's face, as always when there was bad news, was streaming with tears and she was shaking her head. 'No, Miss Rose, I've just come from there. Babby was bein' nursed by Edie Smith but Miss Alice weren't there. Eeh, that babby's comin' on a treat . . . '

'Well, we shall telephone the police and ask them to start a search. She is unfit to be on the loose by herself. Not only is she weak from the birth, she is mad with grief over Charlie. Run down and tell one of the nurses what has happened and that I cannot help them for the moment while I get in touch with the police.'

They found the note an hour later. It was tucked beneath her pillow and at the same time

Rose heard that Sir Harry's stallion, Corey, an absolute beast to ride for anyone except Sir Harry, had gone from the stables.

'I have gone to find Charlie,' the note said. 'Something inside me tells me he is not dead. He is the light of my life and the light has not gone out so he must be alive somewhere. I will find him. The baby is to be called William, dear Rose, but call him Will. His father will like that.'

The search was spread far and wide but it seemed Alice Summers had vanished along with her young husband. Dolly went to pieces which again was not like her for she had been Rose's support and stay for years. But she was older now and she had a great fondness for Miss Alice — Mrs Summers — and having cared for her during her pregnancy, her labour and her grief over the loss of her young husband, she clung to Rose as Rose, as a child and young woman, had once clung to her.

'Nay, I shouldn't 'ave left 'er on 'er own,' lapsing into her native Lancashire dialect as she always did when upset. 'It were my fault, my fault. I blame messen, I do . . .'

Rose took her in her arms and held her tight, her own heart bursting with fear for her friend, her frail, but strong friend who had lost the love of her life and gone out to look for it in the maelstrom of the war across the Channel. Already coming the other way back to England were Channel steamers full of the badly wounded, the very decks crammed from bow to stern and from port to starboard with men who lay still and frighteningly silent, those who moaned or called for their mothers, men with different coloured tags tied to them to denote the condition and urgency of their case to those who would meet them from the ambulance trains.

And rattling through stations all over the country were trains packed with young, cheering, excited men, longing to get over there and do their bit before it all ended. It was a well-known fact that one British soldier was worth ten Germans and the Hun would be defeated very soon. Lord Kitchener had pointed his finger and ordered them to go and who were they to disobey?

★ ★ ★

They never gave up hope. The police found Corey in a meadow where other horses, mares, were placidly cropping the lush grass. Eleven months later the farmer who owned the meadow was astonished at the beauty of the foals produced in the spring of the following year from his mares but remembered the stallion that had been among them for a short time. He had reported it to the police for he was an honest man, but was delighted with the results of the horse's short stay. That had been at Pinfold Farm on the outskirts of St Helens, which was within riding distance from Old Swan and then a walk to St Helens railway station.

She must have boarded a train from there to London, which, of course, was where she could find some way of crossing the Channel to where Charlie had last been seen alive!

★   ★   ★

The committee room of the Woodfall Hospital Corps was dark and crowded. It was above a grocer's shop, and the woman in the drab outfit of a servant climbed the stairs wearily but when she reached the committee room she straightened her back and lifted her head, trying to look as tall as she could. Several women were sitting round a table on which papers were scattered. One woman seemed to be bored with the whole procedure, while the second appeared to be a secretary and was taking notes. She seemed nervy and filled with some anxiety. The third was Dr Emmeline Woodfall who was smoking a cigarette, lighting one from another so that the room was filled with what seemed to be a fog.

'Come in, come in, Miss . . . '

'Mrs Barnes.'

'Well, Mrs Barnes, what can we do for you or rather what can you do for us?' the doctor asked cheerfully.

'What do you want me to do?' the woman asked.

'We need ambulance drivers, nurses, stretcher-bearers, in fact anyone prepared to help out in any capacity. We need women who can speak French and they must be as strong as a horse. We want women who are not afraid to get their hands dirty; some of them have come today with their mothers and have never washed so much as a teacup in their lives. And we want married women. Do you know what this war is about, Mrs Barnes?'

'I do. My husband is missing and I know exactly what the war is about. I want to help.'

'Are you over twenty-one?'

'No, but I am married and I know I have every right to serve.'

'She looks very slight,' the woman who was bored remarked. 'And you did say you wanted women who were strong, Emmeline.'

'I may be slight but I am strong and determined.' The young woman straightened her already straight back.

'Good, then — '

'Hold on, Emmeline.'

'No, I will not hold on, Anne. I know that you and the committee raise the funds but I am in charge of the hospital and I know the sort of girl I want. This girl' — pointing a finger at the figure who stood defiantly before them — 'knows what she is about. She's not yet twenty-one but as a married woman whose husband is missing she has every right to serve abroad. I am taking her. Now, Mrs Barnes, let me describe the place that will be my hospital. It used to be a nunnery in Le Havre and the only servants are French orderlies. You will be on the front line. We will pay you ten shillings a week and your keep. You will have to sign on for six months so are you still prepared to take the job?'

'I am.'

'Good girl. Get yourself some woollen combinations and drawers. We'll send you your uniform in a week or two and — '

'Oh, I cannot wait a week or two. I must go at once.'

The doctor and the other two ladies looked astonished.

'At once. Why?'

'I cannot explain but if I cannot go at once, today, then I must find someone else to take me.' She lifted her head a little higher and with a face like stone stared directly at Dr Woodfall.

'My dear, you do not know what you are asking. There is so much to do, so many preparations. I could do with a month but I have cut it down to a fortnight . . . '

But already the woman who called herself Mrs Barnes had turned on her heel and was heard running down the stairs.

★   ★   ★

The baby was thriving and on the following Sunday, Rose, Dolly and all the servants stood in the church where his parents had been married just a few short months ago. He was a lovely child with Charlie's deep brown eyes — so like Harry's, she thought — his hair beginning to grow into a dark swirl of fine baby curls. He wore the same christening gown that Charlie and Harry had once worn, delicate, old and fragile, a Summers heirloom, edged with the finest lace and with insertions of new blue ribbons. He cried out when the holy water from the font was dribbled on to his head and those present sighed, for it was a good sign. Though it was the twentieth century some of the medieval superstitions still had some currency and the cry drove the devil out.

After the church service they all drove or walked back to Summer Place which, after all, would one day belong to William Summers unless his uncle Harry married and had a son. Afternoon tea was served, all prepared by Nessie and Mrs Philips, even the servants drinking champagne, for this was a special occasion with the poor wee thing having neither father nor mother to cherish him. There were none of the usual presents, silver mugs, silver teething rings and such that would normally be given since the guests were servants and could not afford such things. There were, however, flowers everywhere, grown by Rose's gardeners, in tribute to the son of the house. There was many a tear shed for the child who had no one, no member of his own family to love him though Miss Rose seemed very attentive. They even took him into one of the wards where the wounded were presentable and he was handed from soldier to soldier — much against Staff Nurse's wishes — but the men were delighted, some of them perhaps thinking of their own children. Will, as they were to call him, did not seem to mind, looking placidly into each face, ready to smile though Dolly said it was only wind!

Rose looked splendid, the men thought, because they had only seen her in her plain grey cotton dress and enveloping apron, her hair covered with a white servant's cap. Now she was wearing a warm peach-coloured silk dress with a hat whose broad brim was loaded with roses and baby's breath and pale green leaves. The wounded, surrounded by nurses, were made up with it all, they told one another and Miss Rose was a corker. They were unaware that Miss Rose was ready to weep every night in her bed, tormented by thoughts of a tall, good-looking man with an ironic twist to his wide strong mouth who was fighting in France and who had not written to her. Who could have disappeared with his brother for all she knew into the foul mud they floundered in. The foul mud under which lay hundreds of decomposing bodies, for most of the wounded who died in no-man's-land between the English and German trenches were left to rot since they had enough to do seeing to the wounded; the dead would understand. There was a camaraderie between these men — of all ranks — and their brothers-in-arms who had fallen lived on in the hearts of the men who survived.

★   ★   ★

'How many of you can drive?' the staff sergeant barked, glaring along the line of women who stood to attention in the yard of the Red Cross headquarters in the Mall.

Six of the girls, for that was all they were, girls, some just come from school, put up their hands. The other three exchanged glances but looked hopefully at the sergeant.

'Right,' he shouted and they all wondered why he had to be so loud. Were there a lot of deaf men in the army? 'You three can go. We only want women who can drive and know something about what goes on under the bonnet and can repair it.'

The six hands that had gone up wavered and two dropped their hands and shook their heads. One of those who had put up her hand spoke out. 'I can repair an engine, sir — '

'You don't call me sir, young lady. I am sergeant to you and tell me how is it *a lady* can drive and repair an engine?'

'Well,' the girl said, 'my father had a car, a Morris Oxford and I used to drive it round the grounds and the chauffeur — I used to watch him fiddle about with the engine. I'm not very experienced, that's why I wasn't sure whether to put up my hand but I'm a quick learner and if you could lend me that ambulance over there' — nodding her head in the direction of the vehicle standing by the entrance — 'and if you sat beside me I will show you what I can do.'

'Oh, can you, miss. We'll see about that and why his it that there are nine of you when I was promised eight?'

'I was told to go with the others,' the girl who had spoken told him.

'Hand where is your uniform?' for the girl was dressed in what he called 'civvies'.

'I'll get it shortly, I was told, S'arnt.'

The sergeant was impressed. She even knew how to address a sergeant. He had been given the job of engaging six women to go out with the ambulances the next day and here was one who appeared to be willing to tackle anything. She

115

was, as he said, evidently a lady though she was dressed like a servant and he wondered what her story was. So many of these young women were attracted to the idea of going to France and driving ambulances, or nursing but they had no bloody idea what they were letting themselves in for. What an adventure, he had heard one say to another.

'Never mind, miss, I'll believe you where millions wouldn't. Now, what's your name?'

'Mrs Barnes.'

'Mrs Barnes, his your 'usband hin France, by any chance?' he asked suspiciously.

'Does it matter?' she answered, and the sergeant thought, Well, give 'er 'er due, you can't say she 'asn't got pluck.

'No, but don't think you'll find 'im, my lass, if that's what you was 'opin',' forgetting for a moment to be strict with these ladies.

'Thank you, S'arnt,' giving him a smile so sweet he almost smiled back, 'but when I have leave I intend to try.' The other girls stared in astonishment at her.

'Right then, be 'ere at five termorrow morning. The train leaves Victoria at seven.'

The six of them were the only females on the troopship. They were Barnes, Ewing, Radley, O'Neill — who crossed herself frequently — Mayne and Thorley, for it seemed Christian names were never used. The sergeant who had interviewed them the day before had given them their uniforms which were hideous and was travelling on the same Channel steamer. It was somewhat choppy and the young soldiers who,

116

as they cast off had all been singing and joking, eager to get out there and kill themselves a few of the devils who raped nuns and cut off babies' hands, were for the most part hanging over the rails vomiting into the rippling waves, but Alice and the other ambulance drivers here proved Alice's theory that really women were stronger than most men.

She thought about Charlie, taking him out of the small shrine she had made for him in her heart, the shining memory of the moment when she had become his wife and before that when they had loved one another in her father's summer-house beside the lake at Weatherly. Memories of when she had been a child, she realised that, but now Charlie and this bloody war had made a woman out of her and when she found him — and she would — she would never leave his side again. If he was blinded, maimed, emasculated, and she knew what that meant now, she would be beside him for the rest of their lives. He had blessed her world. He was the beat of her heart and as the ship dipped up and down on the heaving seas and the young soldiers all around her voided their breakfasts into the Channel, she thought about the child they had made with their love. She had left him behind with Rose, dear Rose, who would keep him safe until she and her husband returned.

They were met at Boulogne by a command leader. Barnes and O'Neill were to go with another detachment of ambulance drivers to Number 4 General Hospital at Camiers, the rest to go on by train to Étaples. Alice hoped to God that O'Neill would not be genuflecting and praying all the live long day for she would find it very hard to live with someone who still believed there was a God who would allow this massacre to grind on as it was doing. She had not even arrived at their designated hospital yet and certainly not been in any sort of close contact with the wounded but just standing here on the dock listening to the sighing, murmuring of suffering humanity who lay on the dock waiting to be shipped back to England, was almost more than she could bear. She wanted to go to each man on his stretcher and try to comfort his pain, his *agony* but she must be dispassionate and listen to the instructions the command leader was mouthing at them. She watched a line of soldiers, their eyes bandaged, shuffle up the gangway of a steamer bound for England, each one with a hand on the shoulder of the man in front of him, a doctor leading them, a nurse at the rear and she was almost destroyed by the horror of what might at this moment be happening to Charlie. If he was blinded she would lead him, ease his pain, care for him but first, she didn't know how, she must find him. If he were in some hospital she would scour every one until she did. Charlie . . . Charlie, her heart cried as she followed O'Neill and the others to the waiting ambulances that were ready to go up to the front.

8

The men coming from the line, the walking wounded and the mangled and bloody bodies of those carried on stretchers were astonished and delighted by the dainty little lady who was dressed as an ambulance driver and who smiled as she spoke to them, for she was the prettiest thing they had seen since they left home. She was questioning every one of them about a certain Captain Charlie Summers, though they were sorry to see the disappointment on her face when they sadly shook their heads since they would have liked nothing better than to help her.

'The 19th Battalion, the King's Liverpool Regiment,' she repeated time and time again. 'I cannot find out where he last fought but someone must have served with him and can tell me where that was. In March, it would be. Perhaps Neuve Chapelle or Ypres in early April?'

She walked along beside the wounded men on stretchers, looking from one agony-filled face to another, even holding a hand that reached out to her, for though she worked eighteen out of every twenty-four hours and wore the unflattering hat and long shapeless coat of an ambulance driver she was very pretty and her compassionate smile made them smile through their pain.

Alice Summers had been given her first half-day's leave since she had been sent to the tented hospital in April and it was now

119

September. The Germans had almost demoralised the men at the front with their hideous new weapon, the 'flamethrower' at a place called Hooge. It was called the 'wonder weapon' and was meant to burn the British troops out of the trenches. The German soldier wore a pack on his back from which ran a rubber hose ending in long steel nozzles. Out of the nozzles spurted a vicious stream of liquid fire. The men who were caught in its horrendous river of flame were for the most part killed but a few of them survived it. They were dragged out burned, blackened and bleeding and yet still breathing — wishing they weren't — from the inferno. These were on the stretchers being carried to the hospital at the end of their tortuous journey and would be treated on a special ward. When they had been hastily examined, one of Alice's colleagues would drive them in her ambulance to the docks and the boats that would take them back to the special burns unit in England. It took all her strength to talk to these tormented soldiers who did their best to help the lovely woman who was looking for her husband. What was such an innocent little thing with eyes like pansies doing in this hell on earth but all they saw was her serene and Madonna-like face, not the steel that lay at the core of her. She was stronger than the strongest of them but they did not recognise that, only the sweetness of her, the almost ethereal frailty of her shimmering in the pale sunshine that broke through the clouds.

Alice saw an officer limping along with the walking wounded, a lieutenant, young, with barely the fuzz of a beard on his gaunt face and she wondered how old he was. What he must have seen to make such a boy into an old man she could well imagine after driving her ambulance for four months, but he was polite as he stopped to talk to her, glad to do so for he was but a lad at the end of his tether. He had several splinters of shrapnel in his arm and could not lift it to raise his cap or even manage a small salute, which distressed him as he had been brought up to be polite to ladies.

'Miss, why don't you go to headquarters, to Command and ask in which battle the Liverpool 19th fought. They will tell you and perhaps . . . ' He shrugged and his cultured voice tapered off and his face contorted in pain. He swayed and she put out a hand to him, holding him steady.

'I do beg your pardon, miss, but I must go with my men and am only sorry I could not have been more helpful.'

She took his advice and the next time she had an hour free she walked up the shattered road from the hospital until she reached the headquarters building from where all commands were sent. It was heavily sandbagged and guarded by two soldiers with rifles. They were loaded down with the usual accoutrements of war as though they were to be off to do battle at any moment. Gas mask, rifle, cartridge carriers, haversack, pack, canteen and numerous pouches to carry everything a soldier might need for trench warfare.

'Can I help you, miss?' one asked politely. He looked at her with the admiration all men did,

121

for even in the ugly, concealing uniform she was an extremely attractive woman. She had on the long khaki coat that came to within an inch of her ankle bone and hid most of the thick, black woollen stockings she wore. Her hat did not detract from her loveliness though it was a hideous thing pulled down to her eyebrows. From it escaped curling fronds of her silver-gilt hair.

She was not a woman really, as she still had the innocent, childlike features she had when she first met Rose despite what she had suffered. She had loved and lost her husband. She had borne a son and left him behind, in good hands, she knew that, but Charlie was first in her affections and she would search until she found him or had positive proof of his death. Her face was a pale oval and her huge eyes reflected the many shades of the winter pansies that grew in the garden of Summer Place. Their brightness and the sparkle of laughter they had once shown had gone but they were still exquisite, her eyelashes sweeping delicately nearly to her eyebrows and her cheekbones. They fluttered at the soldier and he fell instantly in love with her as all men were inclined to do.

'What d'yer want, chuck?' he asked kindly, while the second soldier wished *he* had spoken to her first.

'I want to speak to someone in command, if it is at all possible, whoever that might be,' she said softly. 'My husband is missing, believed killed, but I cannot believe it. If I was to tell the commanding officer what regiment he was in he might be able to say where the regiment was fighting in March or April. I don't know whether that is prohibited information but I will look for him until the end of this vicious war, if I have to. Can you help me?' she asked innocently.

'Nay, lass, I can't leave my post but I can send for someone who can.'

At that moment a man with a major's insignia on his sleeves climbed the steps that led to the door the two soldiers were guarding. They both saluted smartly and, like all male creatures, the major's eyes could not tear themselves away from Alice Summers. He had been about to berate the soldiers for talking to a woman while they were on duty when she turned her luminous eyes on him and, again like all of his gender, he fell into them. He returned the soldiers' salute absent-mindedly and turned to her.

'May I ask what your business is here, miss?' but in a soft voice as though speaking to a lost child. She was a beauty and when she looked him fully in the face he could feel the corners of his mouth lifting in a smile.

'I am looking for my husband, Major.' She knew all the ranks by now, for even under the muck, the blood, the compost that French farmers had spread upon their land and which was now insinuating itself into the wounds of the men and was the chief source of the infections to the wounded, their ranks could just about be seen and recognised.

'Does he work here, madam?' he asked, wanting to take hold of her hand and lead her off to somewhere private, for the two guards were watching with great interest.

'Oh, no, Major, he is in the 19th Battalion, the King's Liverpool Regiment. Captain Charlie Summers,' she said proudly. 'I gave birth to his son in April — ' then she shut her mouth like a trap because as a married mother she should not have been out here in France. She opened it again, then smiled radiantly and at once all three men smiled back, unable to help themselves.

The major leaned towards her and actually took off his cap, for he knew he was talking to a lady even if she was in the unattractive uniform of an ambulance driver.

'And what — '

'I would like to know where his regiment was fighting last March or April when I received the news of his . . . the telegram said, 'missing, believed killed' but he is not dead, Major, I know that. I would know it here' — thumping her chest where her heart lay — 'if he no longer existed,' she went on passionately. 'I want to find him or . . . or his . . . his body and I shall not be turned away. I was told that I might find out here where . . . where he fell, and I beg you to help me. I know that these two soldiers' — she began, turning to smile brilliantly at the men guarding the door. They said to one another afterwards it was like a bloody angel touching them, marvelling at her.

'Of course, I understand. If you would come with me to see Colonel Savage he might be able to give you that information.' He led her through the double doors into a wide hall that was filled with men in uniform, hurrying and scurrying

124

here and there with bits of paper in their hands, ignoring each other as though they were ghosts. 'Of course that might be classified information, I'm not sure. The colonel will know and perhaps be able to help you. That is if he is available. Will you wait here, madam?' He touched his swagger stick to the peak of his cap and knocked lightly on a door. A voice told him to enter which he did, closing the door behind him.

Alice sat on a wooden seat placed next to the door of the colonel's room and waited. A quarter of an hour later the major reappeared. 'He can give you five minutes, madam. He is a very busy man, as you can imagine.' And he had not yet set eyes on Mrs Summers, the major thought, which might change his mind for he had had a hard job convincing the colonel that this was a lady who promised not to keep him long.

He opened the door for her and the colonel, sitting behind a cluttered desk, looked up irritably, then, after letting his eyes wander over the face of the beautiful ambulance driver, stood up and smiled. Alice had realised that she was always to have this effect on men and would often take advantage of it!

'My dear lady,' the colonel said, for, like the major, he knew one when he saw one. 'I believe you wish to know something about the disappearance of your husband. Please sit down,' indicating a chair in front of his desk, not sitting himself until she was seated.

'Yes, I know he . . . fell . . . sometime in March or early April but I don't know where. He was in the King's Liverpool Brigade, the 19th Battalion, a captain in the cavalry, but I don't know in which battle he . . . he fell. If you could tell me where his brigade was fighting at that time I can start to look for him there. I have spoken to — '

'My dear madam, you cannot possibly wander round the battlefields looking for one officer. God knows who might be there now.'

'You would know, Colonel, and I don't want what might be restricted information, just the actual battle in which he fell. I shall look for . . . I don't know what, exactly, but there must be some of his regiment still in the lines somewhere, a soldier who knew him. His . . . his . . . body has . . . ' She almost broke down then, for the thought of the masculine beauty of her husband's body, torn apart as so many of the soldiers were, those she had carried so tenderly in the back of her ambulance, those she had seen dragging themselves and their wounds back to the hospital, almost undid her. She drew herself together and both men, soldiers who had fought, for the colonel had not reached his rank without physically fighting, moved automatically to try to comfort her but she lifted her head proudly as though daring them to pity her.

'Madam, I'm sorry for your loss, of course, but I'm not sure I can help you. If you will wait I will consult our records of the different regiments' movements. Please wait here and perhaps Major . . . ' — he looked enquiringly at the soldier who stood to attention — 'could bring you a cup of tea?'

'Major Pearson, sir,' saluting smartly.

'Major Pearson, see what you can do while I

consult with my commander-in-chief.'

'Thank you, Colonel, you are very kind,' Alice murmured softly. They spoke to one another as those of their class had always done. He was a gentleman, she was a lady and was given the courtesy and respect she deserved. She might be on a mad mission that was bound to fail, for by now her husband would be among one of the tens of thousands who were even now decomposing in the soil of Flanders.

She drank her tea which an orderly brought her, captivated by her sweet face and smile of thanks. Major Pearson, with great regret, apologised but he must be about his duties, he told her. When the colonel returned he held a scrap of paper in his hand. He sat behind his desk staring at the paper then looked up sadly.

'Mrs Summers, I have here a list of the regiments who fought at Neuve Chapelle and the 19th Liverpool Battalion was among them. Your husband . . . I'm sorry, if he was there, I have no list of the men, the officers who fell and no way of knowing what happened to those who did not come back. If Captain Summers was in the battle there and did not return he will be believed to have been killed or taken prisoner.'

She leaned forward eagerly. 'But don't you see, if that is the case I must find some of his men who might have seen him fall, or got away with the others who came back.'

'If he had come back, madam, he would have reported to his — '

'Yes, yes, I know, but he may have been . . . been wounded and could not get back.'

'Then where is he, Mrs Summers? He was not a conscript, I take it?'

'No, Colonel, he was a regular soldier who came over with the BEF — '

'Who were seriously depleted, madam.' Then was sorry for his words as her face seemed to crumple, almost to melt in her agony.

She got slowly to her feet and at once he did the same. She might be a lowly ambulance driver and he a colonel in the British Army but he treated her as he would any lady. Besides, she was one of the brave women who had come to this hell-hole to ease the suffering of the fighting man and he admired her for it.

'I'm sorry, madam, if I could — '

'No, no, Colonel, you have been most helpful and kind but at least I know where to start searching for him or men who were with him in the battle.'

His face expressed his horror. 'Mrs Summers, you can't mean you are to go to — '

'I must, Colonel. When I can get time off I will make my way there and search.'

'But it is no place for a female. God knows what you will see there. It was a bloody battle and hundreds of men fell. His unit will have been split up and the men who survived placed in another brigade. To find his . . . his body you would have to dig up every square inch of the battlefield.'

'If that is so I must remember to take a spade with me.'

★ ★ ★

The doctor came every day to examine him, clearly glad of something other than the usual battle wounds that took up his time. He was pleased with his patient and had removed the bandage, revealing the long scar with its neat stitches on his shaved head. The man had borrowed a dictionary from one of the nurses and was teaching himself a smattering of German so that he was not completely out of touch. They were all interested in him, nurses, doctors, patients and orderlies, despite the fact that he was a British soldier, and were pleased when he practised his halting German on them, laughing when he got things wrong, correcting him, congratulating him when he succeeded. It gave him something to do in the empty world in which he lived. It was a frightful thing to have nothing in one's head, no thoughts, no memories except those of the last few weeks.

'*Wo ist* . . . ' Where is this hospital? he was trying to say.

'*Krank-uhn-hows*,' the doctor said helpfully.

'That means hospital, Doctor?'

'*Ja*, hospital.'

The soldier lifted his head and his eyes looked round the ward. He was young, good-looking, lean as an athlete beneath the tight sheets that made it almost impossible to move but he was improving in strength and the doctor knew he would have to go to the prisoner-of-war camp eventually. He would be sorry to see him go, for though he was the enemy he would have liked to have seen the outcome of his delicate work on this man.

'*Was ist das datum, bitte?*' He stumbled through the sentence, referring to the little book the nurse had given him.

'*Zehp-tehm-behn*, my friend.'

September! The soldier's expression turned to one of astonishment and neither he nor the doctor knew why. Into the soldier's mind came a faint memory of daffodils, wild primroses, violets, the rich palette of crocus, tall soldier tulips and narcissi: Spring flowers that grew abundantly under trees that were barely in bud. They flourished in a strip of woodland to which his desperate mind clung but before he could get a good grip on it, it was gone. The flowers he had visualised did not bloom in September so how much of his life had he lost in this place where German was spoken?

'September! But — '

'*Ja, mein freund*, my friend. You have . . . er, been here a long time but . . . er . . . soon prison camp you go.'

The soldier lay slowly back on his pillow and could have wept for he did not know where he was or what he had done to justify taking him to a prison. Had he committed some crime? Dear God, he felt he would go crazy in this mad, mad world. He needed someone, something to cling to. A name — not his own perhaps but the name of someone he had known, even loved, for in this tricky memory of his he knew he had loved a woman and if only he knew her name it would give him some hope that one day this bottomless pit in which he floundered would be resolved. He tried to go through girls' names starting at

130

the beginning of the alphabet, which for some reason he remembered, pondering on the irony that though he could not remember his own name he could bring to mind the alphabet. Now then, begin with A and at once, there it was. ALICE! Her name was Alice. She was the one who . . . who what? What was she to him? Had he loved her? No, it would just not come and thinking, trying to drag the past into the present, made his head ache fiercely.

He laid his throbbing head on the pillow, wanting to weep, then, as the doctor turned sadly away he gripped the sleeve of his white coat.

'Can you not tell me what I am doing here in a German hospital? *Was hilfe ich . . . habe . . . mich . . . verlaufen konnen sie . . . mir helfen?*' His pathetic stumbling to make himself understood reached the doctor's heart which he had thought to be past such feelings after all he had seen of suffering. His own English was stilted but he did his best.

'You Englander . . . prisoner of war.'

'War! *Bitte . . . ich verstehe . . . nicht . . .* ' frequently consulting the dictionary.

'Germany *und* Englander at war. *Du* wounded . . . in battle. *Ich* . . . ah, I learn English but not good. You have nothing to . . . *die identifikation.*'

The soldier looked away hopelessly, his eyes wandering about the ward. There did not seem to be anything else he could say to this kind doctor.

★　★　★

The baby on her lap chuckled in that endearing way babies have and reached out to fumble at the woman's face that smiled down at him. He was quite beautiful and Rose thought how could he be anything else, the son of Alice and Charlie? Her heart was sad that neither of them had ever seen him, for Alice had slipped from her childbed making sure she did not look into the child's face lest he divert her from her purpose before she disappeared from their lives. As Charlie had done.

She was unaware that she was being watched as she took the little boy's hands in hers, then bending her head she blew raspberries on to his bare stomach. He opened his mouth wider and emitted a shriek of delight.

'You like that, don't you, my darling.' She laughed. 'Shall Rose do it again?' which she did and the soldier who stood in the doorway smiled and with a sigh put down his pack and said her name.

'Rose,' softly, tenderly. She looked up, her heart beginning to thump in her chest and there he was, the man she loved; the man who had gone off to war and had, she knew, been in the horror of the Battle of Loos. Before he went he had given Rose the telephone number of his friend at the War Office and told her to keep in touch with him, for not only would Tom Harris know where the 19th would be but might have news of Charlie and Alice. Rose had written to him to tell him of his brother's disappearance and of Alice's determination to find him.

Gently she laid the baby on the floor where a

rug had been spread to allow him to kick his chubby legs. She stood up and slowly moved across the room to where Harry stood, a desolate figure just come from the battlefield. She gently took away from him all the equipment every soldier carried around with him and when they were placed somewhere, anywhere so that his arms were free, she put hers around him and pulled him against her. His head was lowered until it rested in the curve of her neck, her hand smoothing his filthy, tousled hair. He sighed deeply, moaned almost, as though a great weight had been lifted from him. She had taken it from him with her loving womanliness, knowing exactly what he needed.

'You know I love you, Harry,' she whispered. He badly needed a shave, in fact a bath because he smelled of the mud, the blood, from some other soldier, she hoped, the stink of corruption, because Harry Summers had carried in his own arms many of the badly wounded men he commanded to the dressing station or to an ambulance if one was available.

'Yes,' was all he said, lifting his face to hers, his eyes welling with tears, for Harry was not the same man who had left her months ago. Then, 'Will you let me love you, my Rose, before I go back?'

'Let me get rid of this fellow and then I will bathe you and put you in bed,' since she was of the opinion he needed to be cleaned up, fall into a depthless sleep before he loved her, not for her sake but for his own. A proud man had been Harry Summers and he would want her to see him for the first time as he had been before the war took him.

Though they looked for her in the hospital, those who depended on her, patients, nurses, all those who had come to trust and admire her in the last few months, she was not to be found. Only Dolly knew that she and Captain Summers were deep in the comfortable bed in which Harry himself had been born. It seemed only right that the result of that loving had been Harry, then Charlie and that Rose was healing him as best she could in the only way women could heal their men who had been to hell and back.

It was two days later that Harry was first introduced to his nephew and broke the news to Rose and Dolly that he had seen Alice. He had even managed a few words with her. She was well and sent her love to them both. There were tears in the eyes of all three for the woman they respected, admired and, most of all, *loved*.

Now, she was the heroine of hundreds of men. Not just because she carried them to safety courting danger herself, but because she had become a legend as the woman who searched the battlefields for her man.

9

The soldier who, though he was not aware of it, was Captain Charlie Summers, lay on the floor of the cattle truck, his body pressed painfully against the side by the crush of other captured soldiers all around him. They were all officers for though their captive had nothing to tell them he was a captain, it was perhaps his cultured voice, so different from a Cockney or a Liverpudlian, that brought it about. Even the Germans followed the quaint custom that officers should be kept apart from 'other ranks'. At last he could speak to someone in his own language and though he was totally bewildered by the news of 'the bloody war' that was being fought across the wilderness that was France, he was beginning to feel he had a place somewhere in the world. His head had been shaved for the surgery performed by Dr Westmann and the young lieutenant who lay next to him asked him cheerfully where he had picked up what looked like a 'blighty one' as the men called it.

'I don't know,' Charlie answered him hesitantly, wondering how the man could be in such good spirits as a prisoner of this war, whatever it was about.

'What's your regiment?'

'I don't know that either, I'm afraid. Apparently I took shrapnel in my head and it's left me . . . a bit confused.'

'Oh, bad luck, sir,' the lieutenant said. 'When was this?'

'God knows,' Charlie told him listlessly.

'Don't you have your dog tags?'

Charlie wished he would leave him alone and it seemed the boy, for that was what he looked like, a boy in a soldier's uniform, began to take the hint. 'No.'

'Your uniform. Would it not have . . . ' But Charlie was dressed in the assortment of clothing the hospital staff had rooted out for him. Civilian clothes in a drab grey, a shirt, a jacket, old baggy trousers and a comical trilby hat.

Suddenly from across the rocking, rattling truck a voice shouted in what seemed to be amazement. 'Summers? Is that you, Summers? Good God, we thought you were dead, old man. What happened to you? It's me, Jimmy, Major Jimmy Bentley. Jesus, it seems bloody years since I last saw you on the train leaving Liverpool. Remember you couldn't get your mare aboard? You were with a real popsie and your brother. What happened to you? Look, let me get over to you if these chaps would let me through.'

With much cursing and a great deal of shuffling of weary bodies the man who spoke managed to get across the swaying truck until he lay beside a bewildered Charlie. Charlie dragged himself into a sitting position and waited warily for this total stranger who called him *Summers* to speak.

'What happened to you, old chap?' the major asked gently. 'And why are you out of uniform?

When were you captured by the blasted Hun and the battle and . . . and how long . . . '

Charlie stared with wonder at the gaunt face of the soldier and suddenly hope burst in him like a bubble rising to the surface of water. Here was a man who knew him. A man who had given him a name. All the time he was in hospital the others, doctors, nurses, stretcher-bearers, had called him 'Tommy' for that was what the British soldiers called each other. Now here was someone who had known him in the misty past and who could perhaps mend the many holes in the gauzy remnants of his life before his time in hospital. He had no idea where he was, why he had been in a German hospital or how long for and, more to the point, what month it was, even what year.

'You tell me, Major, if you don't mind. I have lost my life and until you spoke now I didn't know my own name. It appears I was in the army. I can vaguely remember a horse; she was blown to bits by . . . I don't know why or . . . or . . . Please, Major, please, give me back what you know of my life and then perhaps the rest will come.'

He gripped the major's arm so fiercely he winced and pried Charlie's fingers from him.

The major could see how distressed this wounded soldier was and wanted to put his arm round the man's shoulders and say 'there, there' as his own nanny had once done when he was a boy but he was being watched by many of those nearest to them so he merely patted his hand and placed it back in Charlie's lap.

'You are Captain Charlie Summers. A cavalry man.'

'I remember horses.'

'You were in the 19th Battalion, King's Liverpool Regiment, as I was. We fought recently at the Somme — '

'The Somme? Where — '

'There is a great war taking place, Captain, between Germany and the British, the French and there are men from many parts of the world involved. If you cannot remember where you were last I cannot tell you in what battle you fell or how you ended up in German hands.'

'I am from Liverpool?'

'As is your brother, Harry. He fought in the Battle of the Somme and I believe there was talk of sending him home on leave. He, as your next of kin, was informed that you were missing a while ago and I believe there was talk of your wife — '

'Wife?' Charlie said wonderingly.

'Yes, and the last letter he had was from someone called Rose.'

'Rose . . . '

'A lady of whom he seemed . . . fond told him that your wife had borne you a son. Now what did they call him?' Major Bentley scratched his head in which something was crawling and which seemed to be the common state of all these filthy, mud-coated, blood-coated, exhausted men. Some of them were merely boys, come straight from the public schools where they had learned how to march and shoulder arms but nothing else that would keep them and the

138

men they commanded alive.

'I have a son, a wife, a brother and — '

'I know, old man, it is a lot to take in all at once but I think it might help you to know that you have a family who care about you but who all believe you are dead.' He stopped speaking abruptly, his eyes unfocused, staring at something that baffled him. 'Though there is a tale that some young woman, a lady ambulance driver, wanders up and down the lines questioning soldiers about her lost husband.'

Charlie gave vent to a gusty sigh that came from the depth of his soul and he felt a great wave of jubilation. He was *someone* at last. Not just Tommy who the rest of the ward thought was out of his mind but Captain Charlie Summers from Liverpool who had a wife and son at home. He could not visualise them, or the place that he had called home. Nothing in fact but what this officer — whom he could not remember nor the incident with the train and the horse — told him but perhaps now that he had these few facts he might put together the rest of his life.

It was very hot and most of the men had discarded their jackets but he in his thin shirt felt no discomfort, for his heart was beating in rhythm with the clackety-clack of the train. None of them knew where they were, nor did they know that the Germans had camps all over the countryside and that in fact they were headed towards a town in northern France and that they were not far from the lines over which they had fought and where his own brother was now in the thick of it.

'What's the date?' he asked the major.

'It's June 28th, Charlie.'

'But last time I asked the doctor at the hospital he said it was September so how can . . . ?'

'How long were you there? If you could remember when you were captured . . . '

Charlie felt reality spinning away from him again, for it seemed large parts of his life had simply disappeared. The guard who stood by the door of the truck where there was a small window lit his pipe and blew smoke through it, quite unmoved by the suffering of his cargo. The shifting, murmuring layer of men had received nothing in the way of food or water since they had left the railway siding where they had been loaded and many of them were dehydrated but there was no water to be had.

Charlie licked his cracked lips and asked the last question. The answer to which he dreaded to hear.

'Jimmy . . . '

'Yes, old man?'

'What year is it?' and was appalled by the answer.

'It's 1916, Charlie.'

Charlie fell back and began to repeat the mantra that was to keep him sane in what was to come.

'I am Charlie Summers from Liverpool, Charlie Summers from Liverpool . . . ' He said it out loud to himself until an officer with a hacking cough and who seemed ready to die,

140

told him to 'put a bloody sock in it, old man'. He turned over, his face pressed into the straw that lined the truck and whispered silently to himself the words that were to keep him from simply dying as many of them did during the next months.

★　★　★

She watched him sleep, her face scarcely inches from his. Dolly had taken over the care of young Will Summers with the help of Polly or Nessie, who fought over who was to bathe him, put him to bed, or feed him He could hold a rusk in his hand, attempting to get it into his mouth, as he did everything from a fold of the rug to the collar of one of the dogs and at fifteen months was walking in a top-heavy sort of way as though he would trip over his own feet. Which he did frequently. Now and again when he fell he resorted to crawling. The dogs played with him in mock fights, often knocking him over but he didn't care, though Dolly was terrified one of the dogs might bite him. It appeared the animals sensed this lively creature who punched them or grabbed at their fur was to be handled carefully and their mouths were gentle as they nuzzled at his neck.

The soldiers, who looked forward to his visits, adored him. Sister argued that such a young child should not be subjected to some of the sights on the wards but he was too young to realise the implications of men without limbs, the men who handled him as though he were made of porcelain, those who were blinded, their faces quite grotesque. Rose argued that it gave them a feeling almost of normalcy. The sound of his infant babbling, his laughter, his feet in their new shoes of which he was inordinately proud as he toddled along the ward, was a memory of happy times before the war.

* * *

No one came near the bedroom that had once been Harry's own. It was placed at the corner of the house with a sharp bend to navigate and was designated too awkward to use as a ward. Rose had helped Harry into a long bathtub in front of the fire and gently scrubbed the filth of the trenches from his thin body, washing his hair and every inch of him, making him groan despite his exhaustion as she worked her soapy fingers about his male organ which stood out from the plentiful mass of dark pubic hair. It did not last long, this evidence of his desire, of his manhood. He was simply incapable of lovemaking in his state and when she had dried him and rubbed his dark, curling hair he had sunk into the bed in which he had slept all his boyhood and young manhood and she watched him fall into the bottomless pit of sleep he desperately needed. He had five days' leave and when he was rested she would climb into bed with him, as naked as he, and bring him back from the horror he had known.

He slept for thirty-six hours. She left him now and then to check on Will and to do the rounds of the wards where all the soldiers knew her man had come home and she would be absent for a while. They did not begrudge it to her, or him. He was a soldier, as they were, and had suffered what they had though he had no wounds to show for it.

'Us'll keep an eye on't babby, Miss Rose,' they told her. Will had become a kind of symbol of hope to these poor, pitiful wrecks whose own lives, even if they did not return to the front, would never be the same again.

When Harry awoke she fed him herself, making him eat the good, nourishing broths, soups, and custards that Nessie made for him and slowly though still thin he began to look like the man who had left her over a year ago and in his eyes was a look that asked something of her. She knew what it was and when she had fed him and returned the tray to the kitchen she went upstairs, telling Dolly she did not want the captain disturbed.

Dolly watched her go sadly for there were so many men longing for what Rose was about to give Harry and that was a respite from the horrors they had seen in the trenches. She sighed and exchanged a sympathetic smile with Nessie. Both were knitting, socks, balaclavas, mittens, scarves, anything to keep their men warm in the coming winter. They had both come to work at Summer Place because that was where they were needed but with Beechworth destined to be the next house authorised as a hospital who knew where they would end up? Wherever two elderly ladies could do the most good. Not much except be there for the ones who cared for the men in the beds. The maimed and blinded, the mutilated and damaged in their poor heads and minds that could literally take no more. For nearly two years these men had been subjected to terrors not just of possible death, which in many ways was better than the wounds that crippled them for life, but of the loss of their innocence, their faith in the men who led them.

'Let's hope there'll not be another babby without a father,' Dolly murmured and a sad tear ran down her cheek, finding its way along a wrinkle that ran from the corner of her eye to her chin.

'Miss Rose loves that there man, Dolly, and will give 'im summat ter take back ter that 'ell 'e come from.'

★ ★ ★

He watched her from the bed, his need of her, now that he had the strength to manage it, very obvious in the bulge under the clean sheets she and Dolly had put him between that morning. His face was a blessing to her for she knew that she would send him back with the remembrance of her in his arms and their loving which she prayed would heal his wounded soul. Though he was whole, as so many weren't, his mind was not, for in it were pictures of the young, baby-faced officers straight from school who had never been with a woman and now never would for they had had their genitals blown off; men who wandered the trenches calling for 'Tich' or

'Jimmy' or, worse than anything, 'Mummy' or 'Nanny'; men who held their blown-off leg in their hands, begging for someone to sew it back on; men screaming as they were caught in the barbed wire, cruelly and for ever entangled until some compassionate pal put a bullet in them. The casualties flowed back across the Channel and some flowed the other way, returning to the front. The smell of gangrene and perhaps the worse sight, not remarked on but heartbreaking just the same, the surgeons who did their best but wept at the sheer waste of it all.

These images were tumbling about in his head but the sight of Rose, his lovely Rose, clean, *whole*, swept them all away as she came into his arms and held him as he, unable to help himself, wept too. Then with her hands and her mouth and the smell of her in his nostrils, it all vanished and rapture came, sweeping them both up on its wave and taking them to a shore where peace was. They slept then but during that night they loved again and again, slept and loved and mended Harry Summers. The man with half a face blown away was himself no more than a misty sorrow in Harry's mind and the words he had spoken to him, the smile he had given and the man's gratitude as Harry looked him straight in the face and did not flinch.

'Thank you, sir,' the man had mumbled through the hole in what was left of his face. All this had tortured him for the months he had borne it but now he knew he could deal with it which sounded hard but was merely an acceptance of life, and death. He wanted Rose to

145

be here when he got back. He had lost his brother and, more than likely, his brother's wife who gallantly and probably foolishly roamed the battlefields looking for Charlie, but here was his saviour in his arms. Their loving seemed to strengthen him and where she had been the dominant one in their desire he now began to make demands of her that had not been in his power in the beginning.

'I love you, I have never stopped loving you,' laying a hard hand against her cheek. 'My heart rises when I see you and my love is as constant as the heavens. Do you . . . ?'

'I have waited for this ever since that day,' lifting her hips to accommodate his masculine need.

'Which?'

'The day at the station. Oh God, I did not know this would ever come . . . '

'This . . . ' His body moved slowly, slowly in and out, then his pace quickened.

'Let me help you,' for she was afraid he was not strong enough for such a pounding energy.

'I need no help. You love me?'

'Yes, oh yes . . . this is . . . I am ready to scream. Dolly will . . . '

'To hell with Dolly. I need this, you know that . . . '

'I am yours to do with . . . '

'This?'

'Yes . . . yes . . . yes, my darling heart. I love you, never leave me . . . '

And so she shouted her love, her passion for this man — yelled, he told her later as he cradled her in his arms. Their climax had been an explosion of love held in and now given free range. She was drowsy with it now but he watched the light slowly beginning to seep round the edge of the curtains and the joy that had been shared with her, just for a moment, made his heart ache for it was to end this day. He felt the desolation run through him, then, like a dog just come from the water, he shook himself; had he not just been given what all the men he served with yearned for. Love! Yes and more than that because he knew this woman would wait for him and the next leave he had they would be married.

When she woke she found him leaning on his elbow looking down into her face. She put her hand on his cheek. 'Such love I have. I am filled with it.'

'I did my best,' he said, grinning.

'Was it . . . ?' then had no need to continue for he turned her towards him and silently, gently, his lips fastened on her nipple and she rose to meet him and he loved her for what he knew would be the last time on this leave.

His uniform had been cleaned and pressed and hung on the wardrobe door in readiness for his departure. From the bed she watched him and didn't know how she could bear it. She had only just found him. *I have only just found him*, to an uncaring God yet he was to go and her heart was breaking, for would she ever see him again and if she did would he be whole and sane as he was now?

'I told you I had seen Alice,' he said abruptly

and she felt ashamed as in her new-found happiness she had forgotten. She sat up and the sheet fell away from her and his eyes went to the sweet roundness and fullness of her breast.

'Sweetheart, don't do that or I shall never . . . '

She sighed since she knew what he meant. 'Tell me about Alice.'

'She was standing outside the hospital and each time an ambulance drew up she accosted those who were able to speak. She was off duty but she would not rest. 'Are any of you men from the Liverpool Regiment?' she was asking and from everyone there was either silence or a shake of an anguished head. Then someone — perhaps a lad from around Old Swan or West Derby — said he was but the regiment had lost so many men those who were left had been integrated into other battalions.

''Was yer lookin' fer someone, queen?' he asked sympathetically, despite his own troubles, doing his best to raise his head from the stretcher.

''Captain Charlie Summers of the 19th Battalion, King's Liverpool Regiment,' she replied, moving to the stretcher and taking hold of the man's hand. 'Do you know him? He has been missing for a year or more.''

Harry sighed and stared out at the garden. 'They all knew her, of course, for she had become famous. Mad, they thought her, but nevertheless they all held her in great esteem. She was not shirking her duties and drove her ambulance wherever it was needed and gave great comfort to the men she brought to the

148

hospital but she cried when I spoke to her. She has the strength of a lion. Who was it said, 'I have the body of a weak and feeble woman but the heart of a lion,' — or something like that? A queen, I think, and that is Alice.' He fell to musing as he buttoned his immaculate khaki shirt. 'That day when Charlie left, you remember when Lady wouldn't get on the train, she wept and was so fragile, so wilting, like a flower dragged from the soil but now I believe if they gave her the leadership of the armies she would have this bloody lot sorted out in no time. She swears she will not come home until she has found Charlie or seen his body, which is impossible. She was going to start on the prisoner-of-war camps, someone told me, which is madness.'

'I know how she feels now, Harry. If you were to — '

'Don't,' he said sharply but she would not be stopped.

'I would do as she is doing. I know it is ridiculous. If every woman who lost her man were to do what Alice is doing there would be chaos but . . .'

He dropped on to his knees beside the bed, running his fingers through her hair, stroking her cheek and neck and, inevitably, the peached peak of her white breast. They could both feel the hot blood begin again and hastily he kissed her, a light kiss, then stood up and strode from the room. She knew he was going to the nursery where young Will Summers was having his breakfast. He would report it all back to Alice if

149

he saw her again and even present her with a photograph one of the men had taken of Will. It might persuade her to come home.

* * *

The shelling had eased off a lot when she spotted two khaki figures stumbling towards her about fifty yards away. She had a revolver one of the officers had given her, saying he hoped she never had to use it but better to be safe than sorry. It remained in her pocket and had never been used. She had smiled at the picture of herself shooting a fellow human being but the two soldiers seemed unaware of her and just kept walking. *They were Germans.* Both of them had wounds, at least they were bleeding, or there was blood on them though she could not tell from where.

'Madam,' one of them said, an officer by the look of him. 'You are English.'

'Yes, I am, but what are you — '

'I have brought my corporal to you, to your hospital which I know is near. He is hurt. I have many hurt but this one is my brother.'

'Your brother!'

'*Ja.* Forgive me, but I must get back to my men. They are . . . I must get back to them but I could not leave Erich, you understand?'

'Well, no. I am — '

'The nearest hospital is . . . German hospital is several miles away. It is in a prisoner-of-war camp where there are many Englishmen: soldiers, prisoners. One of them was helped by a

German doctor. He had no papers but he is with his own now. I thought since a German doctor tended him one of yours might do the same for Erich.'

He laid his brother down in the bit of grass that had first attracted her to the place. There were even wild flowers. After clicking his heels and saluting with great politeness, the officer strode away and disappeared into the distance from where sounds of gunfire could be heard.

Alice looked down at the young corporal in astonishment then up again to where the officer had gone. A small crowd of soldiers had gathered round her, ready to stick their bayonets into the supine figure on the ground but with a sharp word from her they drew back. They all knew or had heard of the mad woman who searched for her husband and would not cross her for the world. She was on a par with an angel to them for not only did she work alongside them she was also a mystical being from another world, or so they believed.

Doing as she ordered, they made a rough stretcher and carried the young wounded soldier back to the hospital.

10

They had more warning — and help — this time when Beechworth opened its doors to the pitiful dregs of humanity who were once men, soldiers who had answered the call and paid heavily for their patriotism. The suffering victims had had nothing in the way of medical care bar the hastily slapped-on dressings at the dressing station hundred of miles away. Their faces were grey with pain but this time Rose and her helpers had everything ready, her home scrubbed from attic to cellars, beds erected, doctors at the ready with a staff of nurses and VADs, some of them borrowed from Summer Place. The men were quiet as though the little bit of life that had been theirs at the beginning of their journey from the front had slowly drained away from them as time moved on. Ambulance, train, boat, train, ambulance: hours had passed and now they were lifted gently from the fleet of ambulances by the volunteer stretcher-bearers who placed them in the beds they had been designated. Doctors and nurses had travelled with them, two of them, and Dr Cartwright from Summer Place, reading the labels that had been tied on to the men, different colours denoting the severity of their wounds, inspected them briefly then directed them to their place in what Rose thought of as a queue, the worst of them first though how these medical men could make such a decision was beyond her understanding. Two men, almost unrecognisable as men so wrapped about were they in various pieces of what looked like rags from the bone yard in Old Swan, were found to be dead, their blood hiding their horrific wounds so that they had probably been dead for hours without anyone noticing.

Some of the farm wives stood by ready to give a hand were it needed, dropping blood-soaked dressings into a bucket, their expressions stoic. They had been brought up to deal with nothing more than a cut with a scythe, a burn perhaps, a child poorly with a fever and even though some of them had loved ones at this mysterious 'front' that was forever on everybody's lips they did not falter. Rose was everywhere at once, taking orders since the doctors knew how reliable she was, giving them to the farm women, even the VADs who didn't know where anything or any place was, and at the end of the day it was only Dolly's forceful command and her own total exhaustion that made her lie down in her own bedroom at Beechworth.

'What about Will?' she said plaintively and was gently pushed down on the bed, covered with a blanket and told that there was a horde of women, servants from Beechworth and Summer Place, only too willing to look after the dear little chap.

'But he might fret if I'm not there,' for it was very evident that Charlie and Alice's son had attached himself to Rose as he would a mother. The bond between them was a worry to Dolly. What would happen when his parents came home? She fully believed they would, she didn't know exactly why but in her heart there was a small place that held the sweet girl whom they had all come to love, and a voice in it that whispered to her that she would not be taken like the Summers brothers. Like Alice she somehow felt that she would know if Captain Charlie, a great favourite of them all, was dead and fully expected his face to smile up at her from one of the stretchers that were now in some sort of order according to the gravity of their wounds.

'Be quiet and do as you're told for once,' Dolly ordered and almost before Dolly left the room, Rose was asleep.

★ ★ ★

'What have you done to your hand, Nurse?' the doctor asked tiredly. Although he was beyond exhaustion as he bent over a bed in which a boy moaned in his sleep, he still noticed that the little ambulance driver who had just brought him in had her left hand wrapped up and his medical training kicked in, for it would not do to have a valuable member of the medical team with an injury.

'Nothing, Doctor. A splinter from the frame of the hut where we sleep. Nurse Paget got it out then bandaged it to protect it from — '

But the doctor had turned away. A splinter! In the midst of the horrific wounds some of these men suffered, a splinter did not seem to matter much in the scheme of things! Alice left the stretcher that she had helped to carry in and headed for the hut where she and the other ambulance drivers slept, hoping for a bit of 'shut-eye' but the alarm bell rang out to tell them that the ambulances were needed again.

'Where to?' she asked O'Neill who was crossing herself as she ran for her ambulance. The Battle of the Somme still raged as it had done since July and the tented hospitals were overflowing with the wounded. Alice had lost count of how many times she had made this run to the dressing station to pick up the shattered flotsam that was once a group of fighting soldiers. From the hospital she would then run them to the railway station where they would be loaded like so many parcels to be shipped back to England.

'Somebody said Delville Wood wherever that is. There's been a big battle there. We're to pick them up and take them directly to the trains. The hospitals are full, they say, and the wounded are just lying on the ground where they were brought in.'

Alice climbed into her ambulance though the damn splinter in her finger was throbbing so much she could barely hold the steering wheel. Some kind soldier, despite a terrible wound to his left arm, had cranked the engine for her, cheerfully smiling as he waved her away and she wondered for the thousandth time how these men, these suffering men, many of them clerks, tram drivers, coal men, milk men, servants, kept going against the odds which said that two-thirds of them would be dead before the week was out.

She and the stretcher-bearers packed the

155

ambulance with wounded men. She had cigarettes in her pocket and having lit several for the men who were in her charge, for it seemed, despite their plight, a 'fag' was a great comfort to the wounded, she then turned in the direction of the railway station, following the line of other ambulances. The train was already at the platform and she reversed her vehicle adroitly so that the rear was facing the train. She knew all the terrible wounds by now, the worst being made by the evil serrated entrenching tools used by the Germans. There were shrapnel wounds which she knew tore off parts of the body and then the ones that were clean, one could almost call it the humane wound of a bullet.

The men were loaded, lying almost on top of one another in the wagons which she knew would be stinking, accepting the conditions in which these poor souls were to lie for there had not been time to clean them and the floors where the patient wounded lay were filthy with vomit, excrement and blood from their last passengers. It seemed no one cared and for a moment she felt a great wave of guilt sweep over her. She thought she had become so indifferent — no, that was not the right word, but it was close and for an instant she wanted to weep. For these brave and suffering men, for the people she loved at home who must suffer agonies at her disappearance, for her beloved husband who could not be found. Dear, sweet Jesus, forgive me.

It took all her strength to climb back into her ambulance and follow the one in front, which was driven by O'Neill. She knew that when she reached her destination she and the others were faced with the task of cleaning their ambulances and the thought demoralised her. Her hand, her whole arm hurt and if she didn't get some sleep soon she would not be able to get over to the enemy prisoner-of-war camp where she meant to find a way in to see if . . . if . . .

The ambulance behind her nearly ran into her as the vehicle she drove began to swerve from side to side, finally finishing up against the stump of a tree. Ewing, who was now in Alice's detachment cursed like a trooper, for they had all learned the language with which the men addressed everybody and everything in this bloody war: lice, rats as big as cats, mud and each other.

Opening Alice's ambulance door she found the driver slumped over the steering wheel. There were shouts and much honking of horns as impatient drivers piled up behind Ewing's ambulance, from soldiers doing their best to get to the front lines, or from them, all in a hurry but Ewing took no notice. From ahead O'Neill ran from her vehicle to see what the hold-up was, leaving her engine running as it was hard to crank it up again.

'What's wrong?' she gasped. 'We are causing an awful hold-up here, Ewing. What's wrong with Barnes?'

'I don't know. She's passed out. You'll have to get a couple of blokes to run her ambulance out of the way and I'll take Barnes in my ambulance. Can you get some help?'

Two soldiers on their way to the trenches were only too pleased to help and within minutes they had the semi-conscious young woman into Ewing's ambulance, then shouldered Alice's off the road. The soldiers who were on their way to the line cheered; the incident had been a welcome break in their weary, fear-filled lives.

The little convoy was soon on its way and when they arrived two stretcher-bearers, seeing the two ambulance drivers struggling to get another from her ambulance, ran to help.

'What's wrong with Barnes?' Nurse Paget asked abruptly, bustling up in what Dolly would have called a 'paddy'. She had wounded men pouring into the hospital and an ambulance driver who was fainting was very annoying. Only a few days ago she had taken a splinter from the girl's finger, which was nothing compared to the terrible wounds of the men under her care.

'Don't know, Nurse, but she'll have to be — '

'What? She'll have to be what?'

'I don't know but . . . '

The nurse tutted irritably then her mind dwelled on the fact that this girl, Barnes, for she was no more than a girl, was the hardest working of the lot of them, and they all worked until they were nearly dead on their feet.

'Very well, leave her there for the moment and I'll see to her as soon as I've got a minute. Sit her on that box there and get back to your quarters. See if you can get some sleep.'

Two hours later a wounded man who lay on the ground at the feet of the young woman heard her moaning. No one took any notice for moaning was a common sound round here but she was a funny colour, he thought, who was himself the colour of putty.

'Nurse . . . Nurse . . . ' He tried to shout but his energy was expended on trying to breathe, never mind shout. When, in a lull, which was very rare, a VAD found her she was beginning to ramble and then, with a gasp that he thought might be her last, she fell off the box and on to another injured man who screamed since she was heavy on the wound he had sustained only an hour ago.

The VAD put her hand on Alice's forehead and drew it back as though the ambulance driver's flesh was burning hers. She ran to fetch another VAD and together they lifted the driver they all thought of as Barnes and took her to another room, one where the exhausted nursing staff could rest for a moment. The doctor was called. When the bandage was unwrapped those who were present gasped in dismay, for the driver had what the wounded themselves feared. What was picked up on the battlefields. The battlefields that had once been the French farmers' pride and joy and which they had carefully spread with manure and under which now lay the rotting dead of two years of war. The tiny splinter when removed had left an open sore that had festered and was pretty close to becoming gangrenous.

'This woman may lose her hand, or even her arm,' the doctor said sadly. 'We all know what this is, don't we? Sepsis, which could turn gangrenous. Treat her with hypochlorous acid.

You know the amount, Nurse. I can do nothing for her here. She must be sent home. Put her on a hospital ship as soon as you can.' He looked down at the moaning, restless woman stretched out before him. In his mind was the horrific war that was wounding and killing men in their thousands, hundreds of thousands, and he did his job in a kind of numbness, for it was the only way he could manage to keep his sanity, but to see a woman suffering the same fate as the soldiers was almost too much for him. His own wife and children were safe at home, thank God. This brave woman, it was said, spent all her spare time, which wasn't much, searching for her husband who was missing and must surely be dead.

Shaking his head he turned away, going back to the nightmare world that was his, leaving Alice Summers to the care of the nurses.

*　*　*

'There's a woman ter see yer, Miss Rose. A lady, I should say. She ses it's important. Shall I send 'er in? She's come in a chauffeur-driven motor car!' Obviously impressed since motor cars were not often to be seen out of Liverpool, for the petrol to run them was scarce as the war drew on.

Tom Gibson, who would have gone to do his bit at the beginning had his age not been against him, stood in the doorway of the tiny room, once a butler's pantry, where Miss Rose did the administration work that had fallen on her shoulders though she would much rather be on the wards at Summer Place or with Will and the dogs as they romped about the garden. Taking a walk through the wooded area at the back of the gardens on this lovely autumn day with the boy tumbling about in the fallen leaves, the dogs, four of them now, counting Harry's retriever, hopefully bringing the toddler a stick to throw, which he did but not very far for he was barely eighteen months old. Ginger and Spice raced round and round and a little rough-haired dog who had shown up at the back door about six months ago did the same. They called the stray Tommy and he seemed particularly attached to the men on the wards as though he sensed they needed him and the nurses had given up chasing him away. No one knew where he came from but he would lie with his nose on his paws, his eyes flickering from bed to bed and when an arm dropped he would sneak over and lick the hand devotedly and the hand would weakly caress his fur. He was bathed regularly which he accepted and everybody loved him, especially Will. He slept beside the boy's bed and seemed to have the gift of knowing exactly where and when he was needed most.

Rose sighed and looked up at Tom. Tom and Nessie had moved back to Beechworth and their own little cottage beside the vegetable garden when the place had been taken over and Mrs Philips, cook to the Summers family, had her kitchen to herself again with Mary to help her in feeding the wounded men and the staff, the doctors and nurses and everybody connected with the hospital.

'Did she give a name, Tom?'

'Mrs Bentley, Miss Rose.'

Bentley! Bentley! Now why did that name ring a bell?

'You'd best show her in then, Tom.'

The lady who entered Rose's small domain was in her thirties, small, pretty and very elegant. She doesn't buy her clothes in Old Swan, Rose thought as she rose to her feet.

'Good morning, I believe your name is Mrs Bentley. I am Rose Beechworth and this is my home which has been turned into a sort of convalescent home for officers. May I ask . . . oh, please do sit down and may I offer you some refreshments.'

'Thank you, Miss Beechworth. A cup of tea would be nice though I hate to bother you when you are so busy, but I think I might have some news — good news, I hasten to add, that might interest you. My husband, Major James Bentley, is in the 19th Battalion, King's Liverpool Regiment and he said in his letter that you . . . that your friend, Alice Summers, is married to one of the Summers brothers.'

There was a knock at the door and a tray, carried by Dolly who was eager to know what this lady had to say to Miss Rose, was set on Rose's desk. Silver, since the motor car at the door was evidently owned by a person of importance. A teapot, sugar basin and milk jug set on a lace tray cloth with the best porcelain cups and saucers. A small silver tea strainer, and

162

a plate on which lemon slices were delicately arranged.

Rose's heart was beginning to leap about in her chest and she wished Dolly would leave but she was bobbing and smiling in the evident belief that Mrs Bentley was about to say something that Dolly felt she was entitled hear.

'Thank you, Dolly, that will be all,' Rose said firmly and as Dolly sidled out, highly offended, she turned to Mrs Bentley, asking her politely whether she took milk and sugar, or lemon but suddenly she could take it no longer.

'Please, Mrs Bentley, what is it? Is it Harry? He is in the same regiment and I cannot bear the — '

'No, no, my dear.' Mrs Bentley smiled kindly. 'As far as I know Harry is . . . well, how can any of us know? It is his brother, Charlie.'

Rose sat down heavily and her heart — how foolish the heart was, leaping and plunging and yet really the organ never moved; she was going mad . . . *was she going mad*? She could hear a blackbird singing and when she turned to the window it hopped across the lawn, then flew over the wall, ready to land on the other side with its raised and fanned tail. A thrush answered in its musical notes, three times as though to outdo the blackbird. One of the dogs was barking in the back, longing to be let out of the stable, and from upstairs came the baby voice of Will demanding to see 'Wose'. Jossy, aged fifteen and who had replaced the gardeners was in the garden, doing what he hoped would be the last of the lawn mowing while Mrs Bentley's chauffeur leaned on the bonnet of the motor car watching him. He was an elderly man and, she supposed, like all the men who were too old for the trenches, he had taken over from a younger man.

'Please, Mrs Bentley, please . . . ' Rose croaked.

'I have had a letter from Jimmy, my husband.'

'Oh, dear sweet Lord . . . '

'He is a prisoner of war in a camp. A camp for officers somewhere in the north-east of France. Six months now . . . ' A spasm of pain crossed her face and Rose wanted to get up and stroke her hand but she didn't think it would be welcome. 'He met Charlie.'

Rose's face lit up like the first evening star on a winter night: 'Charlie, thank God, oh thank the dear God,' then it fell again.

Mrs Bentley stood up as though she would put a comforting arm about her but she sat down again and continued. 'But there is more, my dear. Charlie has been seriously injured — his head. Oh, he is well now but he has lost his past, his memory. Jimmy told me he has informed the authorities so Mrs Summers should hear very soon that her husband is alive but a prisoner of war. When you tell her she will be overjoyed, as I was when . . . I'm sorry . . . '

For Rose's face had fallen into lines of despair. What an irony, was the thought uppermost in Rose's mind, going round like a mouse on a wheel. Charlie is alive and has been found and we don't know where Alice is to tell her. Somewhere in France which was a heaving mass

164

of struggling humanity where it seemed to her no one was in charge. Some of the soldiers who were recovering in this very hospital and who had been in the thick of it had told her. At the beginning of the year the Germans had been at the zenith of their fortune and the Allies almost on their knees. They, with the French, had done their best to defend Verdun, a citadel town surrounded by impregnable forces, a bulwark, a bastion that the French were determined to defend. The dreaded flamethrowers had been used to incinerate them, the massive *Minenwerfers* that could toss huge bombs the size of oil-drums, and 1,200 guns ranged across the narrow front from where the attack came. The casualties were horrendous, the roads almost impassable with troops marching towards the battle and others marching in the other direction. Refugees, ambulances, lost children and mothers frantically searching for them. It had been 'bloody hell on wheels' the soldier had told her and though he had lost both his legs he felt himself lucky to be out of it. And, he muttered in disbelief to Rose, who sat by his bed and held his hand, much to Staff Nurse Long's annoyance, men were still volunteering.

'They don't know what the bloody 'ell they're lettin' themselves in for, poor sods. They should stay at 'ome with their family. Bugger me if I don't think them conchies were right after all. Never mind puttin' them in prison, they should pin a bloody medal on them.'

When Rose had seen Mrs Bentley out she scurried to the kitchen where Dolly and the others were waiting with barely concealed impatience to hear from her who the lady had been and what she had to say.

Rose swept Dolly into her arms and, laying her forehead on Dolly's shoulder, began to weep.

'Not . . . not Captain Harry, my lass, tell me it's not Captain Harry.'

'No, Dolly, not Captain Harry. They'd hardly send a lady in an expensive motor car to tell me Harry was . . . was . . . ' She couldn't even bring herself to speak the word. 'It's Captain Charlie. He's alive, Dolly. He's in a prisoner-of-war camp in France and that lady's husband, a major, who's also a prisoner, recognised him. But Charlie has been wounded in the head and he has no memory. Didn't even know who he was until Major Bentley came across him. The major told him all he knew about himself, Charlie, I mean; he told him about the day at Lime Street station where Lady wouldn't go on the train and Sparky and everything he knew . . . '

'Dear sweet God. Oh, Lord above, thanks be to God. Now Miss Alice — Mrs Summers — can come home and see her babby and the little lad can meet — Why, what's ter do, Miss Rose, are you not glad that . . . '

Dolly reached out and took Rose's hands between hers, doing her best to peer into Rose's face, for her young mistress had hung her head in despair.

'Can you not see, Dolly? We have found Captain Charlie but we have lost Alice. We don't know where she is over there. You know that friend of Harry's tried to discover her, and Harry

166

even saw her once but she will not have joined under her own name and from what the soldiers here say, it is total chaos on the battlefields. She might even be . . . be . . . '

'Nay, I'll not have it, never.' Dolly reared up and her face was fierce with her fury. 'The good God wouldn't let a lovely, good-hearted girl like our Alice be taken, not when her husband's just been found. I'll not have it, d'you hear, so if you won't do it, I will.'

'What, Dolly?' Rose sniffed disconsolately; though she was a strong and determined young woman — what she had done these last months proved that — for once she was at a loss.

'Telephone that there friend of Captain Harry's an' ask him to make some enquiries. He must know folk in high places who can go through records an' find out where Captain Charlie is. Ask about this 'ere Major Bentley. They must know what camp he's in and if they can tell you Captain Charlie will be there. You could write to the lad, when they've found him an' tell him all about his life, his wife, his own little lad and it might bring the poor young man to find himself again. Now stop that worritin' and write that letter.'

11

She lay on the narrow cot that was her bed. It was covered with a thin, lumpy mattress and a worn sheet. Spread over her and the strange hospital nightdress she unaccountably wore, was a flimsy blanket. On top of that someone had laid her long overcoat. In the next cot O'Neill breathed the deep exhausted sleep into which they all tumbled every chance they had, but Alice's brain was straining to make sense of what had happened to her and how she had come to be lying here in a hospital gown, like the ones the wounded men wore.

Her hand gave a vicious twinge and when she attempted to alleviate the pain by moving it she found it was bound in a dressing. Suddenly she remembered the splinter Staff Nurse had removed and marvelled that it could hurt so much. It had only been a splinter after all. Why was she dressed like a patient, for God's sake, tucked up in her bed with O'Neill snoring her head off beside her when she knew there had been a huge battle and every ambulance driver had been needed to bring the wounded to the hospital? Was it over, the 'big push' everyone had waited for? And why . . . where . . . Dear Lord, was she going mad or . . .

Her mind travelled back over the months since she had landed in this pit of hell. How many men had she witnessed, dragged from the mud, the slime, the putrid shell-holes, the blood-soaked trenches, most of them by their own mates, for these men had formed a bond with one another that only they could understand. No-man's-land, and that was what it was, a land on which man could not survive without the comradeship of those who floundered in it with them. Rusty barbed wire, machine-gun fire, 'whizz-bangs' and the terrible crescendo of the shelling that went on for hours and drove men mad. The soldiers were thrown against these fiendish challenges repeatedly and repeatedly she and the other ambulance drivers carried their mutilated bodies back to the hospitals or the hospital trains, the hospitals completely inadequate though they did their best to put the poor battered bodies back together. Through the summer of 1915 she had carried the wounded, at first so horrified by what she saw she felt she could not carry on, but she had.

At the outset she had known that she could not maintain the engine of the overworked ambulance, for despite her protestations to the sergeant at the Red Cross station in London, she really knew very little about them. She just could not understand the intricacies of the tangle under the bonnet, but she had learned and had managed it. She, who had never washed a cup and saucer in her life, had forced herself to scrub the inside of her ambulance of the muck, the blood and other nasty substances left by the wounded men and her hands were a testament to it. The first time the whistle had shrilled out telling them they were needed she had trembled so violently she could not button her overcoat and was forced to accept the cheerful help of the stretcher-bearer to crank the starting handle of the vehicle. Her terror had surely been visible to all the others until she realised they were all afraid and the knowledge had strengthened her. The smell of the wounded men, the sounds, the screams, the whimpers of pain, the whispers begging 'Mam' to fetch them home, the moans, haunted her. They cursed her when she almost dropped her end of the stretcher, jarring their poor tortured bodies. They cursed her in the dialects from the places they had left, Lancashire, Yorkshire, Cornwall, Scotland, London Cockney, Liverpool, reducing her to scalding tears but she carried on, turning her eyes from the white of bones glinting through the red of torn flesh, from blood, vomit, faeces, she dealt with them all. She had learned to let the clutch out gently on her overworked vehicle so that it would not jump forward and jostle them. She had carried cigarettes which she lit and placed tenderly between lips bitten and bloody and she survived and lived only for the hours she could snatch to search for Charlie, or his body; for some exhausted soldier who might have known him among the tens of thousands who had fought where he had.

She dozed a little and was startled to find Nurse Heron bending over her.

'I've come to look at your hand, Barnes. It will need re-dressing. Can you sit up?'

'Of course I can, Nurse,' she said, struggling and failing to raise herself into a sitting position.

She was amazed to find she had not the strength to do as Nurse Heron asked her.

'Never mind, Barnes, if you'll lift your arm from under the blanket I think I can manage. I'm sorry to hurt you,' as Alice winced, 'but it must be looked at again.'

With much difficulty she unwrapped the bandage and with much difficulty Alice did her best not pull away from her. Her hand and arm, even her shoulder were alive with pain and when the nurse finally had it revealed she frowned.

'This is not good, Barnes. I think the doctor had better have a look once more. It is . . . well . . . well, let us say it is in a bit of a mess and you are no use to us if you cannot use it. You cannot possibly drive an ambulance.'

With her good hand Alice leaned to grasp the nurse's arm. 'Please, Nurse, can you not douse it with Eusol? Wrap it in lint and then a bandage. I could wear a glove to protect it. Please . . . please . . . ' Her voice was weak and hoarse and the nurse, known for her steadfast obligation to duty, became curt.

'Barnes, you cannot even sit up in bed, let alone drive an ambulance. Now lie still and I'll send the doctor to you as soon as he has a moment. Do as you're told, Barnes,' she continued sternly, for Alice was struggling not only to sit up but to get out of bed. 'You will wake O'Neill. She has been on duty for fourteen hours and needs her sleep.'

'There you are, you see. All the ambulance drivers are badly needed and I am an ambulance driver. I can't loll about here in bed while the other girls do my work. Just wrap it up, for God's sake and let me — '

'Barnes, remember to whom you speak. You are not fit for duty and the doctor will confirm it, I'm sure. Now lie back and I'll send a cup of tea for you.'

'I don't want a bloody cup of tea, Staff — '

'Remember to whom you speak, Barnes,' Nurse Heron repeated, 'and do as you are told.'

The doctor arrived just as Alice had decided to get out of bed and sod the lot of them. She was driven to resort to the coarse language the men used in their agony but as she did her best to sit up a masculine hand pushed her back.

'Staff tells me you are being obstinate, Barnes, and want to get back to the men. Has it occurred to you that you are a danger to men already weak with their wounds? You have picked up something from *them*, probably from the soil, which has poisoned what is a simple splinter wound and having left it to fester is now beginning to poison you. That hand of yours is swollen and red with inflammation and I know you are in great pain. You have been out here for how long?'

'Almost eighteen months, Doctor,' Nurse Paget said, looking sternly at Alice.

'Eighteen months. Then it's time you had some home leave anyway. And while you are there your hand will be — '

Alice clutched at the doctor's arm with a feverish desperation. She was starting to feel worse than ever but she would recover from this, she knew she would, and if they sent her home,

172

which it seemed the doctor was threatening to do, she could not continue her search for Charlie.

'No, please, Doctor, don't send me home. Nurse will re-dress my hand and in a day or two I'll be up and about again. I'm strong and — '

'Barnes, everyone here knows how you spend every free moment searching for your husband. We are all very sympathetic but you are no longer well enough to remain here. I cannot let you be responsible for bringing in the wounded if you are in poor shape which it is obvious you are. You have a high fever and . . . Barnes . . . Dear God, what is your Christian name?'

'Alice,' she mumbled.

'Alice, you have worked beyond your strength and to tell you the truth I don't know how you persuaded them to let you come in the first place. Look at you, nothing but skin and bone. If you don't go home, have your hand seen to properly, rest and eat well you will . . . I'm . . . well, I hate to say this but I must: you could lose that arm.' He turned to the nurse. 'Dress this hand and then arrange for Barnes to be put on the first available transport for England.'

Alice began to weep but suddenly the world about her, the hut she was in, the sleeping figure of O'Neill grew hazy and her last thought was that O'Neill was simply so exhausted she had slept through all the comings and going of the last half hour, then darkness fell and she herself slipped into the comforting arms of oblivion.

★　★　★

Jimmy Bentley, though he was sympathetic towards poor old Summers who was a good chap on the whole, was becoming increasingly irritated — easily done in their confinement — with the constant questions about their past life.

'Did you know this brother you say I had, Jimmy?'

'Only slightly, Charlie. He wasn't in the regiment when we sailed for France but I was told he was in the fighting in the Somme offensive.'

'Do you remember my mentioning someone called Alice?'

'Not really, old man. You and I lost touch in the battle but if you know the name surely that will bring back memories. Was she your wife?'

Charlie shook his head despondently. 'I can't remember. She may have been a sister or . . . '

'I don't think there was a sister, old chap. I never heard one mentioned. I do know your father was a baronet so I suppose Harry will inherit if — ' He stopped abruptly for he had been about to say 'if he's still alive'.

'If he's still alive I suppose you mean.'

'Well, a hell of a lot of us fell, lad.'

'What was my mare called, Jimmy?'

Jimmy would sigh and do his best to fill in the huge hole in Charlie's life.

'All I can tell you, old man, all I can absolutely recall is the day we entrained at the station in Lime Street from where the troops set out. You were having trouble with your mare.'

'Lady.' Charlie began to tremble as he spoke

the forgotten name.

'Yes, I believe that was what she was called.'

A flash of an ugly picture streaked across Charlie's blank mind, a ghastly picture from which he flinched. There was a shifting haze of red, *blood*, an explosion in which human and animal vanished as though they had never been. *Lady!* And a man, a soldier, holding her bridle who disintegrated in the mist, the scarlet mist of horror.

'Lady is dead, Jimmy,' he said sadly.

'You remember her, Charlie?'

'Yes.'

Jimmy put his hand on Charlie's shoulder. 'She was a lovely animal, lad, but you'd a devil of a job getting her on that train, Charlie. She wouldn't go up that ramp, not if her life depended on it. Had it not been for that lady with the gig-pony, she'd be — '

'What lady?' Charlie's voice was sharp. He gripped Jimmy's arm so fiercely the major winced.

'I didn't know her name, old chap, but she and your brother went to fetch the pony they'd left in the stable yard of the Adelphi. The other one, a real beauty, stayed with you. It was clear she was very taken with you and you with her.' He laughed, then was sorry, for poor old Charlie looked quite pole-axed. 'I'm sorry, lad, I'd completely forgotten the incident but your mentioning Lady being blown away brought it back. She was quite lovely, the lady, I mean and come to think of it . . . ' Hey, steady, old man, perhaps you better sit down,' he added, for

Charlie was swaying like a young sapling in a strong wind. 'I've written to my wife to tell her that you and I have met and asked her to tell your family that you are a prisoner of war with me; the authorities will know by now and soon, when this bloody cock-up of a war has ended, we will both be on our way home. God, I can't wait.'

'Alice,' Charlie whispered wonderingly. Little things, little pieces of the jigsaw puzzle in his head were slowly being fitted together by the miracle of finding Jimmy who was remembering small details and feeding them from his memory to Charlie.

'The tiny glimpses of your past life are infiltrating into your mind and gradually the whole picture will emerge, I'm sure. And if this woman who is looking for her husband is your wife, she should be told.'

'Alice . . . '

* * *

Hundreds of miles away a small boy staggered down the slope of the lawn. It was October and the leaves were beginning to fall. Stopping suddenly, he sat down and clutched a damp bundle of them, studying them with the absolute absorption of the young, concentrating as though he must memorise every one, then calmly he put them to his mouth and would have stuffed them in if Tom, who was 'minding' him, had not left the border he was weeding and flew across to stop him.

'Nay, Master Will, them's not ter eat. Yer'll 'ave

a rare old belly-ache if yer swallow that lot.'

The great beeches that ran on either side of the gravel drive, burned amber. Against the far wall that surrounded the garden there were hedges that glowed with the fruit of hawthorn, wild rose and a feathery tangle of wild clematis. With only Tom and the boy Jossy to work in the enormous garden and the park that surrounded the house, everything was getting out of hand. So many of the gardeners who had once lovingly tended the beauty of Beechworth were gone to the front and so many of them would never come back and it looked as though not only this toddler's pa but his ma as well were among them.

'See, give 'em ter Tom, there's a good lad.' He held out his hand but young Will Summers shouted his displeasure. He was strong, big for his age, spoiled by everyone and he liked his own way. The dogs pranced around him, scenting a game but the gardener picked up the boy and put him in the wheelbarrow on top of the weeds and began to push him up the slope noticing, and not for the first time, that the grass needed cutting, despairing, for he knew things would only get worse. He couldn't manage the whole place on his own, he thought, wondering when this bloody war would end. Archie, Corky, Davy, Billy, gone to the front, filled with enthusiasm, just the kid Jossy left and the old fellow who could only milk the cow and do little odd jobs about the place.

The boy was all smiles now, hanging on to the sides of the wheelbarrow, laughing and shouting

177

to Tom to go faster. The dogs, Ginger and Spice, who had been given to Rose almost two years ago barked and leaped about and the boy screamed with laughter; the man pushing the wheelbarrow had time to think that at least this little lad would never know the terrible time they were all living through.

★ ★ ★

She travelled back by train then Channel steamer, both filled with the wounded who had caught a 'blighty one'. The doctor at the hospital had bandaged her hand and put her arm in a sling and told her she must see the doctor as soon as she got home to continue the treatment of Eusol and peroxide until the hand had healed. He had cut some flesh from the infected finger in an attempt to save the finger and the *arm* too.

She had stood on the deck of the steamer, a cold wind in her face, watching the shore of France vanish in the slight mist and her heart was heavy, for her chances of finding Charlie disappeared with the shoreline. Her eyes were filled with the memories of crucifixion by barbed wire and the swelling corpses she had trodden on as she searched the battlefields, her nostrils plagued by the stench. She had carried gassed, burned, blinded men and even now there were many about her on the deck of the steamer that was shipping them back to England, choking, crippled. She had seen so much death and mutilation she wondered if she would ever be able to live a 'normal' life back home, especially without Charlie. She had vowed she would never return without him and yet she had been forced to by some unforeseen mishap, a damned splinter in her finger and the irony of it made her want to weep, to curse the fates, even to curse God, for surely He could have allowed her this one boon.

She returned to London in October, taking a taxi to the station where she boarded the train to Liverpool. It was crowded with soldiers, some of them going home to die, for most were wounded, and some on leave but even these were not uplifted by the idea. They wore blank faces but just the same they were inordinately kind to her, one giving up his seat for her in a compartment. She was still wearing her unflattering uniform of an ambulance driver, her pretty hair stuffed under the unbecoming hat. They knew she was one of them, noticing how she winced every time the train jolted them. There were a lot of men wincing with far worse wounds than hers but nevertheless they pressed a biscuit on her, a bit of chocolate and at one station a corporal jumped off the train and came back with a cup of tea for her.

'Liverpool, is it, love?' one asked her in the sing-song, nasal tone of a Liverpudlian. 'You bin over there long?'

'Eighteen months,' she had answered politely. 'My husband . . . ' She cleared her throat. 'My husband fought with the King's Liverpool Regiment. I have been . . . ' She could not go on and they looked at her sympathetically, for they were mostly Liverpool men and knew that the

179

battalion had more or less been wiped out.

'I am going home,' she said simply, and they asked no more questions. Questions were difficult to answer even by the men who knew exactly what each of them had suffered.

'Me mam lives in Tuebrook,' another said. 'I used ter work on the land.'

At last they reached Lime Street. There had been many hold-ups because there were trains going the other way, hurrying recruits to London and then the Channel for the battlefields must be fed their daily rations of the young, eager flesh of the boys who had no idea what they were getting into. Those in her compartment stared out at them as they stopped opposite each other and their faces were blank until one said quietly, 'Poor bastards.' He had only one leg and knew he would never have to return.

Another taxi-cab took her out of Liverpool and along the winding lanes towards Beechworth, for she could not stand the idea of going to Summer Place just yet even though it was really her home. Not until she felt stronger. And Rose was at Beechworth, and Dolly, and they would help her to get over the enormous disappointment of being sent home. Somehow it never occurred to her that her son was there, Charlie's son, the baby she had seen for a brief moment some eighteen months ago.

The cab took her right up to the front steps of Beechworth. She had passed through the autumn foliage that lined each side of the hedges that were shrouded with white convolvulus. Thickly drooping blackberries were ready to be

180

picked, the bright scarlet berries of black bryony were visible, while above her a swathe of swallows flew south. It was all so peaceful, so beautiful, she could hardly believe that not so very far as the crow flies, hell reigned on earth that had once been as lovely as this.

The cab driver, an old man, helped her gently out of the cab and up the steps, waiting with her until someone came to answer his aggressive ring of the bell and when the door opened and a little maid peered out he went back and fetched the small bag she had brought with her.

'Yes?' the little maid said.

'Is Miss Beechworth at home?' Alice quavered.

'Who is it?' a voice questioned and then with an energetic pull the door was opened wide to reveal Rose and at her feet a small boy clung to her skirts. Rose swayed when she saw her, her face as white as the pristine apron she wore and then with a great shout that startled the child, she grabbed at Alice, taking her into her arms and began to weep.

'Oh, my dear, my darling Alice. Dolly . . . ' she shrieked over her shoulder, her mouth so close to Alice's ear that she flinched and almost fell over. Alice was held in arms strong and loving, arms that told her she was home now, safe and they would put her right. Perhaps they would make her well enough to go back and continue her search for Charlie. She too began to cry and to keep them company so did the little boy. Dolly, her hand to her mouth, staggered up the hall then threw her apron over her head and wept with them all. All Rose could say was 'Alice, oh

Alice,' over and over again.

Suddenly aware that the cab driver was waiting on the steps for his fare, Rose passed Alice into the open arms of Dolly who couldn't wait to get them about 'their' Miss Alice. Rose ran for her purse and gave the man some money, thanking him for bringing Alice home to them as though he were personally responsible for her return.

The small boy plugged his thumb in his mouth, a habit he had lost months ago but he was unnerved by the actions of those who loved him and in whose world he was the centre, but none of them took any notice of him, leading the strange lady towards the kitchen where it was warm, placing her gently in what was known as 'Dolly's chair'. He followed disconsolately and for a moment he was lost then 'Wose' turned and saw him and held out her arms. He flew into them and stared at the strange lady, resenting her, for Wose and Dolly belonged to him. But Rose stood him on the floor again leaving him alone and once more, Rose knelt by the lady and said to her, 'Charlie's alive, darling. He's a prisoner of war. We have just heard. Oh, darling, Charlie is not dead but in a prisoner-of-war camp and when the war is over he will come home to you and Will.'

Will did not know who Charlie was and didn't care. And he wished the lady would go away again so that Wose and Dolly would pay attention to him. He stamped his feet in temper but nobody seemed to care except Ginger and Spice. He would take them out and go and help

Tom. Tom liked *him* the best.

He pouted petulantly and dragged a chair from the table then reached up and opened the door, running out into the yard, the dogs at his heels.

12

They did not attempt to introduce the bewildered little boy to his mother that first day, or indeed for many days to come. She was too ill and he was too uncomprehending. They had decided they would let him get used to her living at Beechworth before starting on the difficult task of telling him that she was his mother and the equally difficult task of getting her to recognise that this small creature was actually her and Charlie's son. Besides which, she was too ill to be worried with even this important issue. How she had ever managed to get herself from the hospital at Camiers to Beechworth in her state they could only marvel at. She was running a high fever and Dolly was incensed with the medical staff in France who had sent her home alone in such a condition.

Dr Roberts came within the hour although he was up to his tired eyes with the influx from the recent Battle of the Somme; he could not keep up with the positions of the battles and felt ashamed, but there were so many and so many men involved all he could manage was his determined need to help those who came to him and Dr Cartwright. It had all become a blur to both the doctors as the wounded poured in and out, most of them destined for home but some poor bastards back to the trenches.

He looked down at the pretty but strained face

of the young woman who he had been told was the wife of one of the Summers boys, the one who had been missing but was now discovered to be a prisoner of war. She was semi-conscious, muttering to herself and like Miss Rose who stood beside him he was astonished that she had arrived here at all. Not brought by ambulance as were the rest of his patients but under her own steam.

Her hand and arm up to the elbow were wrapped in a soiled bandage, probably put on by the beleaguered hospital at the front.

'Let's have a look,' he said and began to unwrap the poor young woman's arm. What was revealed caused him to gasp in shock. The arm was a suffused purple and red, puffy, swollen and the fingers on the hand were like plump sausages and all from a ghastly looking wound in her wedding finger but where her wedding ring was was a mystery. When he had cleaned the hand he found the ring embedded in her swollen flesh. The wound was oozing pus and the young woman next to him clutched his arm in horror.

'How did she do this?' he asked, wondering at his concern, for he had seen much worse than this on the wards of the hospital. But somehow it seemed worse in the case of a young woman. *A lady!*

'I think she said she got a splinter in her finger.'

'All from a bloody splinter,' he spluttered. 'Why was it not tended to in the hospital at . . . where?'

'Camiers.'

'They were probably so overwhelmed they — '

'She probably had it for days before she told them, knowing Alice. For such a little bit of a thing she was an obstinate beggar. She would hardly consider it worth mentioning. She was strong and wilful and her whole soul was obsessed with finding Charlie, her husband.'

The doctor bent down and sniffed at the exposed hand. 'Well, one good thing there's no smell of cheese so not gangrene but ... I'm sorry, this finger will have to come off and let's hope that will fix it or it will mean the whole hand or even the arm.'

Rose put her hand to her mouth, turning away to stare out of the window where the patient Tom was busy digging at something with Will kneeling beside him; she had time to bless the good man and to thank God he was too old for soldiering because he seemed to be the only one who could manage the extremely despotic little boy at the moment. Dolly was too distraught and Nessie too busy doing her best to do what Dolly usually did, and besides she had to feed those who needed it, staff, nurses, even helping with the menus for the wounded though they had their own cook of sorts, but not much 'cop' Nessie believed and said so to Dolly!

Alice was carried on a stretcher from Beechworth to Summer Place and the room on the ground floor that had been turned into a surgery where Dr Roberts and Dr Cartwright did their best to put together the mangled bodies that streamed into them. She was placed on the operating table on which minutes ago a young

186

lad of eighteen had just had both his legs removed. He was sleeping peacefully on the ward, unaware that his life had changed for ever.

It took no more than ten minutes to cut the inflamed and swollen finger from Alice's hand, a pathetic little piece of her body, the doctors praying in their own way that the rest of her would now heal. Neither of them was religious and their praying was more a ferocious tirade against whoever had done this to the men in their care but somehow it seemed much worse to slice into the flesh and bone of a woman, a brave woman who had probably sent on their way some of the wounded in this very hospital, more than likely saving their lives.

She was carried back to Beechworth where Dolly, in tears, the painful tears of the old, waited for her and when she was settled in bed, still unconscious, refused to leave her side as though now that she was home she would never let Alice out of her sight.

It was November before the Somme offensive ended and in all those weeks Alice lay in her bed and began to be introduced to her son. At first, being inquisitive and having evaded the two women who did their best to guard Alice's door, he opened it quietly and peeped inside. He was astonished to see a lady lying in the bed with her eyes turned towards him as if expecting someone.

'Hello,' she said. 'Have you come to check up on me? They won't let me get out of bed.'

'Why not?' he asked, moving slowly across the rich carpet towards her.

'I suppose it's because I've a poorly arm.'

He glanced at the bandaged arm that lay on top of the quilt. 'Did you fa-de down?' He had many quaint sayings and this one meant had she fallen down which he did frequently.

Alice did not know how to reply so she answered factually. 'I got a splinter in my hand.'

The little boy snorted derisively. 'A *splinter*. Me got splinter one day but me not go to bed. Me brave boy,' puffing out his chest.

'Ah but you're a boy. Ladies are not as brave.'

There was a dog barking somewhere, several dogs, and the boy leaned confidentially on the bed, careful not to touch the lady's arm for she was a very pretty lady. Alice had been almost force-fed on Nessie's custards and broths and indeed anything with plenty of milk and eggs in it and her face had filled out and had lost the dreadful flush of fever. Strangely, she seemed reluctant to get out of bed as though she were not yet ready to face the world despite being told Charlie was alive and would, when this war was over, be coming back to them. It was as if something had at last broken in Alice, perhaps not broken but cracked and needed rest to mend itself. The desperate life she had led for a year and a half, the whistle, the alarm bells, the sounds of ambulances being cranked, not to mention the cries of the wounded, and which had forced the pace of her days, had taken something from her but she had not been aware of it.

'That's Ginger an' Spice an' Tommy.'

'What?'

'My dogs. They all mine.' He was full of his own importance.

'You are a lucky boy. To have three dogs of your own.' She wished the boy would go away. She knew she had a son and she supposed this was him but she did not know him and was too tired to get to know him. She closed her eyes and he patted her cheek.

'You go bye-byes,' he said kindly, then turned to tiptoe out of the room.

★ ★ ★

It was Christmas before she came downstairs and it was only Rose's nagging, as Alice called it, that did the trick.

'Look, sweetheart, you can't lie up there for ever. Will is excited about having a Christmas tree and he keeps asking when the poorly lady is coming down to see it. He seems to have taken a fancy to you and is dying to show you his dogs. Dolly won't hear of him bringing them up to you so you must come down to them. Your hand is healed and your arm is no longer in bandages. The doctor says you are recovered and — '

'My finger, Rosie, my finger.'

'I know, darling, but it is better than losing — '

'My wedding ring is gone with the finger and I no longer feel I am married to Charlie. It is so long since I've seen him, married him; it's all unreal.'

It was then that Rose at last realised that although Alice was recovered physically she was not really herself, the sweet, good-humoured girl

189

they had all come to love in 1914.

The loss of her wedding ring, the absence of the man who put it on her finger, the boy they had made together who was still not hers, had interfered with something in her mind and she wandered about the house and gardens, often with Will and the dogs running round her, her face vague and expressionless, her eyes dulled so that Rose and Dolly began seriously to worry about her.

'D'you think it's shell-shock, Doctor?' Rose asked Dr Roberts anxiously. 'Men who come back from the front often look like she does and she seems to care for nothing, not even Charlie, nor her son. Look at her . . . ' And they both turned to look out of the window at Alice who simply stood on the lawn that ran down to the lake, staring at nothing. 'Her life is empty without that compulsion she had to search for Charlie, and Will might as well be the gardener's son to whom she is kind and to whom she listens when he speaks to her but she never bonds with him. We have told her he is hers — her and Charlie's son — but she simply looked at him quite without interest and said, 'Yes, I know.' I don't know what to do, really I don't.'

'Try not to worry, Miss Beechworth,' the doctor said absent-mindedly, his thoughts turning to the lad on whom he was to perform surgery within the hour. He had been shot in the face, only a glancing blow from a bullet across his forehead which did not disfigure him but which had left him blind, and the devil of it was he didn't know what he could do to bring back his sight. There were doctors who dealt with specific types of wounds. Men who operated in men's heads revealing their brains, others who cared for shell-shocked men who screamed at the slightest noise, men who looked after and did their best for those who had been burned: specialists in their chosen field. Perhaps he should send the young soldier to one of those.

He sighed and patted her hand and Rose was left to realise that the woman in the garden who to all intents and purposes was cured, for the loss of a finger was nothing compared to the loss of a young man's sight, was not really of much concern to the overworked doctor.

★   ★   ★

There was great excitement in April when the United States of America declared war on Germany, for surely this meant that the war would soon be over and perhaps, Rose thought, Harry might get some leave. She had not seen him for more than nine months when he had managed a forty-eight-hour pass. She had gone up to London to meet him and they had spent the whole time cradled together either in the bed of the hotel in which she had booked a room, or in the bath, for he could not seem to feel clean, he told her. Indeed when she saw him climb wearily down from the train and walk towards her on the platform she had scarcely recognised him he was so covered in mud and what looked suspiciously like blood. He was weighed down with the usual clutter a soldier, even an officer, must carry about with him and when she shrieked his name she could see the effort it took to lift his head to look at her.

'The blood?' he asked, crying and laughing at the same time, she didn't know why, but it wasn't his, he managed to tell her. He did not mention to her that it belonged to several young officers, most of them straight from school and ridiculously boyish, whom he had carried one by one from the battlefield.

She stripped him in the warm hotel room and, without a word being spoken, put him in the bath she ran for him then followed him, sitting behind him as he leaned back against her. She murmured soft endearments to which he did not answer, sponged and soaped him, even his genitals to which he did not respond and she realised he was asleep. Exhaustion had him in thrall for almost twelve hours then when he awoke he took her savagely, no tenderness, no words of love, just as though it was the only way Harry could join Rose again in the way they had known on his last leave. Only when his orgasms, many of them, released some inner horror, allowing it to drift into the heavy London sky, did he begin to make love to her. The badness had gone and only the sweetness they had known remained and he spoke to her of his love and longing and dread of going back.

'But when the Yanks arrive it will be the end of it all. I must stay . . . stay alive until then, my darling, for I want this, what you have given me, what I have taken, I suppose I should say, to go on for ever. We will make lots of babies and

. . . and . . . ' He began to weep desolately and she knew that this bloody war had not only torn Alice from her but was going a fair way to taking this beloved man as well. He was on the edge, the precipice, ready to tumble down into the chasm of despair and only times like these few hours with her could drag him back. She supposed they were all like that, or most of them.

They parted at the railway station quite calmly, just a light kiss from Harry's lips on Rose's bloodless cheek, then he turned away and climbed into the carriage. She did not even watch the train leave but took a tram to the train that was to take her way up north and she was aware that anyone seeing them say farewell would think they did not care much for one another. An onlooker would not know that if they had let their feelings show they would both have run screaming into the traffic that crammed the streets, careless of death. She and Alice had died months ago and so had Charlie and Harry.

She got home, moving like a robot up the long drive and into the front door where an ecstatic Will clasped her round her knees and told her loudly that she was very naughty to have left him and she must promise never to do it again.

★　★　★

And now Alice watched as an ambulance came chugging up the drive of Summer Place with its usual cargo of wounded. As it passed her she turned to watch it and, slowly at first, then more quickly, she followed it to the wide front door.

Stretcher-bearers began to unload the quiet men, the fresh batch of wounded, quiet since most of them had come straight from the trenches and had been on the move for several days. Nurses were busy about them, directing each man to the place where he was to be dealt with according to his wounds. There were a dozen of them and apart from the bit of rough first aid they had received at the clearing stations, they still had the mud and filth of the battlefields on them. Grey and silent, close to death it seemed, and the VADs were astounded as the woman they knew had herself been on the battlefields was bending over one of them with the words they all used.

'It'll be all right, old chap. You'll soon feel better when you've been cleaned up.'

'Mrs Summers, you have no business here with these wounded,' Staff Nurse Long told her. 'Please stand aside and allow — '

'Give me some scissors, if you please, Nurse,' to a VAD who stood uncertainly beside her. 'I shall do my best to get these stinking uniforms from these soldiers. There, there, old chap,' for the soldier had begun to moan. 'Don't fret, love, I'll help you until the doctor sees to you.'

They stood, open-mouthed, as the dainty Mrs Summers moved from one soldier to another, soothing, laying her mutilated hand on their brows, murmuring, telling one who whispered for his mam that if he would give her his mam's address she would write to her, or even telephone; no, she understood, Mam did not have a telephone, but a telegram would be sent.

'Mrs Summers,' Staff Nurse exclaimed, 'you cannot go round these men promising things that might not be possible.' But she had to admit that all those who were treated to Mrs Summers's unique handling were looking up into her face as though she were an angel, believing implicitly that she would help them.

'You should be with your own son, Mrs Summers, you cannot possibly — '

'All these men are someone's son, Nurse, and have no one but us. My son is loved and cared for by people I trust. I can be of more help here. I was an ambulance driver at the front and I am well acquainted with the sort of wounds these men have. I pray that my husband, wherever he is, will come home but until then I must be of use to somebody. I would return to the front but . . . '

'Mrs Summers, please . . . '

'If I can shut out the sights, the sounds, the smells, the hell of the Western Front they have all suffered over there — well, you have heard them scream.' She stood up and moved towards what was now the sluice. 'And anyway, you cannot order me about in my own home. I shall put on an apron and cap and help these men to recover as best I can. Take it up with Dr Roberts if you must but let me get on. I must do something now that . . . that I am here.'

'But you have had no training, Mrs Summers,' the staff nurse protested, doing her best to regain her dominance over this woman.

'Really! I should imagine I have seen more wounded soldiers than you have, Nurse, and

195

looked after them until I could pass them into the doctors' hands. I shall do so here.' She pushed past the sister, who stood with her mouth open, and even the soldiers on the stretchers smiled.

It was the start of Alice Summers' recovery and very soon they all began to wonder how they had managed without her. Not for her nursing skills, though she had some of those, but for her ability to quieten a suffering soldier. She even sat with them at night and sang in a whispering voice the songs a baby enjoys at bedtime, holding their hands, and was once seen to kiss a young lad's cheek telling him his mam was on her way. She made it her business to find out the history and home address of every wounded man in the hospital and as she had promised sent telegrams inviting them to come and see their brave sons. These mothers found a bed at Beechworth and in no time at all even Dolly began to look her old self again as she chatted to them, most of them working class like herself, enjoying the cup of tea she put in their hands. They might only stay a day or two, sitting beside the bed of their son or husband but the doctors were astonished at the improvement in the men's morale.

The entrance of the United States into the war did not seem to alter in any way the savagery of the fighting that still continued on the Western Front. A new offensive was started at Nivelle and on the very same day the Arras offensive began. On and on it went and the hospitals were filled to overflowing, week after week, and all the time Alice kept up her own particular healing of the men who came into their care.

And all the time, too, Rose and Dolly watched with bated breath for Alice to notice her little son who, thankfully they thought, was unaware that his own mother scarcely spoke to him. He had become accustomed to having her around the place, to sleeping when she was not at Summer Place in the bedroom at the back of Beechworth which was supposedly a guest bedroom and not a very luxurious one. At Beechworth he played games with the three dogs, chasing them about the garden, interrupting Tom's work as the gardener did his best to do the job of three men, but it was not until he had been missing for a couple of hours, the dogs with him, that they realised the child needed something other than the cuddles and hugs and kisses the women of the house gave him.

Oak Hill, the nearest farm to Summer Place, was tenanted by Dan Herbert who was, like Tom, doing his best to keep everything running smoothly until Sir Harry came home. He had three children, two of them boys who each had a small pony on which they rode to school every day. On this particular day they were plodding slowly up the lane that led to Oak Hill Farm when the dogs, squeezing through the hedge to the side of the woodland belonging to Summer Place, ran across their path and behind them ran a small child who was shouting his head off telling them to come back at once or he would give them a good hiding. The ponies, both young, reared up and one of the riders, five-year-old Alfie, slithered over his rump and fell into the dust of the lane. He was not hurt but he was incensed that the bloody dogs had made him look ridiculous. Alfie turned ferociously on the small boy who followed the dogs through the hedge.

'What the bloody hell d'yer think yer doin' lettin' them bloody fools dash about like that? They had me on me bum an' the 'orse 'as run off an' you, yer little twerp, can run after 'er. Come ter think of it I'll give *you* a good 'iding, never mind them dogs.'

Though Alfie himself was only five years old he suddenly realised that the fool who'd let his dogs run wild and had unseated him was really only a baby. A little lad no bigger than two pennorth of copper. They had neither of the brothers been to Beechworth where their pa helped out Miss Beechworth when he wasn't doing his best to keep Summer Place going while the squire, as they thought him, was off fighting the Hun. This must be the nipper whose pa was brother to the squire.

'You've just sweared,' the nipper said severely. 'Wose said swearing's naughty.'

Alfie laughed. He was the youngest of Dan and Jinny Herbert's children and had been bossed about by the older children all his short life. Now, here was some kid *he* could boss about and he began at once.

'Yer can come an' play wi' us if yer like,' he said loftily, 'but first yer'll 'ave ter 'elp me catch me pony. It were your fault she ran off. Come on, but yer've got ter promise yer'll do as yer told.'

'Oh, I will.'

' 'Onest?'

'Yes, honest to God,' a phrase he had heard Mrs Nessie say to Tom.

John, who was a year older than Alfie and who had watched this exchange with amusement and derision, turned his pony towards the farm, saying as he trotted away, 'Yer as daft as 'e is, our Alfie. 'E's only a kid. Besides, they'll come lookin' fer 'im an' it's nowt ter do wi' me. I'm off 'ome fer some o' Mam's fatty cake,' a delicious mixture of pastry left over from the pies his ma made and which, spread with her best butter recently churned by herself, would keep him going until teatime.

'Can I have some?' Will beseeched.

'Course yer can,' Alfie told him, 'as soon as yer've catched the 'orse.'

It was the start of a friendship that helped Will Summers to be completely happy until his pa came home.

13

Jinny Herbert was horrified to see two-year-old Will Summers accompany her two sons into the yard, the small boy tagging along with Alfie who was *always* in trouble. What the dickens was the lad doing so far from home and what was his mam, or at least Miss Rose, doing to allow the boy out of the garden at Beechworth which was where he seemed to spend most of his time?

She dropped her rolling pin on to the table where she had just finished shaping out the fatty cake and ran into the yard. There were, besides the boy, three dogs who began to chase her chickens which had been clucking and muttering to one another in the yard, and with an earsplitting shriek she rushed towards her sons.

'What the 'ell's goin' on 'ere? What the devil d'yer think yer doin' wi' Master Will?' turning on Will who cowered behind the fragile protection of Alfie's back. 'And you,' glaring at Will, 'where d'yer think you're off to? What's yer mam thinkin' of, letting you wander about at your age? An' them damn dogs'd better leave my chickens alone or I'll 'ave them shot. John,' addressing her eldest, 'get down off that bloody 'orse and sort this lot out. See, get 'old of the bairn's 'and an' 'tekk 'im back ter Beechworth. Nay, don't you dare argue wi' me,' as John began to protest that it was not him but Alfie who had fetched the kid to the farm. 'Now get 'old of 'is 'and and tekk 'im 'ome.'

'Mam, 'e were 'angin' about in't lane wi' them dogs an' the dogs jumped up at Misty and our Alfie fell off an — '

'Never you mind. Get 'old of 'is 'and.'

But Will, used to having his own way, did not want to have his hand taken nor did he want to go home. He and Alfie were friends now and he wanted to stay and play with his new friend and he said so vociferously, but as he was still having some difficulty with longer words he could not make this woman who was so cross understand this so he stamped his foot and when Mrs Herbert advanced towards him he ran away. The gate was still open so he darted through, much to the amusement of the Herbert boys who knew that their mother always won in the end. She'd tan his bottom when she caught him, whether he was from the big house or not, for Mam liked her own way an' all.

The spoiled, precocious son of Alice and Charlie Summers was caught by the outraged Mrs Herbert and she carried him, struggling fiercely, under her arm through the gate that led into the lane, across the field, into the lane that skirted Beechworth and up through the vegetable garden to the back door of the house. It stood open, for Miss Rose was just getting up a search party for the little boy, and the men, even some of the walking wounded, were all milling about waiting to be told where they should start.

'It's about time Alice faced up to her responsibility for her son, Dolly,' Miss Rose was ranting to Dolly, her fear making her voice sharp. 'He wanders about getting in everybody's way, keeping Tom from his work and though we all love him he's getting out of hand. Dear God, haven't we enough to worry about without — '

'Now, now, lass, child means no harm.' Dolly did her best to calm Rose down although her own heart was beating fast with dread. She wrung her hands in her apron and the men shuffled from one foot to another waiting for orders.

A loud gasp of relief went up when Jinny Herbert walked through the door holding the protesting child who had caused such commotion. They all started talking at once, most of them agreeing with Jinny who gave her opinion that the boy should have his ears boxed but Dolly, who took him from Jinny's arms, at once began to pet him. She was astonished when Rose tore him from her and turned towards the door.

'It's no good making a fuss of him. He should be with his mother or we should get a nanny to look after him. He has far too much freedom for his age. Dear God, he could fall in the damn lake or wander off — '

'He did wander off, Miss Rose,' Jinny interrupted, 'an' 'is dogs played 'avoc wi' my chickens. Any road, keep a tight 'old of 'im, if you please.'

She turned her back on them and marched off in the direction of Oak Hill Farm and the fatty cake she had promised Alfie.

★　★　★

202

'Dolly, we must speak to Alice about Will. I know she is more content, more herself since she started to help out at Summer Place and had the news that Charlie has not been killed, but Will is her son and she seems to take little interest in his welfare. Caring for the wounded is helping her to get over the last couple of years but her boy must be given into her hands then when Charlie comes home they can settle down together.' Rose shook her head, not knowing how this little family were to bond. All of them at both houses loved the child and he had had a happy childhood so far, but the truth was that with so many folk to indulge him he was getting seriously out of hand. The wounded in their beds made a great fuss of him, glad to see him wandering along the ward which he did whenever he could escape the notice of the overworked nurses. He would stop at a particular bed, whichever took his fancy, and was not afraid of bandages or even faces that were not quite as they should be or scars that were healing but really no sight for a small child. Some of the men were quiet, some whimpering from pain, other calling out for Elsie or Joan or their mam but when his inquisitive little face beamed at them on their pillows they quietened and did their best to smile.

'I'll get her on her own tonight when she comes over to Beechworth,' Rose said to Dolly.

'See, sit down, lass, and I'll make us a cup of tea, and you, you young imp, sit there and eat one of the biscuits Nessie has made. No, you can't have two. You'll spoil your tea. Here'

— reaching for a pile of books and crayons on the dresser — 'do some colouring in to show Mama when she comes in and try to sit still.'

She moved across the kitchen which even with the door open was warm for it was the middle of summer, 31 July. Rose wondered tiredly how much longer this bloody war would go on. She put the kettle on, feeling the sweat trickle down her back between her shoulder blades and her thoughts winged across the country and thence to the Channel over which so many men had gone, some never to come back, some returning so maimed in mind and body they would never be the same again. Where was Harry? Dear God, it was weeks since she had had a letter from him and then it had been barely more than a note. At least it had told her he was alive. *Then!* Even as she held it she knew, as did many of the women at home, that though he had been alive when it was sent, he could have been killed between it leaving his hand and being delivered into hers.

★ ★ ★

Captain Sir Harry Summers was shouting his head off, saying he didn't know what, encouragement, he supposed, as he went over the top waving his revolver, but it helped to get his seriously depleted men up the ladders and into the almost knee-deep mud in no-man's-land, for the weather in France was not as pleasant as it was at Beechworth. They were in the second wave, crammed into the trenches along the Ypres salient and they shivered in the persistent drizzle

204

that had been falling for days.

He yelled for his men to keep shoulder to shoulder, which was how they were supposed to advance but it was the maddest way to move because they made a solid wall of men, easily mown down by the venomous machine guns of the enemy. And they did go down, like ninepins, he thought, like those in the pubs at home that played the game but this was no game. Men lay in writhing heaps as he and those who were left ran into the vicious fire and though he did his best not to step on the fallen it was impossible for they were so thick in the churned-up ground of mud and blood that soaked into the land about them.

'Keep going, lads,' he heard himself shouting, at the same time condemning himself for encouraging these bone-weary young men to run towards the barbed wire behind which the Germans lay. Down they went, and down, and from somewhere something slammed into the front of his thigh and to his own astonishment he stepped on to the prone body of one of his own men and fell down. Private Joe Turner, he thought it was, and he found himself apologising to the soldier who was already dead. He lay for several moments doing his best to stand up and it was probably his inability to do so that saved his life. He began to crawl through the muck and mud and across fallen men, some of whom cried out in pain, calling to Private Turner to follow him, but he was on his own until he toppled into a hole made by a shell, one of their own that had fallen short of the target, the Hun.

There were several others already in the crater, one of them shrieking, 'Make it stop, please, Jesus, make it stop,' until a tired voice told him to put a sock in it. They huddled together, those men, glad to be safe for a minute or two, if you could call a machine-gun-strafed hole safe, then Captain Summers began to do his best to rally them. But they were not to be rallied. They'd had enough and one of them was heard to mutter that if the officer thought he was getting out of here in broad daylight he'd got another bloody think coming. It was still raining and with so many men in the crater it was beginning to fill up with rainwater. Harry struggled to climb up the slippery walls of the packed hole but he found the leg that had been hit would not hold his weight and it was damned hard to climb with only one leg workable.

'We'll wait until it's dark, lads,' he told them, but he was so bloody tired he had no strength to enforce his will on them and could you blame them for not wanting to move. Poor sods had been fighting valiantly for months in this battle along the Ypres salient, some of them in these same trenches and across this same bit of land, for three years. He himself had not been on leave since last autumn, rallying his men in this hell on earth, breathing in death and destruction along with the stink of rotting bodies and yet here they still were at the end of the first day of the Third Battle of Ypres and he had worked out that they had advanced no more than half a mile.

He must have passed out then, for the next time he came to it was to the sound of a young voice, the voice of a boy, screaming for his mam. Then suddenly the voice fell silent and he realised that one of the other men had hit the lad to quieten him as he was driving them all to the edge of insanity.

It was very quiet and as dark as the inside of the parson's hat, as his old nanny used to say, and he knew that it was time, the only sensible time to make a bid for their own lines.

'Give me a hand, lads. Push me up to the top of the crater and then help one another as best you can. I'm going to crawl on my belly so those who are up for it, and that means all of you who are not wounded, follow me.'

'I'm not goin',' a belligerent voice answered.

'This is an order, soldier.'

'Oh, sod it,' came from the darkness but the men began to inch their way, pushing him upwards until he reached the lip of the shell-hole. He put his head tentatively over the top, just his forehead and eyes and could see absolutely nothing.

'Right,' he whispered, 'follow me.' Slowly, inch by inch, he hauled himself over the lip of the shell-hole and crawled as near to the ground as he could, his belly brushing against the silent dead who lay in a carpet between their position and the trench from which they had erupted hours ago. It seemed to take ages but was actually no more than an hour and he was amazed because it seemed to him that they had run for miles that morning.

The men still in the trench almost cried out as Harry and the few men who had followed him fell in on them.

★ ★ ★

The hedges were bright with wild rose, elderberry and honeysuckle. There were cows knee-deep in clover and poppies as Rose, Will and the two dogs crossed the field from Summer Place to Beechworth. Tommy had chosen to stay behind beside the bed of a soldier who was dying from the gas he had breathed in weeks ago and from which he had never recovered. The dog sensed that the soldier, Billy Collins, who was all of eighteen years old, was near to death and he lay on the polished floor ready to give comfort, as he did to so many of the men should they show signs of distress. Billy, Private William Collins, whose mother was expected any moment, was not quite so tucked up as Staff Nurse Long liked her patients to be since it was so warm, and his arm fell over the edge of the bed, his hand dangling near Tommy's nose. The dog licked it tenderly and the boy, the *soldier*, since he had fought valiantly in France, did his best to open his eyes; though the nurses bathed them each day the lids became glued together with the nasty matter caused by the gas. His breathing was hoarse and when his mother arrived and was taken to his bed she began to weep. This was her baby. She had fought him every step of the way when he volunteered but it did no good, he had gone anyway and now he was to leave her for ever.

'Be brave, Mrs Collins. Try not to cry for it will only upset him. Kiss him, give him a hug and tell him about all the things that are happening at home in . . . ?'

'Preston,' Mrs Collins managed to say, then, with the strength that amazed Alice, who was the nurse who had led him to her son, she smiled.

'Eeh, our Billy, what yer doin' fiddlin' wi' that there dog? I'm that surprised they let the animal in.'

'He has a twice-weekly bath, Mrs Collins. The soldiers love him and he loves them. He often comes in here to comfort those who are — ' She nearly said 'close to death' but quickly changed it to 'who need a bit of fuss. He does them a lot of good.'

'Aye, our Billy always liked a dog. We got one at 'ome called Tinker. You remember our Tinker, lad?' The lad did his best to smile but as his hand wavered in the air his mother took it, sitting in the chair they had placed beside the bed for her. She brought it to her lips and Alice tiptoed away.

Rose sauntered in the late summer sunshine while Will frolicked round her with Ginger and Spice. The cows in the field eyed them suspiciously but the dogs were accustomed to them and took no notice of their presence. Rose had been hoping to get a word with Alice about Will but Alice was always busy and she had had little success.

The perfume of the wild flowers was heavy and sweet and she breathed in deeply. Dear Lord, let me have a letter soon or I shall run mad, she said out loud but Will was rolling in the grass with the dogs and nobody heard her. She had written to Harry only last night, telling him of the enormity of her love for him, of the future that she prayed for to a God she was not sure existed because would a loving God allow the massacre and maiming of so many men, the agony they suffered, the pain she herself felt in her desperate worry over Harry. Her love was strong, steady, the love of a mature woman, patient and honest as she had always tried to be, and she would wait for him until the end of her life. It was not romantic, a dazzling emotion felt by the young boys and girls who were caught up in this war. It was enduring, indestructible, a love that filled her heart and mind and would never change. She had told him so in her letter, begging him to write soon. She knew he was busy; *busy?* What a word to describe what he was doing, but if he could just send her a line, a postcard, to let her know he was still — she hardly dare think the word — *alive*.

She shook herself from her morbid thoughts, or tried to, opening the field gate and calling to Will who was crawling through the long grasses with the dogs barking and jumping all over him. He stood up and ran towards her, the dogs at his heels and when they entered the stable yard Tom was there sitting in the sunshine smoking his pipe. He stood up at once, flustered, for he felt guilty that he, the last man left, apart from the boy, Jossy, to tend to the gardens and even the parkland and wooded areas of Beechworth, should be found lolling about.

'No, Tom, stay there and finish your pipe. You deserve a rest with all the work you do. I don't know where we would be without you what with all the young men at the front.'

'Aye, tha're right, Miss Rose, and gerrin' a real pastin' by the sound of it. Eeh, wharra' waste o' — ' He suddenly remembered that Miss Beechworth's young man was one of those getting a real pasting and he clamped his lips firmly over his pipe. First young Mr Charlie getting lost, though thankfully he was found again, and Sir Harry fighting for his Liverpool Regiment *and* his life in the thick of it.

Will addressed Tom in his own particular way which they all seemed to understand and the gardener listened intently.

'Me come wiv you, Tom. Will come wiv you. That there grass needs cutting,' he told him, using an expression, one among many, that he picked up among the servants. He nodded his head sagely.

'Nay, Master Will, tha're right there and termorrer thi' an' me'll 'ave a go at it.'

'Can Will push, Tom?' meaning the ancient lawn mower.

'Aye, I don't see why not but Sparky'll give us a pull.' Sparky was company for Sir Harry's hunter in the paddock to the side of the house. Though the lad often held him up Tom didn't mind. If it helped Miss Rose and Miss Alice that was something.

★ ★ ★

211

It was three days later, just as Rose was passing it, that the telephone shrilled out. For a moment her heart missed a beat for that was what the machine did to you. It was probably the hospital authorities looking for beds since they all knew by now that a battle had recently been fought in which many wounded had been reported but nevertheless they hated the damn thing. It was known as a 'candlestick' model with the earpiece hanging from its side and with some trepidation she put it to her ear and spoke into the receiver.

'Yes,' she answered briefly.

'Is that the Beechworth House Hospital?' a masculine voice asked politely.

'Yes,' she said again.

'Ah, may I speak to Miss Beechworth?'

'This is Miss Beechworth.' And though she was expecting the call to be about wounded soldiers and any space she might have for them, her pulse raced and she felt the need to sit down.

'Forgive me for interrupting you, Miss Beechworth, but it's Tom, Sir Harry Summers's friend.'

'Oh, please, don't . . . '

'I'm sorry to distress you but I work at the War Office and I have just heard — '

'Please, oh please, don't tell me . . . ' She wanted to scream at him, to swear but she leaned against the wall and did her best to hang on to her fading senses.

'I'm afraid Harry has — '

'Don't you dare tell me he is . . . is . . . please . . . '

'He has been wounded, Miss Beechworth, but

212

not fatally. A leg wound. I should not be giving you this information but Harry asked me particularly to let you know if — '

'Where is he, for God's sake, where is he? Not still at the front . . . ' for she had seen wounded men who came straight from the fighting and the condition they were in.

'No, he is in a hospital in London where he is to be operated on — '

'Not . . . not amputation?' She slowly slid down the wall until she was crouched on the floor.

'I can tell you no more than that, I'm afraid. Wandsworth, you know it? But if you could get up here — '

'I'll be on the first train, tell him.'

'I'm afraid I can't tell him that but — '

But she had hung up and was screaming down the hall towards the kitchen where Dolly and Nessie and Polly stood huddled together as though their proximity to each other gave them courage. They all had their hands to their mouths.

'Dolly, oh Dolly, it's Harry; no, not dead, wounded in London and I'm off to the station to get the first train.'

'Oh lass, whatever next? As if we haven't got enough wi' Mr Charlie and . . . and . . . see, get a bag packed an' go. Me an' Nessie an' Polly'll manage. We'll see to Master Will. Miss Alice'll have to give a hand here an' you know how good Tom is with that little lad. Eeh, I dunno, will this damn war ever be over?' She put her apron to her eyes and rubbed them furiously then gave herself a shake and was her old self. She had looked after this family, Rose's mother and the miscarriages she had suffered and she'd not let the lass down now even though she did feel that the good Lord was laying too much of a burden on her old shoulders.

She sighed as she heard Miss Rose thunder up the stairs and drag a suitcase to the floor, packing it hurriedly with clean underclothes, a nightdress and odds and ends she might need, though what could they be, for goodness sake. She wasn't going gallivanting. She was going to the man she loved who lay in a London hospital where they would do everything they could for him. *If it was not too late.* The dread of gangrene pierced every one of them who had nursed wounded men. The muck they picked up as they lay where they had fallen and even Dolly who had never nursed a wounded man knew that was what frightened those who had.

The station at Lime Street was a seething mass of soldiers and their loved ones who had come to see them off, or to meet them as they came home. Many of those who had come from the battlefields just stood, with the accoutrements of war they were forced to carry everywhere they went hanging about them, waiting for someone to tell them where to go, waiting for orders since that's what they had been doing for three years.

She could have wept for them, these poor bits of flotsam who were going home for what should have been peace but whose confusion was reflected in their gaunt faces.

It was the same on the train that she eventually boarded but these men were going back, knowing what to expect and obliging death and wounds as they had been instructed. The sadness in her for them was mixed with the worry that was infecting her for the man she loved.

Dear sweet Jesus, let it stop soon, she begged, as the man in the shell-hole with Harry had begged.

14

He was lying flat on his back gazing at the ceiling when she entered the ward.

'Are you a relative, Miss Beechworth?' a harassed nurse asked her as Rose enquired at the desk for Captain Summers. 'It is not visiting time, you know.' She looked Rose up and down as though to find some reason why she should not be allowed to enter the hospital, never mind the ward where the wounded officers lay.

'Yes,' Rose lied. 'His mother cannot come since she is not well so I offered to visit Captain Summers in her place. He is my . . . cousin. I have just made a long journey from Liverpool where I am a VAD at a nursing home and cannot go back to her to tell her you would not allow me to see her son.'

'I am not saying you may not see him but visiting hours are — '

'I must see him at once, Nurse. I have a job to do at the hospital which you of all people must understand and I must get back to it as soon as possible. The wounded from the last battle are pouring in and we can barely manage; surely you must realise how important *our* work is?'

The officious nurse relaxed, for she was worn to the bone nursing the sick and wounded who flooded not just into her hospital but others all over the country and this woman whom she was certain was not a cousin of Captain Summers knew exactly how she and her fellow nurses and VADs worked round the clock. She nodded her head towards the stairs and turned away and without a word Rose sped up the stairs heading for the ward where Harry lay.

He lay completely still under his bedsheets except for his hands which moved restlessly, pulling at something as though he hauled at a fishing net. Careless of the men who lay in their beds, some asleep, others unconscious, she almost ran along the ward until she reached the last bed where he lay. He continued to stare at the ceiling and seemed unaware of her presence until she knelt beside him and took his twitching hands in hers, bringing them to her lips in an outpouring of love. She folded them gently in her warm grasp. Silently she spilled out the endless current of her love and when he turned his head and looked into her eyes she bent and kissed his mouth. He was gaunt, sunken-eyed, the lovely chocolate brown of his eyes flat and unfocused as though he were still back on that battlefield where he had stepped on poor Joe Turner's fallen body.

'Harry, Harry, my love . . . what . . . ' She did not know what to say. 'How are you? How badly are you wounded? Does it hurt? What happened?' all seemed so stupid, puerile, as though the wounded man, who stared at her as if he wasn't sure who she was, was a fool for he wouldn't be here if his wound were not serious.

'I don't know what to say except how glad . . . ' *Glad!* What a stupid word to describe the way she felt, the joy that was running through her at the sight of him, of knowing he was alive, wounded, certainly, but alive and back here in England. She had lived a life of worry, with an agonising, ever present expectation that he would vanish as so many of them had done. The unknown was a spectre that stared her in the face day after day after day. Even asleep she had been troubled by dreams of him festering in the muck and mud that Alice had inadvertently told her about. She had not meant to hurt her, to drive her mad with anxiety but Alice had been unable to hold back her own knowledge of the horrors that faced the men who fought 'over there'. And here he was back within reach of her eager hands, arms, lips, but there was something wrong with the beloved man she had known. He seemed confused, *uncaring* of who she was and yet she knew he loved her as she loved him.

'Harry, my love, I am here. Look at me, sweetheart. I am here to take care of you, perhaps to bring you home if they will let me. Charlie is found, did you know? And Alice is back with us. The boy, their boy — dearest, look at me, please, and say you know me, that you love me still . . . '

His face spasmed as though in sudden pain and she gripped his hand, turning to search for a doctor or a nurse. She wanted to know the precise details of his injury but the nurse was bending over another bed, giving a soldier an injection, she thought, and she did not like to interrupt.

'Rose . . . ' Harry's voice quavered and with a gasp of relief she turned back to him.

'Yes, my love, I am here.'

'I stepped on poor Joe Turner's body. I didn't mean to but he . . . ' Again his face spasmed and she realised it was not with pain but with anguish. He was remembering the last battle in which he had fought and though this man — Joe Turner — must have been dead, the fact that he had stepped on him seemed to have made more impression on him than any other memory of that terrible day. Among the many hundreds who had fallen under the first rain of bullets and who scattered the ground like leaves from the oak trees at Summer Place in the autumn, this one soldier obsessed his mind. His spirit seemed to have been broken but if she could just get him home to those who loved him she was determined it would be mended.

'Darling, don't.' She didn't know how to comfort him, to expunge from his mind this one moment of horror when he himself had been injured. What was there beneath the cage that covered his legs? Not — oh sweet Jesus — not *amputation*, not the horrific damage to the life of this active man who had already given so much of himself since the beginning of 1915.

She stood up decisively and placed Harry's hand on the bed where it lay like an upturned leaf, then started again with its drawing in of a net, and walked the length of the ward barely aware of the smell of suffering, of the antiseptic used, the carbolic soap with which everything was scrubbed, a smell with which she was very familiar. She patiently waited until the nurse had finished ministering to the soldier and spoke

219

harshly to her as she left the ward though she did not mean to be harsh.

'Nurse, please, can I speak to a doctor? I have come from Liverpool to . . . to be with my . . . cousin but he seems unable to tell me what has happened to him. He is wounded in the leg but in what way? I work in a hospital and I am used to wounds but if you would tell me where I might find — '

The nurse, not a VAD but a trained nurse, did her best to brush by her agitated visitor. 'The doctor, all the doctors are run off their feet, miss, and have not the time to — '

'To tell a relative what has happened to a loved one! I cannot believe it. I must know what has happened to Captain Summers so I may return and reassure his . . . his mother that he will recover from what has happened to him. The captain seems unable to communicate.'

'He is very ill, Miss . . . Miss . . . ?'

'Beechworth.'

'Miss Beechworth. He was unconscious when he was brought to us — '

'When was that?' Rose rudely interrupted her, then was sorry, for did she not know herself how hard these nurses worked, *overworked*, and hardly had time even to speak to each other, let alone to anxiously demented visitors.

'I'm sorry to plague you when you are so busy, really I am, but perhaps you can tell me the extent of Captain Beechworth's wounds. He has not had his leg . . . ' She could hardly bring herself to speak the word. It seemed to stick in her throat, choking her and the nurse relented, putting a gentle hand on Rose's arm.

'He still has two legs, Miss Beechworth, though it has been touch and go. He was trapped in a shell-hole, I believe, and the wound was not tended to for a couple of days. A shrapnel wound that tore through his thigh, just missing his . . . and, perhaps I should not tell you this but you say you have had some nursing experience.'

'Yes, I have. I shall stay here with Harry, if I may. I promise not to get in the way but I should like to speak to a doctor regarding the possibility of taking him home and nursed in the hospital where I work.'

The nurse looked doubtful. She was obviously also eager to be away. From somewhere on the lower floor there was some kind of commotion and with a shake of her head and a long sigh she began to move hurriedly towards the head of the stairs along with other nurses who had appeared from different wards and a group of orderlies.

'More of them, I'm afraid. There must have been another battle.'

Rose followed her down the stairs, watching the long line of ambulances come from Waterloo station straight from the hospital train proceeding slowly up the drive, the first one stopping at the bottom of the steps. Stretcher-bearers, well used to the drill now, ran to the back of the ambulance and gently lifted the stretchers carrying the sighing, moaning, murmuring wounded and carried them into the hospital. One of them screamed as the orderly jogged the stretcher on which he lay, a pathetic bundle of a blood-stained, mud-stained uniform. Doctors

221

were here and there, hurriedly studying the tags tied to the men denoting the seriousness of their wounds and for the next few hours it was confusion, and out of the confusion came order. Rose Beechworth, calm and steady, was there to help where she could and where she was needed and nobody seemed taken aback to see a woman — not dressed as a nurse but wearing an enormous white apron she had been given — in the midst of it.

When she returned to the ward where Harry lay she was not surprised to see the beds there pushed even closer together to allow for the extra ones on which the newly arrived wounded lay. There was barely room between each bed. Harry seemed oblivious to it all.

She knelt awkwardly again by his side, taking one of the twitching hands in hers and he became still.

'I stepped on Joe Turner, you see,' he said in a conversational tone as though describing a walk in the gardens he had once known. 'He had been hit in the stomach and his insides were hanging out. He had done his best to hold them in, his insides, his hands were . . . a gaping hole in which I stepped but the rest of us crawled back to the trench as best we could though some of them didn't make it.' He mused for a moment or two on the terrible circumstance through which he and his men had lived, slithering across the bodies of their mates, some still horribly alive and crying for water, for their mothers, for Elsie or Maggie and the event seemed to have affected him more than the rest of his experiences of war.

'Darling, try and rest. Joe would not have blamed you for stepping on him,' wondering at the same time how he had come to *step* on a comrade when he had just told her they had crawled back to safety.

But now as they fought in the Third Battle of Ypres in August Captain Summers had managed to stand despite his wounds, doing his best to rally his men before collapsing again on to the still and sometimes squirming bodies of those who had 'gone over' first. As she did her best to soothe him into healing sleep she said a silent prayer to whoever had brought this about that he was out of it now, please, please, God.

Rose stayed in a small private boarding house quite near to the hospital, going every day and staying as long as she was allowed with Harry. The doctors had sewn together the dreadful gaping wound in his thigh which had come close to his genitals, delicately reuniting the muscles, the flesh, the bone that had been shattered, and he was slowly recovering though the doctors told her he would always have a limp. It was not the wound that had crippled him but the festering filth that had been allowed to remain in the leg during the two days it had taken him to get to the dressing station. 'Another day and he would have lost the leg, his ... his manhood, you understand,' — delicately — 'and possibly his life, Miss Beechworth; it is not the wounds but the muck that these men pick up on the battlefields before they can be tended to. French farmers were very liberal with the manure they spread on their fields. But — ' he passed a weary

223

hand across his forehead, then smiled at her.

'You say there are two hospitals nearby.'

'Yes, one of them my own home,' she answered eagerly. 'There are nurses and doctors to continue his care but . . . '

'Yes, Miss Beechworth?' the doctor enquired.

'He seems to be . . . he keeps talking, rambling, really, about a man in his regiment who fell with him — died, I should imagine. It preys on his mind and — '

'There are many who have such things on their minds, Miss Beechworth, and who can blame them. He knows you, does he not?'

She hesitated. 'I think so, though this one particular soldier, in his regiment, seems to be uppermost. He stepped on him; he, the soldier, had taken shrapnel in his stomach and must have died almost at once but Harry put his boot in . . . in the injury and cannot seem to forgive himself.'

The doctor stood up. There was nothing more he could tell her and after taking note of her address and telephone number, the name of the doctor in charge at Summer Place, he told her she could take Harry home.

'I have arranged for a private ambulance to drive us to Liverpool.'

'Good, good. Please keep in touch.' For though Captain Harry Summers was only one of the thousands who had passed through his hands the doctor was concerned with all of them and it broke his heart, he told his wife a dozen times a day, to send those he put together again back to the trenches.

She and Harry arrived back in Liverpool on a warm, sunny day at the end of August when the garden looked full of colour, though sadly neglected since Tom could only do so much with only Jossy to help, especially with that young scamp, Will, constantly by his side and the dogs barking and dashing all over his beds. The lanes they drove through on the way to Summer Place were ablaze with guelder rose, elderberry and wild angelica in a tangle of blossom. The birds were singing, chiefly linnets and warblers, and as they passed between the slowly rusting wrought-iron gates and up the drive they saw men, lying in long chairs, some able to hobble about on sticks, others just standing and staring at nothing, or at the glory of the wallflowers that would soon be over.

They were all there to greet him, since she had telephoned Alice to expect them. Dolly, her face that had once been round and rosy drawn with weariness and sorrow, for she loved Rose and Alice, and Captain Summers, though she had not really got to know the captain's brother Charlie. Tom came across the grass with Will at his heels and the dogs, as usual, 'mekkin a damn nuisance o' theirselves' as Dolly said, getting under everyone's feet. If she had her way she'd get rid of the whole boiling lot of them, but she realised that the animals, sensing the frailty of the wounded men, especially that Tommy, certainly did them a power of good.

Without a word Alice put her arms about Rose and they held one another for several long moments, then Rose stepped away from her, tears on her cheeks and on Alice's. Then it was Dolly's turn before they turned to Harry who lay patiently on the stretcher carried by the ambulance driver and one of the orderlies.

Alice moved to his side, bending down to kiss his cheek. 'Welcome home, Harry,' tears falling on to his pale face.

'Alice . . . Alice,' he murmured, 'how lovely . . . ' then his voice tapered off.

'And this is your nephew, Will, Charlie's boy.' The boy stared down at his uncle. 'Did you fa-de-down?' he asked curiously in that quaint speech of babyhood. All the men in the hospitals had 'fa-de-down' or fallen down.'

Harry looked bewildered and Rose realised that this was as much as Harry could take, until with a bound that nearly knocked the ambulance driver off his feet, Bess, Harry's own dog, leaped up and licked his face in ecstasy. It was many months since Bess had seen him and had at first fretted for him but now she could not be persuaded to leave him alone, even though she was aware with that instinct animals possess he was not the same man who had left her. She backed off, sat down and gently placed her muzzle on his chest. She did not lark about with the other dogs, she was too old, spending most of her time in her basket in Harry's study. She was well used to the constant coming and going of ambulances and their cargo of wounded and did not greet them but somehow she had sensed that her beloved master was home and she had become young again, racing out to meet him.

Harry put out a wavering hand and managed

to lift his head and look down at her. He put the hand on Bess's silky head and smiled.

'Bess, Bess,' he murmured. 'I am come home, Bess.'

Rose's heart lifted with joy for surely this was a sign that he was improving, would improve further in his own surroundings. There were doctors on hand, nurses, women experienced by now in the needs of badly wounded men, and with the love she would wrap him in he would surely recover and become again the man who had left her two and a half years ago.

They carried him up the stairs and laid him on the bed in the room where she herself slept when she stayed the night at Summer Place as she had instructed them to do, for she needed him near her. The dog followed, padding stiff-legged up the stairs, then lay down as close to the bed as she could with an almost human expression on her face that told them she was not moving. She would find her way out into the gardens when a call of nature demanded it but this was her place now.

Out in the paddock, Tom was amazed when Corey, Sir Harry Summers's black stallion, began to race up and down the fence, neighing fiercely, so loudly he could be heard in the house. In his bed Harry smiled, then fell into a deep, healing, untroubled sleep.

★ ★ ★

The wound on his thigh healed slowly and with the help of the man who exercised other soldiers with similar injuries, working their muscles and encouraging them to help themselves, Harry left his bed and began to build up his strength. Rose begged him to take it easy for she was terrified he might recover enough for the army to send him back to the trenches.

'Hold my arm and walk slowly, my love. Use your stick to balance yourself and I'll help you.' They were walking, or rather *wobbling* along the path that led to the paddock since Harry had asked to see Corey who had been making a fuss ever since Harry had been brought home. The stallion was normally quiet, cropping the grass beside Sparky. Sparky was Rose's gig pony but had been brought over from Beechworth to see if he could calm Harry's animal as he had once calmed Lady, Charlie's mare when Charlie had left for the front. His presence had done the trick and though nobody rode the handsome stallion since Harry had gone and Tom was of the opinion he was getting fat he was peaceful enough.

He whickered his delight when Harry appeared at the fence, nuzzling against Harry's shoulder, slobbering over the riding jacket Harry had put on for the first time that day. It positively hung on him for he had lost weight but it was a step in the right direction, Dolly told Rose hopefully.

Rose was drooping over the kitchen table with the inevitable cup of tea in her hand, Dolly's answer to all problems. When Harry was sleeping and she had a spare moment in her busy day she would go to Beechworth and spend half an hour with Dolly and Nessie. She and Alice split their time between Beechworth and Summer Place, for the wounded still continued to pour in, from Passchendaele and Cambrai, battles that became household names all over Britain. And though physically Harry continued to improve his wounded mind did not. He seemed disconnected from Rose and everyone in the two households. He was, or had been a strong man with a strong man's will and resilience but something had gone from him and though he did not mention it again Rose knew with the instinct of a woman for a beloved man that Joe Turner still haunted him. He had seen his men die, many of them, some of them in the most horrible circumstances and though it had saddened him, it had not unbalanced his mind as had the incident with Joe. Though he and Rose had been lovers before he went back to the war he made no attempt to make love to her now, treating her politely, courteously as he did the others. She might have been a neighbour, or friend. She was aware that the shrapnel that had come so close to emasculating him had not done so. She had, hesitantly, consulted with Dr Roberts, embarrassing them both, but the doctor told her that his genitals had not been damaged in any way and that he must be given time for his male senses, his male desires, to return to life.

'The act of love begins in the brain, Miss Beechworth, and Sir Harry's brain is . . . no, not hurt in any way but something in there has gone to sleep, hidden itself away in self-defence, and until it revives he is still . . . ' He paused, fiddling with a pen on his desk, unable to meet her eye.

'Unmanned? Is that what you're trying to tell me, Doctor?'

'Yes, I suppose I am.' He looked up. 'You are to marry him, I believe, Miss Beechworth.'

She cleared her throat. 'We talked about it before he went back to France but since then he has not mentioned it. It's as though he has forgotten.'

'And if I were you I wouldn't mention it. Let him recover in his own time.'

'You won't recommend he goes back there, will you, Doctor?' she asked fearfully. 'Now that his wound has almost healed?'

'No, Miss Beechworth, I can promise you that. He is not fit to fight again. It might damage him further.'

'Thank God.' She folded her arms on the desk and rested her face on them, ready to weep with relief. She had not got *her* Harry back again but the man who had come back to her was safe and with time and patience, which was what all these wounded souls needed, she would return him to himself again. And to her! She no longer slept beside his bed but had moved back to Beechworth. Bess was there with him and when Rose had a little time to spare she persuaded him to walk in the overgrown gardens or into the woodland at the back of the house. Down to the paddock with an apple for Corey and Sparky and though he was still distant, vague in his speech, impassive, never again mentioning Joe Turner, she thought — or was it just hope? — that he was coming back from the far place he had been to since the Battle of Ypres. It was rumoured that he was to receive a medal for the part he had played in bringing back from the dead, so to speak, so many of his men but he was not concerned with the news, treating it as inconsequential and nothing much to do with him.

Alice had received a stilted letter from Charlie which did little to comfort her for it was evident he had no idea who he was writing to and so life — and death — went on, the only positive occurrence being Will's growing attachment to his Uncle Harry and Harry's interest in him.

15

Rose watched as Harry, his hand held firmly by Will's and surrounded by a swirl of dogs, was dragged down the slope of the overgrown lawn towards the small lake on which swam two swans and numerous ducks. Tall weeds grew round the lake since one man, Tom, and one young lad, Jossy, had had no time to clear them out. Once upon a time Tom had been in charge of half a dozen gardeners three of them now dead on the Western Front; one of them brought home to his appalled family with no legs; and the other two still slogging it out in the trenches. Her heart was heavy, for though Harry was home and beyond the reach of snipers, bullets, whizz-bangs, gas attacks and all the obscene weapons that the Germans threw at the British lines, he was, it seemed to her, still there. With Joe Turner, Lieutenant Jack Sullivan who had been his second-in-command and all the other lads he had left behind. With Sid, Arty, Fred, Davy and all the men in his platoon. He had never returned to her, to the woman he had loved and who had loved him with every beat of her heart.

They were feeding the ducks with bits of stale bread from the paper bag Nessie had provided. Rose could hear him laugh and grab the boy who was ready to fall into the water as his enthusiasm and his poor aim got the better of him. Her eyes filled with tears because it seemed the man who had loved her was never to come back to her and unless she did something drastic, something to remind him what they had once been to each other, against the doctor's advice, she was well aware of that, he was to remain like this for ever. While his strength was so fragile, as the doctor told her, meaning the strength of his mind, not his body, she was to let him recover in his own time. But it was breaking her heart.

She was sitting on the old wrought-iron seat on the terrace in one of her rare moments away from her work, the sun warm on her face, the scent of roses lapping round her and when Alice sat down beside her she was startled. She and Alice had never resumed that warm friendship they had known three years ago and she had often wondered why. They had been close when Alice had been found on the doorstep, thrown out by her own father because she carried Charlie's child. They had formed a great attachment to one another up to the day Will was born and Alice simply disappeared from their lives. She had returned, Charlie had proved to be alive but Alice, like Harry, had not been the same person who had left them so abruptly. This hellish war, Rose thought bitterly, seemed to have torn apart friends, family, lovers, even husbands and wives though they had survived in the flesh.

She waited for Alice to speak, for these days they seemed only to communicate with one another on medical matters and Alice, even with Dolly, who loved her, was vague, reticent though always polite, causing Dolly immense distress.

233

'Your son is enjoying himself,' Rose said at last as Alice seemed reluctant to say anything.

'Yes, he has taken to Harry who has been like a father to him.' Her reply was curt.

Rose jumped in before she had time to consider her words. 'And what will Charlie think when he comes home?'

'I don't know.'

'Nor care, it seems.'

Alice turned to her and with a gentle motion put her hand on Rose's arm. Her face was anguished. 'Oh, Rose, what is happening to us all? I seem to have distanced myself from everybody, even my child. I weep at night in my bed for the hopes I had before this terrible war started. That girl, the one who saw Charlie off at the station, has been destroyed and I don't think she will ever return. Charlie will come home to a wife and a child he does not know so what is to become of us? You and Harry are . . . not as you were, or so Dolly tells me. You love one another and yet cannot resume that . . . that closeness; what you had seems to have gone too. I have been obsessed with finding Charlie and now that I know he is alive and will, one day I presume, come home to us, how are we to get on with our destroyed lives? We have become strangers to one another. The only time I can find some sort of order is when I'm on the ward, caring for other women's men. I know what I'm doing is helping some woman, wife or mother towards a happy ending. *Or am I?* Is this happening all over the country? Are there men and women desperately trying to get back the normality they once knew or are we all to be forced to live some sort of charade? It tears me to pieces, Rose. It has been four years nearly and I am still living in this nightmare. All I wanted was to find Charlie, when I went to France, I mean. It was all I was. Alice who was searching for Charlie. Now that has gone and to tell you the honest truth, Rose, I don't even know if I still love him.'

'Alice! After all you have done — '

'No, please don't try to . . . '

'What, Alice?' Rose put her hand over Alice's, leaning closer so that their shoulders touched. They had been devoted to one another while Alice was pregnant. Alice had been like a child, a hurt child who needed protection, someone to love her, to keep her safe but it seemed Alice had grown up, grown away from them and this conversation was the first they had shared in years. She knew exactly what Alice meant but she did not want to lose this fragile link they appeared to have formed in the last five minutes by voicing her own concerns. She knew she still loved Harry, always would. But Harry seemed no longer to return it. Alice had opened up, if you could call it that, doing her best to explain her actions, her feelings, or lack of them towards her adopted family, Rose, Dolly, Nessie, all those who had sheltered her, loved her in her hour of need, which sounded a bit pompous. They appeared to mean nothing to her now and it seemed to Rose she was telling her she had nothing to live for — which was ridiculous — except her devotion to her patients. What was to become of her when it was all over, for one day, please God, it would be? What was to become of Rose who wanted nothing more than to marry Harry and start a family? She was twenty-eight and by the conventions of the day was well past the age of child-bearing. Not physically, she was aware of that, but it was the custom for women to marry young, as young as Alice, and have three or four children clinging to their skirts or in the nursery before they reached twenty-five.

They had read about the Third Battle of the Aisne in May where the first Americans fought in France. In the fierce fighting the German advance had been halted. There had been nearly 130,000 Allied casualties and losses, some of them already dispatched to Summer Place and Beechworth House. The worst of these were men who had been massed in the front trenches and gassed after the initial artillery attack. Rose had done her best to keep the news from Harry, hiding newspapers that reported the outcome of the battles, but he could not fail to have noticed the state of the wounded as they came to the two hospitals.

They were silent for several minutes as they watched Harry and Will larking about by the lake, Rose with astonishment, for was this the serious, self-contained soldier who had been brought back to her? He was laughing as the child clung to his leg, the dogs, excited by the rumpus, jumping up to snatch at the bag of crusts he held out of their reach, then, with a groan of pretended submission, falling to the ground with Will and the dogs leaping on him.

'Dear God, does he not consider the wound he is supposed to be recovering from? If he goes on like this he could open it,' she moaned but Alice squeezed the arm she held.

'No, no, it is completely healed now,' Alice told her. 'I helped Staff Nurse Long to dress it and he is entirely recovered. You know that he has made a couple of rooms at the top of the house into living quarters for himself and is completely independent and — ' Then realising what she was saying she clamped her lips together since it seemed harsh to tell Rose that there was absolutely no physical reason why he and Rose should not resume their loving relationship. Rose had not been allowed to nurse him, for it needed detachment to attend a wounded soldier and the doctors knew that Rose was far from detached. They had heard of Rose and Harry's feelings for one another. That in the past he had been home on leave and had shared her bed, and though as men of their era they could only disapprove, times had changed with the war and who could blame lovers for snatching at the chance when one or other of them could be dead within a week? Women nursed and drove ambulances in the front lines and were just as threatened as the soldiers they ministered to.

'Harry thinks the war will end this year, Rose, now that the Americans are in it,' Alice added hurriedly.

Rose turned sharply and stared at Alice. 'He told you that?'

Alice nodded, saddened again because it

seemed Harry did not speak much to Rose. What had happened to the virile young man they had all known before the war? What was happening to all the young men they had known before the war? Though they recovered from their wounds their spirits still bore the scars; their mind's eye still gazed with compassion, with helplessness at the wholesale slaughter they had witnessed and which they never spoke of, except perhaps to one another. A brotherhood of badly damaged young men who jumped nervously at the banging of a door, shrank from the sound of a motor car backfiring and even, it was said, hid under their beds at night in fear of the dark.

'He has raised a wall between us, Alice,' Rose went on sadly, 'and yet there is no one in this world who loves him more. I don't know what to do. Shall I force him to share his thoughts with me or shall I leave it, as the doctor advises, and wait for him to take the first step? Does he even remember what there was between us? I could be bearing his child.' Rose bowed her head. 'I wish to God I was. I can't bear his indifference to me and I — '

'Don't you think that that is an indication that you mean something to him, deep down? He treats us all as acquaintances, even Dolly who loves him because you do, but he avoids you.'

'Does he?' Rose was astonished and her bewilderment showed in her agonised face.

'Yes, he does and I think he does it because he knows that you love him and he loves you but he cannot manage the feelings you arouse in him. He can't cope with . . . I think he believes his wound has emasculated him in some way and he is terrified that if he took you to bed he would fail you.'

'Oh, Alice, I wouldn't care if he did.'

'But *he* would. He loves Will but then Will demands nothing of him that he cannot give. You would and so he stays away from it. One of the nurses told me he used to ramble in his sleep. He cannot get out of his mind the moment he stepped on one of his own men in no-man's-land, a dying man who was trying to hold his insides together. He had been struck in the stomach with shrapnel and Harry stumbled into the wound. What remained of the soldier's stomach had adhered to Harry's boot and he had nightmares about the blood and . . . and the rest, which he carries around with him. So he has two afflictions to contend with: the soldier he thinks he himself hurt and his fear of letting you down. His mind is not in the right place and until it is he will never recover.'

'Oh, Alice, what am I to do?' Rose began to weep but Alice made no attempt to comfort her. Even Rose's distress did not seem to move her. She continued to watch Harry and Will, her face impassive. Then, as though it took a great deal of effort, she patted Rose's arm, stood up and walked away.

Both Harry and Will stopped what they were doing and watched her go towards the gate that led through the field to Summer Place. Being an experienced nurse, though not officially recognised as one, most of her work was done at Summer Place where the worst of the injured were. Those who were recovering were moved to Beechworth which was considered to be a kind of convalescent hospital. Will waved to Rose and shouted something incomprehensible. Harry smiled at whatever Will had said and shrugged his shoulders and for a moment a thread of something warm moved between them, something of the past, some tiny acknowledgement that they were still Rose and Harry, a couple, then it was gone as Will raced away after the dogs and Harry followed.

She felt a glow somewhere beneath her ribs. It was the first time that Harry seemed to have recognised who she really was — or was she imagining it — and though it was too soon for him to re-form that special bond since his wounds, inward and external, she was certain, with a frail hope, that he was healing and at the same time moving back to her.

Her tears dried as though magically. She rose and with a lighter step turned towards the door that led into what had been the drawing room. There were soldiers there, officers, for in their wisdom the authorities still divided the 'men' from those who had commanded them. One of them who had lost a leg and would have a prosthetic limb fitted as soon as he was strong enough was stumbling down the centre of the ward on his crutches, a nurse solicitously by his side.

'Watch what you're doing, Major, or they'll have you in the races at the Old Swan fête next week,' she called out to him.

With that cheerful spirit that seemed to say

that nothing much had happened to them though most of them had come close to death, he answered her with a blithe wave of his crutch which nearly had him over.

'A three-legged race, Nurse, you can bet on it.'

★ ★ ★

The war dragged on. Names grew familiar to the British public through newspaper reports. Operation Marne was launched in July, beginning the Second Battle of the Marne, and marking the first successful Allied offensive of the war while in August 8,000 German prisoners were taken, so surely, they all said to one another, it would be over soon. Tanks were used at a place called Bapaume opening the Battle of Albert, the weary troops told they were to 'break the enemy's front'. The patients in the wards read the newspapers eagerly for they, of all the British public, knew what this meant. The Germans were falling back under the onslaught. In nearly four weeks of fighting since the beginning of August over 100,000 German prisoners were taken and what was known by the Germans themselves as 'The Black Day of the German Army' marked the beginning of the end.

Nevertheless in September the Germans continued to fight a strong rearguard action but were unsuccessful and news of Germany's impending military defeat spread through the German armed forces and with American troops arriving at the front at the rate of 10,000 each day, Germany reluctantly moved towards peace.

Rose and Alice were at Summer Place giving a young soldier a bed bath, gently sponging what was left of him when the news filtered through. Bobby, he was called, Corporal Robert Ackroyd, who had served in the same battalion as Harry and Charlie and he had not been expected to survive since he had lost both legs to gangrene, and, perhaps worse than that, the will to live. He had volunteered joyously when he was eighteen and marched off in high hopes of a great adventure and having lived through nightmare after nightmare for four years at the age of twenty-two had cautiously believed he would get through it unscathed. He and his pal 'Woody' Woodbine had both stepped on the same land mine in the Allied attack on the Hindenburg Line in October. Woody — lucky bugger, Bobby cried piteously — had been killed instantly but Bobby had survived and his young face stared bitterly from his pillow at the two nurses who were so kind to him.

'Not much ter wash, Nurse,' he told Alice. 'I don't know why tha' bloody bother. Never mind, a savin' on soap, eeh. Me mam was allus sayin' we was 'ard up so there's summat ter be grateful for. Cut down expenses a bit.'

Both Alice and Rose were used to the bitterness that emanated from some of the men they nursed, particularly the very young ones, those who had often lied about their age to 'get in on it'. Others were cheerful in the face of terrible wounds but Bobby wanted nothing but to do away with himself for he believed he was useless and had no future. A young VAD, pretty and shy, stopped to speak to a soldier in the bed opposite and Bobby followed her progress with hopeless eyes. He was a handsome lad, six feet tall or had been on two legs, with the most beautiful eyes, somewhere between blue and sea green surrounded by thick black eyelashes the same colour as his curly hair. He had been a great favourite with the girls before the war and when he was home on leave they had flocked to the street where his family lived, longing to give comfort to one of the heroes of this everlasting war.

But they would no longer flock, for who wanted a man short of his legs, a man who could neither walk nor do any of the things young men like to do. He had played football for his local team, cricket, and was a good dancer, his favourite the waltz since it gave him the chance to put an arm about a slim waist. Now he would be confined to a wheelchair for the remainder of his life which he prayed would be short.

The VAD moved slowly along the wall, speaking to the wounded in each bed and Bobby's eyes followed her. He was not the only one, of course, but when she stopped at his bed she moved to the side of it and sat down on the chair put out for visitors. Bobby's heartbroken mam came each day to sit with her son since she lived in Old Swan but not many of the others had a visitor as they came from all parts of the country.

Rose and Alice had moved to the next bed after carefully pulling up the covers over Bobby's shattered body but they were aware, as Bobby was not, that the VAD, whose name was Dilys Morgan, seemed to have forged a link of some sort with the badly wounded young soldier. Bobby had given up all hope of living a normal life — or as near normal as a man missing his legs could attain — and even turned his head away as she smiled at him.

'Is your mam coming today, Corporal?' she asked shyly, the lilt of Wales in her speech, her pretty face pink with the effort, for her upbringing in a strict Welsh village had not encouraged young boys and girls to approach one another without the permission of their elders.

'I s'pose so,' he muttered.

'You're lucky to have a visitor, is it, Corporal. So many of these lads have none at all, see. Their families live so far away. I haven't seen my mam for months, nor my brothers. I've five, you know, all in the trenches.'

He turned his head on the pillow and looked at her sad young face for it had not, in his own suffering, occurred to him that there were others who might need comfort. He knew, of course, of the horrific wounds many of them sustained. He had only to look around him at this ward in which he lay to see it all, but the nurses, the doctors who worked here, well out of the danger he had known, he had not considered.

'Owen was wounded six months ago but he recovered enough to go back and my mam . . . she . . . I'm sorry, Corporal. You have enough to . . . ' She stood up and hurried to the entrance of the ward watched by every soldier from their beds, those who could see, for many of them had been blinded by the gas.

Rose and Alice followed her because there seemed to be some sort of commotion at the entrance to Summer Place and were in time to see Harry jump down the last few steps of the wide staircase, his face lit up for the first time in months.

'It's over, it's over,' he was shouting. 'I heard it on the radio. I'm just going to telephone my friend at the War Office to confirm it, but an armistice has been signed, an armistice. What's the bloody date? November 11th. It's all over . . . Alice, oh Alice, Charlie will be coming home and we can all be together again.'

He took Alice round the waist and to the astonishment of the nurses and patients who were milling about the wide stone hallway, waltzed her down the length of it while Rose, whose heart was breaking once more, after watching them for several aching moments slipped into the garden where the November fog hid her. She ran down the length of the lawn, passing the amazed figure of Tom, who stared after her, and blundered into the summerhouse.

She cried until she was exhausted, unaware that Harry was running from room to room, from ward to ward looking for her, since his own heart had at last been unlocked, and into it had rushed the knowledge of how much she meant to him.

'Have you seen Rose?' he asked Staff Nurse Long who was doing her best to calm those patients who grew agitated at the slightest unusual activity. It was all she and the rest of the staff could do to stop them from screaming, jumping from their beds or chairs where they sat and running out into the garden to escape the bombardment.

'Rose?' she snapped, doing her best to coax Sergeant Johnson back from the sill where he was intent on jumping from the first-floor window.

'Miss Beechworth,' he snapped back, going to her aid with poor Sergeant Johnson who would spend what was left of his life in a constant state of terror.

'No, I haven't, Captain, and if you have nothing better to do than search for Miss Beechworth then I suggest — '

'It's over, Staff, the news just came through — the bloody war is over. An armistice is to be signed and all the men — my men — will be home.' He wanted to weep with Staff Nurse Long as she dragged the poor jabbering sergeant into her arms to comfort his terrible distress and the sergeant, who seemed to understand at last what his captain was saying, put his arms round her and kissed her soundly.

'Thank God, thank the dear Lord,' they both sobbed and so did Harry for it meant he was released from the frozen desolation in which he had been trapped ever since he could remember. Joe Turner could forgive him now for stepping on what remained of his pitiful wounded body and with that forgiveness he could return the love he knew Rose felt for him. When he found her. When he found her. *When he found her.*

246

They were all going mad with joy, and scenes that were taking place at Beechworth and at Summer Place were being repeated all over the country. But in her quiet room at the back of Beechworth House Rose sat very still and waited for she knew not what. Perhaps for an indication of what she was to do now. She would no longer be needed to care for the wounded. Gradually they would all go home to resume the life they had once known or, as best they could, make a new life for themselves. What would it be like, the life she had known before the war? What had she done, she wondered idly, staring out at the garden where, despite the excitement, Tom was industriously dragging the lawn mower out ready to be hitched up to Sparky. Grass had to be cut despite the end or even the beginning of a war. Nessie was running down the lawn to him, waving her arms and as Dolly would say, 'giving him the rounds of the kitchen'. Rose could imagine what she was saying, on this longed-for day, telling him to leave the damn grass for once and come and celebrate with the rest of them in the kitchen. They had not lost a loved one in the war for they had no children but they had been touched, both of them, by the suffering of the men in the two hospitals. Nessie drew Tom into her arms, soundly kissing his cheek then, taking his hand, drew him up the lawn towards the house and Rose sighed, for she was past tears now but longed with all her heart to be doing the same with Harry.

16

It was the strangest thing, Rose reflected sadly, that now Harry appeared to be his old self again apart from a slight limp he seemed to be totally unaware of her presence in the dismantling of the two hospitals. He was helping with the transfer by ambulance of the badly wounded who were not yet fit to go to their own homes, but to the hospitals that were now emptying of those who were. He still made no attempt to resume the relationship that had been theirs before the war. He seemed to be living within himself, only concerned with his estate and the badly wounded who were leaving it. Now that he was fully and physically restored to health he was engaged in riding round the farms to see his tenant farmers, doing his best to help them to achieve their full potential. She was forced to come to the conclusion that what she had thought of as their true and lasting love had only been what was called 'a bit of fun' to him, as it was to all soldiers who were making the most of what they could — in other words a 'fling' with a willing female before the tide of war washed him into the trenches of the Western Front. She had been available to him and he had taken full advantage of it, as men did.

She was not to know that Harry Summers harboured the same agonising belief about her, only in the opposite sense, a woman filled with pity for a soldier off to war. Not that she was having a bit of fun, for she was not that sort of a woman, but that out of patriotism and pity she had allowed him into her bed.

They moved about each other's lives like polite strangers. Rose was in despair. Here they were, the four of them safe after coming through the worst experience that could be asked of man, or so she thought it, and yet they could not seem to resume the life they had led. She had believed that the reunion shared by Charlie and Alice meant that though Charlie was still missing many parts of his life Alice would repair him and they would continue with their marriage but it was not so. Another bed had been placed in the bedroom where Harry had slept since he had come home and it was there that Charlie settled. Alice did not speak of it to Rose for the Alice they had all come to love over four years ago had vanished in the horrors of the war, leaving in her place this quiet stranger who had waited so patiently and fought so bravely for Charlie. Though he had come home he was not the man she had fallen so passionately in love with. He had chosen to sleep apart from Alice, which was bad enough, but though he could have had any one of the many bedrooms at Summer Place if he so wished he clung to his brother.

Harry was without exception kind and patient with him. He had managed to find a gentle mare for him which seemed strange because Charlie had lived and breathed horses before the war and was capable then of controlling the wildest, but until his brother was a great deal better

Harry felt it would be wiser to start him on a gentle animal with a sweet temper. A young grey mare totally unlike Lady, who had been a bit of a handful but had been blown into a bloody haze on the battlefield, so that there was nothing to trouble his brother with memories. They rode out together to visit the farms on the estate, much to Will's fierce resentment since he had considered Harry to be *his* friend and not this other man's and they were treated to frequent tantrums. Will was almost five years old now, strong and wilful, and Harry was of the opinion that he needed a good 'walloping' for he was thoroughly spoiled. He told Rose so, knowing it was no good appealing to the child's mother.

'Harry, you must try to be patient with him. He has been raised in trying circumstances.' *Trying!* What a ridiculous word to describe the past four years when the boy had not had the benign childhood given to most children. He had been loved, of course. He had been the centre of not only the servants' world but the hundreds of wounded who had passed through the hospitals. They had doted on him and many of them could be said to have been helped in their recovery because of him.

'He has had no mother nor father and though I have done my best to be both, Dolly has petted him, refusing him nothing. Tom's the same. They have loved him trying to make up to him for his lack of — '

'I know that, Rose, and I'm sorry for it but it can't continue. I've been on the lookout for a small pony for him then he can ride out with me and Charlie but until his mother is recovered again someone has to discipline him,' *and it won't be Charlie*, the words unspoken.

'Oh, Harry, please tell me you won't — '

'Won't what, Rose?'

She was going to say 'Beat him' for in the back kitchen Will could be heard yelling that he was going with Harry and no one was going to stop him!

Rose could see the anger on Harry's face change slowly to sadness. For how could he, who was himself only just beginning to recover his own sanity, manage not only his badly damaged brother but this demanding child who was his brother's son? Strange it was that Charlie had not questioned anyone about Will. He must know that Will was his but he ignored him, escaping with Harry into the burgeoning spring countryside, slowly gaining confidence on the lovely little grey that he had called Misty. Dear God, were they ever to get back to normality, to the contentment of the past? To *reality*. She wanted a child of her own but she could not manage it without Harry, could she? And what were Charlie and Alice to do with the rest of their lives with Charlie off each day with Harry and Alice drifting about, staring out of the window, drooping from room to room as though looking for something and with an unhappy and bewildered little boy creating mayhem between them all.

Charlie had been home two months when Alice dropped a bombshell into their midst.

'I wanted to tell you while we are all here

together. I'm going to London at the weekend. I want to help the suffragettes to continue their fight for the vote.'

'But . . . but surely they are bound to get it now the war is won? They stopped all their protests when war was declared,' Rose stuttered, while Charlie looked from one face to another, an expression of bewilderment on his gaunt face. They had spoken of many things to bring back his memory, but universal suffrage had not been one of them. Though the fight was being fought long before he went to war he could not remember it.

Harry shook his head in despair. Was he to be burdened for ever with his brother? He felt great affection and pity for Charlie, but there was no hope of his recovery if Alice left him; no reconciliation between husband and wife and a normal life for Will. Harry had believed — *hoped* — that with his wife and son Charlie would regain what had been taken from him in the carnage of France. His terrible injury, his time in a German hospital and then the prisoner-of-war camp: those days would be repaired by the love he gave and received with Alice. And the sturdy, handsome, winsome boy who was his son. The child needed a father, and he, Harry Summers, needed Rose who had held it all together through the last four years. Sweet Jesus, how he loved the woman who was at this moment staring in horror at Alice and he knew deep in his wounded heart that she loved him but neither of them could move on with this little family hanging round their necks. His guilt racked him but when was *his* life to begin? He wanted Rose. He wanted children of his own. Rose should be mistress of Summer Place, living here with him and the family they should have. Charlie had a wife and a child and must take responsibility for them. But how . . . *HOW?*

They had just sat down round the dinner table at Summer Place, unfolding their napkins; their new housemaid, a niece of Jinny Herbert called Martha, was bringing in the soup that Mrs Philips had made. Martha was very proud of her position as housemaid to *Sir* Harry Summers and for a moment she did not notice the curious tension in the air. She was fourteen and pretty and was even now entertaining the exciting prospect of allowing Jossy, who though he was really a cowman was helping Tom with the gardens at Beechworth, to kiss her behind the stable block! There were several ex-soldiers working about the grounds who winked at her and life could not be better. She was no longer the schoolgirl she had been before the war and enjoyed lording it over Polly, who was a scullery-maid and not considered suitable to be made up to housemaid.

She suddenly became aware of the absolute stillness of those round the table. Martha had never seen the inside of Summer Place before she became housemaid but her mam, who also had been a housemaid before she married Pa, had told her that the gentry always dressed for dinner. Dressed for dinner? What did that mean for goodness sake? Then her mam had told her about the lovely frocks of silk and taffeta and velvet that the ladies wore and the black and white evening suits worn by the gentlemen. Martha could not, for the life of her, imagine such things but then that was in the olden days before the war.

Martha stood as though frozen to the spot, just inside the doorway wondering what was wrong. Was it her? Had she made some blunder? Because if she had she couldn't think what.

Thankfully Miss Rose saw her. 'Leave the soup on the sideboard, Martha, there's a good girl.'

Again Martha hesitated for it was part of her job to serve the soup and she had became right good at it, she had told her mam, spilling not a drop.

'You can go now. We'll help ourselves.'

'But miss, I'm . . . '

'Just leave it,' Miss Rose said, right sharp, she was.

Martha placed the soup tureen on the sideboard and fled.

It had been one of those lovely days that come in spring. Not a cloud in the sky. On the terrace stood urns of lavender and Tom was in his element with his preparations for his herbaceous borders, his rose-beds and the re-growth of the lawns. Will was in bed in what had once been the nursery, where the two Summers lads had played out their childish games. Rose had read to him and he had fallen asleep with his thumb in his mouth, something he had not done for several years, and it was an indication of the uncertainty in his life that he had reverted to the habit.

The old ways were gone and they no longer changed for dinner every day as once had been the custom. Alice wore a dress she had not worn for five years, old-fashioned but attractive. It was composed of a collarless, bloused bodice fastened down the front with a row of tiny pearl buttons which were repeated at the wrist of the long sleeves. It was attached to a plain seven-gored skirt in the semi-princess style, the colour a delicate apricot which touched her cheeks. She looked as once she had done, the only difference being the length of her pale silver hair. It lay like a curly cap on her well-shaped head, the fringe almost reaching her eyebrows. Rose had gasped when she saw it and was sorry and so was Harry but Charlie seemed not to notice. Rose herself was in what she called her usual 'get-up': an ankle-length skirt in a shade of pale coffee, a white, open-necked shirt, a wide leather belt about her waist and her riding boots, as she had ridden over from Beechworth to check on the people she loved and worried about, and to dine with them as was her custom. She had grown thinner since the return and the apparent indifference of Harry Summers. The only one to notice was, naturally, dear Dolly, who begged her to eat up since she was nowt but skin and bone. Dolly had believed that once the brothers and sweet Alice were home, all would be as it once had been but sadly she had remarked to Nessie that they were all going to hell in a handcart and she didn't think she could take much more, shaking her old grey head in sorrow.

'What is this all about, Alice?' Harry asked Alice quietly.

'You cannot change my mind, Harry. I am no use to — '

'I don't think that is true, Alice,' Harry interrupted, knowing what she was going to say. 'You have a husband here,' indicating Charlie who sat open-mouthed, not understanding.

Charlie was not absolutely sure what they were talking about but somehow it made him feel as though he should be involved in whatever it was. He had been home two months and was beginning to feel secure in what they told him was his home or had been before the war. Sometimes he had flashes of memory, some particular event or object brought back a moment from when he was a boy or a young man. The woods behind the house where he and Harry rode; a certain hedge which he knew before they got there on their horses hid a wide ditch and was a bugger to jump; the welcome from the farming tenants, some of whom he recognised in a hazy sort of way; the woman who hung out the washing who had shouted, 'Good to have you home, Mr Charlie.'

'That was Bessie, wasn't it, Harry?' he had said wonderingly but now it was clear from the expression on his brother's face that he was bothered about something. He had known Alice, pretty Alice, but he could not contemplate getting into bed with her, which he knew was expected of him since husbands and wives shared a bed. And the boy, the boy who scowled at him and clung possessively to Harry's leg,

256

shouting defiance and crying broken-heartedly when the woman in the kitchen took him on her knee as they left him behind. This was his son. His son who scratched at his nerves and nearly drove him to violence with his screaming anger. Should he not have bonded with him? He knew he should, or possibly would in time but it was too much for him to manage just yet.

Rose spoke, tears in her voice. 'Alice, you cannot mean to leave us when you are needed so much, whatever you say. You have gone to hell and back, we all know that but you must give it time. A couple of months is not long enough for us all to . . . to . . .'

'To what, Rose? My son prefers you to his own mother and it seems I cannot give him what he needs. I spent eighteen months looking for Charlie, trying to bring him home to me and our son but it seems neither of them care whether I live or die.'

'Don't say that, darling. We all love you so and with time we shall be as we once were, won't we, Charlie,' turning to Alice's husband who was beginning to look distressed.

Alice snorted derisively. 'As we once were! I was a naïve ninny in love with the idea of being in love.'

'And what was I, Alice?' There was pain in Rose's voice.

'Oh, Rose.' The pain was echoed in Alice's voice. 'I don't mean to hurt you but don't you see? For so long I have been helping in the war, helping to bring back the wounded, treated with respect as a valuable part of their battles and I find it hard to just . . . just . . . '

'Be a wife and mother?' Harry said bitterly. 'For that is your role now. Until . . . until I marry, if I do, you are mistress of this house. Or why don't you learn to ride and then you and Charlie could visit the farms on the estate. And I could do with some help with the accounts — paperwork that mounts up — and Rose has enough to do running her own estate, bringing it back to the productive business it was before the war. You could begin to teach your son to read and — '

'No. No, I couldn't, I'm not a teacher.' Her voice rose shrilly, with what sounded like a touch of hysteria.

'Why not? He's four years old and needs some routine in his life. Perhaps in the afternoons you could go up to the old nursery and — '

'No. I've told you I couldn't. I'm . . . no, no, Harry, I beg you. He . . . he frightens me he is so — '

'*Frightens you!*' There was amazement in Harry's voice.

Martha knocked timidly and popped her head round the door. She had come to collect the tureen and soup dishes but on seeing neither had been touched she scuttled out again, closing the door quietly behind her.

'They're 'avin' a right old ding-dong in there,' she whispered to Mrs Philips as though those in the dining room could hear her. 'Sir Harry's glarin' at Miss Alice an' Miss Rose looks ready to start bawlin'.'

'What for?'

'I don't know, Mrs Philips. Sir Harry looks as mad as a march 'are and Miss Alice is cryin'. I think it's summat ter do wi't little lad who's a right hellion an' if 'e was mine I'd give 'im a damn good hidin'. My mam'd soon knock some — '

'Well, it's got nowt ter do wi' your mam, or you, fer that matter, but all I know is that if someone don't do summat little lad'll turn into a bad 'un. Eeh, many's the time I could give 'im a clout but — '

Realising she was saying too much, she clamped her lips together and sat down in her rocking-chair in front of the fire. Martha stared at her waiting to see if she was going to say anything else but Mrs Philips merely looked into the range fire, her old face sagging with sorrow. This house, despite the old man's many ways of frittering away his inheritance, had been a happy one with two lively boys who, though she often scolded them when they became too high-spirited, she had held in great affection. Now would you look at it, such sadness you could feel it in your bones, a loss of what had made it a happy home. They, unlike so many others, had come through the war with the lads unscathed and two good-hearted young women ready for married life, babies; wouldn't she just love one of them to have a baby. Perhaps then that naughty boy, who was basically not a bad lad but wild, undisciplined and needing a father to show him the way of things, would calm down and realise he just could not have his own way all the time. Like Dolly at Beechworth, she shook her old

259

head and sighed for the lovely days before the war.

In the dining room no one spoke then Harry broke the silence. 'Well, since Mrs Philips has gone to a lot of trouble to provide us with a meal, perhaps we could eat now.'

The soup was cold, and the delicious salmon that followed — brought in by a nervous Martha who looked as though she was expecting some terrible scene — was pushed around four plates with an obvious lack of enthusiasm. Nobody round the table looked at anyone else.

Harry said to his brother, 'I don't know about you, old chap, but I could manage a brandy. Should we . . . ' And so, after a courteous bow to the ladies, he and Charlie left the room with great eagerness.

When they had gone, Rose rang the bell and Martha hesitantly answered it.

'No dessert, Martha, tell Mrs Philips, just coffee I think. Perhaps you would ask the gentlemen if they want the same. They are probably in Sir Harry's study. Mrs Summers and I will have ours in the drawing room.'

'Yes, ma'am.' Martha bobbed a little curtsey and almost ran for the door.

'They don't want dessert, Mrs Philips, just coffee.' Martha was almost in tears. 'The gentlemen are in Sir Harry's study. Oh, Mrs Philips, 'ave I ter take it in? I'm that upset what with . . . could Polly take it in?'

Mrs Philips reared up in indignation. 'No, she can't. You begged to be a housemaid here and one of a housemaid's duties is to serve at table.

260

Now get on with it. Set another tray for Sir Harry and Mr Charlie and I'll have none of these ... ' She was about to say *tantrums* but they'd seen enough real tantrums in this kitchen with Will and Martha was really only a little lass and too young for the job. But it was so hard to get decent servants these days what with all the women who had done men's work during the war and received much bigger pay packets not being willing to go into service as once they had done.

'Go on, lass, they'll not bite you.'

A fire had been lit in the drawing room and the two women sat side by side before the comfort of the glowing flames. They sipped their coffee, both of them preoccupied with their own thoughts.

Rose was the first to speak. 'Do you really want to get away, Alice?'

'I feel I must, Rose,' Alice answered sadly.

'But your husband — and your son?'

'I don't feel as though Will is my son, Rose. You are more mother to him than I could ever be. He totally rejects anything I do to get closer to him and to be honest it is only because it is expected of me that I really try. He is a dear little chap and though I gave birth to him, he is not my child.'

'Alice, really, you must not — '

'Let me finish, dear Rose. I married Charlie but he is not my husband, not in the true sense. I have been ... well, I won't say stupid in my search for him since during that time I know I helped other men to return to their families but I

261

was a child when I married him. A fairy-tale princess marrying her Prince Charming. I wore a pretty dress and he was so handsome in his uniform and I thought I would never stop loving him but I have grown up since then. I am twenty-three and I am of no use to anyone. Harry is slowly healing Charlie and you and Dolly give Will all the love and care a child needs. He will grow out of his defiance when he realises that you and Harry are and will always be with him. He doesn't need me. He doesn't need Charlie, his own father, and I don't know what is to happen there but ... but ... Oh, God, I'm sorry, but I love neither of them.

'While I was searching for Charlie I thought I still loved him. It was a story, the brave heroine looking for the hero but again it was no more than a dream. When he walked through the door that first time I was still in that dream. Here he was, the man I had married, to whom I had borne a son and it seemed that I should wrap my arms about him, embrace him, the returned hero come to claim his wife and son but it wasn't so. You see how he is with me. He is rather embarrassed since he doesn't know how to deal with the situation, and neither do I. If he was in his right mind and stronger I would speak to him about it but he is still too fragile and I am afraid that if I make ripples in the calm and peace he feels with Harry I might undermine the strength he is slowly regaining.'

'But, Alice, it has only been a few months. Surely it is too soon to expect the miracle of his complete recovery? Won't you give it a few more weeks? I cannot bear to lose you when we have been brought together again. You are my only friend.'

'Harry loves you, Rose. I have seen him look at you with such longing in his eyes.'

'Have you?' she said with bitterness. 'I haven't. He's absorbed with his brother, putting *him* back to what he was, and with his farms, producing the much needed meat and crops to feed this nation, keeping an eye on the tenants and teaching Charlie the ropes, so he has no time for . . . for anyone. What with Charlie and Will he is fully occupied. I am twenty-eight, Alice. I want children *of my own*. I love Will though he can be exhausting at times but I believe, given time, he will settle. He should be told that you are his mother and Charlie his father. We are all so busy protecting this one small boy. Oh, sweet Jesus, I wish I could just say 'I'm going away' but how can I leave?'

She leaned forward and put her hands to the fire, rubbing them together, her voice soft. 'My grandfather built Beechworth after finding gold in a place called Yackandandah in Australia. Did you know that? No? I promised myself that one day I would go and see the place where it all started. When the war ended, I told myself, and everyone would be back in their place in life. You and Charlie together; I didn't include Harry then, though I had fallen in love with him almost from the first day at Lime Street when we went to see the troops off. Then it seemed so wonderful that when he was home on leave he loved me in the same way. But that has gone,

263

Alice, that dream, so one day I will return to my previous one. Yackandandah! What a wonderful name. It draws me and one day I shall go, but not yet, it seems. I cannot leave Will to servants, dearly as they love him, so if you are to desert him, I must stay.'

Alice was weeping broken-heartedly now, her hands to her face, tears dripping through her fingers. 'Don't, Rose, oh, please don't . . .'

'Don't what? Don't leave Will, is that what you're asking me? You can speak so calmly of abandoning your own child *and* husband but I must stay here and take responsibility for your family. I've done enough, Alice. I've loved you since that day at the station. You were the little sister I had always wanted. And your idea of joining the suffragette movement is a ridiculous one. They have won the right to vote or will do soon, so what can you possibly mean when you say you want to help them? They no longer need it. The war made the difference. Well, my dear,' she said, standing up and smoothing down her skirt, 'I shall leave you with your tears and go to bed. I am tired and I must ride back to Beechworth. And what is to become of Will? It might be as well if I remove him to *my* home which, if I am to be his mother, will be his as well. Dolly will be pleased. Goodnight, Alice.'

17

For a week she did not go near Summer Place. She could no longer bear to be close to Harry, close to the polite stranger he had become. She had come to the end of her tether, which was a stupid expression she knew, but she could think of no other way to describe the utter hopelessness that had invaded her. She had lived only for this time when he would come home to her. It had been the life raft to which she had clung during the past four years. She had wordlessly begged some unknown, unseen being to fetch Alice home to them and for Charlie, merry, mischievous Charlie to be found. Which he had been. Charlie had been released and taken to Camiers and from there, by boat and train, returned to them just before Christmas. Charlie who could be relied upon to lift their spirits. For Will at last to be with his mother and father, and of course, the most cherished dream of all, Harry at her side, in her bed and life as it used to be. It had happened but it had *not* happened. They were all safe, uninjured, by which she meant, no loss of limbs, no blindness, no serious wounds but injured just the same, *all of them*. Will was just a baby and like young children he would adjust to the upheaval in his life but he was precocious. He had never played with children of his own age except for the children at Oak Hill Farm, the wounded soldiers, the servants and herself, she must be honest, had treated him as though he were older.

As Rose walked slowly down towards the paddocks she could see Mary from Summer Place hanging out the washing and for a moment she wondered why Mary was doing Bertha's job. Where was Bertha? Perhaps she had gone over to Summer Place to give a hand. But Bertha's soldier son, wounded in the last days of the war, was home, his leg beginning to heal but he was still virtually helpless. It was all Bertha could do to manage the laundry at Beechworth without coping with that of Summer Place as well.

Foxy and Sparky were in the far corner of the paddock but when they saw her they both ambled across the grass towards her. They poked their heads over the fence and Foxy nuzzled her neck then tried to reach her pocket where she sometimes fetched them an apple.

'I've nothing for you, my lass,' she said sadly, sliding her hand down the mare's smooth neck. She fondled the two of them until they lost interest and began to crop the grass by the fence. But something was bothering her and she turned her back to them, leaning against the fence, her elbows on the top rung. Dolly had not told her that the housemaid from Summer Place was working in Beechworth's laundry. Dolly was getting on, and the war and the consequences of it seemed to have drained something from her, taking that strength she had always shown and leaving her frail and dependent on Nessie, the cook and now more or less housekeeper, the decision-maker in the kitchen. Rose had been so focused on Alice and Charlie and the general air of sadness that hung about the two houses that she had taken little notice of the running of them. Dolly would see to it as she always had done, she had thought if she had thought at all.

A quiver of apprehension darted though her. No, not apprehension, that was too strong a word, more . . . unease. Why was Mary hanging out washing on Beechworth's washing line? Where was Bertha who was usually so dependable? She had been laundress at Beechworth since she was a girl of twelve and had married Arthur who worked as head keeper at Weatherly House. Bertha had given birth to three boys: two had never come back from the war into which they had so gladly flung themselves. Only Sandy had been returned to them. Jimmy and Arnold were lying together in Flanders Fields. They had joined Lord Derby's Pals' Battalion and were killed on the same day.

Bertha, like all the wives, mothers and sweethearts, had aged overnight. She had pulled herself together though she had grieved badly for her two handsome boys, and got on with life, giving thanks for the survival of her one remaining lamb.

Rose fairly ran back to the kitchen where Nessie and Dolly were comforting themselves with a brew. It brought you round a treat did a brew, or so the two women said. They sat in silence, for though Master Will was a handful he brought a bit of life to the place and somehow they missed his lively presence.

Dolly made an effort to rise from her chair by

the fire, saying as she did so, 'Come and sit thee down, my lass, and have a cuppa. There's one left in the pot. It's fresh made — '

'Why is Mary hanging out the washing?' Rose asked abruptly, cutting off Dolly's words, startling the two women.

'Good 'eavens, our Rose. Is that all? We thought it were something life-threatening the way you dashed in. Bertha's not well, nor her lad so Mrs Philips from Summer Place offered Mary. Miss Alice is helping out in the kitchen, muckin' in as she always does. 'I've done harder jobs than this in France,' she ses. 'I won't tell you of some of the messes I've cleaned up in . . .' Well, you know what she's like. She ses she's nowt else ter do so — '

'What about Will?'

'Oh, he's off with Sir Harry and Mr Charlie. Sir Harry puts him up in front of him on his horse and t'lad's made up. Honest ter God, our Rose, yer'd think he were runnin' the estate with Sir Harry and Mr Charlie giving him a hand.' She looked somewhat troubled, taking a sip of tea before continuing. She didn't like the expression on their Miss Rose's face if truth be told and neither did Nessie. 'What else could we do, our Rosie?' Dolly asked the pacing figure of the young woman she had known from birth. 'Me an' Nessie can't manage him, chuck. He's that wilful so Sir Harry, bless him, took him off with them. He's a rare one is Sir Harry. Wounded in France, his pa dead leaving him to manage the place, his brother not right in the 'ead and on top of that there's that little monkey ter bring up. Eeh, I don't know, it's enough to be the end of anyone and this — I could swear, really I could — but this war's caused a deal of trouble, I can tell you. Servants not knowing where they should be, never mind what they should be doing. Me an' Nessie can't keep on chopping and changing between Beechworth and Summer Place like the young 'uns do. It's like it was when they was both hospitals when war was on, everyone where they was needed — '

'Yes, yes, Dolly,' Rose interrupted, for once Dolly got going it was hard to stop her, 'but I don't like the idea of Bertha over there by herself at Primrose Cottage.'

'She's got Sandy,' Nessie put in.

'He's no help to her, Nessie. He can barely get about let alone care for his sick mother. What's wrong with her anyway? I've never known her to be ill.'

'Arthur said she had flu. He was on his way to work and couldn't stop. There's a lot of it about, he ses. The housekeeper, now what were her name, Nessie? Mrs Gibbs? No, it were Mrs Gilly, that's it.'

'For God's sake, what does it matter what her name is? Flu, you say?'

'That's what Arthur said.'

Both women watched her intently.

'D'you think one of us should go over there and see what's what? Arthur didn't say much but yer know what men're like. As long as their grub's on't table, they've gorrer pipe ter smoke and their *Echo* ter read they don't notice owt else.'

'My Tom's not like that,' Nessie protested indignantly.

'Now I'm not sayin' he is, Nessie, but . . . well, I've never 'ad an 'usband but I remember my old dad, that was before I were put in the orphanage — Nay, what's up, chuck?' as Rose flung herself out of the kitchen, leaving the door swinging violently, then ran down the wide hallway, out of the front door and down the short path that ran from the house straight to a gate in the high stone wall. Beyond it were four cottages all belonging to Beechworth, in the first of which Bertha and Arthur Longton had brought up their three sturdy sons. She stopped suddenly at the wrought-iron seat beneath the dining room window, then slowly lowered herself on to it. Was she panicking over nothing much? The last four years had left her, as it had all women with men on the Western Front, with a tendency to fret over the slightest thing. Perhaps this with Bertha *was* just a cold but would Bertha, stalwart Bertha, stay at home for something as slight as a cold? She recalled reading, without a great deal of interest, the piece in *The Times* about returning soldiers and the cautious comment on how many of them, weakened by their ordeal, had caught colds so easily and these colds were turning to influenza. It said that of all the Americans — which was why it had not concerned her — who went to France, half of them died not from their wounds, but from this dreadful sickness called influenza. Peace was here, the war was over, so an illness such as this had not seemed worth worrying about, but now that it might have struck someone she knew and was fond of, it was suddenly of some importance. She felt shame because it was the Americans who had helped to bring the horror of the war to an end.

From somewhere she could hear the squeals of children playing and dogs barked, evidently involved in the children's game. Could she hear Will's voice among them? What was he doing? He was supposed to be with Harry and Charlie. Had they become exasperated with the noisy, self-willed child and left him with the other children in the lane? She wouldn't be surprised. He was enough to irritate the most patient!

With a sudden surge of panic she strode through the gate into the lane, crossing it to the row of cottages where some of the people who worked for her lived. Bertha's cottage, the first one, was strangely silent so without knocking she opened the door and walked in. The room into which she stepped was a kitchen-cum-parlour, usually as neat and clean as a new pin, but now somewhat cluttered. The remains of a breakfast, Arthur's she supposed, was still on the table which was without a tablecloth, something on which Bertha was particularly insistent. She had standards, did Bertha, and they were sadly lacking here.

It was a mild day but certainly not mild enough to be without a fire. There had been one, for the remains smouldered in the grate, but it had gone out and nobody had re-lit it. Sprawled in a fireside chair was Bertha's son, Sandy, his wounded leg and his bare foot propped on a stool. Lying by his side, his nose on his paws, was the family dog, called, for some reason, Tuppence, so it was not Tuppence who was making such a row in the lane.

With a start Sandy became aware of her and did his best to sit up. The dog rose to his feet, and turned round but made the mistake of putting his nose on Sandy's leg, the one with the deep, half-healed wound. Sandy shouted with pain. At the noise Bertha's voice called out weakly from above.

'Sandy, lad, what's ter do? Is tha' dad home, Sandy?'

'No, it's me, Bertha. Rose Beechworth. I've come to see — '

'Oh, thank God, Miss Rose. Did my Arthur call in ter tell yer?'

'No, Bertha. I suppose he was in such a hurry to get to work. He told Dolly you had a cold, though . . . ' She didn't know how to complete the sentence, because Arthur's employer, Alice's father, was known for a hard master and had been known to sack a man for being two minutes late for work. Arthur Longton would be afraid of losing his job, especially with work so hard to come by.

'Can I come up, Bertha?' she asked. 'We've been quite worried about you. Mary's managing but she hasn't your touch.'

'Miss Beechworth, me mam's in a bad way,' Sandy mumbled, his voice hoarse. *And so are you*, Rose thought but didn't say so.

'Stay just where you are, Sandy. I'll go up and see your mother.'

'She's badly, miss, an' I'm no use to her; come to that, to anyone. Me legs . . . '

Rose raced up the stairs, leaving poor Sandy to his rambling. There was a narrow landing with two doors leading off it and with a swift look round she found Bertha struggling as her son had done to rise. She was feebly pushing back the bedclothes with the obvious intention of climbing from the rumpled bed but in a second Rose was beside her, pushing her back on to her pillows. Bertha was struggling to breathe and as she did so in her desperate effort to clear her airways, blood-tinged froth gushed from her nose and mouth.

Frantically Rose looked about her as though help might be standing at her elbow but there was no one. Downstairs poor Sandy was fastened to his chair and could not run for help. But someone must. Could these two sick and wounded people, people she had known since childhood be left by themselves? The agonising answer was 'they must'.

But there were other women in the row of cottages, wives of the men who worked on her land and she could not help but wonder why they were not here helping Bertha in her hour of need. *All* the neighbours helped one another.

She knocked on the door of the cottage next to Bertha's. It was opened by a small, neat woman wearing a pinny. She had obviously been baking, for her hands and arms up to the elbow were dusted with flour. When she saw Rose she almost curtsied but Rose put out a hand and took hers, flour and all.

'Oh, Mrs . . . I'm sorry I don't know your name.'

'Mrs Wainwright, miss.' She was clearly puzzled but very polite since Miss Beechworth was her landlady and had allowed her and her children to stay on when . . . when . . .

'Can I 'elp thi?' Her heart had sunk for a minute when she had seen who was at her door. Her Arnold had been killed at Ypres, leaving her with four children below the age of ten and ever since Arnie had gone she had been worried to death Miss Beechworth might turn her out. Had she changed her mind? Did she need the cottage for a new family? Mind you, Effie Wainwright had worked hard and she had been proud to work up at the hospital so 'appen the mistress might look kindly on Effie and the bairns and let them stay on as she had promised. Her face was pale with apprehension.

'Mrs Wainwright, might I ask a favour of you, a great favour?'

'A favour, Miss Rose?' Effie's voice quavered.

'You know Bertha Longton, I take it?'

'Oh aye, miss, her and me's good neighbours but — '

'She's not a bit well, Mrs Wainwright, and what with poor Sandy unable as yet to get about I wonder if you would sit with her while I fetch the doctor and make further arrangements for her care.'

'Eeh, Miss Rose, o' course I will an' right gladly. I didn't know or I'd've bin round there. Bairns are up lane playin' wi' Jinny Herbert's lads' — so that was where all the noise was coming from — 'but you go on. I'll see ter Bertha. She were right good ter me when my hubby were killed so just let me get this pie in't th'oven an' I'll be on me way.'

But when Mrs Wainright returned with Rose, they found it was too late to help Bertha and Sandy.

★ ★ ★

Dolly and Nessie nearly jumped out of their skins when Rose shot into the kitchen like a bullet from a gun. Not that either of them had seen a bullet let alone one being fired. Ginger, who had been dozing by the fire leaped up and began to bark furiously.

'Aye up, our Rose, what's ter do? Oh, give over, Ginger, do, we can't hear ourselves think. Now then, what's up, my lass?'

'It's Bertha, Dolly,' Rose panted.

'She was coughing blood, Dolly,' Rose said quietly.

Both women became silent, looking at each other with dread.

Then: 'Blood, lass, nay you don't have that with a cold.'

'I know, Dolly, and then — Oh Dolly, they're dead!'

'I'll get over there directly,' Dolly said firmly. 'Oo's with her now? That lad of hers can barely stand.'

'Sit down, Dolly, you're going nowhere near her and neither are you, Nessie. I've an awful feeling it's that influenza, that's coming back

275

with the soldiers. I was reading in the paper that — '

Nessie made a scornful snort. 'Nay, tekk no notice of papers, Miss Rose. They'll say owt ter get yer ter — '

But Rose was through the kitchen and down the hall to the little niche that housed the telephone. The two elderly women sank slowly to their chairs, for they had heard about the speed of the disease in America where their returning soldiers were spreading the illness throughout the land. They were not aware, since neither read a newspaper, that the disease was making inroads in countries all over the world, including their own.

Dr Smith, who had been the family doctor as long as Rose could remember, answered the telephone himself. He sounded weary and for a second it occurred to Rose that he must be getting on. He had seemed old when she was a child.

'Oh, Doctor, thank goodness you're in. I've — '

'Just walked in, my dear. It is Miss Beechworth?'

'It is, but how did you know, Doctor?'

'My memory is not what it was but I remember voices. Is that not strange?' he mused as though talking to himself.

Rose wished he would let her speak, so quite rudely and she was sorry for it, she interrupted him.

'It is my laundry-maid, Doctor. She has died very suddenly. I've just come from her cottage and . . . well, she was coughing up blood and I — '

'It sounds as though it is what they are calling Spanish flu, Miss Beechworth. I'm sorry to say it is ravaging the whole world . . . '

Rose clung to the shelf on which the telephone stood. Why had she not known of this, for God's sake? She had read of the flu in the newspaper but had not realised its spread was of such epidemic proportions. Where else had it settled in Liverpool and its outskirts? Were there men and women, even children, now in the same condition as Bertha and if so how long would it be before it attacked Beechworth and Summer Place?

As the doctor rambled on, his voice calm, steady, but not comforting, she heard voices at the door that opened into the stable yard. Harry was laughing at something but as suddenly as it began, the laughter died away. Dolly was speaking, her voice trembling. Rose thanked the doctor who said he would be there as soon as he could and she replaced the receiver, turning to see Harry coming through the kitchen door into the hall.

He looked the picture of health, his face ruddy, his eyes bright, his dark hair in a windblown tangle on his head. He wore a tweed jacket, beige breeches and knee-high riding boots. Even as her mind scurried like a hamster in a cage she had time to consider how well he looked, how handsome, then she began to babble, her words running into one another. She was bewildered and at the same time entranced by his closeness as he stood before her, strong, steady, calm. His calmness calmed her.

'Rose, start again. Dolly was incomprehensible so slowly tell me what has happened. Bertha she says is — '

'She's dead, Harry,' taking his hands as his reached out to hers, holding them in hers lest she fall. 'There was blood . . . You know what it is, don't you? I can tell — '

'Yes, Rose, so if you would go and join the ladies in the kitchen and well . . . I would be obliged if you would speak to Charlie. He's inclined to get the willies over even the slightest thing. I will take over here and speak to Alice wherever she is. It appears she might be needed after all.'

'Do you know?'

'I don't know but she must be found and brought here. Will must be brought home and made to stay indoors though he won't like it. Charlie will have to be watched for the moment and Dolly and Nessie are the only ones to do it.'

'Why?'

'Because they are here all the time. Can you shout for Tom and Jossy to come to the kitchen door? You'd best get Mary but I think she can go back to Summer Place. I'll go over and see to the other servants and — '

He stopped speaking suddenly, staring in the direction of the strip of garden at the side of the house where two young girls were chattering and laughing together, one with an empty laundry basket on her hip.

'Who the devil are those two and what the hell

do they think they're doing lolling about together as though they haven't a care in the world?'

Rose clutched at his arm.

'It's Mary and Elsie. Perhaps helping with the laundry.'

'Mary must come back to Summer Place at once. Charlie and I haven't been in contact with anyone connected to the . . . the sick people at Primrose Cottage.'

'Arthur, her husband, was here this morning, sir,' Dolly piped up. 'He came to tell us she were poorly.'

'Did he come inside?'

'No, sir, just stood on't doorstep.'

'Then I think we can chance myself and Charlie, plus Alice when she is found, depending on where she has been, returning to Summer Place.'

His face which had been filled with tenderness for Rose froze into a stern expression, blank of all emotion. All signs of his loving feelings for Rose had slipped away and with a brief oath he pushed past her, tearing to the back door and the corner of the house.

'You two girls,' he roared, 'get into the house at once.' Mary almost dropped her basket and Elsie squeaked and grabbed at the laundry-maid.

Rose, who had followed him, said, 'You're frightening them, Harry.'

'They need to be frightened, Rose. Now will the pair of you stop dithering and do as you're told. Both of you wait in the kitchen until I get there. I will talk to you later. Quickly, dammit,' as the two servants almost bumped into one

279

another in their effort to do as they were told.

He whirled about and ran towards the gate into the lane and as he reached where the children were playing caused pandemonium by grabbing Will and holding him under one arm with great difficulty since the child struggled fiercely, and shouted at the rest of them.

'Listen to me, all of you. You are to go to your own homes and stay there until I come and speak to your parents.'

'But we wasn't doing nuffink, sir,' one boy whined.

'I didn't say you were but you are to do as you're told or you will be in a great deal of trouble.'

'Yes, sir,' the braver of the children said truculently, pulling at his brother. They were Alfie and John, Jinny and Dan Herbert's boys.

It did not take Harry long to sort them all out into their respective places in this crisis that had come upon them, the children's outrage having no effect on him whatsoever. They had been having a lovely time with their game and could see no reason why they should all go home. What would they do when they got there? they asked one another sullenly but Harry was adamant. He fought Will every step of the way, threatening to box the boy's ears if he didn't do as he was told for bloody once.

'You sweared then,' Will shouted.

'I'll do something worse in a minute.

'Have you a spare cupboard?' he asked Dolly as he carried the yelling, struggling child into the kitchen. Somehow he must impress on him that he meant it.

Dolly was confused and upset for she loved the little lad and the children were doing nothing wrong in her opinion, but Sir Harry was determined to show the wilful child that this — and he — were serious. She supposed he was right as it would be a disaster if any of them caught the dreadful disease. It seemed thousands were dying of it so it was for the best if the bairns were all kept indoors though she pitied their poor mothers.

'Well, Sir Harry, there's a small one under the stairs next to the telephone but surely — '

'You hear that, boy!' Harry roared. 'The cupboard under the stairs.'

Will began to cry now though he still aimed kicks at Harry. With a sigh Harry sat down, a fascinated circle round him, frightened themselves but at the same time wondering what was to come next. In a strange way the servants were quite enjoying this excitement in their dull lives. With the war over — though they were sorry for those involved in it like poor Mr Charlie who seemed to have lost his mind — it had given them something outside their tedious days to liven things up.

Harry pulled the boy on to his knee, reluctant to do this to him but he must be made to realise the seriousness of what was happening.

'Will, you know Bertha who does the laundry?'

The boy nodded mutinously.

'And her lad Sandy, who was a soldier?'

Again Will nodded.

'Sandy came home from the trenches with a terrible illness that was very contagious — catching. That means he could give it to someone else.'

'His poorly leg? It has a hole in it made wiv a bullet. A nasty German. A Hun did it, Sandy ses.' The boy nodded his head sagely is if to affirm the importance of what he was saying. 'Has Bertha catched a bullet hole?'

'No, lad. Sandy, as well as his poorly leg, brought home an illness called influenza.'

'Oh yes, the girls skip to it. A little bird, I fink.' Scornfully: 'Girls are daft the things they do, Alfie ses so,' looking round at the servants as though to let them know that what Alfie said was gospel!

'Maybe they are, Will, but this illness, influenza, is making people poorly all over the country. They are dying from it. Sandy had it and sadly he gave it to Bertha.'

'That was naughty, Harry.'

'He didn't mean to, Will, but, well, he gave it to Bertha and . . . and . . . well . . . ' Harry looked about him helplessly as though asking for strength to tell this small and innocent child the tragedy of Bertha and Sandy. Will's first brush with death close to home.

He sighed and hugged the boy to him. This was Charlie's son, Harry's nephew and Rose turned away to hide her tears

'Poor Sandy and Bertha have both died, Will.'

Will looked astounded then burst into noisy tears, falling against his uncle's chest, then scrambled from his knee and ran to Dolly. She caught him to her and held him against that deep comforting bosom where the child had so many times found consolation. She petted him and soothed him and the others watched, most in tears. What next? their sad faces asked.

Just when the war was done with and families were reunited this killing disease came along and it looked as though it would sweep all their hopes for peace at last into thin air.

18

The young man almost stumbled as he dragged himself along Lark Hill Lane. He came to a pair of impressive wrought-iron gates set in the stone wall that evidently surrounded what must be a house of some splendour. The gates were firmly closed.

He put out a hand and clung to one of them. For several minutes he stood there, then, putting the small suitcase he was carrying on the ground, he leaned on them in what appeared to be total exhaustion. They were double gates and as he held on to the left one it opened as though it had not been firmly secured. He almost fell as the gate swung open. God in heaven, was it a sign? he thought wearily. He had been tramping for weeks up and down long, gravelled drives such as this one and had been turned away menacingly. Well, could you blame folk with this hellish influenza decimating the population? But this one seemed to be inviting him in. He had decided only this morning that he could take no more. He would find a dry ditch, lie down and let his weary body and soul go where they would.

There were two men, one elderly, the other no more than a lad. They talked quietly together as they worked side by side with their hoes, moving along a bed in which spring flowers were beginning to peep through the soil, skirting the

284

roots of broad oak trees. They did not notice him as they had their backs to the gates but the dog did. A large, golden retriever that began to bark. Not threateningly but in a friendly way. The weary man had had a retriever once in the sweetness of the past, dead now, he supposed, as was his past.

At once the men turned and took several steps towards him, accompanied by the dog which wagged its tail. They held their hoes as though they were weapons and then, as an afterthought, inched backwards warily.

'Now then, lad,' the older man said sharply, but not unkindly. 'We don't want no 'awkers 'ere.' Tom eyed the intruder's khaki overcoat which was threadbare and stained. This was not the first ex-soldier who had come begging in this 'land fit for heroes' as one politician had called it, wrongly, it seemed.

'Forgive me,' a cultured voice whispered. 'I'm begging for one thing only and that's work. I'll do anything. Any odd dirty job nobody else wants. It's been four months since I was discharged and I'm — oh, I'm sorry, it's this influenza thing, isn't it? People are afraid and it's not surprising. I don't think I carry it.' He swayed and Jossy would have darted forward, being a kind lad, but Tom held him firmly by the arm.

'We've 'ad two died of it an' want no more. Miss Rose ses ter let no one in.' Tom was thinking of poor Bertha and her son Sandy from Primrose Cottage. Arthur, husband of one and father of the other, grieved all alone since his two other lads had been killed in the trenches. Miss Rose and Sir Harry had been most insistent since then that no one was to come on to either estate until the epidemic was over. But sweet Jesus, this poor chap, presumably a discharged officer, looked to be at the end of his tether, and as though to prove it, he dropped his battered suitcase and with a whispered moan fell unconscious to the grass.

Tom and Jossy looked at him in astonishment, then at each other not knowing what to do. For humanity's sake could they just leave him there in a heap of dusty khaki, his face almost the same colour as his overcoat?

'What shall us do, Tom?' whispered Jossy. 'We can't just leave poor bugger, but he might have the influenza.'

'Run fer Miss Rose, lad, an' look sharp. I'll stand guard,' as though the prone figure were a dangerous animal.

'Aye,' Jossy replied thankfully. Dropping his hoe, he sped up the sloping lawn and round to the back of the house, for even in this emergency he wouldn't have dreamed of using the front door even if it was quicker. As he ran into the stable yard Fred, the groom and stable lad looked over the half door of the stable in bewilderment.

'What's up, Jossy?' And as he spoke Miss Alice — they could not get used to calling her Mrs Summer — came from the kitchen wiping her hands on a cloth.

'Yes, what's all the fuss about, Jossy?' she asked absently.

At once Jossy turned to her, relieved to have someone of authority in charge. 'Eeh, thank God, Miss Alice . . . '

'What is the matter, Jossy?'

'There's a man, soldier I reckon, been trampin' the streets I . . . well, 'e's fallen down on't lawn. Tom's with 'im but neither on us wants ter touch 'im on account o' this influenza an' Miss Rose an' Sir Harry said . . . Well, we just can't leave 'im there, poor sod — beg pardon, Miss Alice — he looks right poorly.'

Alice took hold of his arm. 'It's all right, Jossy, just calm down. I'll come and have a look at him and — '

'Eeh, no, Miss Alice, what if he's got the influenza thing? Yer mun't touch him. 'Appen if us leaves him he'll wake up an' be on his way. Me an' Tom'll watch him.' Jossy was mortified. He didn't know what he expected anyone to do when he raced up to the house but he certainly was not inclined to allow delicate Miss Alice to come into contact with the poor chap who Tom was guarding with his very life if necessary. 'P'raps it'd be better if Sir Harry or even Mr Charlie' — though what help he thought the poor brother of Sir Harry could manage was a mystery. But certainly not Miss Alice, pretty, dainty Miss Alice, who, if he had known it, had attended to more horrifying crises than he would ever encounter in her years on the battlefields of France. He didn't know what he had been thinking about as he chased after her down the lawn where it seemed she was to examine the chap.

'Nay, Miss Alice,' he panted, 'don't you go touchin' him.'

'And what are we to do with him, Jossy? Leave him here to perish?' Alice rolled the man on to his back, felt his forehead, lifted his eyelids, put her ear to his chest, opened his mouth and peered inside, while Tom and Jossy watched helplessly. Then at last she stood up.

'This poor man does not have influenza, men. He is starving and exhausted. You can lift him and carry him to the house. We'll find a bed for him and I will nurse him. I had plenty of experience during the war.'

The men exchanged glances but Miss Alice had been at the front so they gingerly lifted the unconscious man. One at his feet and one at his shoulders. Tom shook his head compassionately. 'He don't weigh much, Miss Alice, poor lad.'

'Follow me, Tom,' she ordered. 'I'll bring his suitcase.' When she looked inside it she was not surprised to find dusters, brushes, scrubbing soap which he had apparently been hoping to sell. He was one of the 'heroes' of the land and the battles he had fought to protect it.

They carried him through the stable yard, watched by Fred, and into the kitchen where Dolly, Nessie and the others backed away as though the young man Tom and Jossy carried were a leper.

'It's all right, ladies,' Alice said serenely. 'He hasn't got influenza. He's an ex-soldier I should imagine who can't find work and is quite literally starving to death, which I'm sure Dolly and Nessie will soon put right with a bowl of Nessie's soup. Tom and Jossy will put him in a bath and I'm sure Sir Harry or Mr Charlie can find something for him to wear. Then he shall be put in a spare bed where he can rest. Now, don't all stand gaping at him. See, he's coming round so perhaps soup first then between them Dolly and Nessie will have him on the road to recovery. Poor boy, he offered his life to his country and look what it's done for him.'

Lieutenant Tim Elliott thought he must have died on the long weary road he had tramped only to end up in his mother's kitchen. There was Mrs Atkins who baked the most delicious almond biscuits in the world. He and James and Paul used to untie her apron strings and run screeching with laughter as she chased them with her wooden spoon. There was the old dresser and the shining black-leaded stove, the gleaming copper pans, the neat maids in their starched aprons and the ginger cat stretched out in front of the fire.

He had tried, God how he had tried for work but nobody wanted an ex-officer with a first-class degree in history. What good could a man steeped in literature and history be in a country doing its best to recover from a devastating war? He was over-qualified to teach the children of a working-class man, he had been told kindly, so he had joined the multitude of ex-servicemen who were fighting each other now to get work, any work. He couldn't remember when he had last eaten anything and he had threepence three farthings in his pocket, saved for a rainy day!

Now, he realised that he was sitting, not in his family home but at a kitchen table with a horde of women round him urging him to eat up and eat up he did, much to their approval, positively bolting it. He could feel a little strength seep into him for the soup was the best he had ever tasted, better even than Mrs Atkins's, cook at his old home, and she had been the best cook in Sussex. He wondered where she was now. Probably in her grave with his mother and father, and his two brothers who lay somewhere buried in Flanders fields.

At that moment three more people burst into the kitchen, making it even more crowded. There was a very lovely woman, tall with a magnificent figure and short, curly copper and gold hair. Her eyes were the same gold, shot with copper. Despite his desperate weariness he could not help admire her for, after all, he was a man. The two men who came in with her looked like brothers.

'Alice, for the love of God,' one of the men said, not to the lovely woman but to someone who stood behind him, her hand on his shoulder, who, when he turned to look at her, took his breath away. The women were so different but really, he could hardly believe his eyes, they were both so beautiful. Where in hell was he? It *must* be heaven!

'Sorry, old chap,' the man said, turning to him, 'it's nothing personal but this bloody influenza has got everyone a bit paranoid. I believe it's on the wane now but we tried to make sure it didn't get into Beechworth or

Summer Place and now Alice has brought you — '

'It's not influenza, Harry. I think this young man is ex-army and is looking for work. He's starving, worn to the bone.'

Tim Elliott stood up unsteadily. 'Please, all of you, I apologise for intruding. I don't know why I fell over but I'll be on my way now. That soup has — '

'You're going nowhere, lad, so sit down an' stop bein' so daft.'

Dolly had spoken and so Tim Elliott became one of them. The survivors!

19

Their new employee — which he insisted he was and was known to do more work than his frail health really allowed — was called Tim by everyone, even the servants. He was so obviously a gentleman, despite his shabbiness. Alice watched over him for signs of the dreaded influenza but as the days and weeks passed into a glorious spring then summer he began to look as tanned and fit as Harry and Charlie. Tim Elliott, by which name he had introduced himself, was once a lieutenant in the Royal Sussex Regiment. He felt no need to tell them he was titled. He was the younger son of Sir Albert Elliott, now deceased, as were his brothers, so he was entitled to be called Sir Timothy Elliott.

He still wore his uniform jacket, the one with the lieutenant's pips on the shoulder, and when Harry proposed that he borrowed a shirt or two, a couple of long-sleeved jerseys with polo necks and an old pair of riding breeches Tim was inordinately grateful.

'I fought beside your lot at Ypres,' Harry told him abruptly, as though to explain his generosity. 'Bloody good chaps.' And he felt the same about Tim.

Tim was unassuming, eager to do any task asked of him, mucking out the stables, grooming Corey and Pixie at Summer Place. But the best and most appreciated was that Will transferred his attentions to Tim, claiming him for his best friend, dumping Alfie and John without compunction. He followed him everywhere and Tim didn't seem to mind. Alice was of the opinion that the small boy took the place of his own brothers of whom he had been very fond but whom he had lost in the trenches. Certainly he had been the youngest but they had included him in all the games, the tricks, the hi-jinks boys get up to. Tim even began to teach Will, without the boy being aware of it, how to read, to write, to add up simple sums in the games they played. Harry had bought Will a small pony named Molly, and Tim and Will rode out nearly every day.

'How many blackbirds have we seen this morning, lad?' Tim would ask.

'Six.'

'And how many did we see yesterday? Do you remember the ones we heard singing in the meadow?'

'Seven.'

'Very good. Now think hard, how many is that altogether? Don't forget the one that was perched on the branch of the oak tree.'

Silence as Will added up the blackbirds then, triumphantly, 'Thirteen.'

'Good lad. Now take away the three we can see in that hedge there.'

'Ten.'

'By Gad, you're a clever lad.'

'By Gad, so are you, Tim. Now where are we going this morning? Shall we ride over to Ashtree Farm? They've got new puppies and if I'm a good boy and can tell Rose you said so d'you think she'll let me have one? Tommy's getting on a bit and — '

'We'll see, Will. Now then, d'you think you and Molly could jump that hedge?'

'Course. Molly's a good jumper.'

'Righto, race you to it.'

He let the boy win, of course, and Alice watched them from the rear bedroom window of Summer Place. Will was not the only one to take to Tim. Alice might as well have been a widow for all the notice her husband took of her. He had improved enough to have his own room now but he never attempted to claim his rights as a husband. He was extremely polite with her as he was with Rose. It made no difference to the way he behaved towards her and she began to fear he had lost not only a great part of his past but also his manhood. He had nothing to say on the addition to their household although he startled everyone by saying out of the blue, 'I knew a chap once who was called Tim.' This was early on when Tim had been with them for a week or so.

Tim had turned to him immediately, knowing by now that there was something seriously wrong with the good-looking young man who was Alice's husband and who always seemed to hang about on the edge of the company.

'Did you, old chap?' he asked gently, and though she did not realise it then, that was the moment Alice considered the astonishing idea that what she felt for him was not just the emotion of friend, of compassion for a fellow

294

warrior, but something far stronger. All these years — five — she had loved Charlie. Or had she just idealised him, turned him into something he was not? Eighteen, she had been and Charlie so handsome, so dashing, such good company, and he had loved her. That had all gone and in her was a quiet place, empty and ready to be filled.

'Yes,' Charlie said now in a vague voice. 'He was screaming, caught on the wire so I shot him.'

'I know, Charlie. It was necessary, wasn't it. You could not let your chum suffer.'

'Did you know him, Tim?' Charlie asked eagerly.

'Oh yes. Tommy and Fred and Ginger and Sid and Wally.'

Charlie smiled sadly. 'They're still here with me.'

'I know, with me too. I say, why don't you show me the places you go to here on this beautiful estate? Where you go to remember them as they were. We had a few laughs in the trenches, didn't we, as well as the terrible suffering they knew. Did you have a particular pal with whom you would have liked to share these lovely moments you know now? Let's ride over there.'

'I'd like that, Tim.' His face clouded. 'But you see I have to stay with Harry. Harry and I are brothers,' as though that was all that needed to be said.

But Tim was a survivor, as Alice was and though the rest of them did not notice he and she often laughed and chatted to each other when Will was in bed. They walked through the woods, looking for mushrooms, they told Dolly, and as the summer ran into autumn, blackberries. He told her of his happy childhood with his family at home in the south.

Though he knew he must tread lightly, he asked her about her past — and Charlie. 'How old were you when you married Charlie?' he questioned softly. 'I believe it was at the beginning of the war?'

'I was eighteen when we met. Well, I say when we met but we grew up together, the Summers boys and me. Rode to hounds, or up into the foothills of the Pennines, taking a picnic. Funnily we were not acquainted with Rose then. You know what families such as ours are like. My father did not consider the Beechworths *our sort* since her family gained their wealth in trade and she was always busy with her estate. We met, she and I, as Charlie, full of fun and enthusiasm as they all were, set off for France. Charlie and I had been ... lovers and when my father discovered I was with child, he threw me out with no more than a petticoat to my name.' She laughed harshly and when Tim took her hand she let it lie trustingly in his.

'I had met Rose briefly at the railway station when Charlie left and since I knew of no one else who would take me in, I went to Beechworth House. I loved her then and still do. She was my saviour. I was a romantic and when we heard that Charlie was missing I determined to search the battlefields to find him.'

She shook her head and smiled sadly. She and

Tim were sitting in a soft mossy hollow beneath the roots of an ancient oak tree and as their shoulders touched she leaned against him and seemed to accept what was happening. Their horses cropped the grass several feet away and the two dogs, Ginger and Spice, lay with their noses on their paws, their eyes swivelling lazily, their ears twitching at the loud, metallic *chink chink* of the chaffinch in the branches of the trees.

They both sighed. They did not kiss. There was no need. There was no need for words. They knew what was happening to them.

* * *

Rose's love for Harry had never wavered though she often wondered what that episode in their lives during the war had meant to him. Not by a flicker of an eyelid did he show her even a fraction of affection other than that he showed Alice or Dolly or the boy.

As she struggled on with her barren life helping the women in the kitchen or the men in the garden and meadows, trying to teach Will a few simple sums or a word or two, she often passed him as she moved from one house to another and he did the same and on one occasion he spoke her name carelessly.

'Rose, now that Tim seems to have joined our household, I think Charlie and I, and Tim, of course, can stay permanently at Summer Place. We'll take Will since he's Charlie's son. Alice may please herself. She and Charlie have not

297

resumed their marital status and it seems they are never likely to, for I have come to believe Charlie will recover no further than he has so . . .'

He shrugged carelessly and made his way towards Charlie and the newcomer who were laughing together over something in the stable yard.

She felt as though he had deliberately slapped her in the face.

Harry's heart felt as though it were bleeding as he picked up Corey from the Beechworth stables with the intention of riding him across the field to Summer Place. Rose's devastated face swam before his eyes so that had it not been for Corey's instincts he might have ended up in Old Swan instead of his own stable yard.

He wondered despairingly what had made him say and do what he had. He loved her, goddammit, more than life itself, and yet he seemed compelled to treat her as though they were no more than acquaintances. Once . . . once they had been different. Years ago now when he was on leave from the hell of war so why, *why* did he act as he had done? Why? He had loved her from the first time he had seen her on Lime Street station, the day Charlie had set off excitedly for France, the day Lady had refused to get on the train and Rose, later, had loved him. They had been lovers, for God's sake, but since Harry came home a badly damaged soldier — not that that had anything to do with it — they had been cool with one another.

So, what should he do next? he asked himself.

He nodded at Ned as he ran forward to take the stallion who was jibbing with disapproval at the short ride, uncooperative as Ned led him into the stable and began to unsaddle him. Suddenly Harry turned and hurried back into the stable.

'Leave him, Ned. He needs exercise and so do I. I'll take him to . . . to . . . well, leave him saddled and . . . '

Ned was startled but handed the reins to Sir Harry and stepped back respectfully. He watched as his master thundered out of the yard and headed for the stand of trees and then beyond to the moorland where he urged the animal up and up to the start of the lower Pennine Chain. On he rode, his face almost on the stallion's neck, pursued by the expression on Rose's face. He had for a moment or two been transported back to those magical days when he and Rose had been lovers. She had clung to him as eagerly as he had clung to her but there had been so much confusion. All those who relied on him turning towards him for orders. God, oh Jesus God, what was he to do? What was he to do with this love he bore her? Did she feel nothing for him? If not, then why had she been so glad to be in his arms?

Corey was beginning to flag so he reined him in, leaping from his back with the smooth movement of the splendid horseman he was. He left the animal to graze on the wide shelf of grass, flinging himself down and turning on to his back to stare at the blue bowl of the sky. His eyes closed and, relaxing at last, he fell asleep.

She found him there, the strong invisible bond

that both had denied drawing her on Foxy's back to this peaceful plateau. Quietly she dismounted as Foxy whickered a greeting to Corey. She knelt at Harry's side and looked down at his beloved face which was gaunt, thin, the clefts chiselled beside his mouth deeper, more pronounced, his eyelashes, so long and dark any woman might have envied them. His mouth was stern, even as he slept and she noticed that the hair above his ears had white streaks in it which had not been there before the war. He must be thirty-two or thirty-three, she mused. She was twenty-nine and time was racing by at an impossible speed, a frightening speed.

He sighed and without thinking she laid her lips on his. He actually smiled in his sleep. She felt it beneath her own then his arms lifted and drew her down to him. He opened his eyes, unfocused as he woke, then he groaned.

'Tell me I'm not dreaming,' he murmured, his lips opening against hers. 'I couldn't bear it if I was.'

'No, Harry, you're not dreaming. I don't know how it came about. I didn't follow you up here. I just needed to get away from things.'

'I did the same. Is it meant to be, d'you think? You know I love you.'

'No, I didn't. I only know *I love you*.'

'Then why the hell have we been — '

Her lips stopped the words and, now that his arms were around her, she really didn't care how it had come about. She was here where she had longed to be for months, years, and it seemed words were no longer needed. He propped

300

himself on one elbow, his eyes drinking in the luminous, incredulous glow in hers.

'Did you say you loved me?'

'Yes, and did you say — '

'I did and I do, dearest heart.'

Despite his astonishment at this moment he began to kiss her face with a somewhat feverish desperation as though he were afraid this might somehow be an illusion and he needs must make the most of it. His lips slid under her jaw and down her throat to the buttons of the usual white shirt she wore.

'Dear God, I love you . . . want you. I need to take you before you change your mind or fate changes it for us.'

'Please . . . oh please, let this be real. I wouldn't want to live if you . . . if we . . . '

'Be quiet, woman . . . *my* woman . . . '

'Harry . . . Harry . . . '

Their lips clung together while their hands were busy with buttons, belts, until her breasts were revealed, sweet . . . sweet in his hands and lips, her nipples hard and peaked at his touch. He sucked and bit them as her body arched to his and the horses turned in bewilderment, amazed at the sound of their lovemaking. At last it came, an explosion that, because of their long wait, was rapidly over. They were both almost naked. Then it began again, slowly this time as he moved inside her, tenderly then more insistently as the love they shared and which had been denied for so long carried them to the highest peaks of climax, then gradually on to the shores of peace, acceptance, tranquillity. He

301

rested his face on her white, rosy peaked breast, his hand stroking her belly and the glory of the auburn triangle that guarded her womanhood. It was as it should be. They loved one another. Harry and Rose. Rose and Harry.

* * *

Tim had proved to be an honest, obliging hard worker, with Charlie at his side, thankful to have found a settled place at last and Harry and Rose thanked the gods who had sent Tim Elliott to them. He and Charlie were scarcely ever apart though Tim, with an anxious apology, asked humbly if he might have a bedroom of his own. He was sensitive to Charlie's needs but he needed privacy, he explained to Harry who understood.

No one noticed the growing attachment between Alice and Tim, for they were all agog with the unexpected but wonderful preparations for Sir Harry's wedding to Rose Beechworth. Where once Will had clung to Harry, he now would not be parted from Tim who resignedly put up with Charlie and his son. It became a familiar sight for the two men and the small boy to be seen trudging about Beechworth and Summer Place and they all — Harry more than the others — thanked whatever being they believed in, that Will had transferred his attention from him to Tim and Charlie. Another occurrence, or two actually, that escaped the household's attention was the disappearance at odd times — at the same time — of Tim Elliott and Alice Summers.

Harry and Rose had decided on a small wedding with just the family and their servants at the church where Charlie and Alice had been married. And as soon as possible, Harry declared firmly, for his lovely glowing bride-to-be was already pregnant though nobody knew except himself and Rose. A quiet smile and a twinkle in the eyes of Dolly could be seen if anyone was looking for it, since whatever her much loved child did, it could not get past the woman who had brought her up. But Rose was not the only woman pregnant!

★   ★   ★

Dr Westmann often reflected in the year following the end of the war how many of the young soldiers had survived not only his surgery but the war itself. He supposed there must have been hundreds who had come under his knife but he had done his best for the wounded soldiers despite his loathing for war, and no man could do more. When, at the end, he had been relieved of his duties as a military doctor he had returned to Berlin, the home of his birth and to the hospital where he had learned to become a military surgeon. Many years ago, of course, because he was now in his sixtieth year.

The hospital had had many uses, since its history harked back to 1710. It had been a hospice for the destitute, a workhouse for beggars and a maternity home for unmarried mothers, and had expanded over the two hundred or so years since its construction. It was now a military hospital and infirmary as well as a training centre for future military physicians. He mostly did teaching work now. The Charite was its name and it had become second home and focus of the dedicated surgeon's life.

So many young men, but now he also tended to females. He was looking down on one now on his operating theatre table. She was the daughter of one of Berlin's prominent and wealthy citizens, who, knowing of Otto Westmann's reputation, had insisted that he should operate on his only child. It had been a shooting accident at one of the local nobles' weekend parties. A gun, carelessly aimed at flying grouse, aimed by a youngster who should not have had the weapon in the first place, and the result was the pretty young woman with her brain exposed awaiting the surgeon's knife.

For several moments he stood, an instrument in his hand, appearing to his staff to be debating his first move but he was in fact, surprisingly, taken back several years to a day in France when he had operated on a young English soldier. He remembered him, because his wound had been similar to this one. He also remembered a very senior officer, a doctor like himself, barking at him that the bed in which the young Englishman lay could be put to much better use for a German soldier and he, Dr Westmann was to get the English soldier on his way to the prisoner-of-war camp awaiting him. Otto had argued but a direct order from his superior could not be ignored. Dr Westmann would have liked to keep the young English soldier in his care for another week or two since he was not quite convinced that he had removed all the shards of bone in Charlie's wound. Head injuries could be problematic and needed close watching, particularly that one because the young soldier seemed confused as to his own identity. He appeared to be recovered, so with his superior at his shoulder he had reluctantly discharged the young man, making it clear he was not happy about it, to his fate in the prisoner-of-war camp. Was he still alive, that young man, and if so had his, Otto's, own surgery given him his life? Who would ever know?

Adjusting his mask, he nodded at the young doctor he was training and who stood on the other side of the operating table and began.

★ ★ ★

The wedding, though small, for who was there to invite, was quite wonderful or so the servants from the two houses, who *were* invited, told one another. And it was, since who among them had ever seen a man and a woman more in love with one another. Sir Harry was ready to run up the aisle to hurry his bride to the altar and the kiss he gave her made the women's hearts almost burst with emotion though it was inclined to embarrass the men. He took several steps backwards towards Rose who was on the arm of Tom, the gardener, who was giving her away. Charlie stood rigid in his place as his brother's best man, mouthing in a trembling voice what his duties were.

Rose Beechworth, soon to be Rose Summers, was not conventionally pretty but her strong face was radiant. Her hair shone copper and gold in the sunlight that poured through the leaded windows of the ancient church. It was short, curling about her head like a halo. Her eyes, golden as a bright new sovereign, were directed at her groom with a glow of enchantment and at the corner of her mouth the dimple deepened as she smiled, first at Harry then round the church at her people. All the people who had stood steadfastly beside her in so many crises. Not for her the downcast, modest gaze of the conventional bride. She was tall, almost as tall as her groom, with a magnificent shapely figure which did not as yet reveal her pregnancy. She had been brought to the church in the Summers's old, open carriage, the one that had carried Alice to her nuptials, cleaned and painted, repairs to the leather seats achieved with great fervour by Ned, Tom and Jossy, Tom on his dignity since he was to ride in the carriage when he gave the woman away. And why not? Had he not known the glorious bride since the day she was born?

She carried flowers, rosebuds of pink and cream twined with white satin ribbon and walked on flowers too, for the local children had strewn the path with buttercups, daisies and poppies. The church itself had been transformed into a garden with flowers arranged artfully at the end of each pew and draped from the old beams. Alice's doing, Rose knew, looking round for her friend, but not for longer than a fraction of a moment because now Harry claimed her attention and her hand.

Her gown was of white satin, a simple fitted sheath, the hem edged with white lace which was repeated on the cuff of the long sleeve and at the neck. Surprisingly she wore no veil but a tiny Juliet cap made up of white rosebuds nestled in her curls.

She had begged Harry to wear his uniform but he had refused quite brusquely, saying he wanted no reminders of the past to impinge on this long-awaited day. Dolly and Nessie cried as did most of the female congregation but it was soon over with the bride and groom kissing one another with great fervour. The register was signed and then the dash in a shower of confetti and rice to the carriage that would take them to Beechworth. This was a country wedding and the guests were made up of grooms, dairymaids, cowmen and their wives, farmers and their families, enough to fill the small church twice over. Their lives had been so fraught with difficulties and terrible sorrows. The bride and groom looked at one another with a certain astonishment that it had ended with this joy. At last! They had shared a bed for several weeks before this day and their child grew in Rose's belly.

The home-made cheeses, syllabub, jellies, fruit tarts and custards and the magnificent wedding cake, made and decorated by Nessie, were all eaten by the guests as the bride and groom lay in their bed, arms about one another. They did not make love for which lack Harry apologised saying he was too knackered and Rose pondered out loud, asking him if he had seen Alice that day.

'No,' he mumbled into her deep breast, unconcerned it appeared as to the whereabouts of Alice. His beloved was in his arms. He fell asleep. His wife smiled, utterly content, just the same. She would speak to her husband tomorrow, sighing into a deep joyful sleep with his arms about her.

20

Rose Beechworth, or should they call her *Lady Rose Summers* was, by the standards of the polite society of the district, decidedly odd. There were no other words to describe her, for heaven's sake. She had chosen her own *gardener* to give her away on her wedding day so what could they deduce from that? She had relatives on her mother's side though none, as far as they knew, came visiting. She seemed to prefer the company of farmers and gamekeepers, those who worked her land, hedgers and ditchers, farm labourers, *working* with them in the fields, on the moorland and woodland, the stables and, it was said, before she married sat down in the kitchen to eat with them. Mind you, to give her her due, she had done more for the wounded soldiers than anyone in the county.

Rose neither knew nor cared what her neighbours thought and never had. Since her mother died her father had become something of a recluse, making a companion of his only child and she was quite content to work among her people. She had no friends, no woman friend until she met Alice. And there was another one! Alice Weatherly. The only daughter, the only child of Arthur Weatherly whose great wealth came from his shipping ventures; an arrogant man with a great belief in his own worth. He had his toe in the door of society and meant to get himself firmly inside. He did not want to lose his position among the great and the good. It had been an anathema to him — which was putting it mildly — when Alice got herself pregnant while still unmarried. She had only just managed to avoid the shame — *his* — by marrying that nincompoop Summers lad who, it was said, was now a dribbling idiot. At first he had been prepared to forgive her but she had vanished in that daft way of hers in the battlefields of France and after she and the idiot returned home it was too late. He had refused to have anything to do with her since.

The newly wedded couple lazed in bed the morning after the wedding, making love, making plans, at peace with the world and each other, and the servants smiled knowingly, for it was only natural for newlyweds to hide from the rest of the world and Rose and Sir Harry had waited a long time for this day.

But Dolly said anxiously to Nessie they couldn't keep it from her much longer. Miss Rose and her new husband must be told. Preferring Tim, nevertheless the boy had gone off with Charlie, reluctantly, for Charlie was not his first choice as a companion.

But this morning would have serious consequences and they, who were only servants, didn't know which way to turn. Dolly was ready to weep, the hard tears of the old, and Nessie, who wasn't much younger, didn't blame her.

'What are we ter do, Tom?' she asked her husband who hung about at the back door. 'It might be somethink and nothink with Miss Rose knowing all about it but then there's this letter. I really think we should do summat. You've bin over to Summer Place and no one there knows anything about it.'

'Yer'll have ter go an' wake them, lass,' Tom said quietly. 'Summat's wrong an' Sir Harry should be told. That little lad'll be back soon and then what?'

'Eeh, I don't like — not this morning. Not with them only wed yesterday.' She put her pinny to her face and Tom patted her arm.

'You must do it — or Dolly. Dolly knows 'em best.'

They were dozing, Sir Harry and Lady Summers, quite exhausted but in a satisfactory way, when someone tapped on the bedroom door. They had stayed the night at Beechworth since it was more convenient just to drift upstairs after the small party to the lovely, fire-lit, candle-lit bedroom and the double bed where Rose slept. Besides, Beechworth's rooms, upstairs and down, were in a well-kept state compared to Summer Place where Alice was supposed to be mistress. Alice had been allowed to run somewhat wild at Weatherly House, indulged by her father, and had not been trained to be in charge of a large house. She was careless in the running of Summer Place and though Mrs Philips and her maids — for they could now afford more than two servants who did their best, a household soon becomes slack without a proper mistress to oversee its running.

Rose lifted her head from her husband's chest and snapped, 'What is it?' She was only just catching her breath after the last passionate encounter with her new husband and was contemplating rousing him again in the way he had taught her and here was someone disturbing this dream world she could still hardly believe in and in a most annoying way.

'Miss Rose, oh, I'm sorry, but Rosie, sweetheart, you must get up. Me an' Nessie don't know what to do. Tom's bin over to Summer Place but it were no good. Oh please, lass, please . . . an' sir, please . . . '

'Dolly, what are you babbling about?' Rose yelled, at the same time turning one full breast to her husband's mouth, then giggled as his hand found its way to that hidden place at the base of her belly.

'Please come out, lass, 'cos if yer don't I'm coming in,' giving them time to make themselves decent.

'Don't you dare, Dolly Davenport. Oh, God in heaven, what on earth . . . '

'You'd better go, my love,' Harry murmured, making it no easier for her by licking her swollen nipple.

'Goddammit!' Rose reached for her robe, detaching her throbbing flesh from Harry's seeking lips.

'Well?' she demanded of the trembling housekeeper, then frowned at the distraught woman who had been a mother to her all her life. She pulled Dolly into her arms and patted her back as folk do to comfort those in distress.

'What is it, Dolly? What's happened?'

Harry sprang from the bed and pulled his

dressing gown about him but not before Dolly
had got a horrified look at the shaft between his
legs.

It was a lovely July day and the sun had
warmth in it, sidling into the bedroom and
reflecting on the well-polished furniture. It
revealed the rumpled bed and Dolly, even in her
distress, had time to think that there had been
high jinks in it that night.

'It's Miss Alice — Mrs Summers — and Mr
Tim . . . '

'What about them, darling?' Rose peered into
the tearful, crumpled old face.

I'm getting too old for this, Dolly thought as
she shrank into Rose's strong young arms.

'They've gone, lass, gone . . . '

'Gone? Gone where, Dolly?' But there was
something in Dolly's voice and manner that told
Rose all she needed to know. She'd seen it
coming and in her own joy had chosen to ignore
it.

'Nay, I don't know.'

'Are their horses in the stable, Dolly, or at
Summer Place? Has Eddie — '

'Their animals're still there, Rosie, but — '

'What?' Rose was ready to shake something
from Dolly though what she didn't know.

There was a pause then, 'There's this,' and she
held out an envelope with the names of Rose and
Harry on it.

'Where did you find it and when?'

'Just now. Eddie said it were pinned to't stable
door.' Dolly was ready to collapse and might
have done so had Rose not held her firmly.

313

Rose stared at it then took it from Dolly's shaking hand. 'Thank you, Dolly. Now you go downstairs. Sit by the fire, you and Nessie, and have a cup of tea. Harry and I will be down shortly.'

The old lady wiped her nose on the edge of her pinny then turned away to totter to the top of the stairs.

They read the letter together.

My dearest Rose and Harry,

This is the most difficult letter I have ever written, Rose. You have been my sword and buckler so to speak for many years and I love you for it. I would have gone under had it not been for you. And Harry, so staunch an ally to me and Rose and I thank God in whom I try to believe that you and Rose are finally man and wife. I would not have gone had it been otherwise. Sadly or gladly, I don't know which, it has given me the strength to do what I must. No one at Summer Place or Beechworth needs me or loves me like you do, Rose, and it is breaking my heart to leave you. But Charlie, my husband, scarcely acknowledges my presence and my son is not really mine but yours. He turns to you as he would a mother, as you are and I am not. I love Tim and he loves and needs me. I am a mature woman now and know the difference between what Charlie and I had to what I feel for Tim. Charlie was the object of a young girl's dream, dashing and handsome, but what Tim and I share is between a man and a woman. So I

314

*must go and live in another world with him.
Do not try to find us. We are leaving you for
ever.*

Your loving friend,
Alice

Rose wept bitterly in Harry's arms while he
talked quietly to her. 'It's true what she says,
my darling. At eighteen Alice saw Charlie as a
knight in shining armour. In a magical haze
she married him, already expecting his child.
But as a child herself she was incapable of
coping with life when her father threw her out
into the snow.'

'It wasn't snow,' Rose sniffed.

He smiled sadly. 'I know, sweetheart. She
came to you who cared for her but her obsession
to find Charlie was part of that young girl's
ingenuous character. I don't mean she was
insane but nobody in their right mind would do
what she did. But when at last she and Charlie
were together again with their child her dream
finally shattered and became reality. Tim found
her like that and put her together again. I was
aware of their growing attachment, and, I think,
so were you.'

He lifted her chin and looked into her
woebegone face. She nodded then collapsed in a
torrent of tears against his shoulder.

'We must go down and speak to our friends;
yes, they are servants but they have been friends
to us.'

★ ★ ★

315

Charlie and Will had gone off somewhere riding Pixie and Molly and had they been there they would have been more than distressed, at least Will would, so while they were absent Harry gathered the servants into the kitchen at Beechworth where they were crammed like sardines in a tin. Dolly and Nessie were huddled in their own special chairs in which nobody else was allowed to sit, with their scullery-maid, Polly standing behind them. Harry had sent a message to Summer Place asking Mrs Philips to come with the rest of the staff. She was mostly in charge of the household since young Mrs Summers had taken little interest in running it as a wife should. In her previous employment she had had daily discussions in the drawing room with the mistress of the house on menus for the day and the ordering of groceries and other foodstuffs. But Mrs Summers, Mr Charlie's wife, had carelessly told Mrs Philips to do 'what she thought best' which Mrs Philips had tried to do to the best of her considerable abilities. She had three house-maids, Maggie, Mary who was not actually a housemaid since she did the laundry (and Beechworth's as well since the death of Bertha) and Martha. Summer Place was a much bigger house than Beechworth but had fewer servants.

These, though bewildered, walked across to Beechworth, wondering whether they should have changed into their 'best' but Sir Harry had said at once so here was Mrs Philips still wearing

316

her capacious white apron and Martha with her comical ballooning maid-of-all works cap hovering about Dolly and Nessie, their expressions asking what the dickens this was all about. And squashed against the far wall and on the doorstep were the men — servants from the two houses: Eddie and Ned who were stable lads, Tom and Jossy and Mr Ambrose from Summer Place who tended the gardens, longing to smoke their pipes, lifting their caps and scratching their perplexed heads.

Sir Harry and Lady Summers, looking drawn, but steadfast, Lady Summers biting her lip, stood at the head of the table, shoulder to shoulder.

Sir Harry spoke.

'You will all be wondering why you have been summoned, all of you who work in these two houses of ours so to set your minds at rest let me first say no one will be dismissed.' He smiled, or rather grinned and looked so like his brother as he once had been, they all relaxed and smiled too.

'I'm not sure how much you have heard about . . . about . . . ' His face clouded and his wife rested her head momentarily on his shoulder. He bent his head and placed a kiss on her bright hair.

'Well, Mr Tim, Tim Elliott, has left us and taken' — here he was seen to gulp — 'our Miss Alice with him.' There was a concentrated gasp and appalled glances were exchanged and Polly began to cry. Maggie put her arms about her.

'So the plan is this, Rose, my wife'

— twinkling down at her for a moment and they all smiled, even Polly through her tears — 'and I are to live at Summer Place and you are all to come with us.'

Another gasp and a great deal of shuffling of feet among the men. Tom took off his cap and turned it round and round between his big, work-scarred hands. His weather-beaten face took on a truculent expression but when Nessie, who had been told earlier about the plan, stood up from her chair and shot over to him, taking his hands between hers, he calmed down.

'I know this will be an important decision for you all to make though you will be doing the same jobs but in a different place. Dolly and Nessie have agreed to work part-time under Mrs Philips who will be in charge and the maidservants' — smiling his engaging smile at them — 'will continue as they do here. There are many more rooms at Summer Place than Beechworth so more household staff will be taken on and you will all get a rise in your wages. Summer Place gardens and surrounds really need at least three more gardeners to bring them back to what they were, so Tom and Jossy with others we will employ will take over with Tom as head gardener. Mr Ambrose has indicated he wishes to retire and a cottage is waiting for him and his wife.' He nodded at the white-haired old gardener who had loyally tried to keep up the Summer Place grounds without any help. 'The stables which at the moment house Corey, my stallion, will easily take Pixie, Molly and Foxy.'

Sir Harry continued. 'There is plenty of room

for all of us, people and animals, so, after some refurbishments to the house, we will move in September. Now then, has anyone anything to say?'

He looked about the kitchen at the puzzled faces of his and Beechworth servants who, he realised, were bowled over and, naturally, worried about their plans. After much clearing of throats and exchanging overwhelmed glances, Tom spoke at last.

'Er, what's ter 'appen ter Beechworth, sir? I've got a grand bed of asparagus waitin' ter be picked . . . '

'Me an' Tom 'ave allus 'ad us cottage to usselves.' In their anxiety Nessie, as Dolly had done, reverted to the broad Lancashire accent she had almost lost.

Harry held up his hands. 'Married couples will have their own places. Nessie and Tom, you will have first pick of the empty cottages and Tom, you will design and plant whatever you care to in the grounds and take care of the woodlands with the other gardeners. We will employ a game-keeper for the moorland and between you you will be in charge of outdoors and any more men you think are necessary. And as for Beechworth itself . . . '

They all turned to Rose, for this was her home after all. 'We are to let it as it stands to a respectable, responsible family. Only the house and gardens, of course. The farmland, woodland, moorland will remain with us. Oak Hill Farm, Ashtree and Top Bank will continue in the same hands as our tenants. Beechworth House itself and the gardens surrounding it will be in the hands of whoever rents it on a lease from my wife.'

There was a stunned silence, no one knowing what to say or do but Harry and Rose looked at one another with the feeling that on the whole the news and the plans for the future had been well received.

'Let me just say that if any one of you is not satisfied with the new arrangements they are perfectly at liberty to leave and go elsewhere with a good reference and a month's wages. Now, Lady Summers and myself will be in the estate office until lunchtime so feel free to seek us out with any queries. And' — here he paused, his face as kind and gentlemanly as he had always been — 'we sincerely hope that none of you will leave us. You are part of our family. All of you.' He turned to his wife. 'Now, no tears, my love,' and led her from the room.

★ ★ ★

No one came. The younger members of staff were excited, thrilled with anything new as the young usually are, and talked of nothing else for days to come. Nessie and Tom inspected one of the little cottages to the rear of Summer Place and agreed it was quite as good as the one they lived in at Beechworth. In fact it was bigger with a stillroom where Nessie could 'mess about' as Tom called it with her herbs and plants from which she made up her homely remedies for coughs and colds, boils and scratches, minor ailments with which the servants trusted her.

The maidservants were invited to inspect the servants' quarters where, to their delight, they were all to have a room each and with great enthusiasm they began to pack their belongings in preparation for the move.

Beechworth, which had had more money spent on it in the past than Summer Place, had a bigger, more modern kitchen so Lady Summers with Dolly, Nessie and Mrs Philips having their say, began to put into place her plans for a brand-new, up-to-date kitchen at Summer Place.

Everyone was happy, except Will!

He stood with his rosy mouth hanging open when he was told that in future everyone would live at Summer Place. It was not that he disliked the Beechworth servants, he said, but he and Tim had built a tree-house on the edge of the wood nearest to Beechworth and they had all their treasures there. And anyway, where *was* Tim? Will hadn't seen him for weeks, exaggerating as children do, and he demanded to be told where his friend was. He and Charlie had good times, eyeing his own father with a disdainful, airy look, but Tim was his bestest friend and wherever was he, implying that he believed they had hidden him away somewhere.

'You can't let someone else live at Beechworth, Harry,' he said patiently.

He glared round at the circle of grown-ups as if he couldn't believe their stupidity. He stamped his foot and Dolly put her hand to her mouth in distress. Nessie, Rose, Harry and Charlie stood or sat about the kitchen, which already had signs that a move was to be made. Bright copper pans were stacked on the table and boxes containing packets of tea, sugar, flour, all dry goods in the one box, were strewn about. Jars held the results of pear-bottling, jam-making. Dolly and Nessie's chairs would be the last to go. Over at Summer Place hordes of workmen were getting ready to build in the modern kitchen which the older servants such as Dolly and Nessie were rather dreading and to which the younger ones were eagerly looking forward. Hot running water from an independent domestic boiler, a gas cooker, streamlined cupboards on the walls, tall ones used as larders, smaller ones for general storage. They would, of course, retain the butler's pantry, the stillroom and the wine cellar. The room was half-tiled and painted white to give a feeling of airiness, and had a cork floor for easy cleaning, a kitchen cabinet instead of an old dresser on which to stand glass storage jars.

Will was concerned with none of this. He would tell everyone to stay here. Dolly would look after him, he yelled, running to put an arm round Dolly's shoulder. She patted him and shushed him and wept quietly for the frightened child. She could not bear to see the little lad upset so she looked hopefully at Rose, despite knowing it was no good.

'Well, you see, lovey, we can't stay here. Another family is ter stay at Beechworth so — '

'What!' Will roared. 'In our house? Don't be 'diculous, Dolly. This is Rose's house, our house and nobody else is going to come and live here. I don't want to leave here until Tim comes back and if they come and try to — '

'Tim's not going back,' a voice from the far end of the kitchen said. A soft, apologetic voice, hesitant and sad. 'He's gone away, old chap.'

They all, as one, turned to Charlie who was leaning against the wall. Dolly grasped Will more firmly, trying her best to get him on to her lap but he escaped her loving arms and flew across the kitchen, ready, it appeared, to thump Charlie with his small fists, shouting, 'No, no, no, no,' but Charlie caught him, held him close and stroked his dark curls.

'You've still got me, Will,' he said humbly.

'I don't want you! Want Tim. Stay here . . . '

It took over an hour to calm the small, distraught boy and then only because Rose slipped a soothing powder into the milk he consented to drink. When he was finally in a deep sleep in his bed there were more than a few tears shed in Beechworth House.

21

Charlie and Will crouched between the huge, tangled roots of an oak tree in the woodland at the back of Summer Place. They were two small boys, despite one being twenty-five years older than the other. They were watching a squirrel, a beautiful red squirrel struggling across the clearing with an acorn between its small paws.

It was October and the woodland trees were fast losing their leaves which lay in a soggy carpet across the clearing. There had been a lot of rain in the last few weeks and a pool had formed in its centre across which bright golden rays of sunlight fell. The squirrel delicately skirted the pool, careful not to drop the acorn which, Charlie whispered in Will's ear, it would add to its hoard for the coming winter, and the two *lads*, as Dolly called them, remained very still in order not to disturb the wildlife. Reflected in the water of the pool were the misted shapes of beech and oak trees and now and again a shrivelled russet leaf spiralled slowly from branch to ground. Beyond the oak wood lay a swathe of conifers and in the space where they had been cut on the orders of the new gamekeeper at Summer Place, grew grasses, bracken and wild flowers. Charlie told Will that at Christmas they would choose one of the conifers to take home and place in the wide hallway or the drawing room and decorate it with candles, coloured baubles and on the very top would be an angel. It was something that lay secretly in his damaged brain. Something from the past that he had suddenly remembered.

It was three months since Tim and Alice had vanished and Rose and Harry had made no attempt to find them. Charlie, since his injury during the war, had imperceptibly slowed down. Not only in his mind and whatever memories — if any — he had but in his speech and his movements. They had all learned to wait patiently as he trawled from deep within himself an answer to a question. His physical health was good. He ate all Mrs Philips's superbly cooked food that was set before him and was strong and bronzed, spending all his time outdoors with his growing son. He had not at first recognised the boy as his but he now loved him just the same and all he remembered as a boy about his surroundings, about the wildlife that teemed on the hundreds of acres was passed on to Will. Beechworth estate, added on to Summer Place, was an ideal and vast school in which teacher and pupil ranged.

But the boy's education must include more than outdoor pursuits since Will was five years old. Though he could stumble through young children's books, thanks to Rose, and add one number to another up to twenty, thanks, strangely, to the vanished Tim, he needed more than that to progress in the world and make a career for himself. Harry wanted to send him to the same public school that he and Charlie had attended.

When it became apparent that Alice had gone for good and Charlie was in no state to decide what his son should do, it was up to Rose and Harry to see he received a good grounding in basic subjects in order for him to be accepted into a preparatory school, perhaps later go on to university. And so a tutor must be found for him.

But where to start? Again, like Tim, the tutor was one of the army of ex-servicemen, who still tramped this country fit for heroes, in which they all were, looking for work. Mark Newton, Sergeant Mark Newton, aged thirty-five, was at the back of the queue even of these unfortunates because he had lost a leg in the last month of the war and, since he was forced to walk miles every day, it was not healing as it should. He was clever, well educated and had the added attribute of having been a teacher before the war. Those who did need a labourer, a gardener, an odd-job man, would not however employ a man with only one leg. His wife and children had lost their lives in an air raid, killed when a bomb dropped from a Zeppelin on to their home. He was a sad man, numbed by what had happened to him and was on the point of doing away with himself when he knocked on the back door of Summer Place.

Harry said he would give him a try. As children are, Will was fascinated with anything unusual, even gruesome, and was won over at once when Sergeant Mark, as he was for ever to be called, showed him his half-healed stump which had been amputated just above the knee where shrapnel had sliced it. He explained to

Will — and the horrified maidservants who watched — how the prosthesis was removed, fastened back on and the workings of what would have been his own knee. He walked with Will, ran with him and even played kick-ball though it caused him agony.

Harry had been impressed by his patience with the child and, more importantly, how he held Will's interest during his month's trial. Knowing Will's stubborn nature, his absolute refusal to stay in one place for any length of time, his wilfulness and defiance of authority, Harry saw that Sergeant Mark seemed to have a knack of controlling the boy and keeping him every morning for three hours.

'Did you know that Sergeant Mark's grandfather was at the well at Cawnpore? That's in India by the way.' Their horrified faces were frozen round the kitchen. 'It was filled, the well, I mean, with dead ladies and children. The Indians did it.'

'Will,' gasped Rose but Harry silenced her and later told her that most little boys were bloodthirsty monsters but grew out of it and though it was a terrible time in British history — his own grandfather had fought there — Mark had taught Will not only history, but geography too. He had captured the boy's interest and gradually the pair of them spent their three hours without recourse to such horrors as the Indian Mutiny.

'Are you cold, Rose?' Will asked her on one occasion. It was a bitter winter afternoon after he and Charlie had been out on one of their forays, riding this time, and were drinking hot chocolate in the kitchen. 'Shall I *fermer la fenêtre, madame?*' then turned and beamed.

'I didn't know you spoke French, darling,' Rose said, trying to keep the tremor of laughter out of her voice.

'*Mais oui.* Mark taught me, an' me an' Charlie often '*parlez*', don't we, Charlie?'

They all waited for Charlie to answer. It took nearly a minute but they had become accustomed to him.

He smiled his slow, sweet smile. '*Mais oui, bien sûr.*'

'There,' said Will triumphantly and Rose thanked the gods who, in the guise of Mark Newton, had sent this blessing on them. Between them, Charlie and Mark, both damaged themselves, were turning this little savage, as he once had been, into a cheerful, normal child. He still had his tantrums, of course, but usually a word from Mark calmed him down.

The servants had settled into their new places. Tom, Jossy and Wilbur — one more of the army's tramping outcasts and who was the new gardener's boy — were preparing the three acres of garden for the coming spring, Tom tutting over the neglect of a once splendid garden. Harry and Charlie's grandmother had been a keen amateur gardener and the polite and genteel society in which she and the then Sir Walter Summers had mixed had been delighted to receive invitations to their home and beautiful gardens. There had been garden parties, tennis parties, shooting parties, all gone now but the present owner and his hugely pregnant wife were determined to restore it to its former glory, thanks to the wealth Lady Summers had brought to the marriage.

Indoors Dolly and Nessie were happy to take tea in the housekeeper's sitting room while Mrs Philips, who was a good deal younger, supervised her half a dozen maidservants and trained up a new kitchen maid by the name of Peggy, turning out splendid meals with a little help — when they felt up to it — from Dolly and Nessie. It was grand, Dolly confessed to Nessie — since she had begun to feel her age — to sit back but be there if their combined experience was needed. All the girls slept at the top of the house in their newly decorated rooms, one to each room and the men, except Tom who shared a cottage with his Nessie, were housed in the comfortable and perfectly adequate rooms above the stable block.

Only Mark had his own room in the house. At each of the four corners of Summer Place was a turret reached by a winding staircase and in one of them he slept and kept the endless books he bought with his own more than adequate salary. He was a reclusive man and could it be wondered at, Rose said to Harry as she fidgeted in their bed, doing her best to find a comfortable position with the burden she carried. Harry fidgeted with her, doing *his* best to help her since she was very near her time. So near that when Harry was fast asleep she clasped his arm in such a relentless grip she nearly pushed him out of bed.

'What the devil . . . ' he spluttered, but was alert at once, for Rose had heaved herself on to her feet and begun to roam about the room.

'The baby?' he asked tentatively.

'Of course it's the baby, you great idiot.'

'What shall I do?'

'Oh, for God's sake, go and get Dolly.'

'Wouldn't you rather lie down, my darling?' Harry was pulling on his quilted dressing gown, bought for him by his wife at Christmas.

'No, I wouldn't so stop arguing,' she snapped, leaning over the dressing table, her hands gripping the edge as she communed with the pain.

'Right, I'll be off then,' as though he were to take a trip to China.

'And be damn quick about it, Harry Summers. I don't think I'll be long.'

'Shall I stay then?'

'Can you deliver a baby?' gasping as she was gripped again.

A look of horror came over his face. 'No, I bloody can't.' And with a last despairing look at his wife's bowed back, he shot out of the door shouting Dolly's name and waking every last one of the residents except Will who, Dolly said, wouldn't wake up if a brass band marched through his room.

'Goddammit,' Rose hissed through clenched teeth, 'he'll have the lot of them in here if he doesn't calm down.'

But Dolly and Nessie soon had it all sorted out. Dolly was in her element. Hadn't she delivered — well, helped — the very woman who

330

was now to give birth herself?

'I'm here, my lovely lass, and this lot are to go back to their rooms. Sir Harry's on the landing asking every two minutes; he's telephoned the doctor. A new fellow, it seems, who says he's an expert in obstetrics, whatever they are. He's — no, not the doctor — Sir Harry is a damn nuisance like all men. The doctor's called Dr Standish; he'll be here soon. See, take Dolly's arm, pet.' The two of them sauntered about the room as though they were in a sun-lit garden while Nessie got the bed ready with old sheets and towels and an old nightgown was put on Rose and when suddenly she expressed a desire to lie down they helped her gently on to the bed. They paused each time she hung her head and communed with the pain. They were both women who had never borne a child but they had helped in many a confinement on the estate. When the labouring mother was tranquil they moved about the room, then suddenly Rose screamed and bore down upon the pain and collapsed on the bed.

Maggie entered the room with a kettle of hot water, some scissors and a piece of twine, glancing sympathetically at her mistress as she struggled on the bed.

'Don't hold it in, lass, let it go.' They threw the covers off her and opened her legs just as Dr Standish came into the room.

'Ah, good, nearly there, I see,' he remarked cheerfully as a wet auburn crown appeared between Rose's legs, followed by a screwed-up face which at once began to yell with displeasure; then the infant bounded on to the bed in a trickle of blood.

'First the afterbirth then,' as he cut the cord, 'you shall hold your daughter in your arms.' He turned irritably. 'No, sir, you can't come in just yet.'

'Try and stop me,' roared Harry, hurtling across the room, pushing the doctor and Dolly — who couldn't wait to get her hands on the baby — both aside. 'My darling, my darling, my two darlings,' wrapping his arms about his wife and daughter.

Dolly and Nessie faltered at the back of Harry while the doctor disappeared into the adjoining bathroom. When he came out, wiping his hands and forearms on a snowy white towel, he told them that the infant needed bathing and again there was a tussle over who should be the one to do it. Maggie, who had been loitering at the door, flew down the stairs shouting as she went, 'It's a girl, it's a girl,' then they all went mad with joy, for at last this house that had known such sadness was filled with happiness. A mere house and hospital had been transformed into a family home as it had been before the war.

The two elderly women argued as they shuffled into the bathroom. The doctor had gone after putting a couple of stitches in Rose's torn flesh, which she endured with no more than a flinch then Rose and Harry smiled at one another. They cuddled up together, Rose propped up on a stack of pillows, listening to the argument coming from the bathroom, Harry with his head on Rose's shoulder.

'It seems our daughter is no longer ours, my love.'

'Never mind, sweetheart, we might be glad of them during the night.'

'I suppose so. God, I could drop off this very minute. It's hard work being a father.'

She laughed. 'I suppose we should think of a name, my darling.' She hesitated. 'I would have liked to call her Alice but that's out of the question.'

'It is, dearest. We have lost Alice for ever, I'm afraid, but isn't there something else that would be suitable?'

They were peaceful together, listening to the now soft voices from the bathroom. Splashes and whispering and cooing from the two women and in the garden Tom and Jossy were slapping one another on the back as if they had just given birth, watched by a bemused Wilbur, who was still new to the household. In the kitchen they were all sipping champagne which Sir Harry had ordered. The excitement was intense.

'It must be a name that reminds us all of Alice but not *Alice*.' They were silent then Rose whispered so low that Harry could hardly hear her.

'What did you say, sweetheart?'

'I said . . . I said Poppy. The poppies in which so many died. But if you think it would remind us of the war then . . . '

'I don't think we should ever forget it, Rose. It reminds us of those who are lost. Charlie and Alice and so many more who gave their lives.'

In a woodland, unaware of the great 'doings' at home, Charlie and Will sat shoulder to shoulder with their backs against the wide trunk of an ancient oak tree. They were very quiet when they spoke, for they were watching a bird, a robin, Charlie whispered, hovering above a clump of chickweed.

They were totally absorbed, father and son, when two burly men stepped into the clearing. Will frowned and stood up. He was unafraid, for nothing and no one had ever frightened him. He was arrogant in his fearlessness as he spoke. 'What are you doing on Sir Harry's land? This is a private wood and you are trespassing. Tell them, Charlie.'

Charlie got to his feet and some buried instinct told him he must protect young Will since it was evident these rough men were up to no good.

The men laughed and quite casually one of them advanced on Will, picking him up and tucking him under his arm. Will started to yell and kick.

'Put that boy down,' Charlie shouted, his fighting spirit that he had lost in France rising to his damaged mind. He ran forward, ready to tear Will from the thug's arms but the second man aimed a huge fist and smashed it into Charlie's face. He went down like a fallen log and that tiny shard of bone that had worried Dr Westmann all those years ago finally reached a vital spot and killed Charlie without a sound.

'Eeh, what's up wi' 'im?' the first man said uneasily, wrestling with the struggling child, ready to give him a backhander if he didn't shut his gob. He toed Charlie's body with a big steel-capped boot but there was no response. 'We wasn't supposed t'kill bugger.'

By now Will was screaming, calling out Charlie's name, but the man holding him shook him and told him to 'shurrup'.

With one last look at the prone figure lying in a shaft of sunlight that lit his dark curls as though he was already with the angels and wore a halo, they left the glade and sprinted off along a woodland path.

★　★　★

The baby was bathed and had been fed at Rose's magnificent breast, watched by her doting father, and was asleep in the cradle in which both Harry and Charlie and before them several generations of Summers had slept. She lay in perfect peace, her infant needs taken care of, her tiny hand like a pink starfish resting on the satin-edged blanket. Her parents were sharing a delicious meal off a tray beside the bed, for Mrs Philips produced a nourishing clear soup, fresh salmon and vegetables and a splendid tipsy cake. It was almost dark and the lamplight and the firelight were dreamlike as the shadows from them flickered against the wall. They were quiet, the three of them, the man and woman smiling at one another in great content. They had everything they wanted. They had each other, their lovely old home which was being slowly restored and they had their child. What else was there?

They were startled when there was a faint tap on the door. The servants knew better than to disturb the master and mistress, for who knew what state of undress they might be in.

Harry sighed in annoyance and took his hand from Rose's. 'Now what is it?' he asked irritably, opening the door to find Maggie on the other side.

'Yes,' he snapped irritably.

'Yes, sir . . . ' Maggie knew he was not best pleased but she went on bravely. 'I'm that sorry to disturb you, sir, but . . . you see — '

'Yes, yes, get on with it, girl.'

'Well, sir . . . Dolly sent me to . . . ' Maggie faltered.

'What, for God's sake?'

'To see if Master Will was with you; we — '

'Master Will? Of course he's not with us. Shouldn't he be in bed by now? Isn't he — '

'No, sir, that's just it. He's not. We've looked everywhere but we can't find him. Or Mr Charlie,' she said as an afterthought.

'What is it, Harry?' Rose asked from her bed, ready to leap out but Harry shooed Maggie away and shut the door. 'You stay where you are, sweetheart. Don't you dare get out of that bed. It's that rascal Will and my brother. The pair of them have lost track of time and they're off somewhere having what they call, or at least Will does, one of their adventures. I'll go down and find them. Take some of the lads. Don't worry,

336

my love. Stay in your bed and I'll come and tell you when I've found them.'

'But Harry, Charlie's not quite . . . ' Rose was filled somehow with a sense of foreboding but Harry was having none of it.

'I'll give that lad a damn good spanking when we find him. It's about time someone did.' He smiled ruefully. 'Unfortunately I can't spank Charlie. Promise you'll stay with the baby and in your bed. You know what the doctor said. At least two weeks before you can get up.'

'Rubbish,' cried Rose, but she sighed and looked down into the cradle and Harry knew she would do as she was told with her own child. She relaxed on her pillows.

★   ★   ★

The servants were in a right old state of confusion in the kitchen, milling about and telling one another when and where they last saw the lad.

'He had his lunch with us . . . '

'Tucked in like a good 'un . . . '

'Mr Charlie an' all . . . '

'Them dogs was under our feet, wantin' ter get goin' . . . '

'Will you all please calm down,' Sir Harry roared and at last they became quiet. Tom was there waiting for Nessie who would cook them a meal in their own cottage kitchen but the rest of the lads who worked the estate and slept above the stable were over there, ready for a glass of ale and a game of cards.

'Tom.' Sir Harry turned to the gardener.

'Yes, sir.'

'Get the rest of the men and start a search outside,' for by now it was almost fully dark. One small boy and a man with a damaged mind might not be able to find their own way home.

'Yes, sir.'

'And Tom, find out if they were on their horses.' An accident perhaps, they all began to imagine, the women putting their hands to their mouths, for though he was worse than a cartload of monkeys they all loved the little imp. And Mr Charlie was a lovely man, so polite and kind and really only a child himself.

'Have we got those old lamps in the stable? Tom, find out. Or perhaps a torch of some kind.'

Tom was hopping backwards and forwards as his master shouted more instructions to him, hoping he could remember them all. Polly, as was her way, began to cry but a sharp word from Dolly to pull herself together since she might be needed, though none of them could imagine for *what*, staunched the flow of tears.

Harry stepped out into the stable yard where the men waited, Ned, Eddie, Jossy, and even Mark, hobbling on the cobbles on his false leg having heard the hullabaloo, limped to join them. He had not seen Will all day, he told them, it being Saturday and their day off lessons.

Both Charlie's mare Misty and Will's pony Molly were in their stalls so it seemed father and son had gone out on foot. Nessie said she had given them a few of her chocolate buns and a bottle of homemade lemonade because Will had

338

told her they were to have a picnic, 'so they'll not starve' she said as though they had been about to trek across the Sahara Desert.

The sound of the men's voices calling to Will or Charlie could be heard over at Beechworth where the new tenants were just sitting down to dinner.

'Now what's that rascal done?' Edward Atkinson asked his wife. They had been plagued a couple of times by Master Will who could not seem to get it into his child's head that Beechworth was no longer his home and thought he had a perfect right to go there when he pleased.

'Goodness knows,' said Mrs Atkinson. 'He's a real imp.'

The men thrashed about in the stand of trees at the back of Summer Place, venturing out on to the moorland where Sir Harry was rearing his game but got no answer. The were tired after a full day's work and hours of blundering about in the dark wood.

Harry would not let them give up and really neither did they want to. They even peered up into the branches of the sturdy oak trees because Master Will had told them about his tree-house.

It was nearly midnight when they found him. He was lying at the edge of a small glade, his head on a clump of moss, his eyes still wide open. Mr Charlie, dear Mr Charlie who had been loved and admired by them all. Sweet-natured, generous, kind and ready to do anything for anybody.

Not asleep. No, they soon realised, not asleep,

but dead and no sign of Master Will. Harry gently turned Charlie's head, and there was a concerted gasp from the men at the sight of his face. His nose was obviously shattered and bruises had begun to form beneath his eyes.

'Jesus, Mary and Joseph,' whispered Billy who was a Catholic. He crossed himself reverently.

Their master fell to his knees beside his broken brother and seemed ready to weep, as did they all, wondering how they were to tell the womenfolk who loved him, that Mr Charlie was dead and Master Will had disappeared off the face of the earth. Who in hell's name had done this to him, to a man who wouldn't hurt a bloody fly?

22

She was in the kitchen with the rest of the women, her hours-old daughter in her arms when they returned, carrying Charlie's body on a makeshift stretcher made from jackets and stout branches.

'Oh, Jesus Christ and all His angels,' cried Dolly, her hand to her mouth.

She had been doing her best to coax Rose back to her bed. 'It does no good, hanging about 'ere, lass. It won't bring them back any sooner. See, your milk'll dry up if you're not careful an' what will poor babby do then, bless 'er. Sir Harry'll find them tinkers an' fetch them home, you'll see an' — '

When the silent procession carried the improvised stretcher over the doorstep with Charlie's lifeless body on it, Rose began to wail and so did the baby.

'Take my wife to her room, Dolly,' Harry said sternly.

'Dear God in heaven, haven't I bin trying to do just that for the last hour, sir, but . . . Oh, dear Mother of God, what's bin done to Mr Charlie?' staring at his still body and battered face. 'Lad's black an' blue. Who did this?'

She flapped about, tears steaming down her wrinkled old face and in seconds all the women were crying, clinging to one another in horror and distress while the men just stood there with

341

their burden, faces grim, bodies rigid.

'Clear the table someone,' Harry snapped, and as one they rushed forward, taking everything, pots, pans, cutlery, placing them anywhere out of the way.

'Put him on . . . on . . . ' Harry ordered the men and gently, with great respect and care, they laid Charlie on the table.

'It should've bin wiped over first,' Nessie moaned. 'I . . . I were baking; there's flour on it.'

'Charlie won't mind, Nessie.' And before them all Harry flopped down into a chair, put his face in his hands and began to shake with sorrow.

At once Rose thrust her newborn infant into the nearest arms, which happened to be Jossy's. He held her tenderly until Maggie took her from him. Rose knelt at her husband's knee, putting her arms about him. He clung to her and nobody spoke.

Then, 'Who did this to him and why?' Harry wept. 'Look at his face.'

They all looked and turned hastily away, appalled. By now Charlie's face was one whole bruise. Both lovely silvery grey eyes were wide open and unfocused, his nose flattened.

'Close his eyes someone,' Harry said harshly, his face buried in his wife's shoulder. His daughter was yelling her head off by now but no one bothered. Maggie rocked her and shushed her, and it was Tom who gently closed Charlie's eyes, his own blurred with tears.

For several minutes everyone wept, or cursed until Maggie said, 'And where's our Will?'

In the shock and horror they had momentarily

forgotten Will but now they all turned to look in consternation at one another.

'Oh please,' moaned Rose, 'not Will as well. He was with Charlie. He was always with Charlie and he's not come home.'

Harry stood up abruptly, almost knocking Rose to the floor. He helped her up and took her in his arms. 'You're right, my love. We must all go out again and look for Will but you must telephone the police and the doctor and then promise me you and the baby will go back to bed.' He turned to Dolly. 'See that she does, Dolly. The baby's not even a day old yet and — '

'Don't order me, Harry. I just can't go and lie tamely in bed with . . . with . . . ' Rose's face was awash with tears. 'Not with Charlie . . . Charlie dead — killed obviously — and Will missing. I must feed the baby,' whose yells of rage were deafening. 'She needs feeding and I can do that sitting here in Dolly's chair but Charlie . . . surely he should be laid somewhere more comfortable than . . . '

'Charlie doesn't care now, my darling,' bringing fresh sobbing from the women, 'about comfort, I mean.'

'I meant more . . . more fitting.'

'Yes, of course, but please do the telephoning first' — for he knew none of the staff was capable of operating the machine — 'and then promise me to sit by the fire and attend to our child.'

'Poor little mite,' sobbed Nessie and Dolly accompanied her.

The men respectfully returned Charlie on to the stretcher and looked at Sir Harry waiting to be told where he was to be put.

'Dolly, Nessie, which … which bedroom should he be … ' Harry was clearly in such a state the two older women shook their heads in sympathy.

'The front bedroom would be best, sir. If the lads'll carry him up we'll see to him. You get off.'

When the men returned from their task of laying the peaceful figure of his much loved brother on the bed in the splendour of the front bedroom they went out into the yard, taking the stretcher with them, forming a group in the stable yard, waiting to be told where they were to go.

Harry, having seen Rose sitting by the fire with her hungry daughter at her breast, decided to do the telephoning himself, then moved to join the men.

'Tom,' who was older than the rest seemed to be the man to be most trusted. 'I want you to go to Primrose Cottages and then to all the farms and fetch the men to help with the search.' He knew that Will was familiar with every inch of the gardens, the woodland and the immediate moorland. He couldn't understand why the boy should run off from Charlie but perhaps the brutal attack on the man he knew only as his friend had so frightened him he had taken off in terror, but in which direction? The terrible fear that flowed through Harry's mind was that the small boy had been taken for the underground sex trade that went on in every major city. It caused an icy shudder to race through his frame. Small girls and boys — for little boys were sometimes to the taste of foul perverts — would be taken to some place where they would be sold to the highest bidder. He though he might vomit at the images that scurried through his mind like rats in a sewer.

The thought crucified him but he revealed it to none of the men. These were decent, ignorant men, country men born and bred who had no notion of the wicked ways of the world.

For the remainder of the night the weary men searched the estate, eager to help. There was no trace of the scamp; exasperating as he was, he was held dear in every man's heart.

Dolly and Nessie had laid Charlie out and they awaited the arrival of the undertakers. The inspector of police came, since these were important people in this parish and two constables interviewed every man and woman on the estate, terribly embarrassed by Lady Summers who was by this time in her bed to which the doctor had implacably ordered her. As sunrise came and the men returned, one by one they too were devastated and so distressed there was a great deal of sniffing and surreptitious wiping of eyes on sleeves. They stood about in little groups feeling that they should be doing more.

'Go home, lads, and thank you. We can do no more for the present,' Sir Harry told them. 'You must be bone weary. I know I am but the inspector and all his constables will widen the search.'

What the bloody hell could the coppers do that they had not already done? Nobody knew these grounds better than them who had lived here since they were born, some of them. They had peered under every fallen leaf and broken branch but they did as their master bade them and went home to their anxious wives, those who had them, inclined to keep their own children in their cottages or gardens.

'Don't go out o' sight, d'yer hear?' the bewildered children were told, their parents terrified that whoever had taken young Will might help himself to one of theirs.

* * *

A small boy with tear-stained cheeks sat numbly at a table in a plainly furnished room. The walls were painted a dark green up to the dado and above that a sort of dull mushroom shade. The table at which he sat was round and covered with a deep maroon chenille tablecloth and on the table lay several books. Opposite the child was a grey woman! Grey hair, stony grey eyes, in a grey skirt and blouse, a mouth like a parrot and an expression that boded ill for anyone who was foolish enough to try to cross her. She held a ruler in her hand which the boy eyed apprehensively.

'Please can I go home now?' he whispered with a tremble in his voice as though the less noise he made might keep the woman from hitting him. He was to be disappointed. The ruler came into play, lashing across the table and striking his fingers. He cried out and got another crack across his knuckles.

'How dare you,' the woman snapped. 'Speak when you are spoken to, boy. Remember that.'

The boy began to cry desolately but the woman was unmoved.

'Stop that noise at once, boy.'

The child did his best but could not control his deep distress.

'Boy, if you don't stop that snivelling you shall have a beating that will not be pleasant. Now, open your book and read the first line on the first page. *Now, at once.*' The woman did not speak loudly this time but with hissing venom that terrified the child even more. He looked ready to break down completely. The woman sprang to her feet, moved round the table and took the boy's ear in pinching fingers and dragged him to his feet. He was paralysed in his terror and the woman smiled triumphantly.

Just at that moment a large, stout, red-faced man entered the room. At once the woman detached her fingers from the small boy's ear and smiled at the man.

'Good morning, sir,' she said unctuously. 'We were just about to read from our book but I'm afraid the boy is behaving with a quite unnecessary show of what I can only call a tantrum. Though great progress has been made in controlling his intransigence he is still inclined to cry for nothing more than a slap with the ruler. But' — here she simpered — 'I think we can congratulate ourselves his first wilfulness is slowly being driven out. He should be just as you want him to be very soon.'

The man looked at the child who looked at

nothing, his eyes quite unfocused.

'Well, he certainly has quietened down since he was brought here. We can't have that kicking and screaming when he is fully brought into company. You've done a good job, Miss Evans. I congratulate you.'

'Thank you, sir. I do my best with the children in my care and might I say this one was very hard to tame. He must once have been allowed his own way in everything. It really is unbelievable the way parents bring their children up these — '

'Yes, yes,' the man said irritably, 'but this boy must be able to mix in good society, Miss Evans, and the ways of good society must be drummed into him if he is to succeed when you have finished teaching him how to behave.'

'And I shall, sir. His spirit must be knocked out of him first, broken, if you like, so that we might start from scratch, so to speak. I've had him for three months and still occasionally he defies me, but we are making good progress.'

'Yes,' the man said, eyeing somewhat doubtfully the crumpled figure of the child who sat dejectedly on his chair by the table and showed no sign of becoming the boy he wanted him to be. A boy to be proud, to carry on the name that was rightfully his.

'Well, I'll leave you to it then. Perhaps he could be allowed to come down and take luncheon with me. You have taught him manners, the correct way to behave in company as well as to read and write but he seems . . . '

He nearly said *elevenpence-half-penny in the*

shilling which he had heard used to describe those who were backward.

'Oh no, not yet, sir. He's not ready for that,' the woman said positively, for she did not want to lose this position which suited her down to the ground. Extremely well paid and she had only to whip this bonehead of a child to become the person the man wished him to be. An easy task for her who hated children. A comfortable room of her own, servants to wait on her, the best food she had ever eaten. Oh, no, she meant to make this job last as long as she could. She herself had come from a strict, even cruel upbringing which had made her as she was. To torment this small being who could not defend himself awoke the grisly, unnameable thing that had spread its tentacles through her. She was warped, twisted and her impulses were to crush this young child almost to breaking point.

When the man left the room she smiled silkily. 'Now then, where were we?' rapping his knuckles when he failed to answer.

★ ★ ★

Poppy Summers was three months old when the inspector rang the doorbell of Summer Place. Martha, who been made up to parlour-maid, answered the door, smiling and bobbing a curtsey to the inspector of police who stood on the threshold.

'Good morning, sir,' she said politely, opening the door wide for him to enter.

'Good morning, miss. Is your master available? I'd like a word with him, if you please.' A straight-backed, smart man was the inspector in his immaculate uniform. He removed his shako helmet and tucked it under his arm, waiting patiently while the parlour-maid went to enquire if the master was in.

Harry Summers fairly sprinted from his office to the hallway where the inspector stood, hoping for good news but when he and the inspector faced one another he could tell by the man's expression that there was nothing to report. No good news, no bad news. Even as he shook the inspector's hand the man was shaking his head sadly.

Still! 'Is there any news, Inspector?' he asked, knowing the answer.

'No, sir, I'm sorry. Can we go somewhere private?' eyeing Martha who still hung about hoping to have something to tell those in the kitchen.

Harry led the inspector to his office, the estate office and asked him politely to sit, enquiring if he would like a drink, perhaps coffee, or perhaps something stronger. There was no hurry since it seemed the inspector had nothing to say on the whereabouts of Will Summers.

Only this!

'No, no, Sir Harry, nothing to drink, thank you.' He shifted uncomfortably on his chair. 'Only this. I'm afraid the search for your nephew is . . . I have been given orders to end it. My men and constables from other constabularies have searched every inch of Lancashire and Liverpool,

350

knocking on doors — you know what I mean. We have even gone as far as London where children . . . er, stolen children are often taken but have come up with nothing. For three months we have investigated every lead given to us, not only by members of the public but by known offenders. I'm sorry, sir, I know what an anxious time — '

Harry exploded, springing from his chair behind his desk. 'Anxious, *anxious*! Good God, man, a child of five years has vanished off the face of the earth. We are frantic, Inspector, frantic.'

For a moment he had lost his composure, pushing a hand through his already unruly mass of hair, rubbing his face harshly, afraid he would break down in tears. The lovely child, a little tearaway at times, exasperating, wilful, cheerful, loving, loved by them all, had been taken from them and they could hardly bear it . . .

'I'm sorry, Sir Harry. I can't tell you how sorry I am. I have children of my own and can sympathise — '

'I don't think you can, Inspector.' Harry had pulled himself together. 'I'm sorry, it was unforgivable of me to . . . to . . . '

The inspector stood up and the two men faced each other then Harry turned to ring the bell. Martha came running, her face bright with hope but at the sight of her master the hope disappeared and tears formed in her eyes.

'Show the inspector out, Martha,' Sir Harry ordered, then turned his back on them both, staring out into the spring garden. A garden vivid with colour. The lawn was a smooth green, watered each day by the conscientious Jossy. Masses of wild daffodils sprang up across the lawn down to the small lake. Below the trees the lovely blue of periwinkle was spreading, jostling with primrose, and the flowerbeds were a blaze of tulips, lily tulips in scarlet, parrot tulips, striped pink and white. The garden took your breath away with its beauty, and was a credit to Tom and his band of men, most of them ex-soldiers.

Sir Harry Summers saw none of this, his heart breaking as he wondered how he was to tell his wife of the inspector's visit and the news — no news really — on the fate of the small boy who at five years old was either in the hands of some wicked men, or dead!

Turning wearily, he made for the stairs, climbing them like an old man, then entered the nursery where his three-month-old daughter was already doing her best to sit up. She was in the old cradle used by both he and Charlie as infants, lying on her back, her plump legs waving in the air. She grabbed at one foot and did her best to bring it to her mouth. Rose watched her, her happiness with her child etched on her lovely, serene face. She turned as her husband entered but at the sight of his face her happiness, her momentary serenity slipped away, leaving her expression drained and fearful.

'Harry, darling, what . . . ?'

He knelt beside her, then leaned forward to pull her into his arms.

'My love, my dearest love.'

Her voice rose to fever pitch. 'What is it? What

is it?' she almost screamed and the baby turned her head in her mother's direction and the sunny smile that wreathed her face disappeared and she began to wail.

'It's . . . it's Will.'

'Not dead, please say he's not dead,' she implored him.

Into Harry's fevered mind slithered the thought that perhaps it would be better if he was. The alternative crucified him.

'No, darling heart. At least we don't know, but the inspector has just been to say, after all this time they are . . . calling off the search.'

Rose fell into his arms, the pair of them huddled on the floor while the baby's cries reached the kitchen. Dolly listened to it for several minutes, exchanging glances with Nessie. It was not like their mistress, or the master for that matter, to let the little pet cry so long.

'I'm going up,' Dolly declared stoutly while the housemaids stood about, white-faced, knowing something had happened. The inspector had been and now their precious little bairn was screaming her head off and no one taking a blind bit of notice. Polly began to cry.

'Oh, give over do, girl,' Nessie snapped though she felt like having a good cry herself.

Dolly knocked sharply on the bedroom door, the bedroom where Miss Rose — as she still felt the need to call her — and Sir Harry slept, and without waiting for an answer opened the door and marched in. She was startled to see Miss Rose and Sir Harry on the floor, arms about one another while the baby wailed and so did Miss Rose.

'Well . . . ' expostulated Dolly, embarrassed and maddened beyond words. The master and mistress 'at it', for she knew no other word for what they were doing, while the bairn cried her little heart out. But . . . but Miss Rose was in a torrent of tears and Sir Harry looked not far from it.

'Oh, Dolly . . . Dolly,' wept Miss Rose. 'Our little boy is . . . '

Dolly put her hand to her mouth and whispered the same words as Rose had done a few minutes ago.

'Not dead . . . eeh, don't say he's dead, Rosie. I couldn't stand it. Not that beautiful boy.' She broke into a wail of sorrow and out on the landing the female servants who had, knowing something bad was happening, followed her up and gathered behind her, began to weep.

Nessie swept into the bedroom and snatched the distressed, hiccuping baby from her cradle, rocking her in trembling arms.

Suddenly it was all silent as everyone realised they might never see their handsome, winsome, lovable boy again. Their hearts were breaking.

23

They all mourned the boy who had played such a big part in their lives. Dolly and Nessie, the older generation, still wore the black they had donned for Mr Charlie's funeral and it was only the baby, darling of their hearts, who kept them going.

Harry, begged by Rose, who was a wealthy woman, employed private detectives, unaware that Sergeant Mark Newton, who had been unable to keep up with the rest in the search that night, and now had no job with Will gone, kept up his own search. He had become fond of the boy who was bright, receptive and lovable but the other men were inclined to ignore him. What good could a man with one leg be, they asked one another, but not in an unkindly way. He was a nice chap but didn't know the area like they did.

As though to mock their sadness the spring was the most beautiful any of them could remember. Yellow iris crowded beneath the newly greening trees and along the hedgerows that lined the lanes. Harebells spread handfuls of pale blue mist and wood anemones peeped shyly from behind the fallen trunks of oak and beech. Celandine, dog violet and primroses grew madly at the edge of the yew hedge and above them magpies and blackbirds began the anxious task of preparing homes for the arrival of their young.

In April on the day that would have been Will's sixth birthday Rose told her husband that she was pregnant again. Poppy was almost four months old and was at that delightful age when she smiled at everyone who looked into her perambulator and that was everyone on the estate from Tom the head gardener to Billy, the most recent addition to the staff. She was a cheerful, contented baby, growing up in a home filled with sadness.

Charlie's funeral had nearly finished them all off. Their sorrow turned for a moment to astonishment, for it seemed the whole county attended the ceremony. The church and the churchyard surrounding it were packed from wall to wall, inside and out. In the actual church folk stood alongside the pews and across the back, most of them, including some men, weeping for the lovely young man who had given his life into the hands of the brutal war machine. He had come back a broken man only to be murdered by some unknown thugs and the small boy who had been his own son and companion spirited away never to be seen again. How could a family bear up under such desolation?

Poppy had been left at home in the care of Polly, would you believe, who absolutely adored the baby. She had been found not to be the 'daft 'apporth' that Nessie and Dolly had believed and even called her, and Rose was seriously considering making her up to nursery nurse when Poppy was weaned. Given such responsibility, Polly was a different young woman to the girl who had snivelled over the dirty pans. She slept beside the cot in the nursery, giving Poppy's parents not only a good night's sleep, which they needed to run the growing success of the estate, but also the privacy they had longed for in their lovemaking, which led inevitably to another pregnancy!

'A boy this time, my love,' Rose told Harry. 'I want you to have a son to continue the line. To keep Summer Place and the estate in the good order it is achieving. But I only want . . . '

'What, my darling?' Harry mumbled into her shoulder, nearly asleep, complete in the joy they had just shared in their bed.

'I don't want more than two children, I mean. That is if this one is another girl. A son would be perfect so . . . '

'Yes, darling?'

'Can we arrange it so that we have no more babies?'

Harry reared up with a great roar. 'You've been reading that woman Marie Stopes, haven't you? Now I'm not one of those chaps who says that whatever God sends must be accepted, that is if there is such a being, which I seriously doubt after what millions have been through not so long ago but — '

'Harry, Harry, darling love.' Rose tried to calm her incensed husband. 'There are ways to . . . to prevent pregnancy.'

'What ways, apart from complete celibacy? And neither you nor I could manage that. We love each other too much, in . . . in every way.' He thumped back on his pillow, arms folded across his chest, looking so like Will when he wasn't getting his own way, Rose wanted to cry, or laugh. Instead she uncrossed his arms and put her head on his chest.

'I love you so much I'm afraid sometimes.'

At once his arms were round her, holding her to him in remorse. 'Sweetheart, I'm sorry if I upset you, but the thought of . . . dear God, if anything happened to you I wouldn't want to live. Some half-baked way of preventing your having another child is . . . it might be dangerous. To you or the child.'

There was silence, then: 'I've written to the the Mothers' Clinic in London and have received literature on how to plan your family. Condoms are . . . have been used for years . . . '

'Condoms, yes, I have heard of them but . . . '

'You do not want to have anything to do with them.'

'I did not — do not — say that. Let us have the child inside you then we will discuss this again. Our love has been so . . . so . . . spontaneous that the idea of . . . well, let us wait and see.'

Rose had no choice but to accept this answer but her mind which for twenty-odd years had made its own decisions with no need to consult anyone, told her to say no more on the matter. For now!

★ ★ ★

The small boy bowed over the table, a pen in his hand, watching the woman who sat opposite him from under his long lashes. She tapped on the table with the ruler in her hand. It had already twice been cracked across his knuckles and his hands, both of them, were very sore. He wanted to cry or scream as he had done at first, to weep his bruised heart out in fear, but had learned that to do so would only result in further punishment.

'When you have finished those sums I have set you I will check them for mistakes so concentrate or it's the cupboard for you.'

He did his best to concentrate on the simple addition. Two and four make six, three and seven make ten and so on until the last one: seventeen and sixteen make . . . what? his traumatised brain asked. He didn't think he could do it with the grey woman staring down at him with those cruel grey eyes and even as he contemplated 'the cupboard' into which she would fling him his child's mind froze. He must get away from her since he was sure she would kill him. The stout man who came in now and again petrified him just as much and as he saw no one else in this nightmare room there seemed to him a great possibility he might as well be dead. What would they do to him when the woman told the man what a clever boy he was? Since that was unlikely he looked towards the window. It did not open but if he pulled a chair up to it he could perhaps jump through the glass and the frames in which it was set. The woman brought him back to earth with a nasty crack across his little hands but he did not cry out or speak. She seemed incensed that she could get no reaction from this poor tortured child so she smiled.

'I'm going to the bathroom and you're to the

cupboard, my lad, when I return. Think about it while I'm gone.' She smiled again showing him her grey teeth.

She moved to the door and for the first time in six months she did something unusual. She forgot to lock the door behind her.

As soon as it closed he was out in the corridor, catching a glimpse of her as she entered the bathroom. He ran past the bathroom door, down the back stairs, then another set of stairs, and another until he arrived at a door which, when he opened it, led into a little square garden of herbs. Like a hunted animal he hesitated, then jumped across the herbs which smelled heavenly, through another gate on the far side and out into an enormous and immaculate garden centred by a sweeping lawn. Two men were working on the far side but they did not see him as they had their backs to him.

Like a hunted animal he ran until he came up to a high stone wall. There was a gate which he wrenched open and fled through, closing it carefully behind him. He was suddenly in woodland surrounded by magnificent oak and beech trees. Brambles clung to and scratched his legs and though he longed to stop and rest, he ran wildly on. He had no idea where he was but he was away from *her* so he didn't care if he was in the wilds of Africa or the Highlands of Scotland. He wanted to sing and whistle and dance but he knew he must put as much distance as he could between himself and that chamber of horrors and *her*. In his eagerness to escape he ran into the trunks of trees, fell down a dozen times, and from behind him he could hear the voices of men shouting to each other, getting nearer and nearer.

With a silent plea to Rose and Harry to help him, wherever they were, he jumped up and clung to the branch of a horse chestnut tree that had wide, spreading branches, a rounded crown and a towering mass of luxuriant foliage. It made a good hiding place. He and Charlie were good at climbing trees and he knew this one was the best. He went up and up like a small monkey until he was sure he was invisible from the ground, climbing to the top. The bark was rough and scaly. It was an old tree and his legs in their short pants, his hands and arms and face were scratched and bleeding.

He heard the men coming nearer and nearer and as they passed under the tree he began to cry. Silently the tears slid down his little gaunt face which had once been rounded and rosy with good health. He didn't dare move until darkness fell, trying to imagine what Charlie or Tim or Harry, or even Sergeant Mark would do. He knew he could not stay here, for the naughty men might come back and find him. His brain was numb, as was the rest of him. He was a child, six years old, but he had been subjected to a torment that had almost turned him into a shadow of his former self; yet something in him, some spark that he had inherited from Charlie and Alice, but was not aware of, had kept him safe so far. He must leave his frail nest of safety while it was dark. His friends, those he had loved and trusted, had all been brave soldiers in the war and poor Sergeant Mark had lost his leg so he must be brave too.

He slid down slowly, feeling with his feet where the next branch would be, pausing before he reached the lowest one, listening, hardly daring to breathe just in case they — who were they? his frightened child mind asked. Friends of the grey lady? — should be waiting for him at the base of the tree. He didn't know where he was. He didn't know what day it was or even what time of the year. Time had no meaning for him. He was so tired his brain seemed to have gone to sleep. He wanted to scream for Dolly, or Rose, or Summer Place where he had once lived and been loved. It was his home but where was it? *Where was he?* His eyes kept closing but he couldn't sleep in case in his sleep he might fall from the tree.

Being as quiet as he could he slid down the rough bark until his feet touched the mossy ground beneath. There were clouds drifting in a soft breeze across the sky and as they moved slowly a full moon shone and he could see as though a light had been switched on and at once he knew where he was. He and Charlie, and Tim, and even Sergeant Mark had come this way many times on one of their adventures. He was in the stretch of woodland at the back of Summer Place where he had last seen Charlie and the robin. In fact he and Charlie had climbed this very tree.

Beginning to sob with relief, no longer feeling tired and afraid, he ran and ran, dodging familiar places until he reached the gate that was let into the wall surrounding the house and gardens. His home, Summer Place, where were peace and love and safety. The horses, Pixie and Molly, Corey and Foxy, sensed him in the yard and were restless and he distinctly heard Ned say, 'What's up wi' them?' but he did not stop. He reached the kitchen door, turning the handle, weeping with frustration when he found it locked. It was never locked, never, but he was not to know that since his own disappearance everyone, cottagers, farmers, everyone with children on the estate, took no chances. Gypsies, vagrants, those with no fixed address were viewed with great suspicion.

He hammered on the door with his fists, screaming to be let in, for even now the men, the fat man and the grey lady might be hot on his heels. Inside Dolly screeched, Peggy, the new kitchen maid, dropped the saucepan she was scrubbing with a great clatter and Maggie reached for the back of a chair and clung to it.

'Shall us open t'door, Miss Davenport?' Martha quavered.

'We don't know who it is, lass. It might be — ' And outside Will began to scream until his throat was raw. The whole household could hear him and the men in the rooms above the stables threw aside the playing cards and clattered down the outside stairs. The horses were plunging and rearing and Ned shouted to Eddie or anybody to calm them down.

Harry and his demented wife, still in the wisp of a nightgown Harry liked her to wear, burst into the kitchen. 'What the devil . . . ' he began and without waiting to calm the servants he drew back the bolts and flung open the door.

The little boy was on his knees now, his screams turning into whimpers.

'Will,' whispered Harry, dazed, for they had thought him dead. The child on the doorstep was barely recognisable. Harry scooped him up and stepped back into the warm kitchen where the women began to moan. Rose was paralysed with shock, white-faced, white-lipped, trembling with horror, but at the same time a great bubble of joy worked its way up her body and like them all she began to weep at the wonder of it.

'Master Will . . . chuck . . . ' Dolly managed to squeak and the boy squirmed from Harry's arms, stumbled across the kitchen and flung himself at her. He crept on to her lap, her arms came round him and like a newly born babe he put his face in her breast, that which had comforted him so many times in his babyhood and the short boyhood he had known. His thumb went into his mouth and he cuddled himself into the love and safety of her arms.

The men crowded at the back door, Tom from his cosy kitchen and the fire where he read his *Echo* and behind him was Nessie in a warm and respectable dressing gown.

They were all speechless, none of them knowing what to say except Dolly, even at this momentous event in their lives. 'Go and put summat decent on, our Rose.' Jossy was eyeing his mistress who might have been naked for all the good the nightdress did. Then Dolly turned to the men and, unlike her, for she detested swearing, told them, 'And you lot can bugger off an' all. You'll be told in the morning what's happened to our little lad and who's to blame. Bye, if I could get me hands on 'im I'd bloody strangle 'im wi' me bare hands.' She kissed the boy's curls and then began to sing to him the lullaby she had when he was a baby.

'Dolly, you sweared,' the boy said sleepily round his thumb and they realised that this was their boy home again and they could not control their joyous tears.

Harry was stern, though his own face was still wet with tears. 'You had best all go to your beds. Leave Will with Dolly. He's where he wants and needs to be.' He wanted to question Will but he knew this was not the right time.

'I'm stayin' wi' Dolly,' Nessie said firmly. 'We could do with a cup of tea, me an' Dolly, so off you go, all of you. You too, Tom.' She placed a kiss on her husband's cheek and shooed them all off.

'You'll bolt this door, lass, when us've gone, won't you?'

'Yes, love'. And after doing so the kitchen was empty of everyone but Dolly and her and the boy who, for the first time in six months, fell into a deep and untroubled sleep

★   ★   ★

They lay in one another's arms, Rose still sniffing and wiping away the occasional tear.

'Oh, Harry, oh, Harry, oh, Harry,' she kept on saying. Before they cuddled into their bed they had checked on their own beautiful child. Rose whispered, did Harry not think her cot should be lifted into their room? As though afraid that what had happened to Will — whatever that might be — might happen to Poppy. Polly was in her bed but she was awake, ready, should it be needed, to give her life for the small being in her charge and Harry was pleasantly surprised that, being young and with a longing to know what was going on downstairs, she had not left Poppy on her own.

'Everything is marvellous, Polly dear,' Miss Rose said to her. 'Master Will has come home. You'll hear all about it in the morning,' turning once more to gaze at the baby in the cot. 'Now get some sleep. Will is with Dolly but — Polly dear, you will be shocked when you see him. He . . . he has been ill-treated, but those of us who love him must restore him to the Will we know and love. We'll go now and tomorrow we will find out what has happened to him, who has done this terrible thing to him. Now go back to sleep and when Poppy wakes bring her straight to us.'

But when tomorrow came and the next day and the one after that it seemed the terrifying experience that their Will had suffered had changed the cheerful boy they had known irrevocably. He was bathed by Dolly and the scratches that the brambles and the rough tree bark had made on his wild dash through the woods were soothed with comforting salve but it seemed the torment he had gone through would not let him be. He screamed in the night about a 'grey lady' who hit his hands with a ruler, which indeed were cracked and sore, and so his little bed was moved into Dolly's bedroom in order that she would be there when he needed her.

'Who is the 'grey lady', sweetheart?' Rose asked him, gently trying to draw him on to her lap, for Dolly was showing the strain of her constant nursing.

'Bad, she was bad, Rose,' he began to whimper, then reached out for Dolly who it seemed was the only one who could comfort him.

Harry telephoned the inspector of police who said he would be right over to question the child, for kidnapping was a major criminal offence.

'Inspector, I beg you to wait for a week or two. Will is in a dreadful state. He has been abused; no, no, not sexually. At least our doctor does not think so but I wanted to let you know he is back home with us. I'm letting the doctor see him again and he will let us know when he is up to being questioned and if . . . if . . . '

'I understand, Sir Harry, and will wait to hear from you. The villains will be long gone after all this time. If the child remembers where he was we can take action.'

'Thank you, Inspector,' he replied and hung up.

Dolly was in her rocking-chair, gently rocking the badly traumatised child as though he were no older than the infant daughter of Rose and Harry. The boy's thumb was firmly plugged into his mouth. The maids moved about the kitchen almost on tip-toe, speaking in whispers, afraid to alarm the pathetic little boy who had mischievously plagued the life out of them six months ago. Mrs Philips had made some almond biscuits especially for him because they had been his favourites but he turned his head away and shrank from her. They all wanted to weep for this terror-stricken child but when they heard the doctor's voice in the hall once again they breathed a sigh of relief. He was a lovely man was Dr Standish and would soon sort out what was to be done with the severely damaged child.

But it was not the doctor who brought their Will back to them but the baby who Rose had brought down to the kitchen to fetch the bottle of milk that was warming on the stove. Poppy was doing well on the mixture of her mother's breast and Mellin's baby food and was halfway to being weaned. Rose wanted to help her husband on the vast estate that was Summer Place and chafed at being tied to the nursery.

Poppy noticed Will at once and staring into her mother's face with that intensity babies have began to babble and point, then laughed as though she and her mother shared a huge joke.

Will stirred in Dolly's arms and though he still clung to her with one hand he sat up and looked curiously at the baby. They all watched and waited, waited for they knew not what, but when Will spoke they wanted to hug each other for surely this was a start.

'Who that?' he asked, reverting to the baby talk of years ago.

'She's Poppy, darling,' Rose said quietly. 'She is my daughter and Harry is her father. We would

368

like you to be her big brother. Would you like her to sit on your knee? No, no, you don't need to leave Dolly's lap but Dolly would like you *both* to sit on her knee. Is that all right, sweetheart?'

No one dared breathe and when Will, settling himself firmly on Dolly's knee, held out his arms, Rose placed the laughing baby on his knee, hoping poor old Dolly could bear the weight of both of them.

'Poppy,' Will said and the baby chuckled and patted his cheek. Rose stayed close, ready to catch Poppy should Will drop her but he smiled down at her in wonder and then up at Rose. He clearly didn't understand but he looked so kindly at the baby they all began to relax. Poppy waited for this new face to speak.

'She my sister?'

'Yes, darling.'

'Rose and Harry her mama and papa?'

'Yes.'

'I got no mama and papa.' Sadly.

'Yes you have, Will. Harry and I are going to be your mama and papa and Poppy is your little sister to play with. Do you remember Polly who worked here in the kitchen?'

'No?' Then cringed back against Dolly as if expecting a blow for the wrong answer.

'That's all right, my love, Polly sleeps in the nursery with Poppy and you could sleep there, too. Would you like that?'

They stood like statues, the kitchen-maid, the housemaids, Mrs Philips, Nessie and Rose.

'I never had no mama and papa,' he said tearfully and they were choked with emotion, all of them. What he said was, they supposed, quite true. Charlie had been no more than a child himself and Miss Alice had run off with another man but Will had never lacked for love from them all. Now it seemed he was to be Miss Rose and Sir Harry's son, so how was that to be achieved?

Dr Standish chose that moment to walk into the kitchen and he and Harry watched this miracle, for that was what it was. The baby and Will seemed to find each other fascinating so they both left quietly and made for the front door. James Standish was a compassionate man and he could see already that the boy was responding to the love that was being wrapped around him.

'You intend to adopt the boy, Sir Harry?' he asked tentatively.

'We do, Doctor. Can you think of any reason why we shouldn't?'

'None. You'll make a nice little family, sir, and if there is anything I can do to help or you feel the boy needs me you have only to telephone.'

'I will find the bastard who did this to the boy, my brother's boy, and I'll give him the biggest hiding he has ever had in his life.'

'I have one request, sir.'

'What is that, Doctor?'

'That I hold your coat while you do it.'

24

It became a familiar sight to see Will pushing the perambulator with Poppy chattering away to him and pointing to anything and everything that caught her attention. He seemed to know what she was saying, at least Polly who walked behind them thought so. Everyone noticed that Polly was very protective of both of them, following them round the garden and on most days into the stable yard where the men made a big fuss of them. Once upon a time Will had given the horses and his pony a lump of sugar on the flat of his palm as Eddie showed him but now he just kept his distance, for the animals came nuzzling their heads over the stable door looking to him for a treat and it alarmed him, as so many things did these days.

''Ere, Master Will, give 'em a bit of apple,' Eddie said, but Will shook his head. The stable boys were saddened. Where was the vivid child who had driven them to distraction with his tricks? *That* Master Will wouldn't have been seen dead pushing a perambulator!

They did not venture far from the house as the young dare-devil was not the boy he had once been. He was haunted by the 'grey lady' who often walked through his dreams or rather his nightmares, screaming for Rose or Harry, his mother and father as they had become. Poppy was his sister and he was astounded when Rose

371

told him he would have another brother or sister very soon.

'Can it be a brother, please, Rose ... er, Mother?' he pleaded.

'Why, darling? Would you not like a little baby girl to play with? You and Poppy are great friends. She loves to roll on the floor with you and soon she will learn to walk.'

'When, Mother?'

'She is nine months old now so it should be soon.'

The solemn little boy considered this. 'She can walk in the garden with me?'

'Yes, and when she is old enough Father will get her a pony and Molly and you can ride out in — '

'Oh no, no, no, Mother, please not outside. The grey lady might get her and hit her hands.'

Rose swept him into her arms and held him tightly, kissing him; it had begun to be clear to them that the grey lady was a monster who might never leave him. She rocked him and kissed him, telling him how much they loved him and that no one would ever hurt him again or take him away from them. And — with Sergeant Mark guarding and encouraging him — the little boy gradually gained more confidence.

In November 1921 Rose was delivered of another girl, a bonny girl who was the image of Will, the Summers strain coming through again. Harry and Charlie who had been brothers: Will, who was Charlie's son and Harry's nephew, had the same glossy dark curls, deep brown eyes as Poppy, the only difference between them being

Poppy's copper-golden hair and eyes the colour of a golden guinea like her mother.

Will was not best pleased since he had wanted a brother but they all thought it was a good sign: perhaps it meant that Will was regaining some of his spirit. He already had a sister who was placid, good-natured, ready to please everyone, and the games they played, watched over by Polly, were all of Will's making. Poppy was walking now and the interest she took in the new baby was perfunctory since she loved Will, and followed him — when she could — wherever he went but never beyond the high walls that surrounded the well-kept gardens of Summer Place. Will's pony grew fat in the lush pasture near the stable yard and Harry wondered if Will would ever ride her again.

But Eloise, or Elly as she was quickly named, soon made her requirements known and by her first birthday she ruled the nursery. Will, now seven years old, was annoyed by her wide and wicked smile and was amazed at the effect it had on everyone.

'Why does she get her own way all the time?' he shouted. 'That's my teddy, ball, drum, kitten' — the one he had picked from the regular arrivals in the stable. No one told him the rest would be drowned! 'It's mine, not hers,' and when told they must share their toys burst into angry tears. Lisa, cousin to Maggie, had been added to the nursery staff since Polly protested she could not manage the three of them.

'She's very strong and very noisy,' Lisa was heard to complain to Dolly. 'She'll take some quietening down, Miss Davenport, I'm telling you, when the time comes.'

But the time, said her doting mother, had not yet come when it was necessary to explain to her that a young lady must behave herself since she was barely walking; but surely, Lisa commented to Polly, that when she put her fist in Will's eye then staggered off down the sloping lawn, shrieking with laughter, it must come soon. She reminded them of the lad before he was kidnapped. Will had been told he must not hit his little sisters and Poppy, whose bottom lip quivered when the tiny girl bashed her big brother, hid her face in Lisa's skirt and was overcome with tears for it was obvious Will longed to strike back. What a to-do, Lisa moaned, and in her opinion the child needed a good spanking but Sir Harry and Miss Rose did not believe in it. Her mam had often given Lisa and her siblings a thick ear and it had done them no harm but that scallywag, meaning Elly, needed a firm hand.

★   ★   ★

Rose and Harry, being unconventional parents and it being a wet day, were in the drawing room sharing the *Sunday Times* newspaper. There were toys everywhere, littering the carpet, on the window-sill and on every chair. The children were playing some game that Will had contrived. Lions and Tigers it was called and when Maggie knocked and entered saying there was a Mr Arthur Weatherly to see them, they both, for

374

reasons unknown to Maggie, put down their paper and stared at each other in consternation.

'Show him in, Jenny,' Harry told her at last, his eyes still on Rose.

Will was crouched on top of a round table because he was the lion tamer and the two little girls were under the table 'in the woods waiting to be captured' when the visitor walked in, eyebrows raised as if he couldn't believe his eyes since he was a firm believer in children being seen but not heard.

Will became very still and every vestige of colour left his face when he saw who it was. His worst fears, his terror, his horror at the memories this man had been a part of rose in his throat and he began to moan. The moan grew wilder and wilder and like the lions his sisters were playing he sprang from the table and flung himself into Rose's arms. He was a big boy, tall, handsome and he was a handful for Rose to cope with but he burrowed in her lap almost as though he were trying to get inside her so that she was knocked back against the arm of the sofa, his moaning rising in pitch to a series of demented screams.

'Dear me, what a display and from such a big boy. I am surprised. Are all visitors treated to this performance?'

Harry rose to his feet but he was constricted in his movements by the two little girls who clung, one to each leg, crying piteously, frightened by Will's screams and therefore of the man who had caused them. Harry leaned towards the fireplace and rang the bell but he had no need to because those in the kitchen were shocked beyond measure by the sounds coming from the peaceful Sunday afternoon drawing room. All except Dolly!

The door opened even before Harry's hand had left the bell. She marched across the rich carpet, ignoring the visitor, for she knew who he was and, staggering a little because of her age, she plucked the terrified child from Rose and, screeching for help, was joined by Lisa and Polly who lifted the two little girls into their loving arms and carried them from the room. They were taken to the kitchen where a horde of women were waiting to comfort them. Elly and Poppy were soon appeased with a lap to sit on and a biscuit each, smiling round the room at the faces they knew and trusted, amazed at their big brother who was curled up on Dolly's knee. He kept begging Dolly to 'send him away, please, send him away'.

In the drawing room all was silent until Arthur Weatherly spoke.

'Aren't you going to invite me to sit down, old chap?'

'No.' Rose and Harry spoke as one.

'Well, I must say — '

'You have nothing to say that will interest us,' Harry said icily, for by now he understood who had taken their Will, treating him cruelly, and, not with his own hands, of course, since a man like him would know where to find men who would, for a price, attack Charlie.

'Now I wish you to leave because I have a telephone call to make to the inspector of police.'

376

'Now then, that's no way — '

'You bastard, get out of my house before I give you the hiding you deserve.'

Arthur Weatherly smiled. He was not afraid. He was a man who feared nothing and no one. His smug expression and the way his portly figure seemed to lounge said so. He had been a dinner guest at the same functions as the Chief Constable and soon Summers would realise that they moved in the same circles.

'Well, if that's the attitude — '

'Get out.'

'I only wished to know the whereabouts of my daughter who — '

'You threw her out when she was pregnant and she came to us for protection eight years ago.'

'And, believe me, if we knew you would be the last person — '

Weatherly interrupted Rose rudely, watching as Harry moved protectively towards her. He had done his best to get his grandson from under the roof where he had been molly-coddled and into his own home where he could bring up the boy as his grandfather thought best. He had broken the boy's spirit and had been ready to claim his right as the child's next of kin, his guardian, his solicitor had informed him, but this couple, Sir Harry and Lady Summers, had stolen the boy from him. They seemed to think they had a prior claim on him, a stronger claim. True, the child was the son of Sir Harry's brother but he was also the son of Alice Weatherly who was *his* daughter.

He spoke sneeringly, sure of his ground. 'You haven't heard the last of this.'

'And neither have you. We are puzzled by one thing. Who is the grey lady who haunts my son?'

'Your son!' Weatherly said incredulously.

'Yes. My brother's and now mine.'

'We'll see about that,' Weatherly said, turning towards the door and as he did so Harry went for him, his face a mask of loathing.

'No, Harry, no!' Rose screamed when suddenly the door opened and there were Tom, Jossy, Ned and even Sergeant Mark on the threshold of the drawing room.

'Do you want this chap ter leave, Sir Harry?' asked Tom and when Lady Summers shrieked hysterically, 'Yes, oh yes,' terrified Harry might do Weatherly some serious damage, Tom said pleasantly, 'Please go peacefully, sir, or we might have to help you,' obviously hoping it would be the latter.

'Get out of my way,' Weatherly snarled, jostling against Tom, almost knocking him over. He had not reckoned on the devotion of the staff at Summer Place. It took three of them to manhandle him to the top of the steps that led down to the freshly raked gravel driveway. Arthur Weatherly's immaculate motor car stood at the bottom and his chauffeur, open-mouthed, clearly didn't know what to do. He sprang from the driver's seat and ran round to the passenger door, opening it, ready for them to fling his master in. They did so but with such force that Weatherly landed across the back seat with his head jammed against the opposite door. His chauffeur wanted to laugh and congratulate the men who were standing at the foot of the steps, for Arthur Weatherly was not liked by his staff. They had all known, of course, of the silent child in the nursery and the woman who had him in her care, poor little sod, but they had been led to believe their employer had a perfect right to his grandson, his daughter's child. It was a mystery to them that no one from Summer Place had come enquiring after the lad but they had been threatened with the loss of their jobs if they went 'tittle-tattling' — Arthur Weatherly's words — beyond the walls of Weatherly House. When the boy had suddenly vanished eighteen months ago they had whispered and wondered what had happened until today when their master had ordered out the motor car to take him to Summer Place.

They were further to be enthralled when, an hour or so after their master arrived home, his face mottled with rage, the Chief Constable of the county called and was shown into Mr Weatherly's study.

'Well, Thomas, this is a fine 'how d'you do',' his housemaid heard him say before the door closed. She would have given a week's wages to put her ear to the keyhole and listen to their conversation.

Sir Thomas Fowler, though he had dined in the same company as the man behind the desk with an expensive cigar between his lips, could not say he liked him. Sometimes it was diplomatic to show friendship to the influential and very wealthy: they could be generous with their donation to police funds.

'It is indeed, sir, and a very serious one. Sir Harry Summers wants you arrested for kidnapping the child William Summers and though the boy is your grandson, I'm afraid — '

'*WHAT?*' roared Weatherly and the servants in the kitchen looked anxiously at one another. Since Miss Alice disappeared out of their lives, years ago now, their master's temper could be touched off by the slightest thing. His boots not polished to his satisfaction, his shirts poorly ironed, and, he thundered, was it not possible for Cook to vary his meals. She'd better buck up her ideas or she could take her foot in her hand and find another job. Cook, who was sixty-two, knew she would never find employment at her age and was frightened and constantly in tears, ready to slap the kitchen-maid a dozen times a day. Not a happy household!

'I'm sorry, sir, but I must ask you if you took his nephew — '

'*MY* grandson and I resent your attitude, Inspector. I shall report — '

'And the death of Sir Harry's brother who was apparently with the boy at the time. He had been beaten to death, sir. Have you any knowledge of that?'

The Chief Constable's face was grim. Arthur Weatherly stood up, pushing back his chair so forcefully it fell into the fireplace where a fire was lit. Fortunately it fell just short of the blazing coals.

'I shall be speaking to my solicitor about this, Inspector. Now I would be obliged if you would leave my house at once,' he blustered like the bully he was.

'Very well, sir, but I shall be back, probably with a warrant for your arrest. I shall need to question your servants and — '

'If you don't leave my house I shall have you thrown out, you . . . you . . . How dare you come here and threaten me as if I were some common fellow from the slums of Liverpool. Do you have any idea what I could do to your career?'

Sir Thomas Fowler sighed because he could see a great deal of trouble ahead, pondering on why this arrogant man had waited so long to accost Sir Harry Summers on the matter of the small boy who was his grandson. He stood up and made for the door, leaving Weatherly spluttering and fuming in a way that would have alarmed his doctor. He felt a good deal of sympathy for any child who fell into this man's hands.

* * *

Sir Harry Summers's solicitor stood up politely as Sir Harry and Lady Summers entered his office. They exchanged handshakes and murmured about the weather and such. When they were seated he sat down himself and waited for Sir Harry to speak.

'What do you know about adoption, Mr Hopkins?' Harry said abruptly and to Mr Hopkins's astonishment reached for his wife's hand.

'Adoption! You are planning to adopt? I

understood you had two daughters — '

'Yes, yes, we do but I also have a nephew. My late brother's boy. With Charlie dead and the boy's mother vanished — well, you might as well know the complete truth. She ran away with another chap. She was still married to Charlie at the time so . . . well, it, or rather she, doesn't matter now.'

'Harry, darling, don't.'

He turned to his wife and gently squeezed her hand. 'I'm sorry, Rose, but I meant she is not involved any more. She never cared about Will, you know that. I'm sorry, sweetheart. I know how fond you were of her.'

'I loved her, Harry. She was my friend. That's why I want to keep her son safe.'

Mr Hopkins felt quite embarrassed as though he was a spectator to something private. These two obviously thought the world of one another but he hadn't got all day, had he? He cleared his throat. At once they both turned towards him and he was quite surprised at his own reaction to Lady Summers's exceptional looks. No wonder Sir Harry thought so highly of her.

Now that she had become a mother Rose was even more lovely than she had ever been. Rose in her early thirties had taken to motherhood and, surrounded by her husband's love, her children's need — and she included Will — and her servants' devotion, had flowered into a true beauty. There was a serenity, a calmness, a sense of peace about her that warmed all those she met. She had three children who blossomed in her protection and a husband who was her rock.

Harry, still holding her hand, began to explain. 'My brother, Will's biological father, was badly wounded in the trenches. When he came home he didn't even know us. He was . . . ' Here his voice trembled and his wife leaned towards him and Mr Hopkins thought she might embrace him but Sir Harry pulled himself together with a visible effort.

'You must pardon me, Mr Hopkins. My brother and I were very close.' Again he hesitated, doing his best to keep his emotions in check. 'He and Will, perhaps not surprisingly, became friends, though Charlie could never be a real father to Will . . . '

'Yes, Sir Harry?'

'I sometimes think that their closeness was . . . oh, I'm sorry, Mr Hopkins. Charlie was beaten to death in Will's presence and Will was kidnapped and though we can't prove it we believe it was Arthur Weatherly, the boy's grandfather, who was behind it. He came to our home on the pretext of finding Alice, his daughter. We don't believe him. We are convinced he had Will for six months. The boy managed to escape him, but by God, if you'd seen the difference in him. He was spoiled, I admit, but he was very lovable. A cheerful, endearing child who was so abused that he is now afraid to go out of the garden. He was with us, playing with our daughters, when Weatherly walked into the room and at the sight of him Will was almost paralysed with terror.'

Harry stopped and turned again to his wife as

though for comfort but he could not go on.

'We want to keep him with us,' his wife continued. 'We want to return him, if possible, to the boy he was. He screams in the night about a 'grey lady' who struck him. We think Mr Weatherly wants to take him so can we legally adopt him? We cannot expect a young boy to be restricted to the house and garden. He used to play with the children on the farms. He had a pony and was afraid of nothing; we loved him — we still do — and he had a happy upbringing. He has a tutor, a clever young man who lost his leg in the trenches and Will is recovering from his ordeal — or was — until he saw Weatherly. We have informed the police and they are doing their best to find evidence. His servants, Weatherly's, I mean, will, I'm sure confirm that a child was kept in the nursery at the top of Weatherly House so this means that if Weatherly took him it will link him to Charlie's murder. He *was* murdered, Mr Hopkins, and he should be made to pay for his crime. Don't you agree?'

Mr Hopkins was a professional man but Lady Summers's tone of voice, her obvious distress touched him.

'First I must tell you that there is no legal way to adopt a child in this country. It's difficult to describe or explain. Some countries, like the United States and many Commonwealth countries, have a legalised adoption system. What you could do, though, is to go to court and Sir Harry could apply to become the boy's guardian.'

'Very well, can we ask you to set the wheels in motion?'

'To make yourself your brother's child's legal guardian.'

'If there is no alternative, yes.'

★ ★ ★

It was a week before Sir Thomas Fowler called on Sir Harry Summers. Will was curled up on Rose's lap with the two little girls doing their best to join him, his thumb in his mouth. The sight of Arthur Weatherly *in his home where he had felt safe* had put him back months so that even on such a lovely day, the sun shining from a cloudless blue sky, he could not be coaxed outside. Rose was reading them a story and Harry brooded over his copy of *The Times* and it seemed that the whole household was holding its breath in fear of what Weatherly would do next.

'Ah, Sir Thomas, have you news about . . . let's go to the study,' nodding his head towards the children, even the little girls subdued by the atmosphere.

'Well,' Fowler began when he was comfortably seated. 'We have interviewed every member of staff at Weatherly House but they had nothing to say that might incriminate their master in the death of your brother.'

'For God's sake,' Harry exploded, 'where did they think the boy had come from?'

'They were told he was Weatherly's grandchild, the son of Weatherly's daughter but they were not to spread gossip about it. Who were they to question an important gentleman like their master? They were just servants and they knew nothing about the boy's father who, they were told, had died of wounds incurred in the war.'

'But — '

'I'm sorry, sir, but there seems to be no connection between Mr Weatherly and your brother's death.'

'God in heaven!'

'Sir Harry, I must tell you Mr Weatherly is taking your kidnapping of his grandson to court and you will be summoned — '

'The bastard, the bloody bastard. I wouldn't let him have custody of my dogs — he is a monster. My nephew is at this moment on my wife's lap with his thumb in his mouth. He is terrified, and has regressed to his babyhood. If the justices could see him . . . Jesus, I'll swing for that man, Inspector.'

'Calm down, sir, you must fight in the courts for the boy and any sign of intemperate behaviour will go against you. You have exactly the sort of household in which to bring up the boy. Mother and father figures who love him and whom he trusts. Two other children and servants who are devoted to the boy, whereas Weatherly is known as a hard man.'

'Will talks of a grey lady who hit him.'

'Believe me, she will be found. The hearing should be soon. I gather your solicitor has put in a claim for you to become the boy's legal guardian.'

'Even if we get what we want, how can we ever know peace? How will our boy ever be as he was?'

Harry's voice was bitter and even Rose's loving arms in their bed at night could not demolish his fears. Afterwards he slept with his head on her breast while she re-lived that day when Alice, dear Alice who started all this, trembled at their kitchen door. Where was she? Where had she and Tim Elliott gone?

★   ★   ★

The atmosphere was tense in the courtroom. Everyone who was acquainted with the Summers family and Arthur Weatherly were crammed into it, peering and whispering, wondering if the boy in question would be there. Weatherly sat on a bench, obviously longing to get up on the stand and tell the world about his claim to his own daughter's son. *His* grandson who, when this charade was over, would at once be re-named William Weatherly.

The judge had just taken his seat when there was a stir at the door. There was barely room to accommodate a mouse but the woman who thrust her way through the mass was so heavily pregnant that out of respect they let her through.

Rose stood up and without a word opened her arms and Alice Weatherly — or Alice Elliott as she now was — walked into them. 'Rose, darling, I read about it and if they think I would let them take my son, *your* son, and give him to that man, they must be off their heads.' She turned to

387

Harry and after a moment's hesitation, for this woman had caused more chaos in his family than . . . but she was here for them. She had been through hell herself. She had known and seen what every soldier in the land had, searching for her husband, Harry's brother.

Further along the bench Arthur Weatherly stood up, ready to leave, because he knew he had lost. His face was ghastly and his mouth opened and closed but no words came and as the silent crowd watched he shouted her name.

'Alice!'

'Go to hell,' said Alice contemptuously, and watched with no emotion as he fell, his face smashing the floor as his heart, taxed beyond its capacity by his rage, stopped beating.

* * *

Summer Place was in an uproar of joy as Miss Alice and her husband greeted old friends and new but the one who all the fuss was about tumbled off Dolly's knee and rushed to meet his old friend. Tim got down on his knees and took the boy in his arms. Will gabbled telling Tim that Harry and Rose were his mother and father now, wanting to drag him out to the paddock where the ponies were and did Tim know he had two sisters now and here they were and did Tim like them? They certainly liked him when he lifted them up and put them on his shoulder and they giggled in his ear. Without even saying goodbye to Dolly Will galloped along beside Tim and that was the last they saw of them, but they were having a great time by the sound of the childish laughter.

Rose and Alice exchanged loving glances which said, how could they have known all those years ago that that chance meeting should lead to this?

Dolly rocked in her chair with Nessie opposite her.

'Put kettle on, Maggie, there's a good lass.'

REFLECTIONS FROM THE PAST

Audrey Howard

When Abby Murphy discovers she's heiress to one of St Helens' largest glass works, her whole life is turned upside down. Torn from her poverty-stricken family and forbidden to see her childhood sweetheart, Roddy Baxter, she is forced by her tyrannical grandfather to become a lady. Then Roddy disappears and soon it seems inevitable that Abby will have to marry her grandfather's chosen successor, Noah Goodwin, and bear his children. Trapped in a marriage where she is little more than a possession, Abby is determined that nothing will stand in the way of her steadfast passion for Roddy. But is she prepared to give up everything she has now for a love from the past?

PAINTED HIGHWAY

Audrey Howard

They are as different as two sisters can be. Vibrant and headstrong, Ally Pearce loves working on the *Edith*, her family's narrowboat, proving she's the equal of any man on the Leeds to Liverpool canal. Betsy, delicate, calculating and sensuously beautiful, wants only to become a 'lady' — and will use the most unladylike means to become one. When Doctor Tom Hartley enters the sisters' lives after a tragic accident, both are attracted to him — but for very different reasons. Tom seems blind to Betsy's ruthlessness, and Ally is devastated when her sister announces that they are to be married . . .